Praise for Summer Heacock
and *The Awkward Path to Getting Lucky*

"Readers who love hilarious, bawdy humor with a heaping dose of swoon will adore Summer Heacock's special debut!"
—Amy E. Reichert, author of *The Coincidence of Coconut Cake*
and *The Simplicity of Cider*

"Chock-full of hysterical one-liners and strings of profanity, the novel will make readers want to slap the protagonist upside the head with a glitter brush in order for her to come to her senses. A delicious summer treat with just enough sass, sex, and edible glitter."
—*Library Journal*

"Funny, fast, smart-as-heck and absolutely delicious. I devoured it."
—Gemma Burgess, author of the Brooklyn Girls series

"Undoubtedly memorable, hilariously quirky and surprisingly relatable, this novel digs deep into the complexities of intimate relationships and how easily the lines between sex and love can blur. Get lucky by making this one-of-a-kind novel part of your summer reading list!"
—*RT Book Reviews*, Top Pick!

"Full of voice and a cast of characters that are side-splitting funny. Between the shenanigans and drool-worthy cupcake descriptions is a modern day exploration of one woman's quest for happily ever after."
—Karma Brown, bestselling author of *Come Away with Me*
and *The Choices We Make*

Also by Summer Heacock

The Awkward Path to Getting Lucky

Crashing
THE
A-LIST

SUMMER HEACOCK

mira

mira

Recycling programs
for this product may
not exist in your area.

ISBN-13: 978-0-7783-6928-8

Crashing the A-List

For questions and comments about the quality of this book, please contact us at
CustomerService@Harlequin.com.

BookClubbish.com

Printed in U.S.A.

For Lola and Miles:

my Puddin' and my Little Sir.

Mommy loves you more than lobster ravioli and I promise to one day write a book you can read before you're legally allowed to drive.

Today is not that day.

Crashing
THE
A-LIST

1

This is the worst couch that has ever existed in the history of couches.

I hate this couch the way my third-grade class gecko hated the dick-weed kids who kept trying to pull off his tail, just to see if it would grow back.

There's no way my brother picked this out. It had to be Trina. I'm taking it as a sign of how much he loves her that he proposed to someone who bought a floral-printed corduroy couch, probably thinking it was retro-chic.

In reality, it's an upholstered monstrosity that will be serving as my bed for the foreseeable future.

Being the best little brother in all the land, Tom helped me drag all my worldly possessions to a storage unit this morning. All that's left are three suitcases full of the items I will need to live as a nomad until I can find—and afford—a new apartment. In the meantime, my trio of suitcases and I have been invited to stay at his enviable one-bedroom in Astoria. He also kindly plotted to keep busy this afternoon to allow me time to "unpack."

Because unpacking, he rightfully assumed, would translate into me sobbing like a soap opera character over the state of my pitiful, ridiculous life. So he and Trina are currently in the kitchen, leaving me to deal with my feelings with as much dignity as possible under the guise of pouring "Welcome to our home!" wine.

Unfortunately, there's not a lot of silver lining to be found at the moment. I'm seven months into my thirties, I've been unemployed for four of those months, and I'm relying on my little bro for a roof over my head.

And, well, then there's this couch.

Though I guess I'm not technically unemployed at the moment. Tomorrow I start working at the same E-Z Storage I moved my entire life into a few hours ago, sorting through abandoned and repossessed storage units.

I flop down onto the charcoal-gray stuffed chair that sits across from the hateful couch out of spite.

I don't even understand how this all happened. A few months ago, I was a busy, working gal. Living the dream, savoring adulthood with a full-time job as an assistant editor at a Big Five publishing house. I had it all sorted out. My twenties were for career and foundations and savings accounts and growing up. My thirties would be for basking in the fruits of my hard work—for being able to afford my own apartment without a roommate, finding love, and starting a family.

Or whatever the hell it is people are supposed to do in their thirties.

Then one day, the Big Bad Wolf of e-retailers, Alkatraz,

took over our house in a massive merger. A week later, I was zombie-walking through the streets of Manhattan with a pink slip in one hand and a sad little box of personal items from my desk in the other, my Minerva McGonagall bobblehead nodding pitifully inside the cardboard with each step.

In the spirit of adding insult to injury, my roommate, Delilah, the chef at an Indian fusion restaurant fifteen blocks from our front door in Brooklyn, decided to enforce the clause in our lease that called for eviction after three consecutive months of unemployment.

To hell with her, anyway. Her paneer lasagna wasn't nearly as impressive as she thought it was.

I'd followed all the adult rules. I had three months' worth of my salary in savings, a 401(k), a master's degree, and a damn fine résumé.

But those things mean absolutely dick when unemployment is laughable at best in terms of support, when you've got a master's degree worth of student loans, and when a quarter of your industry has been laid off and are now cage-fighting recent college graduates to the death for a handful of open jobs.

The one bright spot in this whole situation is Tom, prodigal fella that he is, who's saved me the mortification of moving back up to Buffalo with our parents.

I couldn't. I just could not.

I can accept defeat in a lot of ways. Losing my amazingly suitable apartment that was perfectly Park Slope adjacent. Giving up near-nightly takeout and drinks and general merriment with my friends. I can even accept the idea of my furniture living in a cold and dark storage unit, as there's nowhere to put an ottoman when you're homeless. Those things I can take.

But not moving back home. Never gonna happen.

Instead, I'm mooching off Tom and Trina and jumping

into the world of manual labor while the hunt for a new editorial job continues.

And sleeping on this couch. I fucking loathe this couch. I have a very real ambition to set this couch on fire one day, and am seriously inclined to like Trina less just for having purchased this nightmare.

It's likely a troublesome sign to resent the couch this much when I've lived here for exactly an hour and a half.

I shake my head, trying to clear away the negative thoughts. New goal: find a way to be firmly back on my feet in time for Tom and Trina's wedding, which gives me just under four months to get my shit together, and then I can gift them a new sofa. Something elegant and plush. Something I can crash on with slightly more comfort in the event that my career gets sucked up in the vortex of e-retailers and hostile takeovers again.

Well, there's some positive thinking.

"How's it going, Clara?" Trina asks, poking her head out from the kitchen. I've always thought her long, wavy red hair is such an interesting texture, as though it couldn't decide if it wanted to be curly or straight and landed firmly in the middle.

"It's awesome," I say, nodding at nothing. "Absolute perfection."

Tom's head appears above hers. "Wine time?"

My shoulders slump. "Wine time."

They walk out into the living room, and Tom hands me a generously poured glass of red before taking a seat next to his betrothed on my bed. I mean, the couch.

While Trina is about to become the lone ginger of the family, Tom and I couldn't look more related. We both have the same espresso-colored hair and eyes that are an odd hazel-green blend, which he and I dubbed "greenzel" as kids. The hair came from Dad's family, but the eyes are Tom's and mine alone.

Of course, the one difference is our height. Tom seems to have inherited all the available tallness in the family. The rest of us look like we should be baking cookies in trees.

"So," Trina says, looking around the room. "All settled in?"

I blink at her for a moment. "Well, only two of my suitcases would fit in the coat closet, so I'll have to leave this one out, if that's okay? I'll just…tuck it over there by the wall."

Trina makes a face that indicates, no, that will not be okay, because we are clearly messing with the carefully selected decor here, but Tom speaks first. "Totally fine." He takes a cheerful drink from his glass. "You're going to turn this all around so fast, it won't matter anyway, right, babe?" He gives Trina a little pat on the leg.

"Absolutely." She smiles, visibly unconvinced.

I really shouldn't be so judgy of her. Or her couch. She's actually a very nice person. I've always liked her. And if the roles were reversed here, I can't imagine I'd be thrilled that my down-on-her-luck future sister-in-law needed to camp out in my living room only a few months before my wedding.

I slug down a healthy amount of pinot. "Thanks again, you guys," I say sheepishly. "I promise I'll stay out of your way."

"You can make it up to us in babysitting someday," Trina says. Tom and I both start choking on wine.

"You're not…?" I cough.

She laughs a tinkling little laugh. "Oh god, no. Not yet. But eventually!"

Tom's eyes get just a tiny bit wider as he grins his way through this declaration. "Absolutely! Clara will be a great aunt." He leans over and gives Trina a quick kiss.

Ugh. I clearly didn't think this all through. The pride-crushing reality of living with my little brother, who's not only professionally stable as a successful graphic designer, but also about to be married.

And here I am, with my sad little suitcases, unable to remember the last time I went on a date.

But none of those things are anywhere near as terrifying as the sudden realization that I'm going to have to watch these two exchange puppy-love looks and the smooches of a happy couple every single day.

"Oh!" Trina announces. "I forgot to tell you! Uncle Charlie says if you find anything you like in the storage units, you can keep or sell. He's planning on trashing all of it anyway."

I wince. "That's really nice of him. And he's sure he doesn't want to try and sell them, like on those reality shows?"

Trina's uncle is sort of the storage king of this borough. Apparently there are other kings for the other boroughs, but quite honestly, I don't give enough of a damn to ask about them.

"He says those shows are basically fake." She shrugs. "He just wants them cleared out, I guess."

My hands fidget awkwardly with the stem of my wineglass. "Oh, okay. Well, uh, thanks again for sending me his way."

I'm very grateful to be working at E-Z Storage. After four months of job searching with nary a bite, my panic is starting to grow, and I'm willing to do whatever I can to boost my dwindling bank account. Student loan companies aren't particularly magnanimous about financial crises, and without the money from the Storage King of Queens, the chances of digging myself out of this mess will dwindle to nothing in a blink.

Plus, sitting around here all day constantly refreshing job postings online is maybe the most depressing thought possible. I need to be doing something to make myself feel productive. Anything, really.

"No problem!" Trina says, smiling genuinely.

We sit there silently drinking wine for a few minutes. I'm becoming more and more conscious of the fact that I'm majorly intruding on a coupled life that is still in its beginning days, and I assume the bewildered expression on Tom's face indicates he's still analyzing the babysitting comments from earlier. Trina appears blissfully unaware of all these things.

"So," I finally say with a sigh. "Who's hungry? Dinner's on me."

"No way," Tom protests. "Our treat."

I shake my head at him. "Nope. You're saving my ass here. The least I can do is buy you guys dinner."

Tom concedes defeat, Trina smiles, and I realize that actually, yeah, it really is the absolute least I can do.

2

Late October in New York is not the wisest time to take on an outdoor job when you're a slightly spoiled former office worker who is used to wearing low heels and accent jewelry.

But alas, here I am, regretting the decision not to wear sweats under my jeans and wondering if fingerless gloves really count as wearing anything at all if the tips of your fingers fall off from the cold.

"You must be Clara!" I look up to see a man with salt-and-pepper hair that's considerably more salt than pepper, an orange safety vest, and a bushy gray mustache walking across the parking lot toward me.

I give him a little wave and stick my hand out to shake his. "It's so nice to meet you, Mr. Bishop."

"Please," he says in a friendly baritone, shaking my proffered hand. "It's Charlie."

"Charlie." I smile and nod. "Thank you again for taking me on for this. I really needed the job."

He shrugs and starts walking. I stand in place just long enough for it to be weird and then scramble to catch up to him. "Nothing to it! I normally just hire some college kids to do it every few years, but the guys who used to come in during the summers when they were off school are all grown and gone. Just never took the time to find replacements. Gettin' old, I guess. It's been two years now, and I'm losing more than I care to in clogged-up units. But it's easy enough work. You'll be fine."

We head across the lot over to the third unit in a row of ten. He pulls a ring of keys out of his pocket and undoes the padlock on the front of the door. In a quick movement, he yanks the rolling door up.

I'm trying to keep my most professional face on, but it gives way to disgust. This eight-foot-by-eight-foot unit is full of everything that has ever existed. Moldy furniture, piles of clothing, junky old electronics, just…everything. And what the hell is that smell?

"All right," Charlie says, turning to face me. "Here's the first one on your list. These'll open all the padlocks on the units we've repossessed." He passes me the keys and pulls a folded piece of paper from the pocket of his aggressively orange vest. "Here's the list. You've got twenty-three altogether."

He hands me the paper unceremoniously and reaches back into his vest pocket for another set of keys. "This is our truck." Charlie gestures to an ancient diesel pickup truck with an extra-long bed about twenty feet away. I know exactly nothing about cars, but even I can tell this is a behemoth of a vehicle. "Throw all the junk in the back, and at the end of the day, you'll drive it across the city to the dump. Park behind the front gate and leave the keys in the glove box. The guys there will unload the stuff and bring the truck back in the morning."

He jabs a finger back at the unit. "Now, some of this'll be too heavy for you to move on your own, sofas and fridges and whatnot, so you just jot those down on your list for each unit. I've got guys coming on the weekend to get the big things out. We can sometimes sell 'em off. Also, keep an eye out for things like stocks and bonds or safes full of cash. That stuff I don't wanna toss."

I nod, but my eyes wander back to the unit, searching in vain for the source of the smell.

Charlie claps me on the back. "Everything make sense?" he asks.

My eyebrows shoot up. "Um. Yeah. Sure! I've got it." I glance down at his vest. "Do I need to wear one of those? Is it a safety thing?"

He looks down at himself and brushes off his neon attire. "No. Somethin' wrong with my vest?"

I blink. "Nothing. It's lovely. Great color on you. Brings out your eyes."

Charlie snorts. "When you're finished, I'll cut you a check." He starts walking back toward his car on the other side of the lot. "My number's on the top of the list if you need me. If you find anything you like or you think's worth somethin', it's yours. Consider it a finder's fee. And don't stay after dark, 'cause that's when the weirdos come out."

I stiffen. "Hey, just because I'm a girl…"

He turns around and raises an eyebrow. "It's not 'cause you're a girl. Hell, even I won't stay out here after dark."

I can feel my eyes bulging. "Great. Good to know. Thanks."

Charlie laughs and climbs into his car, which I am just now noticing is a shiny, newish Lexus. Being the Storage King seems to be working out well for him. "Good luck!" he calls. I pretend to study the list, looking as cool and collected as possible while he drives through the lot. I look up to see him give me a short wave before he's on the street, disappearing from view.

Now it's just me and a smelly storage unit. Well, me, this stinky unit, and twenty-two others that I'm sure will prove to be just as palatable.

I fold up the list and stuff it into the back pocket of my jeans, then tuck both sets of keys into my coat pockets. I take a deep breath and turn to face my Everest.

Okay. So, this really isn't too bad. All I have to do is move the stuff in here into the back of the truck. I'm not big on treasure hunting, so the job shouldn't take too long. It's a simple Point A to Point B scenario. No big deal. Might not be particularly glamorous, but a little hard work never hurt anybody.

I can totally do this.

3

"I can't do this!" I sob into my cell phone.

"Yes, you can!" my best friend CiCi says back.

I sniffle loudly. "No, I can't! I'm still on the first unit and the sun is starting to go down! I'm not even half done with it! Everything is gross and heavy and it smells like beets!"

"Beets?"

"Beets!" I shriek. "Fucking beets! And I don't even know why! There aren't any beets in here! D'ya know what *is* in here, though, Ci?"

There's a moment of silence. "Do I?"

"Well, let's see," I muse sarcastically. "There was the old couch at the front that I tried to clean off and ended up finding a stash of used condoms on. God knows how long *those* were there for. Then when I got back a few feet, I came across a dead snake hiding under a box of newspapers from 2003.

And finally there was the giant trash bag full of old mildewed clothes that burst open when I tried to lift it, and a nest of petrified dead baby rats fell out!"

"Jesus, are you serious?"

I choke on a sob. "This is horrible! No amount of money is worth this!"

"But it's five thousand dollars, though, right?" she asks. "That's a lot of money, cupcake. And okay, yeah, that's disgusting, but they can't all be that bad, right?"

I hiccup. "But what if they are?"

"Then we can take a wee bit out of your savings and invest in a hazmat suit? I dunno."

Laughing, I wipe my nose on my sleeve, trying really super hard not to think about what the fabric has touched today. "That's a lot easier to say when you aren't the one who's going to smell like beets for the rest of your life."

"How about this," she says. "You said you still have to drive the truck to the dump, right? Gimme fifteen minutes and I'll meet you, and we can ride over together."

"You'd ride in the scary truck after dark with me?"

"Honey, if there was a body in the back of that truck, I'd still ride with you and I wouldn't even ask questions. Hell, I'd bring a shovel and an alibi."

"Love yer face."

"Love yers, too," she says. "Hopping on the train now. See you in a few!"

She clicks off the line, and I turn back to the unit that's barely half-emptied. I remember how I'd fantasized about setting Trina's hideous couch on fire, and think that those flames would have been a waste. This is where the inferno belongs.

I'm also getting a tad bit concerned about my sudden pyro

tendencies. Unemployment is not proving beneficial to my mental health.

I debate crawling in the cab of the truck and hiding until CiCi gets here, but my desperate need for that money coupled with the knowledge that I will be cursed to smell like root vegetables until I finish unloading this damned unit sends me shuffling back inside.

How could people put all this stuff in here and just leave it? Though I honestly can't understand why anyone thought these things were worth saving in the first place.

Although, based on the gross couch, I'm thinking this might have started out as a storage unit and morphed into a love den. Maybe someone was having an affair, and the only secret place they could run off to for their dalliances was this storage unit. Then once the marriage broke up or the affair was past its prime, the unit became a forgotten place, or perhaps a painful reminder of infidelity?

Or maybe people are just completely disgusting. I mean, my damn.

These units were owned by someone, though. Actual people. People with lives and families and possessions.

Maybe even people who had their dream jobs and lost them all in one fell swoop and couldn't afford to keep their storage units anymore. Maybe these are filled with items people would have given anything to keep hold of, but they were grabbed by overdue debts and corporate greed.

I can't picture Uncle Charlie as the face of corporate greed, though. I think it's the mustache. That poofy of a mustache couldn't be on a bad guy.

Although, now that I think about it, Charlie did have this hint of an oddly intimidating vibe that I can't explain, though it was slightly cloaked by the mustache.

And three rows over from where I stand now is a small unit crammed with my own life. Boxes upon boxes of books, the clothes and shoes I had to pack away, and my blessed mattress, shrink-wrapped to death.

This is all so depressing. I don't have a lead on a job. I don't have a lead on an apartment, not that anyone would lease to the unemployed. Most of my worldly possessions are sitting here in a temperature-controlled cement dungeon. And a metropolitan telltale heart in the form of an auto-payment from my meager checking account each month to E-Z Storage will continue to remind me of what I had and what I'm nowhere close to edging back into.

I fling a stack of old magazines into the back of the truck. What if one day my checking account runs dry, and my payment doesn't make it? What if Charlie has to lock up my unit and it's taken away? Some poor schmuck might wind up sorting through my things and judging me based off what they found. Maybe they'd wonder what kind of life I'd led to lose all those things.

My life wasn't upper-class by any stretch, but I prided myself on having a few nice items that I'd worked for. Like, I own a great mattress. It has a little remote, and I can change how firm it is at my every whim. For years, I shopped thrift stores to mix and match newer items for my professional wardrobe. I packed my own lunch each day. I cut a lot of corners that, while now I'm glad I did, at the time, I hadn't really needed to.

But I wasn't about to scrimp on my mattress. That thing was worth every penny. Watching the deliverymen cart away the full-size I'd slept on since eighth grade and smoothing down the sheets on the luxuriously huge queen felt like my official invocation into the Hall of Adults.

I almost sold it. In a moment of overdramatic worry, I determined I had no use for a mattress, so why bother holding on to it when it could be sold for cushion money? I even went so far as to place a Craigslist ad for it.

A mechanic from Crown Heights answered the ad. He was so happy to find it. Personally, I'd be too icked out to buy a used mattress, and in the guy's defense, he *was* suspicious at first. But I'd taken immaculate care of it. I'd even kept the expensive mattress protector on the entire time I'd owned it. I wanted to keep the warranty valid, after all.

He was a nice guy, but I definitely would've gotten screwed in the deal. Only a few hundred bucks for a three-thousand-dollar mattress. I had to give the guy credit for his haggling skills.

But at the last minute, I freaked out at the thought of someone else sleeping on my one piece of material pride and joy, and sent Mr. Mechanic on his way before pulling the ad.

I suppose if you hear the story from his perspective, he was seconds from a great deal and had it ripped away by a cruel mattress tease. He'll tell it from the stance of his good fortune gone awry. He was a nice guy, and it was my fault for jerking him around.

No. Screw him. I worked hard for that mattress. I interned under a hellish acquisitions editor at a midlevel publishing house that went from procuring literary fiction to trying to "stop the pussification of America" by buying books from every Reddit troll gone viral. That's not even including the author who wrote on a fucking Tandy computer, forged before the earth's crust cooled, and sent every chapter in a separately saved file on goddamn floppy disks, written in a word processing program that hasn't existed since 1994. And each of this author's books contained some variation of the phrase "Her tits tittered tittily."

I worked my way up from that dick editor to earn that mattress. So I don't care how nice the mechanic dude is. It's *my* mattress.

"Uh, Clara?"

I wheel around, still scowling. "What?"

"You're snarling at a lamp," CiCi informs me.

I look down, and sure enough, there's a little bendy desk lamp clutched in my hands. I continue glaring at it for a minute before I accept that my being pissed at this lamp isn't going to bring my bed out of unit 118.

I sigh and fling the lamp into the back of the truck. "Hey."

CiCi assesses the situation calmly. "So. How's it going?"

"I miss my mattress."

"Who wouldn't?" She scans her eyes over the contents of the unit and scrunches her nose up. CiCi has what one might call a moneyed face. Her parents are the kind of rich that people rally against, and my blond-haired, blue-eyed pal definitely looks the part. Well, until she opens her mouth and a myriad of profanity falls out, anyway.

"Holy fuck-sticks, you were serious!" she says as she prances inside and starts looking around. "Oh my god, who keeps this stuff? I don't even know what this is— AHHHH! SNAKE! It's a snake!"

"It's dead."

She runs past me and stands by the front of the truck, clutching her chest. "I didn't even know we had snakes in New York! Why the hell are there snakes? Isn't that why people live in the city? To get away from snakes and shit?"

"Maybe someone smuggled it in?"

"They smuggled it in to let it die in a storage place?"

I throw my hands up. "Yes. It was all part of their master

plan to throw off the snake-smuggling authorities. Misdirection, and all that."

CiCi snickers and then studies me. "Cupcake, you look like hell."

"Thanks." I make a sad face.

CiCi's my best friend because she's amazing, and feisty, and all the things I strive to be. She's also a kick-ass publicist. So while I am banished to the underbelly of the city's abandoned junk, she's still out and about in the professional world I long to rejoin.

She looks over at the truck, which is taunting me with its giantness. I hate driving in the city's traffic at any time, but with this monster, I don't know what I'm going to do.

"Okay," she says, furrowing her brow. "You've had a shit day, yeah?"

"Yep."

Pulling in a deep breath, she looks at me seriously. "Here's what we're gonna do. First, I'll drive you over to the garbage place or whatever, because I know what an awesome driver you are. Then I'm taking you out for dinner because, damn, you've earned it."

I feel tears welling up in my eyes and fling myself at her for a hug. She clutches me back for a moment before pulling away with a jerk.

"Between those things, we will stop by my place so you can shower and borrow some clothes." She takes a fearful sniff. "Because seriously, though…beets. You absolutely smell like beets."

4

"So, how is it?" Tom asks me as we huddle around the center island in his kitchen.

"Technically, it's probably horrible," I say with a shrug. "But I'm doing okay with it. I may have to set aside some money for a chiropractor when all is said and done, but it's not completely crap."

I can say this now, as the second unit I opened after sealing off the first was far less crowded and filled with things like plastic boxes of dishes and old tools. The stuff was heavy, but it was all stacked and orderly and made the rest of my day go smoothly. I was able to lock down that unit by the time the sun started to disappear, which made me feel pretty accomplished after the debacle that was yesterday.

"That's good," he says, taking a sip of wine. With a small laugh, he adds, "I didn't think you'd stick with it."

I want to unleash outrage on him, but I can't muster the energy for it. "Yeah, me either." I steal his wineglass and take a deep drink. "But hey, I'm in it now. I couldn't leave Brutus behind. He's my pal."

"Who's Brutus?"

"The truck."

"The truck?"

"The big orange diesel pickup I have to drive to the dump at night," I clarify. "We spend a lot of time together, and I figured that if I gave it a name, it might be nicer to me when I'm trying not to die in rush-hour traffic driving what is essentially a trash-filled battering ram."

"Whatever works." Tom laughs as he fills himself a new glass and tops off the one I stole.

"And tonight, I will sit on Gertrude in there and scour any and all websites listing job openings, and I will also send annoying check-in emails to everyone I know, to see if anyone has any bites. I have officially reached the point where I am not above begging for favors."

"That's the spirit," he says, and clinks his glass to mine. "Also… Gertrude?"

I shrug again. "The couch."

"You named our couch?"

"I really did."

He raises an eyebrow. "Should I be alarmed by your new fascination with naming inanimate objects?"

"Likely so. But don't stop me. It's working, so I'm rolling with it."

"Fair enough."

We take a moment of silence to sip our wine. Or maybe I'm sipping wine and he's mentally rating what level of lunacy naming his couch actually counts as.

"So," he says, his voice dragging out the word. "Mom called today."

I whine. Yes, I'm thirty years old, and I just whined.

"Is she still mad?"

"Yep."

Our mother is currently not speaking with me due to my refusal to return home during my current job/living situation crisis. I've tried to explain the irreversible damage my limping home as a failed adult would cause to my psyche, but she remains unconvinced. She maintains that no matter my age, I'm her child and should be sitting on her couch eating PB&J with the crusts cut off while she makes passive-aggressive comments on all my life choices.

"I'm not going back to Buffalo," I declare. "I'm actually scared that when we go home for Thanksgiving, she's going to lock me in the basement."

Tom considers this. "That's a genuine risk. But cut her a bit of slack. Our entire family has lived within fifty miles of each other for at least four generations. The fact that we *both* moved away is like the highest sin we could have committed."

"We're still in the same state. It's not like we emigrated."

"Might as well have," he says, assuming a scandalized expression that eerily resembles our mother's. "I mean, we aren't birthing children to be raised in the school system where Uncle Jack is a vice principal! We're as good as shunned!"

"No one should ever have to go to a school where their uncle is the vice principal." I shudder. "You'd think he'd go easier on family, but Uncle Jack was all hell-bent on proving he wasn't nepotistic."

"How many times did we get detention from him in high school?"

I try to calculate. "I honestly lost count. Remember when

he gave you one because you were walking on the wrong side of the hallway between classes?"

Tom snorts. "Oh god, I'd forgotten that."

I take another sip. "It's a special type of hell to see Veep Uncle Jack the Hard-Ass at school, followed by sweet old Uncle Jack who gave us better presents than Mom and Dad at Christmas. All through freshman year, I thought he had dual personalities."

"Looking back, I think it was his way of apologizing. He had a reputation to maintain," Tom offers.

I shrug. "I prefer the Dr. Jack/Uncle Hyde approach."

"It's nice to see unemployment hasn't damaged your grounding in reality at all," my brother says.

I hear the sound of the front door opening, and a few seconds later Trina is standing in the kitchen with us, holding giant take-out bags from Pandora Dragon.

She gives us both a giant smile. "Cooking is for suckers."

"I knew I was marrying you for all the right reasons," Tom says, relieving her of the Chinese food and giving her a kiss. I pointedly stare at the bags and realize it's a lot weirder seeing your little bro smooching his intended inside their own home than it is literally anywhere else. I feel very intrusive.

We take our food and feast while piled on Gertrude watching *Friends*, because sometimes you just have to embrace being a cliché.

After dinner, we lounge about, and I check my email on my phone. Not a single response to any of the résumés I've sent out. It's only been a few months, but the creeping fear of never finding another editing job is growing. I certainly wouldn't be the first person thrust out of their chosen profession and into the horrors of having to pick a new career.

I'm not particularly sure I'm qualified to do anything else, though. What do you do with a master's in English Lit besides working in publishing, or maybe teaching?

Oh god, I'd be the worst teacher ever. Not only am I strangely terrified of teenagers, but I can't imagine having to teach little kids anything. How do you impart knowledge on small people? It's genuinely scary. I'd probably be the teacher who tried to inspire them to love reading and wound up inciting a riot over banned books or something.

Actually, that doesn't sound too bad. We can call that plan B.

"So," Trina says with a yawn as we finish stashing leftovers in the fridge and remnants in the trash. "What kind of units are you doing tomorrow?"

"I don't look until I'm ready to start cleaning," I answer.

"Why not?" Tom asks.

"Because if I looked in them, I'd have to spend all night panicking about the hell that's waiting for me in the morning. And right now, the worst thing in my head is sex couches and beet smell." I shudder. "This way I can pretend that's as bad as it's gonna get."

Some things are best left to be lived in the moment. Like falling in love.

Or, you know, stumbling onto dead snakes.

5

This is the most ass-numbingly boring thing I have ever done. It actually has me missing the physical and olfactory assault of the beet unit.

I seem to have stumbled upon a paperwork-hoarder's wet dream. And of course, this is exactly the type of stuff that I'm supposed to be carefully sorting through, according to Charlie. Boxes upon boxes *upon boxes* of what looks like every record some business owner ever had from the mideighties to late nineties, by the look of things.

I whimper to no one. This is going to take forever. This isn't just hoisting boxes of ancient and cracked china into Brutus. This is sifting through a million trees' worth of paper looking for some random bond or something valuable.

I suddenly hate Charlie and everything he stands for on this planet.

Obviously I need coffee.

I close the unit up and head down to the gas station mini-mart two blocks away.

The cashier greets me with less friendliness than I'd care for. I give him my very best smile. He narrows his eyes at me.

I pour myself a monstrously large coffee from the little self-serve station. There's a sign informing me I can save fifty cents per coffee by bringing in my own reusable mug. I will roger that. Fifty cents is fifty damn cents.

It's still jarring to me that four months ago, I could have dropped fifty cents on the sidewalk and not even noticed. Not that I was fiscally irresponsible, but I would have had it to spare and just told myself it might make another person's day to find fifty cents.

I kind of hate myself for that now. It makes me feel all entitled and elitist. Although, I do think finding fifty cents now would rock my world, so maybe there's more to my original theory than I'm giving credit.

I head to the register to pay and set my coffee on the unnaturally orange counter. It coordinates a little too well with Charlie's vest.

"Hi," I say.

"One-seventy-five," the cashier says.

I hand over two dollar bills and read his name tag. "Rufus. That's a cool name. I like that."

He hands me back my quarter. "I was born with it."

I don't quite know how to respond to that. "Okay, then." I pocket my change and pick up my coffee. "Lovely chatting with you, Rufus."

I can feel him scowling at me as I head back into the chilly outdoors. I don't know why, but I suddenly feel the need to

get Rufus on my side. He's my only potential ally in this battle of forgotten storage relics.

I open up today's unit again and sigh. This looks like today's,
tomorrow's, and possibly forever's unit. Why would anyone
keep this much paperwork? They had scanners and computers
in offices in the nineties. I mean, I was in grade school, but
still. The internet had to be in play during the dates on at least
some of these papers.

I take measured sips of my coffee to avoid too many bathroom breaks. I don't want to earn any more ire from Rufus,
and the gas station looks to be the only available bathroom
for many blocks. Charlie doesn't have an office on the lot, so
there's no dedicated E-Z Potty for me to utilize. Plus, this
coffee is spectacularly bad, so the urge to chug isn't strong.

I'm not entirely sure what I'm looking at with these papers.
I think they're invoices, but I can't tell what for. There isn't
any letterhead, so for all I know, this could have been the be-
ginnings of a Fortune 500 company, lost to the wastelands of
E-Z Storage and Charlie's grabby hands.

Okay, no, that's stupid. No one with a Fortune 500 company is going to let their storage unit get behind in payments.
Probably. Hell if I know what someone with a billion-dollar
company might do.

For every worthless box I sort through, I take great satisfaction when the time comes to fling it into the back of Brutus. Each one seems to take about twenty minutes to filter
through all the pages. Multiply that by eleventy trillion boxes,
and I should be done with this unit by the time my not-yet-
conceived children graduate college.

There's a fun subject. My nonexistent children who have
no chance of existing unless I get my feet on the ground and
find someone to, uh, make babies with.

Yeah, that's not exactly how I want to start a relationship. "Hi! Great to meet you! Shall we spawn now?"

This is why I'm single.

But seriously. I had plans. And I was so close. I really loved my job. It was stressful and exhausting, and I was technically doing the work of at least three people, but it was mine and I was good at it. The track was laid, and I was well on the road to being ready to meet the right guy and settle down and do all the things.

It does sting a bit to watch my little brother strolling into domesticated bliss while I'm just sitting over here with my unemployment checks and boxes of papers.

I should probably be recycling these papers, now that I think of it. Charlie didn't say anything about a recycling center, but it feels outrageously un-green of me to just throw all of these boxes into a dump somewhere.

I call CiCi. "Do you know of any recycling centers in the area?"

"Why? Are you branching out in your trash removal?"

"Sort of. I hate throwing all this paper into a landfill. Yuppie guilt."

"If you ever call yourself a yuppie again, I will punch you in the face. With love."

I snort. "Noted. But really. Any ideas?"

"I'll see who my office uses for recycling and get back to you," she says. "Find any buried treasures today?"

I pop the lid off a new box and start rifling through the stacks of papers, balancing my phone on my shoulder. "Not a damn thing."

"Any more dead reptiles?"

"Not yet, but the day is young."

"That's the spirit, cupcake."

"How's work going?"

"I feel like a jerk talking about work with you," she says, and I imagine her making her squinky face.

"Just because the world of the job-having has cast me out doesn't mean I begrudge others the joy of a paycheck." These invoices look a little different from the last ones. They say CRANSON as a letterhead in an ancient-looking font, presumably an early ancestor of Comic Sans.

"Well, I've got a new author who is supposed to be the next, *next* James Patterson with a book launch coming up, so that's cool."

"The next, *next* Patterson?"

"The 'next Patterson' label was taken by that guy last year who released the first book in a series about a professional swimmer who solves crimes, remember?"

"Oh, right," I say. "Yeah. That book was really bad. I couldn't get three chapters into it."

"In chapter four he went into great detail describing his swimmer's body. It picks up there."

"It's the simple pleasures."

"Simple, hell. It's like I could smell the chlorine and see the Speedo."

"You say strange things."

"And you love me for it."

"I really do." I frown at the papers in my hand. "Okay, these invoices are bizarre."

I hear her chomping on something through the phone. "What's bizarre 'bout them?"

I let out a laugh. "You're eating sunflower seeds, aren't you?"

"They help me focus! Shut up. It's these or smoking."

"I'm not sure which is a more unattractive habit…"

"Shh," she says. "If it was good enough for Mulder on *The X-Files*, it's good enough for me." I listen as she spits out a shell. "What's on the papers?"

I flip through a few more pages and gasp. "Oh my god."

"What!?" she hisses at me.

"CiCi... I think whoever owned this unit was running a brothel. Or was a pimp. Or... Wait—do pimps give receipts?"

"Well," she says, taking a moment. "I mean, maybe a reputable pimp?"

"That's a big oxymoron, hon."

"You're an oxymoron."

I scan another couple of pages. "Seriously, though. I think this is the invoices for the, erm, customers? It looks like it's listed by who they, uh, hired? Dated? And then there's a number for what they...ordered? I don't know how to explain prostitution. This is hard."

"So were they."

"You are the classiest damn person I know."

"Does it have the names of the customers?"

"Yeah."

The sound of her spitting out what I assume was a cheekful of sunflower seeds into a trash can explodes in my ear. "Text me what unit you're in. I'll be there in twenty minutes."

6

"Oh my god," CiCi says, bouncing with glee. "These people were absolutely running some kind of escort thing. A ring? What's the terminology?"

"I'm not hip on the vernacular," I say, rolling my eyes.

She parks herself on a box and starts flipping through stacks of paper. "This is way more fun than answering the ten thousand emails in my inbox."

"You're so responsible." I sip the wonderfully overpriced latte she brought for me and feel the urge to kiss her. "But you bought me this, so I'll let it slide."

She chews on her thumbnail and furrows her brows as she reads. "Okay, so it looks like these Cranson people had, like, what? An escort service? And these were the customers…" She points at the page in her hand. "And these were the, uh, escorts. So this must be what they paid to have done? But what do the numbers mean? Is it like ordering a value meal? You'll take the number three, and supersize it?"

I laugh. "That's definitely what it looks like to me. I wonder if the menu is around in any of these boxes."

"Clara," she says, looking at me with fiery blue eyes. "Do you realize there could be incriminating things in here? What if we find some politician's name on the customer list? Or the *escort* list?"

I go wide-eyed. "I didn't even think of that. Oh god, can I get in trouble for seeing this stuff? Is this illegal?"

"Hell if I know." She shrugs. "But, oh man, what if there really were? Some crappy family-values politician with a fuck-ton of escort receipts? You could sell that or something. Pay for a whole damn apartment if you get the right creep!"

"Isn't that blackmail?"

"It's only blackmail if you tell them they have to give you money, or else you'll give it to TMZ. It's just business if you take it right to TMZ."

I make a face. "That's horrible. I couldn't do that to someone."

"Well, I absolutely could, and I'd split the money with you." CiCi snorts. "This is real life. And we could do it anonymously."

I shake my head. "I'd feel so gross. I don't think I could live with that."

Now she rolls her eyes at me. "Lady, come on. You're living on a couch and sorting through trash. This could seriously mean a lot of money. We can't all make it through life on rainbows and kitten kisses."

I frown at her. "I know that. But come on—this is ridiculous. We haven't even found anything interesting other than that we *think* it's an escort service."

"Then let's look faster," CiCi says. Her smile gleams with wicked delight.

Three hours later, the sun is starting to go down, I haven't had anything besides crappy coffee and a latte in the way of sustenance, and we are still up to our armpits in invoices.

Not a single interesting name has appeared.

"I think we're on a wild dick hunt here, hon," I whine.

"Can we have pizza delivered to the unit? I'm starving."

I scoff. "I love you, but I'm not eating anything inside one of these things. That's how the Black Plague started."

"I'm questioning the historical accuracy of that statement." She stands up and pops her neck.

"Can we go?" I groan. "I still have to drive Brutus to the dump."

She pouts. "Okay, one more box each, and I'll help you drive him. Two boxes, and I'll buy dinner?"

"You're a woman obsessed."

She gives me a toothy grin. "We can have sushi."

I glare at her. "Fine. Jerk."

She climbs over a stack of boxes, obviously trying to up her luck by moving on to a new area, and I begrudgingly lift the lid off another box.

"Don't forget to look for stocks or bonds or whatever," I mutter.

"Yep. Got it. Totally invested." She rifles through the pages like her life depends on it.

I'm looking at another box of invoices. Stupid invoices. Even if I found the pope himself in here, I don't think I could go through with selling someone out like that.

Though CiCi's not wrong—I've heard the icky news outlets will pay a lot of money for this sort of thing. And beggars can't be choosers, and all that.

I'm just not sure if I haven't yet reached beggar status, or if I'm unwilling to admit I've reached it. Either way, this doesn't feel great.

"You know," CiCi says, scowling at what I'm guessing are disappointing names. "We don't know the names of all the politicians. What if we're looking at them and just not recognizing them?" She pushes one box aside and yanks open another one. "Maybe we should start looking up the names?"

I scoff. "Are you freaking kidding? That would take forever. Like, all of our actual lives. I'm not spending the rest of my existence trapped in unit 234."

She slumps. "Well, maybe just the fancy-sounding names? Anything that sounds like Benedict Worthington the Third or something."

"Is…is there a politician named Benedict Worthington the Third?"

She shrugs. "There could be? I don't know! That's why we should look them up."

I shake my head. "Ci. Come on."

"Okay, but if they sound even kind of familiar, we should Google."

I stamp my feet in a very toddler-like manner. "Fine. But I'm getting crab rolls tonight."

"Understood." Her voice sounds positively gleeful.

I make my way through my pile, then scoot the box out of the way. I'm pretty damn sure CiCi is on at least her third box. Cheater.

I pull off a new lid and my eyebrows go up. These aren't invoices. I pick up some papers and gasp.

"What!?" CiCi shrieks. "Who'd you find? Is it that senator from upstate? Please let it be the senator from upstate!"

"I think I found the escorts…"

She comes flailing over to where I'm sitting, tripping spectacularly over several boxes. She scramble-crawls the rest of the way to me.

"You are way too into this."

"Shut up," she pants. "Show me!"

I hand her a stack of what look like head shots with résumés stapled to the back. But where credentials or job experience would normally be listed, there are likes and dislikes—things like workout preferences, sexual preferences, and at the bottom of each résumé, a list of what they like doing with clients.

"Oh. My. *God*," CiCi whispers.

My eyes bulge. "This is surreal."

She bursts out laughing. "Clara, oh man. This chick says she likes a glass of pinot grigio and watching *Melrose Place* to get her in the mood. That is the most nineties fucking thing I've ever heard. This is amazing."

I can't help myself—I'm captivated. These profiles have *everything*. Every gender identity, every orientation. The pages detail any sexual scenario I could possibly imagine, and just…a whole bunch I could not. Some who are willing to role-play. Some who will provide bondage. There's even one guy who will only accept a client if they wear a suit.

My hunger and impatience are soon forgotten as we take turns reading the most impressive and mystifying ones out loud.

"Oh god, okay, oh man," CiCi says, bouncing on her cardboard box. "This guy says he's had over five hundred sexual partners and can show you things you've never even dreamed of." She holds up a picture of a very pale guy who looks more 1985 *Dungeons & Dragons* than superstud, posing in yellow boxer shorts adorned with hedgehogs. "His quote is, 'Let me lead you into temptation.'" She practically falls over laughing. "What do you say, Clara? Shall we look him up? I need some temptation!"

I snort. "Girl, these are over twenty years old. I can't even fathom what that guy looks like now." I make a face. "Oh god. I just fathomed…"

"Then there's this gal," she says, showing me the photo of a woman with more obviously permed hair than she has face. "She will only accept clientele who are willing to perform all sexual acts in a water-based environment."

I blink at her. "What…what does that even mean? Like, a bathtub, or the Hudson? There's a wide margin for weird there."

CiCi giggles and keeps sorting.

"Oh, here's a Google-able name!" I say. "Caspian Tiddles-wich. He's not a Third, but that's still pretty fancy-pants."

She laughs. "That's a badass name. I bet he never got beaten up in kindergarten at all."

I look at his picture. He's all floppy curly hair, pale blue eyes, and long limbs. He's more clothed than most of the other people in the pictures, and he looks really young and uncomfortable. I think he was aiming for a steely, sexy gaze, but it's coming off more terrified and angry.

"Aww," I say. "Poor thing is nineteen. He's still got a baby face and everything."

"Hey, some people are into that."

"Ew!"

She frowns at me. "It's not 'ew.' It's a job, and just because everyone is all puritanical about sex workers doesn't mean they should be. Nobody says 'ew' when someone works as a dentist."

"Okay, I do, but that's because I hate dentists." I contemplate that and nod. "But you're right—I need to dial back my prude."

I glance back down at the photo in my hand. "Just look at this kid, though," I tell her. "He looks kind of miserable.

What if he was just trying to pay his way through law school or something?"

"Then he's probably a successful lawyer? Maybe we found the moneymaker! What was his name again?"

I flip the résumé back over. "Caspian Tiddleswich."

"Wait." She freezes. "Why does that sound familiar?"

I stop and think for a beat. "You know what? I think I've heard it, too."

CiCi squeals at top decibel. "This is it! This is the politician! It has to be!" She yanks her phone out of her pocket and feverishly starts typing. While she waits for her results to load, I look at Caspian's picture again.

The wheels of my brain click to a stop, and I gasp.

"CiCi…"

Without looking up from her phone, she says, "What?"

"I think I know who this is."

Her head pops up. "What, really? Is he a senator?"

My jaw flops open, and I can't answer. There's no way this can be the same man. It just isn't possible.

CiCi looks at me expectantly for a moment, and then her phone finally loads and her gaze jumps back to the screen. She gasps louder than I did.

"It can't be," I whisper.

Her eyes look dangerously close to falling out of her head. "No way. Oh. My. God."

She holds up her phone, and I see what I already knew. There he is. I've seen that face a hundred times before. On television. On movie posters. In commercials for outrageously expensive German cars. Flying across the screen in that comic-book flick I saw on my last real date an age and a half ago.

Caspian Tiddleswich. The very British, impossibly famous movie star.

7

A couple of hours later, we're huddled in a booth at a Japanese restaurant in Astoria, clutching the escort résumé of one Caspian Tiddleswich, former male companion, current English actor sexy man. Every time our waitress comes by, we thrust the paper under the table, like we've got nuclear launch codes and she's an enemy spy approaching.

"This is ludicrous," I hiss over the table. "It can't be the same guy!"

CiCi pounds back another shot of warm sake. "It's not like it's a common name, Clara!"

I massage my temples. "Well, what the hell are we supposed to do with this?"

"Call TMZ!" she trills.

I grimace. "Are you kidding? This could ruin somebody! And this isn't like some jerk-faced politician spouting about the evils of feminism and abortion ruining American family values while he goes around boffing his interns. He could be a nice person!"

"Yes, but he's a really famous nice person! And all those gossip places would pay a hell of a lot more for dirt on a famous actor than a politician!" She pauses for a moment, thinking. "Probably. I actually don't know what the going rates are."

Our waitress comes over and sets plates of tempura rolls, crab rolls, and sashimi on our table. We both smile stiffly at her, looking like cats that ate a flock of canaries. She smiles back, but looks a bit unnerved as she hurries away.

I pop a piece of crab roll in my mouth and chew. "Jeez," I say through a mouthful of rice. "I just remembered I sometimes watch that show *Poirot* he does for the BBC. It's really good."

"Oh, yeah!" she says happily, picking up a bite with her chopsticks. "I've seen that! He's really good in it. All sexy in a weird lizard man kind of way."

I blink at her. "What...what does that even mean?"

She shrugs and eats her sushi. "I don't know. It's weird. He's kind of odd-looking, but he's really hot. I don't get it. Wouldn't kick him out of bed for eating crackers, though."

Disbelief is the kindest emotion I am capable of giving her. "Okay, well, all I can see now is this pitiful little nineteen-year-old kid. Come on. We can't sell that kid out to a tabloid."

She thinks on that and swallows. "But he's not a nineteen-year-old kid anymore. He's got to be almost forty and stupidly rich with private jets and shit."

"No more sake for you," I say, and push the bottle away from her. "You always add 'and shit' to things when you start to get tipsy."

"Thanks, Mom," she huffs, taking a nibble of pickled ginger. "You've got to admit this is really cool. And he's famous!

Famous people are used to this sort of thing coming out! And it's not like he doesn't know he was an escort. He's probably been expecting this to blow up for years! We'd probably be relieving him of two decades of anxiety."

I gape at her. "That's the most ridiculous thing I've ever heard. Ever. In all of life."

"Maybe not my best argument," she admits. "You could seriously sell this, though. So much money! A pretty new apartment! Your real bed that isn't a hideous corduroy couch!"

I'm stricken with a bite of tempura halfway to my mouth. My bed. God, how I miss beds. I can't think of many things I wouldn't be willing to do for the joyful comfort of my real, live mattress.

But could I live with myself if I ruined another person's life just to better my own? Probably not.

Okay, really not. I just couldn't do it.

Still, CiCi is right. He's a big-shot actor. They're used to this sort of thing, right? Or at least they expect it. It's part of the gig.

I grimace at my disgusting line of thinking and set my chopsticks down.

"You look like you're going to be sick," she says, nonchalantly edging the sake bottle back her way.

"This is making me feel icky."

"The sushi? Tastes fine to me."

I blow out a frustrated gust of air. "No, the potential destruction of another human being, CiCi."

Pouring me another helping of sake so as to distract me from noticing her filling up her own glass, she says, "Think about it. He probably did this escort thing because he needed the money back then. It's not something he's particularly proud of, considering he's never mentioned it publicly that I've found online, but he did what he had to do." She points her chopsticks at me. "That's what you're doing. You're in a bad way. You're just taking care of yourself. You don't have to feel good about it, but you're looking out for you."

I scowl. "You know, I'd bet actual money that's what drug dealers say when they recruit new drug dealers. If I had any money to bet, anyway."

"I think your knowledge of the underbelly of the world is somewhat limited."

"Yes! And let's keep it that way! I don't want to be a part of any underbellies!"

Sighing, she takes a sip of sake. "Well, what if it turns out Mr. Tiddleswich is actually a huge twat-wagon? What if he's one of those actors who's a complete prick to other people and makes everyone around him miserable? Like a reptilian-looking Jared Leto."

"He doesn't look like a reptile."

"A little bit, he does," she insists. "But seriously. Think about it—what if he's a holy terror, and this coming out and knocking him down a couple of pegs is exactly what hundreds of poor crew men and women have been waiting years for? It wasn't a terrible idea when it was a jerk politician. A jerk actor doesn't seem like that big a leap."

I prop my elbow up on the table and plop my chin into my hand. "It's possibly the exhaustion, or more possibly the sake, but that actually made some sense to me."

"YES!" she says. "So, should I email places? There have to be lots of gossipy sites that would eat this up."

"NO." I snatch the sake bottle away from her. "No emailing. But how about this—we do some research on him. The internet is full of creepy insider stuff on famous people. If he turns out to be some super-jerk, we can *maybe* reevaluate the possibility of selling this."

Her eyelids are moving a bit slower than they should be. "I guess that sounds okay."

"Promise me," I insist. "No telling anyone anywhere that we have this. Or that we know anything at all about it."

Sloshing her glass a bit, she juts her pinkie finger out at me. "Promise."

8

Another night on Gertrude has me waking up feeling a lot less humane about ruining Caspian Tiddleswich's reputation.

I also might need to cool it on the copious drinks with CiCi on the nights before I hit the bricks at E-Z Storage.

It's outlandishly cold outside today. I immediately regret my choice to dress like a normal person, thinking movement would keep me warm. Turns out sitting on my ass in a storage unit sorting through papers doesn't do much for raising one's body temperature. I pull my green gas station work gloves—acquired during my last visit to the mini-mart in a futile attempt to win over Rufus—over my fingerless ones and suck back the last dregs of my now-frigid bodega coffee.

It's just a loose estimate, but I'm figuring there are seven billion boxes left in this godforsaken unit. And thanks to our discovery of Sir Tiddleswich last night, I open each new box with the same comforting feeling I assume bomb disposal officers feel when they get an unexpected UPS delivery at home.

When you add in my depressingly empty inbox with no news whatsoever on any potential job that could get me out of this soul-sucking freezer where dreams go to perish... I'm not feeling my most chipper today.

Maybe I'll go see if Rufus is working again. Who knows— he could be the missing sunshine in my crappy day. I think I'm wearing him down.

"How's it going?" a man's voice sounds out.

I scream and instinctively fling my empty coffee cup toward the door of the unit.

It lands with a pathetic *thlump* at the feet of Charlie.

"Oh my god, you scared the heck out of me," I wheeze, clutching at my heart.

"Thank goodness you were armed," he says, nudging my fallen cup with the toe of his boot. "Rough neighborhood and all."

I force out a little laugh. I'm not sure what to think about Charlie. He looks like someone's friendly old grandpa, but I've been getting some serious undercover mob boss vibes from him since we met. Between his Storage King status, the fancy car, and the weirdly confident and unflappable posture he throws off—Charlie just has an air about him I can't quite place.

He definitely strikes me as someone who sits with his back to the wall in a restaurant.

"Next time I'll be packing Red Bull. You've been warned," I say.

He snorts. "Just wanted to see how it's comin' along. The boys at the lot said you've been bringing by good loads every night."

I smile. The landfill guys think I'm doing an okay job, at least. "Yep, I was on a roll until I hit this unit. It's all papers. But I'm looking through them really carefully, just like you asked."

He peers around me. "Finding anything good?"

My stomach lurches. He told me to look for anything that seemed valuable, but did he mean things like the escort receipts? Does he know what's in here? What if he knows what I've got?

I left Caspian's résumé tucked in the very bottom of one of my closet suitcases back at Tom's apartment, but I feel like that damn thing is pasted on my forehead right now. A scarlet letter of extortion. I swallow a little too hard.

"Not so much." I shrug, trying to sound casual. "Just a ridiculous amount of receipts so far. It's kind of a paper-hoarding situation. But I'm flipping through everything just to be sure."

He smiles, and his big gray walrus mustache pulls up at the ends. It makes him look like the Quaker oatmeal man. "Makes me glad I'm not paying you by the hour."

I laugh because, honestly, what the hell else am I going to do?

Very really going to do a quick internet search on Charlie tonight, just to see if he's ever been connected to people sleeping with the fishes in any way.

"I'll let you get back to it," he says. "I just stopped by to pick up this week's payments from the deposit box at the gate and wanted to see how it's going. Keep up the good work."

"Thank you. I'll sure try."

Charlie taps the empty coffee cup with his toe once more, then turns around and heads back to his Lexus. I can't decide if I've just now noticed how potentially scary he is, or if it's the guilt of what CiCi and I have been doing in this unit that's got me so on edge.

Suddenly I'm not in the mood to mess with Rufus, either.

I sit back down on a box in the middle of the unit and get back to filtering through invoices. CiCi has been texting me all morning demanding I look out for other fancy names, because she thinks it will be more fun to catch someone who isn't an actor. And by more fun, she thinks I'll actually agree to sell the person out.

Despite my insistence on morality, if I found, say, a belligerent Secretary of State on an invoice, I'd be really damn tempted. There isn't much I wouldn't do right now to get the feeling back into my legs. It is wicked cold.

I wonder how it would work. Would CiCi email TMZ, and then we'd have a check in a week? Because if I could get out of here… I'm pretty close to selling out my own mother.

That's horrible. I wouldn't. Probably.

And I don't think I would be able to just walk away without finishing the job I signed up for with Charlie. I made a promise, and I stick with my promises.

Even if that promise is horrible and freezing and slowly trampling my will to live.

Picking up a sorted box, I waddle over to Brutus and hoist it inside. If I did make a lot of money from selling out Tiddleswich, my first priority is securing a place to put my mattress and sleeping on it for days and days.

I wriggle back into the middle of the unit and pick a new box. I fight a quiet, but very real, urge to set it on fire just to get myself warm.

This box isn't invoices. Nor is it résumés. Thank everything. I want to get back to all the boring, unidentifiable paperwork.

I pick up a page and start reading.

#1 STANDARD ESCORT FEE: $50/hour

#2 ALL-INCLUSIVE MASSAGE: $100 for 60 minutes

#3 SNUGGLING: $100 for 60 minutes

#4 GIRLFRIEND/BOYFRIEND EXPERIENCE—An evening with the escort of your choice doing those things couples do: $350

#5 THREE IS NEVER A CROWD—You and your significant other with the escort of your mutual choosing: $500

#6 ROLE-PLAYING—Act out your deepest fantasies with the escort of your choice: $400

"Oooooooooh my god," I whisper to no one. It just keeps going and getting more and more frighteningly specific.

I quickly take my phone out and ignore the fifteen new texts from CiCi, take a picture of the escort services, and send it her way.

Not three seconds later, she texts back: DON'T. FUCKING. MOVE. I WILL BE RIGHT THERE.

And right here, she is. In less than the usual twenty minutes, even. Somehow, her enthusiasm has managed to bend the laws of space and time.

"Gimme, gimme, gimme!" she squeals, glomping into the unit. I've already moved on to another box, but I point to the stack of menus and she dives right in. "Oh my god. This is amazing. Wait—people pay for cuddling?"

"Sometimes you just really need a hug, I guess," I say, shrugging.

She looks up at me. "Do you need a hug? Am I being a bad friend?"

"Do I have to pay you a hundred bucks an hour for a hug?"

She scoffs. "Two hundred. I'm high-end, cupcake."

Laughing, I drag another box off to throw into Brutus. "You know, I'm actually making progress in here today. I might get this unit done before my hair goes gray."

"See? That's the right attitude," she says, barely paying attention to anything but the paper in her hands. "*Wait.* You can hire an escort for role-playing? Role-playing what?"

My face squinches up. "Naughty nurse? Sexy maid? I'm thinking any of the usual Halloween costumes they sell for women would work."

CiCi slaps the paper down on her lap. "You know, that's a good point. Why are all of our costumes things like 'Slutty Supreme Court Justice,' but all the guy costumes are frickin' Captain America with extra muscles sewn in?"

"We should write our congressmen about it."

She nods, then perks up. "Oh! I spent the morning looking up Tiddleswich!"

"Don't you have a real job?" I frown. "You're going to get fired if you keep running away to help me find the companions of days gone by."

"They can't fire me—I'm awesome." She snorts. "But okay. So this Tiddles-dude is actually all polished and cultured and Shakespearean. Like, actual Shakespeare. He's been Hamlet and Othello and all of them. He's even been nominated for two Oscars. He wasn't super famous until the *Poirot* show, and now everyone is swooning over his cheekbones and manly voice."

"Oooh," I say, standing up to stretch. "He really does have a sexy voice. The cheekbones are just unfair, though."

"Amen," she says, scouring the menu again. "But from what I saw, he doesn't have a girlfriend, never been married, isn't a big tabloid guy. He doesn't go clubbing so much as he drinks like a respectable British guy and swears a lot, but in that kind of endearing way. Not in the entitled asshole way."

"So he's not a Jared Leto?"

Her face crumples with resolute disappointment. "No. He actually seems like a really normal person. Outside the alien cheekbones, of course."

"Of course."

I settle back into sorting through boxes, and CiCi alternates between looking up potentially interesting names and actually doing her real job while sitting on stacks of escort résumés.

After a couple of hours, we take a break for lunch, hoofing it a few blocks until we find a little taco place with only three tables. As much as I suspect the questionable food safety of those tacos, I can't deny that they were delicious. Even if we did eat them while standing outside in frigid winds.

When CiCi and I get back to the unit, she kicks back in the corner on a pile of boxes and gets back to work. I'm just dusting off my hands after flinging another sorted load of papers into the bed of Brutus when my phone rings.

"Hello?"

"Hi," a man's voice says. "May I speak with Clara Montgomery?"

"This is she."

"My name is Michael Dunlop, from Feather Bound Publishing. You put in a résumé for an editorial position?"

I flail my free arm and dance in place. "Yes! Yes, I did.

Thank you so much for getting back to me!" CiCi looks up, and I point excitedly at my phone.

"I'm doing preinterviews before we bring in our final potential applicants for in-person meetings. Do you have a few minutes to answer some questions?"

"I certainly do," I say, pacing in the front of the unit.

He starts into his spiel about Feather Bound, and what they do, but I'm not listening as well as I should. I'm distracted by the sudden look of terror on CiCi's face. I mouth the word *What?* at her.

"Don't panic…" she whispers. "And don't turn around."

Naturally, I turn around.

There is a pigeon standing on the stack of boxes right beside me. Its little bird eyes are inches from my face.

"AHHHHHHHHHHHHH!" I scream and scramble backward, tripping over god knows what and sending papers—and the pigeon—flying around the unit.

"I said not to turn around!" CiCi yells, stumbling over to me. She shrieks as the pigeon dive-bombs her head, and she lands on the floor next to me, flailing her arms. "What the hell is wrong with this bird!?"

"Get it out, get it out!" It's flapping around the ceiling, trying to find something to land on or some way out or possibly plotting how to best peck out our eyes.

"I don't fucking speak pigeon!" she hollers.

All I can hear is the sound of our terrified wailing, the fluttering of papers flying around me, and the wind-slapping sounds of the beast's wings over our heads.

I drop my phone and grab a box lid. Waving it over my head, I try to guide the demon bird toward the entrance of the unit. CiCi grabs another lid, and after a solid minute of feathers and horror, the damn pigeon gets the gist and flaps back out into the gray sky.

We both stand there, clutching our box lids, panting, waiting for it to return.

"What. The hell," CiCi gasps.

I shake my head and try to catch my breath. Out of the corner of my eye, I see my phone sitting on the cement floor.

"Oh crap, oh crap, oh crap!" I cry, diving for it. Hoisting it to my ear, I cry, "Hello? Mr. Dunlop? Hello?"

But the line is dead. The line is so very dead.

9

"Really, it's not that bad," CiCi assures me from atop Gertrude. "I hear Feather Bound isn't as stable as some of the other independent publishing houses. You probably dodged a bullet there."

I take a gulp of wine straight from the bottle. "No, I dodged a pigeon."

"Think of it as a sign from the gods. You weren't meant to have that job, and they sent the pigeon to tell you."

I drink faster.

Getting outrageously drunk seemed the only recourse for the day. Tom had dinner plans and Trina was at some drinks thing for work, so I brought CiCi back to the apartment with me to wallow in misery and wine. A very large amount of wine.

"I'm going to be living on my brother's couch forever," I

say hopelessly. "That was the first nibble on a job I've had in months. My life is an actual nightmare."

"What I'm hearing here is that you're ready to throw Caspian Tiddleswich under the bus."

I take a bigger drink. "No. You know what I think? I think that pigeon was Odin or the universe punishing me for even *thinking* about messing with another person for my own gain. That's what it was. A karmic pigeon."

"You're drunk."

"Yes, yes, I am. And I'm serious. Think of what would happen if I tried to sell it!"

"What? A pigeon would drop a piano on your head?"

I blink at her. "You're drunk, too."

"Damn skippy, I am." She takes another pull.

I flop back onto the couch and hug the bottle. "I wish I could undo all of it. Maybe send him an email saying I found the stuff and I destroyed it and no one will ever know about it and all is well in the universe. If I fess up to being a horrible person, and then burn all the evidence, it'll purge my sin or something."

"I know you're not Catholic, but speaking as someone who spent her high school years being reprimanded by nuns, I'd say you've got the Catholic guilt thing down really well."

"It's nice to know I'm doing something right."

CiCi leans forward and sets her bottle down on the coffee table. "Tell you what. A friend of mine works for the place that did the publicity for the audiobook he narrated a year ago. Maybe I could get his email address."

My eyelids are sticking to my eyes. "Really? Caspian's?"

"Maybe." She yawns. "Would it make you feel better?"

I consider this. "You know, it just might."

She pulls out her phone and fires off a quick text. "There.

If the universe wants you to air it out, the email address will come."

We both stare at the phone in her hand for a few minutes, waiting for the universe to confirm my fate. After a while, we decide the universe is off getting drunk, since it's Friday night, and I order us a pizza.

Hours later, our bottles are empty, the room is spinning, and we've been trying to find something to watch on Netflix for at least a week and a half.

She scans the choices on her laptop for the hundredth time and gasps. "Oh my god. *Poirot.* We have to watch this."

I try to unpeel my tongue from the roof of my mouth. "I still haven't seen season three."

"The universe totally wants us to watch this."

"Um-phmph."

She clicks Play, and we settle in. There are two Caspian Tiddleswiches on the screen, and it takes me a good five minutes to realize this is just my vision, not an actual part of the show.

"He looks really weird in a fake mustache," I muse. "And I don't get why he dyed his dogs."

"Is that what happened? I thought he just got new dogs. You've got to admit he looks pretty hot in those dressing gowns."

"Whatever—I'm in it for his suits. That man can *wear* a suit," I declare. The character of Poirot appears on-screen shirtless, and I can feel my tongue hanging out. "Never mind. He doesn't need the suits."

"Ooh, look at him, all muscly. I read he had to buff up to be in that new space assassins movie. In all my years on this planet, I've never given a fig for intergalactic assassins, but if he's going to be strutting through space looking like that, I'll buy a ticket."

"It's the least we can do," I say. "Go pay to see his movie. We were planning to ruin his life and all."

"Balance." Her phone pings, and she holds it up. "Dude."

"You called me dude."

"Shut up," she says, slapping my arm and sort of falling over beside me on Gertrude. "Look. My friend didn't give me his email."

I frown. "Oh. I guess no clear conscience for me."

"No, *look!*" CiCi slaps me again. "She gave us his *phone number.*"

I gape at the phone. "What do I do with that?"

She slaps me yet again. I try to slap her back, but miss. "You. Call. Him."

I sit straight up, and the room spins faster. "I can't call him! Are you deranged?"

"I'm sending it to your phone," she says, poking at her screen. "Just call and tell him everything you would have said in the email! The universe wants you to call him. And the universe also really wants you to get him to go on a date with me wearing one of those dressing gowns."

"The universe wants that?"

"Hey, the universe hasn't gotten laid in a hot minute. The universe is *due.*"

I rub my eyes. "Are…are you the universe?"

Staring off into absolutely nothing, she sounds completely awed when she says, "I think I just might be."

The front door opens, and in walks Tom, stopping short when he spots his sister and her best friend collapsed together, surrounded by empty wine bottles on his couch. His ugly, ugly couch.

"Bad day?" he asks tentatively.

"We got attacked by a pigeon, and then I lost a potential job," I slur.

"That is a bad day."

"I think I need to sleep," CiCi groans.

"I think you need to pass out and make sure you're not on your back when you do," I mumble, trying to wiggle into a horizontal position beside her.

Tom laughs. "My big sister, ladies and gentlemen."

I sit up and glare at him. "Who are you talking to when you do that? I mean, really."

Trying hard to use his best serious face, he fails and offers to drive CiCi home.

"You are a god among men, Tom Montgomery. If you weren't the little brother of my pal and engaged to another woman, I'd totally date you and shit."

"She's drunk!" I call out. "She's 'and shit'—ing stuff!"

My poor brother helps a stumbling CiCi gather her things and guides her to the door. "Oh, hey, Clara. You should absolutely call that guy." CiCi dramatically taps her nose. "You know, that *guy*. And confess your sins and ask him about the dressing gowns. I really like those dressing gowns."

"I like his suits."

"Um, Clara?" Tom says, propping CiCi up with his arm. "Did you say you got attacked by a pigeon?"

"She really did," CiCi says, clutching the door frame. "I saw it. The actual whole universe sent a hit-pigeon to smite your sister."

I can tell Tom is using everything he has to not smile. "Well, I hate to break this to you, but I think he used an air strike."

I blink at him and try to make sense of his words. CiCi

loudly sucks in air. "Oh my god," she says. "I didn't even notice. You absolutely have bird poo in your hair and shit."

I press my lips together and nod. "Of course I do."

CiCi falls over giggling, Tom barely catches her before she hits the floor, and he can't keep his own laughter inside anymore.

He leads CiCi out, and I stumble off the couch into the bathroom and spot the pigeon remnants right above my ear. Fuck that pigeon.

I very clumsily wash that bit of my hair off in the sink, feeling that an actual shower right now could be potentially dangerous. Then I head into the kitchen, still pawing at my head with a towel. I pour myself a big glass of water and start sipping, knowing this might be my only hope of not waking up feeling like a deflated, hungover tire.

I pick up my phone to send CiCi a text asking her to let me know when she gets home safe, when I see the last message from her is that phone number.

What if the discovery of the bird poo was the universe reminding me I still need to atone? That buying a movie ticket and destroying the papers isn't enough?

I think of Tiddleswich as Poirot, all shirtless and detective-y, and wonder if he'd get a lot of detective role-play requests if he was still in the escort biz. Or if, back in the day, did he really get paid a hundred bucks an hour to cuddle someone?

I wonder if anyone would pay me to cuddle them for a hundred bucks.

The universe has spoken. Well, the bird poo got the message across, anyway.

10

It took me three more days to finish unit 234. The last two days were a lot more bearable, since I wasn't as blindingly hungover as I had been the first. CiCi even came by on Sunday and helped out. I didn't hear a peep from her all day Saturday, other than a pitiful text letting me know she was alive, marred with autocorrect mistakes. I'd imagined her typing it out with one hand in bed with her eyes closed, and she informed me later that this was accurate.

I've now moved on to new units, our brush with blackmail all but forgotten. The first unit after 234 was full of bags of old clothes and most were in relatively okay condition, so after clearing it with Charlie, I arranged to have someone from the homeless shelter a few blocks over come pick them up. Maybe a little philanthropy will help undo some of my bad karma.

My phone rings just as I'm finishing loading up Brutus with

what appears to be cases of old mechanical parts and waiting for Charlie to come look at a few financial-looking things I found in an old lockbox. I think there might be a couple of ancient savings bonds here, but honestly, Charlie seemed more excited at the prospect of the engine stuff when I told him.

I pull the phone out of my pocket to answer. "Hello?"

It's Charlie. "I'm running late, so just leave everything in the unit. I'll come by when I'm done here and check it out."

"Okay," I say. "It's unit 159. I'll lock it up before I go."

"You can leave the truck, too. I'll take it over tonight. I want to see if there's anything worth saving in those parts."

"I can wait around so you don't have to!" I say, not wanting him to think I'm shirking my duties.

"Nah, go home. You're doing good. Take a night off."

"Thanks, Charlie."

I hang up and think of Charlie as a friendly grandpa type again.

Then my brain jumps right into wondering what's got him tied up at the moment. Fixing up cement shoes, perhaps? I keep meaning to Google Charlie. I also make a note to look up if people really do the cement-shoe thing. I'm not sure how practical that would be as a means of offing someone, but the phrase had to come from somewhere.

It's dark out, but I'm still getting home earlier than I normally would. And, lucky me, Tom and Trina are off on one of their painfully sweet date nights, which means I've got the place to myself for the evening.

Riding the train home, I do the math in my head and realize I've only got eleven units left before I can collect my five thousand dollars. That's a nice thought.

What's less nice is that, after that eleventh unit, I'm out of a job again. Other than a few vague emails acknowledging the receipt of my résumé and promises to contact me if I seem like a good fit, I'm not getting anywhere with my job hunt. Which means I'm also no closer to moving off Gertrude and out of Tom's house.

My brain is telling me to be fiscally responsible for dinner and stop off at the market to buy things to cook for myself.

My stomach and my depressed self both agree I should order in curry and chalk it up as a mental tax write-off.

Back at the apartment, I race into the shower to wash the storage stink off myself and yank on my cozy space-cat pajama pants and favorite threadbare T-shirt that has the Tenth Doctor on it. CiCi gave it to me for my birthday years ago, and it always puts me in a good mood.

Curry ordered, mindless television on in the background, I scour Tom and Trina's bookshelves to find something to read. Aside from packing up my mattress, having to part with most of my books was the worst thing about losing my apartment. All the copies I couldn't bear to do away with were divided up between one of my closet suitcases, CiCi's apartment, and a big box sent to the storage unit. Several more boxes that wouldn't fit were sent back to my parents in Buffalo. My mother seemed to find this encouraging, in that it meant I'd probably come crawling back to stay, since I've always said home is where your books are.

It's hard to argue with that logic, but still no. Nope.

The doorbell rings, and I grab money from my purse and glomp to the front door. I open it to find a man on the other side. A man who isn't holding curry.

"Um. Hi," I say, feeling more than a bit confused.

The man stares down at me with unusually pale blue eyes. He has hair so dark it's almost black and is a good foot taller than I am, and he looks a little familiar, but I have no idea why. He doesn't seem pleased at all, and it's just occurred to me I've opened the door to a stranger in New York City. I very carefully pull my phone out of my pocket just in case I need to speed-dial 911.

"Can I help you?" I ask tentatively.

"I'm looking for Clara Montgomery," the man says with a thick English accent.

The voice does it. I *do* recognize this person.

Caspian Tiddleswich is standing at the door.

I gasp and—dropping my phone and the curry money—clap my hands to my mouth. "Oh my god. You're…you're… Oh my god…"

"May I come in, please?" Caspian fucking Tiddleswich asks. His voice is even more godlike in person. I can't feel my legs.

Can Caspian Tiddleswich come into my brother's apartment? My hands still clamped to my face, he can't see my mouth hanging open. Sure. Sure, he can come in. I nod, and slowly shuffle to the side so he can enter. As he passes by, he swiftly picks my phone up off the floor.

I shut the door behind him and finally drop my hands. I'm having a hard time remembering how to breathe. There's a voice in my head wondering if I've had either a stroke or an unforeseen psychotic break, since I'm obviously hallucinating the movie star currently in Tom's living room.

"I assume you're Clara," he says. Oh god. He says my name like Cl-AHR-a. English accents really do make everything better.

I nod, trying with everything I have not to squeal like a tween at a boy band concert. "Would…would you like to sit?" I glance at Gertrude and make a face. I wave my arm toward the charcoal-gray stuffed chair across from the couch, and he glides over to claim the seat. Jesus, he walks the way he sounds.

Caspian sits back in the chair and stares at me as I carefully lower myself onto Gertrude's cushions. I notice he's still holding my phone. "Um," I say. "I'm not trying to be rude, but why in the world are you here? I'm a little concerned I've had an aneurysm."

He scoffs, his face a mask of bitter amusement, and I'm so shocked I almost flinch. "You're not trying to be rude? It's rather late to be bypassing rudeness, don't you think?"

"Excuse me?"

"It's unfortunate enough you've gone to the lengths to extort money from me, Miss Montgomery. Let's not add in the embarrassment of your pretending to be an innocent at this stage in the game."

I blanch, but my heart is racing. He knows. That has to be why he's here. But how the hell could he know? Did CiCi do something with those pages? As far as I know, they're still locked up tight in the bottom of my suitcase in the coat closet.

"I'm sorry," I say, trying to keep my voice level. "But I honestly have no idea what you're talking about."

"Oh, for god's sake," he growls. Caspian reaches into the inside breast pocket of his jacket and pulls out his own phone. He scrolls for a moment and then holds it up in front of him. A second later, my slurring voice comes through the speaker.

"Hello! My name is Clara Montgomery, and this message is for Caspian Tiddles… Tiddles-something. Tiddles-something." My hands slap back to my mouth, and I make a panicked sound. "You don't know me, because why should you? But I know youuuuu. Well, I don't actually know you. But I've seen you on stuff. In stuff. Grammar is hard. I'm an editor. Or I was. I'm not right now. But I clean out storage units and whatnot now, so that's fun. No, actually, it's not fun."

Caspian is staring daggers at me from across the room, and

I think I'm going to throw up as my drunken voice rambles on. "So, anyway, I found this stuff from, like, waaaaaaaaay forever ago when you worked for Cranson. Did you really cuddle people professionally? That sounds like a cool job. But I don't think you tell people you used to be a professional cuddler. I don't think I'd tell people if I cuddled professionally. But I wanted to let you know that I found your, like, résumé thingy, and I've got it. But it's okay, because it's really safe and I'm going to take care of it. I'm on the case! *Like Poirot*."

Past me's voice devolves into giggles. Present me wants to burst into flames. "My friend is really into you in the dressing gowns, by the way. She wanted you to know that. Personally I prefer the suits, but that scene without the shirt, whoooooo-boy. I don't think you look like a lizard. And if I weren't to-tally completely broke, I'd hire you for cuddling. The number three, right? Or hell, after the shirtless stuff, I can see why people would shell out for the role-playing, damn. I'd order a number six with a side of three."

More giggling. I'm going to die.

"So. There's that. But anyway. I've got the thing, and I'm going to take care of it. You watch. I'll take care of eeeeeeeeeverything, sir. Sir Tiddles. TIDDLESWICH! Ha! I knew I'd get it. That's a funny name, though. Caspian Tiddles-wich. Kind of sounds like the noise a bare ass makes on a leather couch in the summertime. So. Yeah."

The sound of a very drunken me fiddling with my phone echoes out through the room, and the line suddenly goes dead.

I can't breathe. He calmly places his phone back inside his jacket pocket and stares at me.

"Oh my god," I groan into my hands. "Oh my god, oh my god, oh my god. This isn't happening."

"Naturally, I waited for further instructions from you," he

says evenly. "And when none came, I decided not to sit around waiting for you to sell the information to the highest bidder."

I half claw at my face. "Wait—what? What instructions?"

He huffs out a quick blast of air. "This will go a lot faster if you at least attempt some honesty. I can imagine it's far less amusing to extort someone when they're sitting in front of you. We can't all hide behind the bravery of what I have to assume was an unhealthy amount of alcohol. But since you set this in motion, I intend to finish it. What is it you want from me, Clara Montgomery?"

His Cl-AHR-a is now considerably less endearing than it was a moment ago. I pull my hands from my face and wave them in front of my chest. "I'm so sorry. You've got the wrong idea, I swear. I wasn't trying to extort you. I don't even remember calling you! Oh my god, this is so embarrassing."

"Come on," he says acidly. "Don't lose your nerve now. I can't even fathom the lengths you must have gone to in order to find information about my time at Cranson. No sense clamming up now."

His demeanor is so solid, it's disconcerting. Add in his already dark features with an angry glare, the menacing voice, and I am either about to run screaming from the apartment or pee myself.

"Look, I understand why you're upset. I do," I say pleadingly. "But I didn't go looking for anything, and I'm not trying to get anything from you. I'd thought about calling you that night, but I was planning to tell you that I'd found those papers and I was going to destroy them because I thought maybe you'd worried they'd get found one day or something. I promise, I was trying to do the right thing."

He lets out a single laugh, and it's terrifying. "Yes, of course. That all makes absolute sense."

I stand up off the couch and decide against dropping to my knees to beg for understanding. "This looks really bad, but I wasn't going to do anything with what I found! And the reason I wanted to call—well, technically I wanted to email you, but couldn't find your email—was because I *had* considered seeing if there would be a way to sell the information, but then I realized how horrible that was, and this pigeon attacked me, and I wanted to restore balance to the universe. Confess my sins, you know?" I can hear myself stuck in a rapid-fire babble, so I wring my hands and add, "I swear I don't usually talk this much. Except when I'm drunk. Evidently."

"You've quite literally just admitted you'd intended to sell what you found," he points out, shaking his head.

"God, no!" I say, hands flailing around my face again. "Why would I do that? Why would I call you to tell you I was about to out you to the world? That's ridiculous!"

"To see if I'd be willing to pay more than whatever gossip rag you'd roped in." He's glaring harder now. "I've no intention of playing games with you, Miss Montgomery. Be glad that I'm dealing with this on my own, because I could easily involve the police. Still toying with the idea, actually. But if you're willing to act sensibly here, I think we can leave them out of it for now."

My heart sinks down onto the floorboards and stays there.

Then the doorbell rings, and I yelp.

"Are you expecting someone?" He frowns.

"No!" I insist. My head is spinning. "Wait—yes. Food. I ordered food."

His expression turns to irritation mingled with a hint of abhorrence.

This is a nightmare.

I look over and see my dollars still lying on the floor. I

scramble over and scoop them up, opening the door as narrowly as possible to prevent the delivery gal from having any opportunity to spot my visitor. I fling the money at her, yank the bag of food from her hands, trill, "Keep the change!" and slam the door in her face.

I turn around, clutching my dinner, and assume a deer in headlights stance.

"Um...dinner. It's curry. Do...? Are you...hungry?"

He makes a confused face. "Are you mad?"

I'm completely exasperated. I stomp over and drop the bag on the coffee table and wheel around to face him. "I'm sorry! I was trying to be polite! I'm not hip on the proper etiquette for the moment when a famous person barges into your apartment and yells at you over a misunderstanding!"

"But this isn't your apartment, is it?"

I freeze. "How could you possibly know that?"

"I looked into you," he says coolly. "Former publishing employee, laid off several months ago, living with someone with the same last name. You're unmarried, so I'll assume your brother? Broke and desperate—the perfect combination to try your luck in the tabloid market."

"Hey," I snap. "You had no right to dig up information on me. That's so creepy!"

He laughs another humorless laugh. "That's your defense? After what you've managed to dig up on *me*?"

"I didn't dig anything up!" I feel tears burning in my eyes. "I found it by accident and had a moment of moral weakness because for a second I thought it would be nice to be able to afford a place to put my goddamn mattress. But I never would've done it! I was trying to tell you I was going to destroy the papers!"

"And did you?"

"Did I what?"

He spreads very long fingers out over the arms of the chair. "You say you meant to tell me the information was being destroyed. So I'm asking if you did. Destroy it, that is."

I frown. "Well, no. I didn't think about it again."

The corner of his mouth curls up. This is a much scarier expression in real life than it was in *Poirot*. "Naturally not. So, let's get down to business, shall we?"

"Jesus," I say, losing my temper. "Enough with the Bond villain theatrics." I stomp over to the coat closet, yank out my suitcase, and violently pull back the zipper. "I don't want anything from you. I never did. I made a mistake, and I'd lost a potential job, and I was having a bad fucking day, okay?" I pull the papers I have on him—the résumé and the "menu"—out of the suitcase, double-checking to be sure they're both there, and march over to his chair. I shove the papers into his chest. "Take them. I don't want them. I didn't do anything with them, and I never intended to. Take them and get out, please."

He carefully gathers the papers in his hands and looks at them. A flicker of an emotion other than derisive resentment crosses his ice-blue eyes, but it's gone again as quickly as it came.

Carefully folding them, Caspian tucks the pages into an inside pocket of his jacket. He takes hold of my phone again and very abruptly shoves it in front of my face.

"Excuse me. What the hell are you doing?" I ask indignantly.

He calmly pulls his arm back and starts silently scrolling, and I realize he used the goddamn facial recognition to unlock my phone. A moment later, he turns it back so I can see. A picture of the Cranson "menu" I'd taken and sent to CiCi.

"And how many more pictures do you have, Clara?"

I grab my phone out of his hand, and I feel the first of the tears falling down my cheeks, leaving a corrosive trail. I quickly delete the picture and show him the screen. "There. It's gone. There aren't any more. I sent it to my friend CiCi— just that picture, nothing about you—and I will make sure she deletes it, too. Okay?"

"Because I have every reason to trust you."

I scream at him out of frustration. "God, shut up! I'm sorry! I'm really sorry! I screwed up, but I didn't mean to do anything wrong!" Tears are absolutely everywhere, and he looks unnerved for a moment. "I don't know what I can show you or say that will get you to understand I didn't mean for any of this to happen. So if you're going to call the police, just do it, okay? This playing-with-your-food game is getting old."

He stands up in a quick motion, and I stumble backward a few steps. Famous person or not, I'm alone in the apartment with a very angry guy who is *much* bigger than me.

"I didn't start this!" he yells back at me.

The front door bursts open, and quite suddenly, Tom is inside, Trina a few steps behind. "I heard shouting," he says, assessing the room. His eyes fall on Tiddleswich, and Tom stiffens up. "Clara, what's going on? Are you okay? Who is this?"

"Holy crap!" Trina gasps. "You're that guy! That actor guy with the really long name!"

Tom's face screws up in confusion. "Who?"

"The posters are all over the city! He's the guy in the Nebula Force movie!"

My brother's face goes blank for a moment while he processes. Then, a second later, "Well, why the hell is he in our apartment, and why is Clara crying?"

Trina stands there gaping, Tom is trying to hold his best

tough-guy stance, and our visitor looks surprisingly contrite. And, even more alarming, possibly speechless.

"Um." I clear my throat. "It's actually nothing." I quickly wipe the tears from my face and straighten up as much as I can. "Mr. Tiddleswich had been planning to write a book under a pen name for my old house, but it all went under with the merger. We ran into each other earlier and were talking about his options, and I got a bit overly emotional about not being able to do more since I'm still unemployed. Think I scared him a bit." I add a pathetic chuckle at the end for good measure.

"Oh," Tom says lamely, and stands down. "God, I'm sorry. We didn't mean to interrupt anything. I heard all the yelling and got worried. We can leave you guys alone." He starts scooting Trina, who is still gaping, back toward the front door.

"No!" I yelp. "I mean, that's okay. He was actually just about to head out. I've taken up too much of his time tonight, anyway."

"Are you sure?" my brother presses. "Don't stop on our account."

I shake my head, and I know I'm seconds from bursting into tears again. I turn to the celebrity in the room. "I think we're finished, aren't we?"

He looks at me for a moment, his expression unreadable. Carefully, he reaches down and buttons his jacket. "Yes, I think we are. Thank you for taking the time to speak with me tonight, Miss Montgomery." He turns to Tom and Trina. "My apologies for the confusion."

He gives me a quick side-glance and then leaves through the still-open front door.

Caspian Tiddleswich has left the building.

11

"I am so, so, so sorry," CiCi says for the seven hundredth time. "This is all my fault."

"It kind of is, but I love you anyway," I tell her with a sigh as I throw another box of old newspapers into Brutus.

"I can't believe he came to Tom's *apartment*!" she says quietly. "And he yelled at you! This is like being trapped in some surreal reality show."

I stop for a moment and look at her. "Shouldn't you be at work? Like, I know you have a banging trust fund and all, but I still think it would suck to get fired because you're rescuing your damsel-in-distress pal all the time."

"Cupcake, you got verbally beat down by a celebrity last night, and it's my fault," she says. "This is what sick days are for." She grabs a newspaper-stuffed box of her own and flings it into the truck. "The least I can do is help you out today.

And buy you lunch. And dinner. And shoes. Do you want some shoes?"

"You don't have to buy me shoes," I say, laughing.

"I still think you should have let Tom kick his ass. He's tougher than he looks."

"No way. Caspian Tiddleswich is a *big* dude. You weren't wrong about him getting all beefy for that space flick. And he's got that whole dark-and-sinister thing going."

"Well, I'm not going to see his stupid movie *now*. He's a prick, and I hate him."

"Amen. I don't think I can watch him in anything ever again. Which kind of sucks, because I really liked *Poirot*. I was about to finish season three."

My phone buzzes, but I ignore it. I'm determined to get this unit finished before lunch. The nervous anxiety of my brush with Tiddleswich has given me a newfound burst of determination to finish this damn job so I can focus on finding a new editing gig full-time.

CiCi's guilt seems to have given her a similar surge of energy, and she's being outrageously helpful today. If we keep this up, I'll be down to nine units by the end of the day. Hopefully.

My phone buzzes again. Then again. And again.

I throw a stack of collapsed cardboard boxes into the truck and pull out my phone. Before I can even get past the lock screen, it buzzes again—I have a handful of texts from people I know casually. Ooh, maybe they have job leads!

CiCi pulls out her phone after a buzz of her own.

I open the first text and scream. An actual, full-lung scream.

There, in a text message, is a screenshot of a crappy gossip website, and in that screenshot stands Caspian Tiddleswich and me. In my jammies. In Tom's living room.

"OHHHHHH MY FUCKING GOD," CiCi shrieks.

I close the message and start opening the other ones—more screenshots. Former coworkers and acquaintances coming out of the woodwork, asking me if I know Caspian. Are we dating? Are we friends? Can I get him to narrate an audiobook?

"Holy shit, holy shit, *holy fucking shit*..." CiCi whines.

I drop to the cement and stare at the screenshots. One has a bigger picture with the caption, *"TIDDLES-WHAT!? CASPIAN BREAKS GIRLFRIEND'S HEART WITH GAY SHOCKER!"*

"OH MY GOOOOOOOOOOOOOOOD."

"What is happening!?" I cry. "This is a nightmare—please tell me this is a nightmare! How did they even get a picture of him in the apartment!?"

"They're saying you're his girlfriend!" CiCi points out.

My phone starts ringing. An agent I'd done several deals with at my old job. Oh Jesus. I send it to voice mail. It immediately starts ringing again. This time it's a former colleague who was laid off at the same time I was.

CiCi's phone is also sounding off like a siren.

"CiCi, what the hell do I do!?"

Another text comes in.

This is Caspian. I need to speak with you. Immediately.

I scream like the phone has burned me and throw it onto a bag of old clothes. I collapse forward and hide my face. "This is it. I'm going to prison. He's going to have me arrested. Oh my god."

CiCi appears beside me. "What? Did he call you?" I weakly point to my phone, and she picks it up, reading the text. "Oh, shit. Um. Don't go! Just don't answer him!"

I grab the phone back and stare at the fatal text. "I can't do that! He was ready to call the cops on me last night, and this is a million times worse! Where the hell did that picture even come from!? OH CHRIST, MY MOTHER IS CALLING! CiCi, help!"

She yanks my phone out of my hand and holds the power button down until it shuts off. Like holding a tiny pillow over its little phone face until it stops twitching and goes quiet. Then she puts her own phone on silent and stuffs both of them into her pockets. "Close this unit up. Let's go drop off Brutus early, and get the hell out of here."

She doesn't have to tell me twice. We scramble to load everything into the truck, and I lock the unit up behind us. CiCi takes the wheel and all but squeals the tires as we flee E-Z Storage.

After leaving Brutus at the dump, we hightail it back to CiCi's neighborhood. I'm not even sort of hungry, but she insists I eat something. "Carbs help with anxiety," she tells me.

"I don't think that's true," I say in a zombie voice.

"It is for me!" She shoves a fistful of french fries into her mouth. We've retreated into a little burger joint not far from her apartment and are currently hiding in a booth.

"I'm going to have to message him back," I say. "Yesterday morning, my biggest concern in life was when I'd find a job and be able to sleep on my own goddamn mattress again. Now it's that I might go to jail for extortion of a famous guy."

"You aren't going to jail," she says through her mouthful of potato. "I won't let that happen. And anyway, his lawyers can't put you in jail. The prosecutor has to do that."

I slam my head down on the table and moan. "I can't afford a lawyer. Oh my god, CiCi, what did we do?"

"I'll tell the cops it was me!" she says suddenly. "I started all of this anyway. I won't let you go to jail for it!"

"I'm not letting you get arrested!"

"Well, I'm not letting *you* get arrested!"

We stare desperately at each other for a moment and then silently start eating fries again. She's right. They are oddly helpful.

"I'll message him back." I swallow hard. "I'll message him back, and we can talk, and I'll beg him to understand. This all started as a huge misunderstanding anyway, but I definitely didn't do anything wrong here. I didn't take that picture. And he's the one who just showed up at Tom's apartment. And it's not like I'm thrilled that a photo of me ugly-crying is now plastered on the front page of Perez Hilton, you know?"

"Maybe there were paparazzi outside?" CiCi suggests. "I mean, they are super sneaky and follow celebrities around. You said the door was open when Tom came in, right? Maybe one of them got the picture then?"

"Maybe?" I think for a moment. "That really could be! They have those scary cameras that can take pictures from, like, miles away, right? So if that's it, this is on him! They wouldn't have been there if he hadn't stormed in like a big jerk!"

"Basically, yes. This is *all* his fault."

"I...I don't think we can go that far."

CiCi sighs and shoves more fries in her face.

12

"**D**id we really have to meet here?" I ask, frowning.

"Is there a problem?" Caspian Tiddleswich replies.

We are in the same position as last night—me clinging to Gertrude, while he's all long limbs and cheekbones in the gray chair, which is starting to look a bit like his throne—but at least I'm wearing real pants this time.

"No offense, but I don't feel particularly comfortable being alone with a guy who may or may not want to murder me."

He rolls his eyes. "I'm not planning to murder you. I would hire out for that, anyway."

"That's not very fucking comforting, you know!"

"Oh, do calm down," he says with a sigh. "I'm certainly not here to offer comfort, but I'm not going to hurt you."

"Then what are you here for? The delightful banter?"

"How much did you get for the picture?"

"Excuse me?"

"The picture you sold. I assume you fared well. Even my own team was thrilled to have a shot of me with a *girlfriend.* The press must have lapped at your hands."

I stare at him for a moment. "Are...are you actually serious right now?" I ask, astonished. "I didn't sell that picture, and I certainly didn't take it. I know you're not actually Poirot, but I was *in* the goddamn picture, and it's not like I have magical camera powers or something. I thought maybe there were paparazzi outside."

"I saw no paparazzi here last night."

I throw up my hands. "Then I don't know, but I didn't take the stupid picture! You were literally standing right in front of me. Did you see me go all Mr. Fantastic and manage to stretch my arm across the room to take one with *me in it?*"

"Perhaps it was your brother?"

I glare at him. "Look, I'm trying to stay as civil as possible, but if you start accusing my family of things like this, we are going to fight, do you hear me? It's bad enough you've decided I'm some criminal mastermind."

"Of course you're not," he says calmly. "You're just a desperate, money-hungry girl lacking the brains to pull off a quick scheme."

I swallow the burn of tears that swims through my throat. "Well, I think you're a pretentious, overly hyped prick with outrageous delusions of being far more important than you actually are."

Caspian brushes a piece of invisible lint off his slacks, looking completely unperturbed. "Now that we've settled on that."

I grab a pillow and slam it into my lap. If I have to punch something, I'll probably do less jail time for the pillow. "Yes, let's move on. What do you want? You organized this little meeting, after all."

"Yes, I did." He sits up straighter in his chair. "You've complicated my life a bit, Clara."

"Yes, but the important thing is that you haven't overreacted at all," I snark.

The corner of his mouth twitches ever so slightly. "I've spent the day thinking how I could handle the situation. Obviously, I could go to the police."

My heart skips in my chest. "Fine. Call the police, then. You're a dick for believing what you do, but whatever."

He gives me a pointed glance. "I've also entertained the possibility that you were genuine in your drunken and horribly misguided phone call."

My mouth falls open in surprise. "Oh."

"You could have made the situation considerably worse for me last night, and judging by the reactions from your brother and his companion, they had no ideas as to why I would be here—which leads me to believe they had no knowledge of what you'd discovered about my…history. When I left, I'd decided to just let it all lie."

"I feel like you're about to say 'but.'"

"But…"

"Goddamn it."

"That was before the picture of us landed on the front page of every gossip site this morning."

"I didn't do it," I whine and throw my face into the pillow.

"I'm almost inclined to believe you," he says. "But as I said, you've created complications for me, and as one good turn deserves another, I've thought of a way you can make it up to me."

I sit back up and take a deep breath. "Fine. What?"

"I'm in the city doing a show, which I assume you know."

"Actually, I didn't. Because not everyone is obsessed with your greatness, Mr. Tiddleswich."

He carries on as though he doesn't hear me. "I'll be finishing my run two weeks from now. The night before I head back to London, there will be a premiere for my new film."

"Okay?" I shrug. "Good for you?"

"As I said, my management team tends to fret over my not being seen in a relationship with anyone, and they've been trying to orchestrate various scenarios for me to be coupled off."

"That's a weird thing to fret over."

He sighs and shakes his head. "I agree. But while it's not my concern, it is tiresome for it to be thrust at me repeatedly. That's where you'd come in."

I blink at him. "I'm sorry—what?"

"You'd accompany me to various public places, a function or two. The press thinks you're my girlfriend, and that we had a row last night. The plan would be to show us happily made up, doing things as a couple, until we unfortunately split up the night of the premiere before I return home."

"You're fucking kidding me right now."

"Do we really need so much color?"

"Fuck, yes, we fucking do. You can't be serious."

"I'm very serious. This would appease my team, give the press something to titter about before the movie opens, and allow me to focus on finishing my show."

My brain can't begin to process what he's suggesting. "You want me to pretend to be your girlfriend? In real life, that's a thing you're asking me to do?"

"I considered hiring you for your cuddling services, but I think you'd overcharge me."

My cheeks burn. I hate that he made me blush. "Why

would you even want me to?" I blurt out. "You *loathe* me. And that's a mutual feeling, I assure you."

"This is merely a means to an end for me." Then a small smile touches his lips. "Although, after the stress you've put me through, I'm a bit pleased at how miserable you'll be. But if you'd prefer we dealt with the situation through legal channels, I'd find that entertaining as well."

Until this moment, my thoughts have been swirling too fast for me to sort, but they quite suddenly stop. Like someone threw a box of puzzle pieces into the air and they land, perfectly positioned.

There's not enough air in my lungs as I stammer, "You're... you're blackmailing me."

He smiles. "You're quite quick. Not as much fun on the other side of the table, is it?"

"Oh my god, I wasn't trying to blackmail you, you absolute cock of a person!"

"I'm prepared to believe you any second now."

"This is fucked up," I snap. "And as much as the mere thought of you repulses me in a way I can't accurately express with words, I'm sure there are dozens of star-humping groupies who would be happy to step in as your rent-a-date. Why not get one of them to do it? Isn't that why jerks like you become actors in the first place?"

He releases a slow breath, and I see a muscle in his jaw working hard. I'm both terrified and annoyed beyond reason. "No," he says, through nearly clenched teeth. "My career motivations were different. My private life is no one's business, despite the media's differing opinion on that subject." He seems legitimately angry, but for the moment, that anger doesn't seem to be directed at me. "So, no, I wouldn't be comfortable attempting to find a random woman to fill the role."

I scoff. I can't help it. "But you have no problem forcing me to?"

For a split second, his determined stare almost breaks, but he regroups. I've never known someone to keep this level of eye contact for so long. It's the most disconcerting part of the whole mess. "None of this would have been my first choice, either," he offers. "But this didn't originate with me, if you'll recall." Before I can pull in air for a verbal, and likely profane, rebuttal, he continues, "And I'm willing to bet the information I have on you is enough to ensure your discretion."

I'm being forced to choose between my dignity or a felony record, and my brain can't settle on one emotion.

I'm scared. There's nothing I wouldn't give to make him disappear from my life.

I'm guilty. I made a mistake that I'm being punished for.

I'm on the edge of hysterics. The whole scenario is so surreal, and there's no room for rationality.

I hug the pillow to my chest, holding it against me like armor. "What would I have to do?"

"Nothing untoward," he says, far too calm for my liking. "We'd go through the public motions of dating, but nothing over the top. Go for coffee, have dinner, that sort of thing. You'd attend my show at least twice, and we'd be seen leaving together. You'd attend my premiere, and that night, we'll be seen squabbling in public, leading to our inevitable breakup. Then I'll go my way, you'll go yours. Behind the scenes, we will continue our mutual disdain, as is our wont."

"Look, I'm sorry, but I can't afford that stuff," I tell him earnestly. "I really can't. We aren't all movie stars. And as much as I'm sure it will end up being less than the cost of a defense attorney, the fact that I'm living on a couch should make it pretty clear there's no way in hell I can swing paying for any of the things you just mentioned."

He stares at me for a moment, absentmindedly pressing his middle fingers to his thumbs. I've never felt more awkward.

"I'll provide whatever is required during our time together."

"No way," I say, shaking my head with fervor. "Nope. Not a chance. I don't want anything from you. Not even a damn cup of coffee."

"Oh, for god's sake, do calm down," he retorts, rolling his eyes at me again. "I'm not speaking extravagances. Travel costs, meals, what have you. Quite plainly, you'll be doing me a favor as well as atoning, so it's not a hardship."

I scowl at him. "And what kind of assurances do I have that if I do this, and make a complete fool of myself, then you won't turn around and call the police on me anyway?"

"I could have my lawyer draft a contract if you'd prefer."

"Oh Christ, no," I sputter. "I don't need you putting your ridiculous delusions about what you think happened down on paper. And I can't afford my own lawyer to look it over to be sure I'm not getting screwed."

"You'll just have to take my word for it, then."

"Because you seem like such a stand-up guy."

He looks down at the floor. It's the only time he's broken direct eye contact for more than a second since he got here. "I am, actually. Well, I try to be." He gathers his mood again and returns to staring. "When I'm not dealing with potential criminals, that is."

My shoulders slump, and I wrestle with my thoughts, desperate to conjure up something, *anything*, to wriggle out of this. I come up empty. "I can't believe you're blackmailing me."

He smiles. "Yes, but the important thing is that you haven't overreacted at all."

13

"You have to go to the police," CiCi hisses as she helps me sort through yet another storage unit. "This is extortion!"

I fling a trash bag full of moth-eaten old blankets into Brutus. "I'm going to choke to death on the irony of what you just said."

"I'm serious!" she says, separating usable clothes from trash. "What if he's some murdering rapist celebrity guy? That can happen!"

I straighten up and glare at her. "Why? *Why* would you say that, CiCi?" Brushing my hands off on my jeans, I try to catch my breath a bit. "I don't think he's a legitimate danger. I just think he's pissed at me and finds the prospect of humiliating me to be hilarious. And what would I even tell the cops? That I'm being blackmailed by the guy I seriously considered blackmailing first?"

For the first time since this whole fiasco started, CiCi looks defeated. She sits down on the edge of an ancient plastic storage container, and her shoulders slump. "This is all my fault."

I sigh. "I went along with all of it. And I'm the one who made that stupid phone call." The memory of my slurring, drunken voice stumbles through the recesses of my mind, and I shudder.

"So what happens now?" she asks, waving her hands around helplessly. "When do you have to...?" A strange expression crosses her face. "Oh my god, I just realized you're his *escort*. Clara, he's making you be an escort!"

I throw a moldy pillow at her as hard as I can. "I am not!"

"I don't mean in a sex way!" CiCi picks up the pillow and walks it over to Brutus, deep in thought. "But that's actually what a lot of escorts do. They just act as companionship for people who are lonely, or who need dates to things." She flings the pillow into the bed of Brutus and looks irritatingly impressed. "You know, as far as revenge goes, that's actually pretty genius."

I squint thoughtfully. "Huh." Not wanting to give him any more credit, I carry on. "Anyway, I think I'm just sort of on call for the next two weeks? He beckons, I go meet him, that sort of thing."

CiCi snorts. "You're his on-call girl."

I raise an eyebrow at her. "You're better than that."

"Yeah, that was low-hanging fruit," she admits as she grabs a box of holey blankets to lug to the truck. "So he can't give you any kind of schedule?"

I shrug. "I'm sure he could, but that would be playing fair. Where's the fun in that?"

"At least he said he'd pay for everything, right?"

A flash of rage rushes through me, and I throw an old coffee can full of rusty nails into the pile. "Yes, ugh. I *hate* this. I don't want to accept anything from him."

"Well, I say you turn the game on him and have some fun with it yourself! Order the lobster! Tell him you need a fancy new dress for the premiere!" CiCi suggests excitedly.

"Not a chance. Captain Cheekbones can deal with me wearing whatever is left in my suitcases to his douchey premiere."

I take a breath and check my email on my phone. Good Lord, there's at least ten new emails from my mom. If I'm not careful, I'll open Tom's front door one day to see Mom standing there with a roll of duct tape and a detailed plan to drag me back to Buffalo. I fire back a quick reply.

Everything is fine, weird misunderstanding, will call soon. Love you.

I scroll through the dozens of acquaintances who suddenly find me much more interesting now that I'm "dating" a movie star, and grumble to myself.

"Are you growling at your phone?" CiCi asks, holding up a men's flannel shirt to check for holes. "Because when my great-uncle started doing that to his TV remote, we had to put him in a home."

"I can't get away from Tiddleswich," I say, exasperated. "A week ago I barely even knew who he was. Now my entire life is all the Tiddles, all the time."

"Did you really say his name sounded like an ass squeak on that voice mail?"

"I stand by that assessment," I tell her, still scrolling through emails on my phone. She giggles and starts pawing through a box of ancient romance novels.

My inbox is a nightmare. I don't even know how to respond to most of these. I can't be honest and quell the curiosity by responding with short and sweet summaries of the lunacy that is my actual relationship with Caspian Tiddleswich. But writing back with anything playing into this comedy of errors feels gross in ways even the nastiest E-Z Storage units can't make me feel.

I can't delete them, I can't archive them, and I can't respond to them. This is breaking my decadelong streak of an orderly inbox and making my eye twitch.

Another thing I can add to the list of things to hate Caspian for, clearly.

A lone email that doesn't have His Royal Tiddles as the subject line catches my eye. "Oh my god, CiCi!"

She abandons her dusty stack of bodice-rippers and comes running straight over. "What? What is it?"

I squeal and start bouncing in place. "McEnroe Publishing wants me to come in for an interview tomorrow at ten! Oh my god!"

She joins me in the squealing and bouncing. "Ooh, they're a great house! That's fantastic! You'd be so good there!" She grabs me in a rib-cracking hug, and we keep bouncing. "I knew things would start happening!"

I mentally tally the time needed to get to and from Manhattan and realize I'll have to start my E-Z Storage cleanup in the afternoon in order to attend the interview. I'm supposed to meet Trina for dress fittings for the wedding after lunch, too. I'll have to put in an extra burst of energy today to make up for the time I'll be missing.

I send back a professional, yet enthusiastic, email to McEnroe and try to sound more like I'm just pleasantly looking forward to meeting with them, and less like I'm going to hump their legs with glee upon arrival.

As soon as I click Send, my phone starts ringing in my hand. The Tiddleswich calls. I whine before raising the phone to my ear. "What?"

"Good afternoon to you as well," his outrageously English voice says.

"Pleasantries aren't our thing. What do you want?"

"I need you in the city tonight for dinner. I'd like to meet at seven thirty to discuss a few things, and then I have a reservation set."

I close my eyes and start counting to ten. I make it to four. Through clenched teeth, I ask, "And what kind of dinner is it? How am I expected to dress, Your Majesty?"

"I imagine clothing ought to suffice. I'll text you the address."

The line goes dead. I scream at the top of my lungs, causing CiCi to drop to the ground like an air strike is imminent.

"Too much time in the units getting you down?" Charlie's voice comes from beside Brutus, and I scream again, albeit in a very different way, wheeling around to face him.

"Oh god, you scared me," I pant. "No, I just… Um, bad phone call. I'm sorry. I won't do that again."

"That's not even close to the weirdest thing that happens in these units, so if it helps, holler away," Charlie and his mustache say.

"Oh, this is my friend CiCi," I say, pointing to my wide-eyed friend. She gives a stiff wave. "She's been helping me out a bit. I hope that's all right."

"No skin off my nose." He shrugs. "Just wanted to see how it's going here."

"I've only got six units left," I say proudly. "That reminds me! I was going to call you this afternoon. We found a box of jewelry. I doubt it's worth anything, but we don't know how to tell what's real and what's fake. Thought you'd want to look." I point to Brutus's front seat, and Charlie reaches inside.

He pokes through the contents, opening up a few of the ring and necklace boxes, giving each piece a close eye. "I'd say these are probably worth something," he says after a moment.

"Oh, cool," CiCi says, her fear forgotten. "We found treasure. That's awesome."

"Anything in here you ladies want to keep for yerselves?"

I shake my head. "No, we couldn't. But thank you."

Charlie paws through the bounty again, taking out a purple velvet ring box and a long navy bracelet case. He flings the ring at me, and the bracelet at CiCi. "Finder's fee," he says with a smile. "You ladies have a good afternoon." He picks up the rest of the jewelry, and a moment later, he and his mighty soup strainer are gone.

We wait until he's out of earshot before we open the boxes. I look down to see a painfully gorgeous emerald ring with little diamonds scattered around the center gem. I gasp.

So does CiCi. I look over. She's staring at a diamond tennis bracelet that, even with however long it's been stuck in that box, is glittering like it's been freshly polished.

"I like Charlie," she says, eyes still huge. "Like, he's my new favorite person."

We carefully stow our goods in her purse and continue cleaning out the unit. This must be why Charlie is such a successful business owner. He certainly knows how to motivate an employee in just the right way.

I'm choosing to believe it's that, and not that he was ever the Godfather or similar.

"Okay, Sweeping Beauty," CiCi says around five. "We need

to get this stuff put away. You should probably go home and get cleaned up before you go meet the evil Prince Charming."

I squeeze my hands into fists. "Tell me it would be wrong to punch him."

"I'll do no such thing. But come on. I'll drive Brutus."

14

With the extremely helpful information that "clothing" is what I should wear, I retreat to CiCi's apartment to shower and rifle through her closet, thanking my lucky stars that she and I are both hobbits of roughly the same size. She's got a full inch on me at five foot three, but that's close enough to work. CiCi hops on People.com and tries to look up what famous people wear to dinner. Apparently, as long as I'm wearing something between ass cheek–baring shorts and a prom dress, I should be fine.

In the end, as I have no idea where we are going, we decide I'll fare best in skinny jeans, flats, a low-cut white shirt, and a fitted blazer. CiCi tosses some of her dangly necklaces on me, and it all comes together. I look like I could be coming from work, or going out with friends.

She insists I wear the ring that Charlie gifted me earlier. "It looks expensive, but not over the top. It'll be perfect," she says.

As much as the occasion is a source of frustration, actually sculpting my normally frizzy hair into a shiny, smooth updo and slapping makeup on my face is a nice change of pace. CiCi is some kind of sorceress and really knows how to make my greenzel eyes pop. It's been weeks since I felt the need to pretend to look human, and getting out of my unofficial E-Z Storage uniform is a real treat.

And on the one hand, I'm pissed that it's Halloween and I'll be missing my and CiCi's annual tradition of wearing costume footie jammies—me in Wonder Woman and CiCi in Darth Vader—and watching horror movies with pizza and beer. On the other hand, I'm not unhappy at having an excuse to get off the storage lot early, because my gods do the wildlings come out in scary force on Halloween, even before the sun goes down, and I wasn't looking forward to that.

Coiffed and pouting, I spend the interminably long train ride trying to focus on a fluffy rom-com audiobook so I don't start panicking about what I'm about to do.

That effort is not panning out well.

I hit Midtown and try to find the address Tiddleswich sent. A few blocks later, I'm standing in front of the Four Seasons and working really hard not to turn tail and flee. The hotel is all windows and looming columns and classic NYC architecture and doormen. It's gorgeous, but also intimidating, given my current circumstances. The people coming and going are impeccably dressed, and I'm pretty sure I just saw a famous Korean pop star—whose name I can't remember—gliding inside with about twenty people tailing him.

I linger on the sidewalk, watching the masses matriculating by, and notice several photographers lounging around a car parked by the sidewalk. They have giant cameras on straps around their necks and enormous cardboard coffee cups perched on the hood of the car. They're talking casually with each other, but their eyes reflexively wander toward each new person who passes by.

I'm starting to feel a little sick.

I send a quick text to Tiddleswich. I'm outside. How do I get in?

After an awkward moment of standing here, staring at my phone, he replies. Go to the lobby. I'll come down.

I tuck my phone in my purse and try to look as though I know exactly what I'm doing as I head to the entrance. A friendly-looking guy wearing a full bellhop ensemble grandly opens the giant glass door to let me inside.

The lobby is absolutely massive. There are uniformed staff members everywhere, pushing luggage carts behind people who don't even sort of notice their existence. Phones are ringing, the constant hum of hollow chatter echoes up to the high ceiling, and the babbling sound of the fountain to the left of the elevators resonates through the glitzy labyrinth.

A moment later, one of the elevator doors opens, and there stands Caspian Tiddleswich, wearing a dark gray suit with a wine-colored button-down shirt opened at the collar and no tie. Under normal circumstances, if I were to see a man like Caspian in this state, I'd be a few steps beyond tempted to stop and gawk at the view.

Alas, knowing what I know—and loathing how I loathe— all I can do is force my face not to register my disdain and disgust while hoping no one can see how clenched my hands are under the cuffs of my coat sleeves.

Without stepping foot into the lobby, he motions me toward him. I huff and roll my eyes before pulling my shoulders back slightly and heading into the elevator.

"Back up, please, Jacob," he says to the uniformed attendant.

I don't remember the last time I was in a place that had an actual dedicated elevator attendant. Now that I think about it, I'm not sure if I've ever been in one, or if I'm incepting my own memories with years of watching movies full of such clichéd extravagances.

Jacob pushes the button and turns to smile at me. "Ma'am."

I smile back. "Hi, Jacob."

Sir Tiddles turns to me. "Did you find it all right?"

I can tell he's only making casual conversation in front of Jacob to keep up appearances, and my first instinct is to start shouting about what a tool he is. Instead, I attempt to take the slightly higher road. "No trouble at all," I say, mustering an exaggerated toothy grin. The corner of his mouth twitches.

Fifty-two floors of silence later, the door opens, and Jacob grandly motions for us to pass. "Have a wonderful night, sir. Ma'am."

I give him a friendly smile and follow Tiddles into what is quite obviously the penthouse. It's just as audacious as I would have expected, and it has at least four times the square footage of my last apartment.

Okay, maybe five times.

"May I take your coat?" he asks, holding out a hand.

"Are we standing on ceremony now?"

He shakes his head. "My mother would be disappointed if I didn't."

I inadvertently glance sideways. "Is…is she here?"

He laughs genuinely, and the sound is disconcerting. "No, but it's hard to break habit."

I slowly peel off my coat and hand it to him. As he hangs it up by the door, I take the opportunity to look around more. The place looks tidy, but lived in. I'm guessing he's been here for a few weeks at least. There are small stacks of books lying on various surfaces, and tiny bits of evidence that a real person exists within the confines of a hotel room that, despite its grand efforts to appear homey, is really just a sterile floor model of what homey is supposed to look like. Things like an empty teacup and saucer on a table by the massive picture window. A blue sweater hung over the arm of an antiquey-looking chair beside some prefilled bookshelves.

Those personal touches would be almost sweet if they didn't belong to a man I know to be an absolute cock.

"Have a seat," he says, gesturing toward a fancy dining room table.

I carefully ease myself into a cushiony chair that definitely costs more than my first car back in Buffalo did. "What exactly am I doing here?" I ask, sitting back and crossing my arms. "I thought we were supposed to be lying to the world at dinner."

He leans back in his chair as well, but keeps one hand on the table. "Well, as we are about to venture forth as a *couple*, I thought it might behoove us both to discuss parameters."

"Such as?"

"What you are and aren't comfortable with, for starters."

A bitter laugh escapes me. "I thought my comfort wasn't your concern."

He smiles. "Emotional comfort will be in short supply. But despite your notion that I'm the villain in this tale, I assure you I'm not actually evil."

"Evidence to the contrary, sir."

"A hint of civility might make this go easier." He raises an eyebrow at me. "In public, the goal is to appear as though we are dating. Currently, our demeanors suggest a less than romantic attachment."

"Well spotted."

"Ahh, yes. There's the civility I long for." He grins. "In all seriousness, I'd like to make this as believable as possible, but I don't want to cross any lines. What kind of public physical contact are you comfortable with?"

I choke on my tongue. "Wh-what?"

"You're very dramatic."

"Says the *actor*." I try to clear my throat of tongue. "What are you talking about?"

"Hand-holding, hugging, a kiss on the cheek. I'm in no way suggesting we snog on the street, but since there are always photographers everywhere, our body language will be very important. However, if those things are outside your comfort level, we can work around that."

My face squinches up. "Oh."

He leans forward and puts his elbows on the table. He rubs one very long-fingered hand over his face and through his hair. "Look, this is unpleasant, and I understand that. I just… I'd really prefer to be left alone, honestly."

"Are you gay?" The words fly out of my mouth before I can stop them. I slap my palm over my lips, unsuccessfully trying to cram the question back inside.

His arm flops down on the table unceremoniously. "No. No, I'm not gay."

I can feel my cheeks blazing red. "I am *so* sorry. I had no right to ask that. Seriously, I apologize. That was beyond disgusting of me. I swear that wasn't me doing the thing where people think they're entitled to personal details from celebrities or something. I just wondered why you're going to all this effort to appear to have a girlfriend."

He sits back in his chair again. "If I were gay, I'd have no issue whatsoever acknowledging it, publicly or otherwise. I just…prefer to keep my private life *private*. That's the whole of it. I tend to avoid dating inside the showbiz pool, and this lifestyle is a lot to inflict on someone who isn't used to it. It's not quite as apoplectic in London, but here, the pressure is immense."

Then, as if he suddenly realizes he was being conversational, he adds, "Not that any of this is any of your business, nor do I owe you any sort of explanation."

My eyes narrow. "I already sincerely apologized for the question. Calm down." Then a thought pops into my head and I frown. "Wait. We're supposed to look like a couple, but we can't stand each other. If you're worried about body language, this seems like a bad equation."

"Yes, well, this will require some performance on your part." He waves a dismissive hand in my direction. "Only in public. Behind closed doors you can flood our space with apathy as you see fit."

I'm fighting the urge to whine. "Look, I get you're an actor and this is your whole thing, but I'm not in the habit of faking my way through life. This feels gross."

"Then I'd hope you'll think twice the next time an idea of extortion enters your mind, yes?"

"All right," I snap. "That's about enough of that. You say you aren't the villain? Well, neither am I. I made a mistake, but I never intended to do anything wrong. You can believe me or not, but you're the one who's now trying to hurt me *on purpose*. And if you want me to go along with all of this nonsense, that is the last time you get to say a single word about extortion, or blackmailing, or any of it, do you understand me? One more word, and you can find yourself another damn fake girlfriend."

"Fair enough," he says lightly. "Any other caveats?"

Now that I've got the floor, I don't quite know what to do with it. "Uh, yes. I'll be civil to you, if you can at least be polite to me back. I'm not an actor. I can't throw on happy faces and adoring looks when someone is openly picking on me and taking digs."

"I can agree to that. What else?"

I shift restlessly in my chair. "Um. The…touching…stuff. All the things you mentioned are fine, I think. But if you try to kiss me on the mouth, I will punch you in the face. Like, actually, literally punch you. Right in your stupid cheekbones."

"So I take it the being mutually nice to each other hasn't started yet?"

"Sorry. That was rude."

"It was."

I fidget. "Sorry. Again."

He glances at the watch on his wrist. "We'll have to leave soon. Shall we move on?"

"To?"

"Backstory. It will come up eventually, so let's discuss how we met."

"Because you crashing into my brother's living room all angry and terrifying isn't what you're going for? I don't know. I think it's got a truthy ring to it."

He smiles. "Not as such."

15

"One last thing," he says as we wait for the elevator to reach the penthouse. "My friends generally call me Cas."

"That's...nice?"

He closes his eyes and pinches the bridge of his nose. "I mean you. *You* should call me Cas in front of other people."

"Oh." It's true—calling him Sir Tiddles out loud instead of just in my head would probably be frowned upon. "What have I been calling you?"

"You haven't. You sort of just speak *at* me."

I try not to laugh. "I'll make a note."

After he pulls a wool coat on, I glance down at his pants and realize his suit is all but identical in color to his "throne" at Tom's, and I giggle.

His eyes meet mine. "I assume you have a reason for laughing at my trousers?"

"Not a good one." I look down at my outfit while I put my own coat on. "I meant to ask, am I dressed appropriately? I still don't know where we're going."

He gives me a quick scan. "You're fine. It's just dinner at Fracas. Do you know the place?"

I nod. "I've done a few business drinks things there. Bit trendy, isn't it?"

The elevator door opens, and Jacob greets us with a smile. "A bit," *Cas* concurs.

"You don't seem thrilled about it."

"I tend to prefer more low-key venues, but those would defeat the purpose of this little adventure."

As we close in on the ground floor, he turns to me and takes my hand in his. "All right, take a breath and do try not to look panicked."

My eyes go buggy. "That is the exact thing you say to someone when you want to incite panic."

The elevator doors open, and he leads me across the lobby, keeping ahold of my hand. I take the breath he suggested, but before we even come close to the windows, I can see the photographers still huddled around the car outside spot him. They instantly spring into action, cameras in hand. Caspian squeezes my hand extra tight and pulls me closer to him as we hit the exit.

The flashbulbs are unfathomably bright. I shut my eyes tight to try to close them out, but when I open them again, all I see are residual stars and more flashes.

I turn my face into Caspian's arm to shield myself from the lights. All around us, the photographers are shouting at him. "Tiddleswich, over here! Who's your girlfriend? What's her name? Look this way, Caspian!"

It's only a few steps from the hotel entrance to the car waiting by the curb, but it feels like walking through a never-ending fire gauntlet. Fortunately, our driver already has the door opened for us, and Caspian ushers me in first before climbing in behind me. The door shuts, and the driver jogs around to the front and slides inside. The whole time, there are actual human bodies pressed up against the windows, trying to take pictures through the heavily tinted glass.

We pull away from the curb, and I whoosh out the breath I've been holding in since we hit the lobby.

"Holy shit," I whisper. "That was horrible. Is it always like that?"

He shrugs. "Generally. Normally I'd leave through the back, but we're on a mission, after all."

"Lucky us."

"Indeed."

We ride in silence for several blocks, but I keep checking out the back window, half expecting to see a dude with a camera hanging off the bumper.

"I don't get it," I say, still looking over my shoulder. "Why would you do something like this if you don't want to? Subject yourself to all…that?"

He stares blankly out the window and answers, "Sometimes we have to do things we don't enjoy."

I unintentionally scoff at him, not sure if he was meaning to be derisive or not. "It's not like you're some newbie starlet trying to make their way in the world. Surely you should get to set the terms of—"

Caspian turns to me and makes the laser-focused direct eye contact that has yet to not make me feel like I'm going to be physically ill on the spot. So quietly that I know there's no chance the driver can hear him, he says, "You've hit your quota on personal questions for the evening."

I'm torn between a flush of residual embarrassment over my astonishingly inappropriate question from earlier, a surge of anger, and a sliver of fear, but I brush all of those aside for a wave of panic. We've arrived at the restaurant.

We pull into a drop-off line of sorts, where valets are taking cars and drivers are letting out various important people. "Oh god," I groan. I can see a whole new set of cameras flashing away. My jaw drops when I see people posing on the sidewalk by the entrance. "Do people really do this on purpose? Go to a place like this and—what? Freaking model on the street?"

"Some do. It's not really my area, but as I said, this isn't the type of dinner locale I would normally choose."

We get up to the entrance and a valet opens the car door for us. As I climb out behind him, Caspian leans in and whispers under the cover of the chaos. "Arm around the waist. Acceptable?"

Feeling a bit of emotional whiplash after going from his personal question embargo to this, I nod and try to smile, squinting hard against the new barrage of flashes. His arm casually wraps around my waist, as discussed, and he leads me into the restaurant, calmly ignoring all the whoops and shouts for his attention.

The hostess greets us instantly, all blindingly white teeth and eyeliner. And boobs. I'm not sure how her low-cut black tuxedo vest-style top is keeping her ladies inside, but it's an impressive feat, and I find myself trying to figure out how to compliment her and ask for tips in a way that wouldn't come across as offensive. She takes our coats with a giant smile and hands them off to another employee.

"Right this way, Mr. Tiddleswich. We've reserved one of the private rooms for you, as requested."

"Yes, thank you," he says as we follow her toward the rear

of the restaurant. The chatter in here is surprisingly loud, but even over the din of famous people eating what I assume to be famous foods, I can still hear the shouting of paparazzi through the windows. The sounds and visuals combined with the feeling of my hand in Caspian's as he guides us around fellow diners is a full-scale assault on my senses.

The hostess leads us through a curtain and into a private room with a small table set for two. Caspian, ever committed to the ruse, goes to the trouble of pulling my chair out for me. I play my part and smile, doing my best to look like a woman with a case of the smittens and not a woman who is pondering whether I could stab him in the hand with a fork and not get into any actual trouble for it.

After taking our drink order—a gin and tonic for me, a scotch neat for Mr. Tiddleswich—and alerting us to the chef's specials—a delicately poached sea bass and bacon-wrapped squab—our hostess informs us our waiter will be with us shortly and retreats, leaving us in an uneasy silence.

Caspian picks up his menu and peruses the options quietly, so I awkwardly do the same. Menus that don't have prices on them scare me. Will I be paying twenty bucks for the citrus-marinated quail breast with edible flowers, or two hundred?

CiCi's voice echoes in my head, and I'm inclined to order the lobster with filet, but while *Cas* here can suck it as far as I'm concerned, I don't want to go out of my way to be financially petulant. Maybe if he sees I'm not the evil wench he's concocted in his mind, he'll let me off the hook to some degree.

Not a word passes between us the entire time we stare at our menus, and even though I've known for a good four minutes what I'm planning to get, I just keep staring. Finally, mercifully, a young man in a crisp white shirt and perfectly pressed black pants appears carrying our drinks.

Setting the glasses on the table, he greets us. "Hello, Mr. Tiddleswich, so nice to see you this evening." He turns to me and says, "Welcome to Fracas, ma'am." With a calm but dazzling grin, he asks, "Are we ready to order?"

"Yes, thank you, Marshall," Caspian says with genuine friendliness. I quickly scan Marshall's uniform for a name tag and, finding none, can't for the life of me figure out how Caspian is on a first-name basis with our waiter. "Clara?"

I offer him a beatific smile, determined to nail my part of this ruse, and go with the pumpkin ravioli with sage and brown butter. Caspian orders the duck.

"Excellent choices," Marshall says, taking our menus. "Is there anything else I can get for you?"

Caspian looks at me as though he genuinely cares whether or not I have needs I'd like Marshall to meet, but I pleasantly shake my head. Caspian smiles up at him, and Marshall is on his way, tugging the curtain closed behind him.

The second we're alone again, I can't help myself and blurt out, "I thought you said you hate coming here."

"I do."

I wave vaguely at the curtain. "But you know our waiter by name."

He shrugs casually. "I've had to take a few business meetings here before. Marshall waited on me during one of those meetings."

I stare at him, and I'm sure my curiosity is on blatant display across my face. "You remember his name from one meal?"

Caspian stills and looks almost disappointed. "Do you not endeavor to treat waitstaff as people?"

"Of course I do!" I half snap. "But you're... I mean..."

You're a fancy movie star. I guess I just didn't expect someone like *you* to do that." I don't know where I thought this line of dialogue was going, and I suddenly hate myself for not having better control over my mouth. I slump down in my chair a bit and finish pathetically, "It's just impressive that you do. Most people don't bother, famous or not."

Sitting back in his chair and taking a sip of his scotch, Caspian looks at me, wearing an unreadable expression that has me squirming miserably. I'd give anything to have the safety of the menu to hide behind again.

After what could have been several miserable seconds, or maybe three straight days in the sights of an unblinking Brit, Caspian stands up, drink in hand, and says, "If you'll excuse me."

"Uh…sure?" I say ineptly as he walks out of the room, the curtain falling silently in his wake.

A heavy sigh falls out of me, and I flop my forehead down on the table loudly. This is so completely miserable.

I take out my phone and fire off a text to CiCi.

I swear to Odin's beard, this is the most horrifying experience I have ever had the misfortune of participating in.

Seconds later, her reply beeps in. Is he being a prick?

I don't need a moment to muse on that one. Yes. Yes, he really is.

Order. The. Fucking. Lobster.

I shake my head and tuck my phone away with a sigh.

Against what most would consider better judgment, I pick

up my drink and chug until only the ice cubes and wedge of lime remain.

As the warmth of the gin spreads through me, I look around the room. Soft lighting, rich burgundy fabric on the curtains, deep ebony woods. Paintings by probably famous artists hang on the walls. The tablecloth is as crisp and white as Marshall's shirt; the stemware is delicate and spotless. The carpet squishes luxuriously under the soles of my shoes.

Many minutes of silence and fidgeting pass before Marshall returns with a tray and another waitress carrying a crystal pitcher of water. She silently fills my glass as Marshall sets down a plate of magnificent-looking ravioli in front of me.

"Mr. Tiddleswich sends his apologies. He's been caught on a call and requests that you begin without him," he informs me.

"Oh. Will he be long?" I ask, trying to sound like a caring girlfriend.

"He didn't say, ma'am. Is there anything else I can get for you?"

I shake my head. "No. Thank you, Marshall."

"Enjoy your dinner, ma'am."

Marshall and the nameless waitress scurry away, and I sit, staring at the now-still curtain for a moment. I'm inclined to wait for Caspian out of manners, but then I realize they didn't even bring in his food. I suppose they're probably waiting for him to return before they serve it.

With a shrug, I set my napkin on my lap and tuck in. It really is a spectacular dish, and I find myself gleefully enjoying the experience of a solitary meal in one of the fanciest restaurants in the city. No Caspian to stare at me while I chew, no paparazzi standing outside the window waiting for me to do something embarrassing, like dribble sauce on my shirt.

Time passes, and my plate is all but licked clean when Marshall comes back in. Picking up my dish, he asks, "Would you care for dessert, ma'am?"

"I really shouldn't until Caspi—I mean, until Cas comes back," I say. "Has he said when he'll be finished yet?"

"No, ma'am. Would you care for another drink?"

I shrug. "Sure. Why not."

Marshall scampers off and returns several minutes later with another gin and tonic, then disappears again.

This time I handle my drink like an adult and sip. And sip and sip and sip.

I check my phone. According to the time stamps on my texts with CiCi, it's been an hour since Caspian stepped out. Not that I'm dismayed to be without his company, but where the hell did he go?

My mental clock ticks away as I poke at the ice cubes in my glass with the stirrer. When those have fully melted, I absent-mindedly suck down the gin-flavored water.

It occurs to me that if they're waiting to serve Caspian when he returns, that means I'll be forced to sit here uncomfortably as he dines, trying not to be the monster human who watches someone else eat. I can't help but wonder if this is an intentional ploy to make me squirm all the more.

I store that thought away and take out my phone, playing a rousing ten hands of blackjack in a card app I've got tucked away for boring subway rides. When that amusement wears thin, I check my email and try to organize my inbox. I tinker with the placement of the icons on my home screen. Eventually, I open up Netflix and start watching a recommended documentary on polar bears.

When my phone battery drops below 20 percent, I shut it off and tuck it back in my pocket, dropping my chin into my hand and staring at the wall, feeling an unpleasant numbness spreading through my ass.

Just when I'm about to stick my head through the curtain to see if an apocalypse occurred and I'm all that's left of mankind, Caspian comes strolling back in.

"Shall we go?" he says, as if this is a perfectly normal thing.

"What?" I frown. "You've been gone for over two hours. You haven't even eaten."

"Yes, I have," he clarifies. "I ate in another room while I dealt with some business. I've already taken care of the check."

I blink at him and feel my jaw clenching a bit. "Are you serious? I've been sitting here by myself all this time."

The corner of his mouth twitches, and I see an unformed grin in his eyes. "My apologies. Shall we go?" he repeats.

My jaw drops the tiniest bit. So it *was* a squirming plot, but an even crueler one than I'd suspected.

Since I absolutely refuse to give him any satisfaction, I plaster on a grin of my own and say, "Absolutely."

My legs feel a bit wobbly after experiencing life as a veal for several hours, and I almost tumble over the chair, but thankfully he's already looking back out toward the main dining area and doesn't see.

As soon as we enter the land of other humans and their watchful eyes, Caspian places his hand on my lower back and guides me back to the hostess station, where the girl with the pearly teeth and outrageously perky breasts already has our coats waiting. Ever the faux gentleman, Caspian helps me into mine before pulling on his own. Below my adoring-girlfriend exterior, I am seething with irritation and confusion.

The bulbs start flashing as we prepare to head back out into the night, and Caspian smiles what anyone else would consider a genuine smile as he takes my hand and leads me through the door held open by the hostess.

Screams for his attention and the clicking of picture after picture pierce my ears as my eyes are assaulted by the strobing lights. Some of the photographers get so close they knock right into me, and Caspian wraps his arm around my waist, pulling me in close as though he's the most caring and protective boyfriend in all the land.

His driver is at the end of the sidewalk, already poised with the door open. I dive inside and Caspian follows, ever so calmly. I'm trying to remain dedicated to my show of not letting him see me sweat here, but on the inside, my heart is pounding and I want to cry a little. The paparazzi onslaught is not a subtle one.

The driver walks around and climbs inside, and we're off at a snail's pace, dodging overly intent photographers who won't get out of the way of the car. I want to take a moment to snap at Caspian for ditching me in the private room while he did who knows what, but I can't fully deliver sass until I blink the spots out of my vision. Those flashbulbs are bright as all hell.

He says exactly nothing to me, and before I've even gotten my proper vision back, I realize we've pulled over to a curb.

"I believe this stop will get you home," he says coolly.

"What?" I say, still blinking and trying to ease my pulse back into a normal range. I look out Caspian's window and see a subway entrance, and I realize I'm being banished from the car and back into the real world, where a forty-minute subway ride awaits me.

I glance at the dashboard and see I've got about eight minutes before the final train to Astoria heads out. Caspian has taken out his phone and looks wholly unconcerned with any of the night's events.

The driver starts to get out, I assume to open the door for me, but I put my hand on his shoulder. "That won't be necessary," I say before I smooth down the front of my coat and climb over Caspian's lap, making sure to step directly on his toes as I open his door and slide out. "Dick," I whisper as I pass him.

I make it to the sidewalk and resist the urge to violently slam the door. Without a second glance—or maybe there was, and I couldn't see through the cartoonishly tinted windows— they pull away from the curb, and I'm left flabbergasted before I remember I now have seven minutes to catch the train, unless I want to take a painfully expensive Lyft ride I can't afford back home.

Dating a celebrity definitely isn't all it's cracked up to be.

16

I'm hustling down the sidewalk to get to my McEnroe interview on time, trying to ignore all murderous Tiddleswich thoughts while mentally preparing answers to all the usual interview questions. The sounds of my twinkling ringtone echo from my pocket, and I pull out my phone, praying it isn't Mr. Posher Than Thou calling.

It's CiCi. I put my headphones in and answer.

"Hey, sugar tits," she coos.

"You are way too peppy for my current mood," I sigh. "What's got you so chipper?"

"One of my clients just hit the *New York Times* bestseller list for her third book in a row. I'm queen of the castle today. How're you? How was the first date?"

"Ugh!" I growl.

"So, it went well?"

I launch into an account of being dragged out in front of photographers for the benefit of Captain Cas, only to be left in solitary confinement with the perk of gourmet food for over two hours. Followed, of course, by the humiliating drop-off at a random subway stop mere minutes before my train left.

"Okay, that guy is a twisted fuck," CiCi concludes.

"You'll hear no arguments from me," I say, rushing across a street before the walk signal ends.

"When do you have to see him again?"

I sigh. "I don't know. I'm at his beck and call, so I assume it won't be a lengthy sojourn."

"Do you want me to start researching celebrity hit men?"

"Let's hold off on that one," I say, somewhat reluctantly. "In the meantime, all the congratulations on your client, sweets. That's awesome."

I can practically hear CiCi beaming through the phone—and also the sound of her rummaging in a bag of sunflower seeds. "Damn right it is." I picture her twirling in her office chair, which I have witnessed firsthand on more than one occasion. "All right, I better get back to my actual job or something. Good luck at your interview, and let me know how it goes as soon as you're done, lady!"

"Will do, madam. Love yer face."

"Love yer face right back."

I tuck my phone back into my coat pocket just as I hit the lobby of McEnroe. I pass through security and sign in, resuming my interview question prep in my head as I ride in the elevator.

The waiting area of McEnroe Publishing is somehow bare and cluttered at the same time. The furniture is minimalist and sparse, but the wall of bookshelves is stuffed to bursting with not only books, but little trinkets and figures. Looking past the staging area, I see that the house favors an open floor plan for the employees over individual offices or even properly isolating cubicles. I know open floors are all the rage in millennial companies, but as far as my chosen field goes, I've yet to meet an editor who doesn't need a cone of silence to fully function. Either because it's easy to be distracted by office noise and conversations, or because many of us tend to talk to ourselves and our manuscripts as we work, the need is the same.

While I have fairly set feelings on the office layout that I would gladly be willing to abandon for the chance to work at a house as prestigious as McEnroe, I still haven't quite decided how I feel about the decor before I'm ushered into a conference room for my interview.

Three people stand upon my entering, all situated around the long conference table. The room has the same vibe as the waiting area, with an entire wall of bookshelves, filled to the brim.

"Clara," the first woman says, reaching her hand out for mine. "So wonderful to meet you. I'm Donna Miller, head of acquisitions, and this is Shay Glau, and Ethan Johnson."

"Pleasure to meet all of you," I say, and shake hands all around. "Thank you so much for having me in. I've heard wonderful things about McEnroe." This feels like a canned compliment, so I quickly add, "Obviously your reputation is well above the fold, so thank you for even considering me today."

"We've heard wonderful things about you as well!" Shay offers.

My cheeks flush a bit. "Wow, thank you. You'll have to let me know who to send a fruit basket to."

They all laugh and look at me excitedly. We chat for a few

moments, with Donna explaining the history and company philosophy of McEnroe, and I'm feeling pretty good about them so far, but I'm also nervously fidgeting my hands under the table, waiting for the inevitable question assault that usually comes in an interview.

"How is this all sounding to you?" Donna asks.

"It sounds amazing," I say with a smile. "Though I wouldn't have expected anything less from a publisher that's managed to thrive as well as yours has in this economy, honestly."

Shay smiles proudly and says, "Wonderful! We'd be thrilled to have you join our team."

I blink at her. "Come again?"

Ethan chimes in, "Yes, we'd love to add you to our roster, Clara."

I keep smiling, but I know my confusion is plain on my face. "But…you haven't even asked me anything yet."

"Your résumé speaks for itself," Shay offers with a wave of her hand.

"Actually," Donna says, "I do have a question." I turn to her expectantly. "Do you know if Caspian is planning to publish anything in the future?"

"Excuse me?"

"We know he's published short stories in the past," Ethan adds. "But if he's looking to do more, we'd be very interested in facilitating that."

"Caspian." I draw in a shaky breath. "You want to ask me about Caspian?"

"He's one of the rare celebrities who seems to have actual writing talent," Shay says with a chuckle.

"Don't you want to ask me about—I don't know—my vision for the editorial process? My strengths, weaknesses, goals? If I'm a team player? Anything?"

Donna looks down at what I assume is my résumé. "What I've seen here is all very impressive," she says. "I think you'd be a good fit with our staff."

I stare back at their expectant faces awkwardly. "Well, okay, then. Um. I'd like a few days to consider the offer, if that's all right."

"Of course!" Ethan says with just a hint too much enthusiasm. "I'll email over all the specifics, things like salary and the benefits package for you to look over. If you'd like to get together to discuss any of it, we're available. I know Caspian is a very busy man, but he's welcome to join in as well! I know how important career decisions are for a couple."

My eyebrows shoot up, and I force a smile onto my face. "Yes, of course. Lots to discuss."

And that's it. I shake their hands again, they chatter among themselves about what an attribute I'd be to their company, tittering over Caspian's upcoming movie, and show me to the door.

I'm in shock, but I'm professional enough to keep my calm until I'm out of the building. The last thing I need is security camera footage of me screaming profanity in the elevator.

As soon as I hit the sidewalk, I yank my phone out and dial CiCi.

"How'd it go!?" she trills into the phone before I can even say hello.

"Caspian Tiddleswich is ruining my goddamn life!" I yell, causing other pedestrians to jump away from me.

"Okay, cupcake, walk me through it."

I spend the ten-minute walk to the train ranting and raving about the world's most ridiculous interview. "Can you believe that!? I could have been the shittiest employee in the world, but they think I can land them a deal with Sir Tiddles, and what the hell!?"

"Ugh. They always say it's who you know."

"I don't want to know him!" I say, descending the subway stairs. "And I don't want a job just because I fell ass over ankles into contact with him. I want a job because I'm a damn good editor and I can bring a lot to a new house. This is bullshit!"

"Maybe it's not so bad," she suggests, and I hear the sound of cracking sunflower seeds. "Maybe this just gets your foot in the door. Then once you're working there, you can wow them with your badass editing skills. And what if this is the universe paying you back for suffering through Caspian's crap? Is it really the worst thing in the world if you use his name to get an awesome opportunity?"

I angrily swipe my MetroCard and storm through the turnstile. "Yes."

I can hear her considering the notion on the other end of the line. "Yeah, okay, it is."

"This is infuriating."

"Is the money good at least?"

"I don't even know yet. They said they'd email it all over later. This sucks. I've waited months for an opportunity like this, and now it's got Caspian stink all over it." I sigh and glance down the platform. "My train is coming, though, so I need to hang up."

"Okay, but just take a breath. This might not be as terrible as it sounds. Go home and relax for a bit."

"I'd love to, but I have a bridesmaid dress fitting with Trina I'm already late for."

"Oh, yikes," she says, and I can almost see her wincing. "So, turmoil in tulle?"

"Exactly."

"Do you ever stop and wonder if maybe you were a murderous dictator in a previous life or something?"

"Every single day."

"Okay, go do the dress thing, then rest. Love yer face."

"Love yer face, too."

I hang up and climb on the train, still fuming.

My rage has not dwindled even slightly when I trudge into the little boutique bridal shop to meet Trina forty minutes later. It's a nice place, hidden in a quiet corner of Queens, and they stock a lot of carefully maintained designer gowns from various decades. So while there's that classy bride vibe, it also has the essence of a quirky vintage store.

As soon as I enter, a woman dressed in chic, well-tailored black clothing welcomes me. "Hi, there," she says with a smile. "Can I help you with something?"

"Yes, hi," I say, trying my best to shake off the storm cloud of rage I've been carrying for the last hour. "My name is Clara Montgomery. I have an appointment with Trina Prince to try on a dress?"

"Of course! Miss Prince is already in her gown, so if you'd like to follow me, I'll take you back to the fitting rooms."

I follow her through the shop, admiring rack after rack of magnificent dresses. I have to stop myself from ducking away to study some wickedly intricate beading on a Vera Wang from the nineties as she leads me to an open area with six dressing rooms surrounding a giant round blue velvet ottoman in the middle. There are mirrors everywhere, which, at the right angle, give the impression of an infinite bridal universe.

"I'll be right back with your dress," the woman says, leaving me to gratefully plop down on the ottoman.

Surprising no one, it's vastly more comfortable than Gertrude.

A moment later, one of the blue curtains pulls back, and out walks Trina with another attendant. She's wearing what I assume is her wedding gown, and it's so beautiful, I can't help but gasp.

"Oh my gosh, you look gorgeous!" I trill.

Trina bounces a little in place. "Thank you!"

It's a mermaid-cut dress that poofs out at her knees. The bodice is, like, 90 percent sparkly crystals sewn onto the fabric. In the bright lights of the dressing area, it gives her a sort of sophisticated disco ball look.

"Ten bucks says Tom bursts into tears the second you appear down the aisle in that thing," I tell her. "Heck, I'm getting a little weepy myself over here."

"He'd better," she says with a laugh. "It weighs about seventy pounds."

My attendant comes back and hands me a garment bag. "There you are. Do you need any assistance getting into the dress?"

I look back at Trina. "Will I?"

She considers this. "I don't think so? Maybe with the zipper, but it's not, like, a lace-up corset or anything."

I smile and shake my head at the attendant. "That's too bad," I say, crossing over to one of the empty dressing rooms. "My boobs look great in a corset."

"They are the gift that keeps on giving," Trina agrees as I slide the curtain shut.

Putting the hanger on one of the hooks, I carefully unzip the bag and await my fate. Bridesmaid dress roulette is a dangerous game. I've seen far too much peach taffeta to remain an innocent.

But to my surprise, the dress is...not bad at all. It's a spaghetti strap, floor-length silk number in a rich navy blue, and the back cuts open to show a short pleated mauve train.

I know every bride tries to play the "You can totally wear it again!" game, and it's almost never true, but this dress would actually work fairly well for the stupid movie premiere.

Somehow, I don't think Trina would support that. Not before the actual wedding, anyway.

I wriggle out of my clothes and slide the dress on, impressed with how well it fits. I'd probably be even more impressed if I'd remembered to bring a strapless bra, so my ratty old violet straps weren't ruining the scene up top.

I push the curtain aside and step out.

Now it's Trina's turn to gasp. "You look amazing!"

"Sorry about the bra straps," I say with a sigh. "Promise I'll remember a different bra on the actual day of."

"Oh, that's fine! It really looks great on you!"

"Well, thank you. And thank you for not picking a dress that makes me look like a badly frosted cupcake."

"Your cousin Marissa's wedding?"

I tap my nose and shudder. "I'd pay big bucks to destroy all photographic evidence of that day."

The attendants have scampered off to do other things while Trina and I make notes about our respective dresses. What could be let out or taken in, too short, too long, etc.

After a few more moments of twirling, she pops into her dressing room and comes back out again holding an envelope.

"Hey, uh, Clara?"

"Yeah?"

"I really need to talk to you about something. Something important."

I straighten up, feeling a sinking sensation in my stomach. "Okay. What's going on? Is Tom okay?"

"Yes! Tom's fine. Everything is fine," she says, but I'm not comforted. "I just… I did something, and I feel like I need to come clean with you about it."

"If you're about to confess to cheating on my brother or something, I think this is going to go poorly," I tell her, really hoping that's not what's about to happen here. "Although, I'd have to admire the dramatic effect of confessing it while we're dressed like this, not gonna lie."

"You're so weird," Trina says with a nervous laugh. "It's nothing like that." She squeezes the envelope in her hand a little tighter before handing it to me. "Here. This is yours."

I take the envelope, eyeing her suspiciously. I open it and pull out a check from TMZ. Made out to me. For seventy-five hundred dollars.

"Whoa!" I sit up straighter. "What is this for?"

"That night when Tom and I came home, and Caspian Tiddleswich was there, well… I was so stunned to see him standing in our living room, and I, uh… I took some pictures of him with my phone."

My jaw drops open. "Oh my god, it was *you*? Why would you do that?"

She's obviously mortified. "I don't know! I wasn't even thinking. I just started clicking away, and he didn't see me. And then, well, I emailed them to that website, and they were all excited because he looked mad and you were crying, and they offered me that money for the photo."

"Holy shit. I can't believe it was you who sold the picture. Trina!" I drop down onto the blue ottoman, gaping at the check. "I… How…? What in the world made you think to do this!? How did it even occur to you to sell it?"

Her entire face turns so red it almost matches her hair, and her expression shifts from straight guilt to a guilt/shame hybrid.

"I…" she says in almost a whisper. "I love celebrity gossip sites."

I blink at her. "Say what now?"

Trina looks so embarrassed, I want to stand up and hug her, but I'm adhered to the ottoman by shock.

"I love the tabloid stuff," she explains, looking like she wishes the floor would open up and swallow her whole, wedding gown and all. "I have since I was a kid. I would even buy the magazines when I was younger."

"I…I don't know what to say to that."

She shrugs pitifully. "I don't, like, stalk them all day or anything, but I like to scroll through the stories in bed because it always takes me forever to fall asleep, and Tom passes right out, so I just lie there and read until I'm ready to sleep."

I take a deep breath and let it out slowly. "I mean, I get that. We all have our things. I'm weirdly obsessed with watching those videos of people coming out of anesthesia after they have their wisdom teeth out," I offer, hoping to ease her awkwardness. "But how did you even know *how* to sell them a picture?"

"Oh," she says, perking up a bit. "They always have a banner or button somewhere that tells people to call in sightings or send pictures in. Like, for sightings, they say it's better to Tweet at them, because then they can get someone there faster and—"

I wave my hands in front of my face. "Okay, no, I get it."

Her mortification and shame return. "I'm so sorry! I was in bed and scrolling through TMZ, and I was kind of half-asleep, and I thought it would be cool if it would bring in a little money to put toward the wedding, so I just…sent it in. I swear, I didn't think it would blow up like it did! I thought they were going to put one of those black bar things over your face and no one would even know it was you. I felt so bad afterward that I had them write out the check in your name."

I press my fingertips to my temples. "Trina. Oh my god. Do you have any idea how much trouble this has caused?"

She starts pacing in front of me. "I didn't know you guys were dating! You said it was an old work thing, and I didn't think it would be a big deal since you obviously weren't working together anymore. If I'd known you were a couple, I wouldn't have sent it, I swear. Why didn't you tell us?"

I clamp my mouth shut. "Uh. Well." The horror of having to lie to my own soon-to-be family bubbles up. "He's a very private person, you know? And…it's really new, so I didn't want to make a big thing out of it."

"Seriously, I am so sorry, Clara." Trina drops onto the ottoman beside me, tears in her eyes. "At first I thought I'd split the money with you, since you could definitely use it, and I'd put my part toward the wedding, and it would be no big deal." She bites her lip. "I really am sorry."

My shoulders slump. "You know what? I can understand that. A lot. I forgive you."

"Really?"

"Of course. It could happen to anyone."

She leans over and hugs me. In the hall of mirrors, my guilty reflection stares back at me from a hundred directions.

"Look, I'll tell Tom what I did, I promise. I just wanted to clear it up with you first, you know?"

"It's fine, really."

The sound of my phone buzzing from my purse carries across the room, so I carefully peel Trina off me and go to fetch it. I look down, and there's a text from his highness himself.

Drinks tonight, 8.

A low growling sound forms in my throat. I type out and delete at least a dozen possible responses, all in the vein of *Fuck you for your adolescent horse shit and for tainting the first real job lead I've had since I got laid off, you prick, and while I'm at it, fuck you for existing*, but in the end, I send At your service.

"Are you okay?" Trina asks carefully. "You look a little wired."

I throw my phone back into my purse with a little more force than necessary. "I'm swell. I get to go sort through other people's trash for a few hours and then go out with my super famous, dreamy British boyfriend. So. *Yeah. I'm living the dream.*"

"Uh, Clara…"

I snap myself out of my rage blackout. "Yeah?"

"Can you maybe help me up?" I realize she's rocking back and forth, kind of like an upside-down turtle. "This thing really does weigh, like, a thousand pounds, oh my god."

I snort-laugh a little and reach out to pull her up. "Oh, wow, you're not kidding. That is heavy."

Trina looks me dead in the eyes and says with total seriousness, "He had better cry *so freaking hard*."

17

While I'm sure this level of bitter rage probably isn't healthy, it's done wonders for my productivity in cleaning out units. The hate-fire of plotting all the different ways I could sucker punch Caspian Tiddleswich in his stupid lizard nose is fueling an almost superhuman burst of physical strength. If I keep this up, I'll have this crap unit marked off my list by the end of the day.

At least this one seemed like it was owned by relatively normal humans. There's nothing in here but boxes of old clothes, dishes, and other things I assume they wanted out of their house, but didn't quite feel ready to do away with. The saddest things, to me, are the boxes of books, left crammed away in this dark and forgotten concrete tomb.

I set them aside on Brutus's front seat and make a note to drop those and the bags of usable clothes off at the women's shelter on 17th Ave before I take him in for the night.

I put my headphones in and hit Play on some feisty music. Angry rock combined with the burning fires of my Tiddles-loathing will get me done with this unit by the end of the day for sure.

Sitting on an unopened box, I crack the lid on a plastic storage container and sift through the contents inside. These look like a hodgepodge of toys from the eighties, but none in good enough condition to be worth anything, nor to be passed on to a shelter.

I pop the lid back on and, just as I stand up with the box, I realize I'm not alone.

I quickly yank out my earbuds and stare at the random man standing in front of me. "Hello?" I say, fairly stunned. "Can I help you?"

"Do you work here?" the man asks. He's maybe in his forties, a week or two into growing a beard or just not feeling inclined to shave at the moment, wearing a beat-up puffy coat over dingy jeans and sneakers that have seen better days.

"Not exactly," I answer. "I'm just clearing out abandoned units for the owner. There's a number on the sign out front if you want to get ahold of him."

"Oh." The man sort of stares at me and then at the unit and then at me again. I'm suddenly very aware of being a not particularly large woman alone in a giant lot with who knows what kind of people coming in and out. I could wind up cleaning out a unit with dead bodies stashed in it, for all I know.

And this could be the guy who put them there.

And here I am, in the back of an eight-foot-by-eight-foot unit, with a strange dude standing at the entrance.

"Is there something else you need?" I ask tentatively.

"Nope." He keeps looking from me to something outside the unit and down a ways. "Thanks, though."

"No problem," I reply with a smile as I scan for ways to get the holy fuck out of this unit.

Creepy Dude takes one more look down the long row of units and calmly walks away.

My heart is beating much harder than I'd like it to be, and I'm pretty damn desperate to get out of here until I know that guy is gone. I slowly make my way to the opening, peeking my head around, but I don't see him anywhere. Still, I'm weirded out enough that it feels like time to pack it in for the day.

I throw the bin of toys in the back of Brutus and reach behind me to slam the unit closed, locking it back up. Then I jump into the truck and make my way off the lot toward the shelter and the dump before I head home to change for drinks.

A few hours later, I'm on a train, heading for Midtown and the bougie bar where I'm supposed to meet my Lord Commander.

My phone buzzes in my pocket. Once upon a time, I reacted to phone alerts with no identifiable emotion. I would just pull it out of my pocket, check to see what had come in, and that was the end of it.

Now I have an almost Pavlovian fear response to any buzz or beep the damn thing makes. Even with Caspian's new Darth Vader text alert sound, the second my phone makes any noise at all, my entire body clenches up and my heart pounds out a rhythm that I've decided is the bass line for the song my subconscious is writing, called "Fuck Caspian Tiddleswich and All He Stands For."

I remember a time when I wasn't an outrageously bitter person, and even though it was only about a week ago, it feels like that memory is eons old.

I swipe my screen and am greeted by an email from the VP of the young adult imprint at Polar House. My heart stops pounding out revenge sambas and launches right into gleeful K-Pop.

Polar House is one of the Big Five houses. The top of the game. I'd submitted an application there, but hadn't even dreamed of hearing from anyone. My résumé is good, but I never thought it would be considered Polar House good— not in a self-deprecating way, but because their standards are absurdly high, and it's next to impossible to get a foot in their door, even as an unpaid intern.

Hell, I'd be willing to sleep on Gertrude a whole lot longer if it meant getting a coffee-wrangling intern position at Polar.

Mara Aaronovich, in all her Polar-y magnificence, writes that she would like to meet with me for lunch tomorrow to discuss the open associate editor position they have on the YA imprint they are so very famous for. I nearly miss my stop rattling off an eager acceptance and start doing an actual happy dance in my seat before I realize I'm not alone on this train and people are side-eyeing me pretty hard.

Whatever. If they'd just landed an interview with Polar, they'd be doing a choreographed jig up and down this car.

As I make my way through the station, mentally combing through the limited professional wardrobe I currently have stored in Tom's coat closet, all my enthusiastic zeal suddenly comes crashing to a halt when I remember where I'm headed and why. The various blazer options in my head are replaced with images of a certain British pain in my ass falling down open sewer grates.

Oh Christ. I turn a corner and trudge down the block toward Clicks, the painfully trendy bar where I'm to meet my fictional flame. There's a collection of photographers on the sidewalk, staring through the window and absentmindedly talking to each other, and I have to physically force myself to keep moving forward, as my gut instinct is to turn tail and haul ass to literally anywhere but here.

There is a very deep-rooted part of me that's unspeakably enraged at being put into situations where I am forced to ignore thirty years of fine-tuning my internal compass in favor of parading in front of paparazzi for the benefit of a psychological sniper who loathes me.

I almost tuck down inside my coat, or at least yank the collar up to cover my face, but I realize that will just draw more attention to myself. Instead, I pull out my phone and pretend to be very interested in something on the screen as I make my way to the door.

For the sake of authenticity, I fire off a text to CiCi that reads, This text exists because I'm trying to look terribly busy and important. Also, I changed my mind and think it's time to start researching celebrity hit men and alibis, because I'm not going to make it through this nightmare with Tiddleswich in one piece.

The fact that I'm not anyone of actual import combined with my ignoring all the hubbub on the sidewalk pays off. Just as I'm about to pass the door, I turn on my heel and push my way inside. I smile smugly to myself as chaos and glaringly bright camera flashes erupt in my wake, quickly extinguished when the door closes behind me.

Just as I'm about to tuck my phone back in my pocket, I see a message pop up on my screen.

I've got a shovel ready to go. Just saying.

I almost laugh out loud, but there is suddenly a very tall, very British presence standing in front of me. He looks happy to see me and bends down in what, to everyone else, likely appears to be a kiss on the cheek. For a hot minute, I have to appreciate his skill as an actor. Even I almost believe he's being genuinely welcoming.

My appreciation is quickly burned away by disgust and wondering if people like him even know when they're bullshitting the world. Still, I plaster my most endearing smile on my face, trying to lock in the "loving girlfriend" look, but I know my skills aren't up to his level.

"Does it get exhausting, not having an actual personality of your own?" I ask him, still smiling beatifically. "Or does lying to everyone all the time get easier after a while?"

Caspian's adoring expression doesn't falter for a moment as he replies, "I assume it's no less tiring than spending your days trying to defraud others for money, but you'd be the expert on that."

I am so out of my league here with the beaming facial expressions while lobbing sentences made of razor blades.

A feeling of annoyance builds on my brow, and I have to fight hard to keep a smile intact. I really need to give up on the sassing while we're in front of an audience, because I am not at all equipped for this game.

He takes my hand, a previously agreed upon acceptable form of physical contact, and I fight an internal and petty as hell urge to dig my nails into his palm.

Once upon a time, I was a normal person who didn't have frequent thoughts of murdering a celebrity or attempting to draw blood in a public place.

Those were the days.

People's heads turn as he leads me through the bar. I'm not sure what it is about famous people that makes them stand out the way they do. Even if I didn't know Caspian was famous, I would find myself looking twice in his direction. Aside from him being a very large—and fairly imposing—figure, he just has that sheen that all celebrities seem to have.

The handful of times I've come into contact with stars in the city, they've been remarkably easy to spot. Once I passed Anthony Hopkins on the sidewalk, and even though there were no cameras or stalking fans to be seen, it was like the man had a glowing marquee following him around, shining brightly to draw the eyes of all of us who walked past. He was dressed in a nonspecific way, had a hat on to protect against the chill of the winter, and yet it was still like walking by the sun, the way he stuck out.

Caspian is damn well no Anthony Hopkins, but he's got that unspecified glowing aura, too. It makes me unspeakably angry that it exists at all for people like him.

We make our way back into what I am assuming is either a tiny little VIP room, or something he managed to have set up specifically for him. He's obviously been here for a bit, because I see a script lying out on the table with various writing implements and notebooks opened up around it.

Caspian pulls out a chair for me, and at first, I can't understand why he's bothering to keep the ruse going when we're in such an isolated space. A biting response is just making its way across my tongue when I realize a waiter has followed us inside our little slice of hell.

Allowing myself to accept the proffered chair, I smile kindly at the waiter, who introduces himself as Lionel and declares he is here for absolutely anything we might be needing for the night.

"Hi, Lionel," I say, taking my coat off and letting it sit on the back of the chair behind me. "Nice to meet you."

"Can I get you something to drink, ma'am?" Lionel asks. I refuse to let my Tiddles-venom leak out onto others, so I manage not to bristle at being called "ma'am." I'm only thirty years old, damn it.

Caspian sits beside me, and I see a glass containing what looks to be scotch sitting in his improvised work area. If I could stomach the stuff, I would order the same, just to appear like one of those couples—the ones who are so disgustingly smitten, they even start ordering the same things.

"Gin and tonic," I say, smiling. "Thank you." Lionel gives a little nod, and as he turns to leave, I look at Caspian and—making sure I'm overheard by our waiter friend—say in my most irritatingly adoring voice, "How was your day, *dear*?"

Once Lionel is gone, Caspian picks up his glass and takes a sip. "That had to be painful for you."

Any traces of adoration fall from my expression. "I may actually vomit."

"Cheers," he says, tabling his scotch and picking up a highlighter.

Oh, goody. It looks to be one of those nights where I've traveled across the city to sit next to a pompous, silent statue in the shape of Caspian Tiddleswich, when I could have been doing absolutely anything else at all that wasn't a huge waste of time.

Well, screw him. Tonight, I came prepared. I have a portable charger for my phone in my purse, and every free game app I could load on this thing ready to go.

I refuse to let him see me sweat.

I'm three rounds into a maddening game where I'm trying to maneuver a pixilated Iron Man through broken pillars when Lionel appears with my drink.

"Thank you," Caspian and I say in a perfect unison that makes me bristle with annoyance. Lionel inclines his head at us and heads back out.

I suppose it's mildly endearing that Caspian is at least polite to waiters and the other service industry folk I've seen him interact with. Either that, or it's all part of his bizarre public facade, and therefore all the more gross.

Iron Man crashes into the fifteenth pillar, and I internally sigh. I plan to show my date nothing but stony silence unless otherwise required by the presence of another human being.

Although, the more I think about it, the more I have to concede that even a fake persona that is kind to waiters and elevator operators is still a huge step up from many people I come into contact with, who seem to believe that every barista they meet is deserving of whatever verbal abuse they can come up with.

The moment of positive thinking about Caspian unnerves me enough to make sure all audible alerts and buzzes are turned off on my phone as I start texting CiCi.

Another riveting date in total silence. Although he actually stayed in the room this time, so that's either progress or punishment. I can't decide.

Definitely punishment.

Touché.

Is he at least being less of a douche this time?

I almost snort out loud, but cover up the sound by pretending to clear my throat and taking a drink.

AHAHAHA, no.

He is intently focused on whatever task he's performing. I try to casually see what he's reading, but the text is too lightly printed, and all I can make out is the giant watermark covering each page that states this is Caspian Tiddleswich's script. I read somewhere once that studios do that watermark thing for scripts they can't risk being leaked.

Naturally, he's up for some fancy part, or has already been cast in one. The thought of him being paid tens of millions of dollars to star in something that's just going to make him all the more famous is beyond irritating—and because the world is a cruel place, I have to assume he will end up an action figure or on the T-shirts of every kid I see for the rest of my life—while I sit here smelling like stale storage units and employment desperation suddenly has me steaming with anger.

An idea that's been rattling around in my head ever since Trina's confession flashes to the front of my mind, and before I can talk myself into doing this with some semblance of class or calm, I'm digging through my purse for the envelope she gave me. When I finally find it, I slap the check from TMZ down on top of his stupid script and say, "Here."

For a moment, he looks up at me without actually moving his head at all, which, if I'm being honest, unnerves me a bit. This guy has the steely glares down cold.

"And what might this be?"

"It's the check for the godforsaken picture that cast me into this role of indentured servitude, your highness," I snap, a little more harshly than I intended. Then the whole day of Caspian-centric shenanigans comes flooding into my thoughts, and I am torn between crying and throwing a drink in his face. The sycophantic grins of the McEnroe staff, huddled around that table; the look on Trina's face as she confessed; his smug, ridiculous, not-at-all Anthony Hopkins sheen—just all of it.

"I didn't sell the damn thing," I tell him. "And before you even ask, I have no intention of telling you who did—I won't

let you throw them into your imaginary debt as well. But…
there's the money for it."

He calmly—so irritatingly calm, god—picks up the check
to examine it. "This is made out to you."

"It's like I'm with the actual Poirot," I say, feigning a gasp.

Now he tilts his head up, and his steely gaze is replaced
by mild irritation. "You do realize how ridiculous you look,
right? Trying to pass this off as not belonging to you while it
bears your name, and no one else's?"

I grab my drink, throw the watery remnants back, and stand
up. As I wrestle my coat on, I say, "I can't think of anything
I care less about than how things look to you."

Leaning back in his seat, he continues to hold the check
while he scans me for…something. "And what would you like
me to do with this?"

I make my way toward the door of the now-stifling VIP
room. "Cash it. Donate it. Burn it. Choke on it. I honestly don't
care. I don't want it." Angrily yanking my purse up my arm,
I add, "And while I hate to deny you the joy of ditching me
on a corner later, I'll be making my own way tonight. Dick."

Turning on my heel before he can make another wry comment, I do my best to sashay out with dignity, but I'm pretty
sure it comes off more like a petulant stomp.

My hubris doesn't last long beyond passing through the
door. Through the front window of the bar, I see there's still
a small gathering of photographers on the sidewalk.

As the blood drains from my face, Lionel comes running
toward me, looking eager to assist. "Ma'am, can I help you?
Did you and Mr. Tiddleswich need something?"

My eye involuntarily twitches both at the "ma'am" and the
idea of Mr. Tiddleswich and I needing anything in a joint capacity.

"Uh," I say, trying desperately to think of anything that might alleviate the horrors of the day. I decide to embrace cowardice. "Actually, Lionel," I say, lowering my voice, "would it be okay if I slide out through the back or the kitchen entrance or something?"

He gives me a knowing, professional nod and leads the way as I shake my head at myself.

In a string of bad days, today somehow manages to stand out as one of the least pleasant.

18

This morning, I was up before Tom and Trina to try to knock out a storage unit before heading back into the city for my lunch interview with the VP from Polar House.

I'm running on very little sleep—couch sleep at that—and the more I throw random things into Brutus, the more I'm regretting my morning choices. Somehow, the prospect of showing up to lunch reeking of stale old newspapers and moth-eaten clothes with giant bags under my eyes doesn't seem like the greatest first impression I could make.

CiCi, goddess that she is, appears around nine with a latte in exchange for all the details from the night before.

"I can't believe you gave him that check," she says, wrinkling her nose at a bag of shoes that look as though they were worn to death before being tossed in here. I see one in particular with duct tape keeping the sole attached.

"I wasn't going to keep it," I say with a sigh. "It's practically blood money."

"Okay, I hear you," she says, rubbing her palms on her pants, "but you're killing yourself digging through other people's ancient trash for five thousand, and that was a heck of a lot more, hon."

I peek into a box and see stacks of old magazines. "There is nothing I could have spent that money on that wouldn't have wound up screaming at me, 'Tell-Tale Heart' style, for the rest of my life."

"It's not like you haven't earned it," she says, sitting on the open bed flap of Brutus. "You could have considered it compensation for humiliation and suffering."

The sound of Darth Vader's breathing emanates from my pocket, and I pull out my phone with a snarl.

Lunch today. Meet me at the theatre at noon and we will leave from there.

"Fuck!" I shout. I see CiCi jump out of the corner of my eye.

"What?" she shrieks.

"The sadist wants lunch! What the hell!?"

"Nooooooo!" CiCi gasps. "He can't do that! Not today!"

"No," I growl, "he can't." I start typing.

Sorry, Your Majesty, I have plans.

He writes back instantly. Yes, you do. Lunch. With me. Meet at the theatre at noon.

My heart is in my throat, and I start to panic. I can't even find the breath to explain to CiCi before I'm hitting CALL.

"What?" is his charming greeting.

"I seriously can't come at noon," I say into the phone, trying my best to control the desperation in my voice and failing miserably. "I have a job interview, and I can't miss it or reschedule this close."

"Our arrangement isn't about convenience to you, if you'll recall," he says. I can hear him moving around, and I am horrified and annoyed that he's just going about his day while he's in the process of ruining my life.

"I can meet you after," I beg, despite myself. "Seriously, I will go wherever you need me to go after the interview, but I can't cancel this, Caspian."

"Oh, I'm 'Caspian' now? What happened to 'Your Majesty' and all your other flattering nicknames?"

CiCi's watching me with captivated curiosity. I flash her what I assume is the look of someone pre-stroke.

"Look, we have our mutual hate, and that's great and all, but I'm not canceling this interview. I need this job. You can't make me do this."

"You can't possibly need the job that badly if you were able to so generously hand over your hard-earned tabloid money to me," he says, and my stomach drops. "Our arrangement stands. Noon."

The line goes dead.

"Oh my god," I yelp.

"He can't be serious!" CiCi yells.

"Why, *why* did I have to be such a sassy snot about that check with him last night?" I wail. "What did I think was going to happen when he saw my name on it?" My email chimes, and I clutch my phone so tightly I worry I may crack the screen. "Please, oh *please*, let this be Mara from Polar emailing to say something came up and she can't meet me until dinner or tomorrow."

It's the promised email from Donna Miller at McEnroe with the job offer details.

"Is it from Polar?" CiCi asks, reading over my shoulder.

"No," I groan, scanning the email. "McEnroe. Figures I'd get an offer at a place suffering from Caspian fever."

I feel CiCi shrug. "I mean, at least the money isn't terrible?"

I shake my head violently. "This is as good as that check from yesterday. It's got Tiddle-stench all over it."

"Yeah, but I still think you should have kept that check, so I'm kind of not against you taking this job."

I tuck my phone in my pocket and turn to her. "No way. I want a job offer because I earned it, not because of—" I freeze, a horrible thought forming. "Oh Jesus."

"What?"

"What if Polar is like McEnroe? What if the only reason they contacted me at all is because they heard about Caspian?"

CiCi blinks at me for a good fifteen seconds. "No way," she insists, but her tone suggests less than solid resolve. "You said it yourself—you're great at what you do. If they saw your résumé at all, they would know that. That's why they want to interview you."

"Oh my god," I whimper. "I don't think I could stand it if Polar is all star-fuckery, too. What if I stand up Caspian for this interview and it ends up being exactly like McEnroe and then I'm still unemployed and he goes to the police, CiCi?"

I can see the wheels turning in her head, and as much as she is trying to look resolute, doubt is written all over her face. "No. It's not even a possibility a place like Polar would even give a shit about someone like Caspian. They've published presidents and stars way bigger than him. I bet real money they don't even know about the two of you, and even if they did, they wouldn't care in the slightest." Now she's starting to look convinced of her own monologue. "You definitely need to go to this interview, because they are going to be blown away by the awesome that is you, and Tiddleswich can go fuck himself."

"I can't argue about him needing to go fuck himself," I say, pulling my phone back out to check the time. "But the rest of that has yet to be proven. And shit, I need to lock all this up if I'm going to have time to wash the unit stink off me and make it into Midtown by noon."

"For your interview, right?" she asks, gathering our empty cups and throwing them into Brutus as I jog out of the unit and pull the sliding door back down. "You have to go to it. You can't let him mess with your career like that."

I mean to nod, but instead it comes off as a weird spinning combination of yes and no.

"Look," she says, walking over to the driver's side of Brutus, "I'll drop you off back at Tom's and take the truck over, because that will give you more time to focus on getting ready for *your interview*. Deal?"

My head continues to spin.

I'd hoped that showering and getting dressed in my chosen blazer would give me the time and confidence I needed to stop panicking about whether or not it's worth it to blow off Caspian to meet with Mara, but nope. As I walk up the steps from the train station, my body is fighting itself trying to decide which way to head once I hit the sidewalk.

Every minute, I think I've reached peak internal hate for Caspian Tiddleswich, but it just continues to build.

I stand off to the side of the steps, making sure not to get trampled by lunchtime commuters, and realize it's time to woman up, here. I've gone round and round inside my head about all the possible horrible endings my choice here could lead to, but ultimately, I know what I have to do.

Feeling as though I may puke right here on the sidewalk, I head in the direction of lunch with the Polar VP. As I walk, my mind can't stop picturing my heinous drill sergeant, who is likely sitting in a Broadway theater at this very moment, watching the clock and gleefully counting down the minutes until he can call the cops and have me thrown in whatever prison caters to the whims of the rich and depraved.

I take as many deep breaths as my lungs will allow and try to ready myself mentally for the meeting. I've dreamed of interviewing with Polar House since I was a wee baby editorial intern back in the day. As much as he's succeeding at destroying everything else good in my world at the moment, I refuse to let Caspian sink this opportunity for me before I even meet the woman.

Then it occurs to me that a job offer from the house of my dreams will mean very little if I'm stuck rotting away in a jail cell, and the panic surges once again.

I find the restaurant and make my way inside. The hostess smiles at me. "Can I help you?"

"Yes. I'm meeting someone," I manage to croak. "Do you know if Mara Aaronovich is here yet?"

"Clara!" a voice calls out. I see my interviewer stand up from a booth off to the side of the restaurant and wave. I slap on a professional grin and wave back.

The hostess guides me over to the table and sets a menu down. "Your server will be right with you," she says and leaves us to it.

"Mara," I say, reaching out to shake her hand. "It's a pleasure."

"That's very mutual," she replies as I take my seat. "Did you have any trouble finding the place?"

"Not at all!" I say, pleased with how confident I sound.

I may never be as good at putting on airs as Caspian, but at least I've managed to drown my nerves and residual fear for the time being.

Mara Aaronovich is a very sleek woman. She's got gorgeous dark, curly hair that's smoother than any curl has a right to be, which is pulled halfway back and out of her face. Her suit looks perfectly tailored, and I can safely assume she didn't have to iron the hell out of it after digging it out of a suitcase from the bottom of her brother's coat closet.

I pour myself a glass of water from the gleaming glass pitcher on the table, and Mara launches into a thoughtful welcome and tells me a bit about Polar.

"You're having a heck of a year," I say, taking a sip of water. "If I'm remembering right, you've got four of the top ten YA bestsellers this week, yes?"

She lets out a humble laugh. "We've got a great team, and some incredible authors, it's true."

"I'm honored to even be considered for that team," I say truthfully. My Caspian nerves aside, I'm struggling a bit to keep myself from fangirling all over my menu.

"From what I hear," Mara says, taking a sip of what looks like iced tea, "you're having quite a year, yourself."

I nod a bit solemnly. "Yeah, it was really sad to see my old imprint eaten up by a company whose main contribution to society seems to be free overnight shipping, but things happen."

"Well, yes, that," she says with a light chuckle, "but I was referring to your personal life as well!"

My hand freezes halfway to my water glass. "I'm sorry?"

Mara smiles. "I don't mean to pry," she says, leaning forward with a conspiratorial look. "But do you know if Mr. Tiddleswich is writing anything new right now? I know young adult wasn't the genre for his short story collection, but honestly, I thought his writing was incredibly versatile. I believe he could easily create some amazing content for kids if he was interested."

"You're asking me if I could get Caspian to consider writing YA?"

She chuckles again, and my heart falls right into my shoes. "Trust me, we are very willing to be flexible. Any of our imprints would be thrilled to look at whatever he wants to work on."

I feel like I'm trapped on a roller coaster and I'm about to hit a giant loop, but I can see the track is missing halfway through the turn, and there's nothing I can do to get out of the car.

Our waitress appears as I try to remember how breathing works. "Hi, there! My name is Nicole," she announces. "Are you ladies ready to order, or do you need some more time?"

I realize my hand is still frozen in midair, halfway to my water.

"I'm…" I stammer, letting my hand drop to the table. Mara is still staring at me with her professional smile intact, and I use every molecule of my person that I still have control over to muster a poker face. Somehow, I think collapsing into a screaming tantrum about how Caspian Tiddleswich irreparably fucks up anything he comes into contact with isn't the career-boosting move I need to make right now. "I'm gonna need a minute."

19

I ride the train in stunned silence, trying to comprehend a life in which I flipped a coin in my mind to either favor my career and go to prison, or abide by the rules of blackmail, and that coin was destined to come up tails, no matter what.

I'm racing to the theater, hoping beyond hope that even though it's two full hours after his demanded time, my showing up at all will inspire Caspian to go easy on me.

At this point, I assume his version of mercy would be to have me drawn and quartered in Times Square, but even that seems preferable to spending the rest of my days in an orange jumpsuit.

How I sat through the remainder of that interview, pretending not to be horrified by the spectacle of it all over salads, I'll never know.

Mara—unsurprisingly, given her motivation for contacting me in the first place—said she would be in touch soon to discuss my future with Polar House. Words I've waited my entire adult life to hear, and instead of jumping for joy, I had to fight to keep from sobbing as I shook her hand in farewell.

And while all I feel physically capable of doing is limping my bruised ego and crestfallen career ambitions back to Tom's to nurse those wounds with a pint of ice cream and an equal serving of hard liquor, instead, I'm off to shed what little dignity I've managed to cling to over the last few months by begging my blackmailer to have a heart.

An organ I have little evidence he actually possesses.

The crush of people wandering through Times Square is the last thing I'm in a place to maneuver through, but here I am. It's slightly after the lunch rush, so instead of ten billion people crammed into a handful of city blocks, it's closer to an even million. Being bumped by tourists as they stare at the screen of their phones taking pictures is something most New Yorkers have accepted as an unfortunate facet of life. The same goes for the topless women adorned in body paint trying to hand out flyers. Somewhere in the back of my mind, I wonder how all the naked folks manage to stand it in this cold weather. I think back to my own shivering in the storage units and have to give credit where it's due.

At the moment, my coordination is sluggish, and I feel like I'm in a wretched game of pinball, being pinged from topless flyer distributors to a tourist couple from Georgia, into a costumed Woody Woodpecker and back over to a guy wearing a sandwich board for a club opening in Hell's Kitchen.

It's not hard to find Caspian's theater. There's a giant ten-story-high neon-lit poster above the marquee with his face slapped on it. The show is a modern-day rendition of *A Midsummer Night's Dream*, but—if I read the online article correctly—it still contains all the original Shakespearean dialogue. It's evidently a revival of something Caspian starred in a few years ago for the Royal Court Theatre in Britain, and is now running with various famous folks stepping into the role off and on.

It hits me now that, in my panic to get here, I never actually thought about how I would get inside. There isn't a show running at the moment, so the front doors are locked up tight. And as much as the idea of texting Caspian to ask him how to gain entry seems like yet another thrilling blow to my self-esteem, I know that would likely end with a sarcastic message from him and me crawling back to Queens with my tail between my legs, living the rest of my days waiting for the sound of police sirens to pull up to Tom's front door.

The stage door seems to be my best bet. I find my way around and see several people lined up against the theater wall, bundled up tight and holding...pictures of Caspian.

Yep. I'm in hell.

I try to nonchalantly pass the group of ten or so and make my way toward the security guard, ignoring the angry stares of the folks who are sure I'm cutting in line.

"Back of the line, ma'am," the burly guard says before I even get to him. I glance back and see satisfied looks on the faces of the waiting fans.

Why do people keep calling me "ma'am"? Whatever happened to "miss"?

I stay my course up to the beefy ma'amer and quietly say, "I'm here to see Caspian Tiddleswich."

The guard—Jared, according to the name tag on his uniform—starts laughing. "Yeah, I figured." I fight to keep from scowling. "Like I said, back of the line."

The people in line start laughing as well, and I decide I've had enough mocking from the universe today.

I stand up straight and give Jared my most haughty look, hoping it's at least marginally impressive, since I've never once managed to look haughty in my entire life.

"Actually," I say in my most sophisticated voice, "my name is Clara Montgomery, and I was invited. I'm running late, but Caspian asked that I meet him here."

Okay, so perhaps haughty was not my best choice here. Irritation plays across Jared's face, no doubt because a thousand other humans have likely used that exact line to try to wiggle their way into a theater stage door, and right when I think he may be about to throw me out of this alley by the scruff of my neck, a woman behind me gasps.

"You're his *girlfriend*?"

I turn and see the awed faces of Caspian's fans staring at the phone of one of the women. God bless busybodies with Google on their phones. The lady holds the screen up to show Jared, and I try to not visibly flinch at the picture of Caspian and me walking out of the hotel together the other night, hand in hand.

As much as I am desperate to get out of this situation, I don't have it in me to lie to complete strangers. So I just give them a kind smile and turn back to the guard, throwing him a knowing look with a raised eyebrow for good measure.

He's squinting, as if debating between risking his job by kicking me to the literal curb, or trusting the Google-fu of a superfan. In the end, he mumbles into the radio clipped to the shoulder of his coat. I have a moment of internal terror when I consider that Caspian may have told the theater nothing about me at all, and him asking me here at all might just be another one of his plays to humiliate me in public, but a few seconds later, after a garbled reply comes back, Jared's entire posture changes.

"I'm very sorry, Miss Montgomery," he announces, moving to open the door for me.

Oh, sure. Now I'm a "miss."

"That's completely okay," I say, offering a forgiving smile while also dying a little inside.

"Hey!" the Googler calls after me as I start to walk inside. "Can you tell Caspian we're out here, and that we love him? Please?"

I turn back, and her expression is so very earnest. All of them are, honestly.

"I will," I say, warmly. "I promise. And thanks for your help."

She beams, and I smile back before heading inside, hearing Jared close the stage door securely behind me.

Now that I'm actually inside the theater, I seem to have forgotten why I was so dead set on coming here to begin with. I look around at the veritable labyrinth of tunnels, and just as I start to feel particularly claustrophobic, another security guard appears with a welcoming grin.

"Miss Montgomery?" he asks.

I quickly scan for a name tag. "Yes, hello, Jose," I say politely.

"I'm here to bring you up to the dressing rooms," Jose says with genuine friendliness. "It's easy to get a bit lost down here."

I laugh. "You're not kidding. If you hadn't shown up, I think I would have just stood here looking pitiful forever."

Jose leads me through eleven thousand twists and turns, and I can't imagine how people keep these caverns straight at all. I'm a little surprised we don't see the skeletons of those who never found their way propped up against the walls on our journey.

After what seems like miles of hallway later, we reach a

higher floor, and things start to look more like a theater and less like a stone dungeon where I will spend the last few moments of my life. We occasionally pass busy-looking people wearing headsets, either studying papers in their hands or talking to someone we can't see. No one seems concerned at the sight of Jose and me on our quest.

Eventually, I'm led through a hallway of dressing rooms. There's the giant group room full of mirrors with blazing light bulbs protruding from the sides, and farther on, we come across the individual rooms. The bigger the part or the name of the actor, I assume, the larger the nameplates.

Sure enough, when we reach Caspian's door, his nameplate is the biggest of all. Although, if we're going by the sheer volume of letters that make up a name, Caspian Tiddleswich was always going to take up a lot of real estate, no matter how high his celebrity star might hover.

Jose knocks several times before turning to me and somewhat sheepishly saying, "They said he was backstage, but it's always good to make sure, you know?"

Part of me wonders how much of that is rooted in good manners, and how much is based on giving whomever is behind the door time to hide a lover who is not a specified significant other from said significant others, or, in a more eighties world, finish up whatever narcotic they happen to be partaking in before the door opens.

After a moment, when it seems safe to assume the room is free of Caspian, mistresses, or cocaine, Jose opens the door and peeks his head in.

"You can wait inside," he offers. "I'll have them let Mr. Tiddleswich know you're here."

Joy, I think to myself. "Thank you so much, Jose. And thanks for the guided tour," I add with a laugh.

"Anytime, Miss Montgomery," he says.

I step inside, and the door shuts behind me. Suddenly, I'm alone in a room that feels like the fairly sacred space of a man I want to punch in the kidneys.

In all my Caspian-focused scenarios, this one feels the most intrusive and cumbersome.

There's the typical mirror with lights that are created to mimic the surface of the sun, but where the group area was a mash of spots to accommodate a large group of bit players, Caspian's room is much more spacious, with lush pale gray carpeting; a red velvet couch that looks like it was created years before I was born, and yet still appears more comfortable than Gertrude; a private bathroom; and a coffee table lined with loose papers and an elaborate floral arrangement. Off to the side is a desk, also covered with stacks of paper and, if my eyes are correct, the script I saw Caspian tinkering with last night.

While few things in Caspian's life have interested me thus far, I have to admit, I am tempted to peek into that script to see what movie it's for. Then again, I'm also tempted to toilet paper his dressing room before fleeing back out the stage door like a coward, so it's obvious my judgment is askew at the moment.

Moment.

When hasn't my judgment been askew lately? I wonder bitterly to myself.

Before I can dig into my bad choices any further, the door opens behind me, and I jump out of the way. I had been too frozen to move anywhere beyond the exact spot Jose left me, so even with my evasive maneuvers, I am nearly bowled over by Caspian as he enters the room.

He seems both annoyed and amused to find me lurking in his doorway.

"I, uh…" I stammer, looking nervously around the room. "I didn't want to, er, invade your space, so I just…"

"Someday," he says, moving past me and walking over to his desk to take a seat, "I'm hoping you'll replay comments like that back in your mind and realize how absurd you sound."

I blink. "Excuse me?"

He turns in his chair to face me and crosses his legs at the knee, resting his hands in his lap. He's dressed in navy slacks and a gray sweater that's the exact same shade as the chair he commandeered at Tom's, and I find that more than a little unnerving. It's not the first time I've seen him adorned in that color, and I know it's totally irrational, but I feel like either he or the universe is doing this to me on purpose.

I'm starting to think it's less about the chair he's actually sitting in, and more about him just always sort of looking like he's about to be crowned.

"What I mean," he says, speaking to me as if I'm too slow to tolerate, "is that you have no problem invading my personal life at all, but you draw the line at sitting on a couch without express, written permission."

In spite of knowing that I'm on unsteady footing with him for being so late, I glare at him and snap, "Oh, goody. You're in one of your patented Prince Charming moods. How fun for me."

He grins at me, and it's not a friendly grin in the slightest. For a quiet few seconds, I'm not sure what to do. I wind up awkwardly shuffling my weight from foot to foot, waiting for him to say *something*.

Taking a pointed look at his watch, Caspian says, "I do believe the instructions were for you to be here at noon. As it's half past two, I have to wonder if you never learned to properly tell time."

A swell of panic washes through me, and I feel wobbly. "Look, I couldn't miss that interview," I say, hoping I don't sound as desperate as I feel. In hindsight, though, I suppose I could have easily missed the goddamn interview. Another Caspian-touched moment of hell that I didn't need in my memory banks.

"As I mentioned before, your grandstanding check disposal last night indicates otherwise," he says, and I realize this must be what mice feel like in front of really big cats.

"Okay," I say, my hands fidgeting at my sides, "I get that you're determined to take everything I do in the worst way possible, but I gave you that check because I don't want it. Not because I couldn't use the money—I absolutely could. The check was only made out in my name because the person who sold the photo felt so bad about it that they were trying to make it up to me. So do whatever you want with the damned thing, because I'm not going to touch it."

He opens his mouth—to throw another verbal barb my way, I assume—but I keep going. "Some of us aren't millionaire movie stars, and we have to hustle to job interviews to try to make ends meet. I'm sorry that the scheduling wasn't great, but you never give me any notice, and you've never made me meet you during the day before, so there wasn't any way for me to prepare in advance."

"Your day planner doesn't interest me," he says, sounding far too mellow given the circumstances. I regret not TPing his fracking dressing room. "That's not our arrangement. Any conflicts are your problem to solve."

"That's not fair," I insist, trying so, so very hard to keep my cool. "I've done every degrading thing you've asked of me while you glibly threaten to throw me in prison for something I didn't actually do, and you're dancing around like this is all some super fun game. Well, it's not. Some of us have lives in the real world, and they don't always match up with whatever sadistic demands you may make."

He stands up, and it's so unnaturally fluid and fast, I instinctively back up a step. I hate that he's so very freaking tall.

"You don't get to complain to me about the inconvenience to your life," he snaps at me. Whatever I said that yanked him out of his Ice King demeanor was certainly effective. Unfortunately, that wasn't my goal. This time. "That's the problem with people like you. You think someone like me doesn't count as a real person because my life is different from yours. This isn't a game to me, either. I have a family of my own that you didn't give a damn about when you dug up that information and threatened me with it."

"Oh my god, I didn't threaten you!" I cry, exasperated. "Enough with the revisionist bullshit. And between the two of us, who's the one doing the actual blackmailing here? I made a horrible mistake that I fessed up to, and I have done nothing but try to make it right. *You're* the asshole who has spent every minute since getting off on torturing someone he doesn't even know!"

"Oh, come off it," he says loudly. We've both entered a volume not at all conducive to my original plan of begging. "Your extorting damsel-in-distress act is exhausting."

"You know what?" I yell. "Nothing is worth this! It's not my fault you can't win over a woman in your *real life* with your dazzling personality, and you have to ransom strangers into pretending they can stand to be around you! You want to talk absurd? How about that you're so goddamn full of your own magnificence, you haven't stopped to wonder if there's a reason you're alone, you absolute prick."

Now it's his turn to take a step back. I can feel the rage

and humiliation of the last few days tangoing across my face.
Much to my utter frustration, tears soon join that party. "So,
fine. Take the voice mail and the paperwork and all of it to
the police, and have me arrested. Truly. Have at it. Because
no matter what happens to me, no matter how long I rot in a
cell for your overdramatized version of the truth, every minute there will suck less than a single second of the time I've
had to spend with you."

I turn and yank open the dressing room door, and just before I stomp away, I remember my promise to the people in
line, although I doubt this is quite how they intended I deliver it.

I glance back at him. "By the way, if you can pry yourself away from your own magnificence to mingle with lowly
commoners, there's a line of people who have no clue what a
depraved piece of shit you actually are wanting to meet you
at the stage door." I head into the hallway and call over my
shoulder, "Get fucked, Mr. Tiddleswich."

I slam the door shut behind me and storm off back the way
I came.

20

"**P**romise me you'll come visit and bring plenty of cigarettes that I can trade for protection and shampoo and stuff?" I say to CiCi, clutching a bottle of Moscato.

Admittedly, the last time I mainlined wine, it ended in the most horrible way possible, but I think I've reached rock bottom as far as poor life choices go. A bottle or three isn't going to damn me any further.

"You won't go to jail," she says, patting my foot. We're curled up on Gertrude, and I'm getting day-drinking drunk while she tries to convince me I'm not bound for the Big House. "I won't let that happen. I was just as involved, and I'll make sure everyone knows what really happened."

I take a long pull from my bottle. "Do you really think either of us would stand even half a chance against an army of lawyers funded by one of the richest actors in the world? Because while I think jail would definitely be less shitty with you there with me, I don't see what good it will do for both of us to get sent away." I gulp some more wine. "And besides, who's going to smuggle me in the cigarettes if you go down, too?"

CiCi ponders this for a moment. "He can't seriously go to the cops," she says unconvincingly.

My life from the last few weeks flashes before my eyes, and I start to cry. I want to blame it on the booze or my anger, but in reality, I'm just scared. "Oh god. What am I going to tell Tom and Trina? They're going to find out I've been lying to them about all of this. And my parents? My mom is going to lose her shit. I thought the most disappointing thing I could do was move away from our godforsaken bubble of suburbia and not stick around to repopulate it with a parcel of grandchildren, but man, was I wrong."

"Hon, they'll understand."

"Will they?" I hiccup. "Because I sure as hell don't. None of this is normal stuff you confess over Thanksgiving." CiCi reluctantly nods in agreement. "And here I've been so stressed about finding a new job, when I won't even be around to work one." I sniffle, and a new batch of tears starts flowing. "I can't believe I finally got an interview with Polar House, and all they wanted to talk about was Caspian. That's all my entire life is right now. Everyone around me only seeing him when they look at me."

I want to take another drink, but I'm crying too hard now to even lift the bottle. "That's all anyone is ever going to see from now on. The woman who defrauded Caspian Tiddleswich. The disappointment. The criminal."

CiCi resumes patting my foot, and I know it's because even she can't find a silver lining to the mess I've created here.

Maybe I have all of what's going to happen next coming.

I was digging through those boxes in the Cranson unit looking for someone to blow a whistle on. I tell myself I wouldn't have done anything with whatever I found, but do I know that for sure? Is that just a lie I tell myself so I can sort of live with the things I actually did?

I lean my head into Gertrude and let the tears fall. For all the hell I give this couch, at least it's never debated selling someone's dirty secrets for money.

Everything I did was with the dream of getting off Gertrude and back to my mattress. Which has all worked out spectacularly, let me say. Sleeping on Gertrude, in retrospect, seems a lot more palatable than sleeping on those little cots in prison.

At least I *had* a Gertrude to sleep on. What kind of spoiled brat am I? I have a warm apartment to stay in, and food to eat, and sure, it's not a long-term career option, but I have a job for now at E-Z Storage. That's more than a hell of a lot of people will ever have, and yet I've spent the last few weeks wallowing in my own self-pity.

Wallowing so hard that I let myself consider hurting other human beings just so I could get back to whatever imagined, fluffy little life I thought was waiting for me to return.

Caspian Tiddleswich may be a major dick, but he's not entirely wrong about who I am as a person.

"When do you think he'll do it?" I whisper, still leaning my head against Gertrude. The couch that has never judged me, despite having every reason in the world to do so. "Like, do you think he's with his lawyers right now? Will they come and do the whole handcuff thing? Lights and sirens? Will Tom and Trina have to be here to watch? Or will they just come home one day and I'll be gone and I won't answer my phone and they won't know why. Until they do. And I honestly can't decide which is a worse thing for them to have to think."

"You know," CiCi says, reaching over and stealing the bottle from me to take a sip of her own for the first time, "I'm not convinced he's actually going to turn you in."

I stare at her as she hands the wine back. "In what world is he not going to throw me under every available bus he can find?"

"Well," she says, deep in thought. "He can't out you for anything without outing himself as well. Even if he manages to keep the Cranson stuff secret—which I know you're a better person than that, but I'm not, and I will shout that shit from the rooftops—but even *if* he kept that from getting out, he did parade you in front of every photographer in Midtown while pretending to be your boyfriend, and him going to the cops now would mean having to explain that."

I sniffle again. "He would probably just tell people I forced him to, or something."

"Because that doesn't sound completely ridiculous," she snorts. "That you, a tiny woman living in her brother's living room, managed to force the giant action star to escort you to all those fancy restaurants."

I open my mouth to counter, and maybe it's the wine or the exhaustion, but I have to admit she makes a good point. "Do you really think he'd consider all that before he brought in his lawyers?"

"If he doesn't, they would make damn certain he considered it. It's their job to protect his image as much as anything else, and let's be honest, he's knee-deep in all of this, too. If he were one of my clients, that's the first thing I'd think of. I'm not seeing how he could spin this to not implicate himself as well. There's no way to pretend every single thing that happened was all you. There're too many witnesses."

I want to tell her he probably has contingencies for that.

I want to argue that he would sooner die than let his image take a single hit while I'm on the loose, ruining lives. I want to find any way to keep my doom and gloom intact, because I can't bear the thought of thinking I may make it out of this in one piece, only to be taken down by a celebrity SWAT team when I least expect it.

So for now, all I can manage is to ask, "Is that really possible?"

CiCi pulls the bottle away from me, taking a defiant drink. "Yeah. I think that's really possible."

I allow myself a tiny, hopeful smile. It's not much, but it feels like more than I had.

21

Thankfully, CiCi took the wine away from me before I ended up drooling drunk on Gertrude—and also before I could make lurid calls to any more famous actors.

I feel I owe her a dinner for being the reason I'm able to make it through my day here at E-Z Storage without a hangover. I debated taking the day off and waiting for my imminent arrest, but on the off chance CiCi is right and Caspian is too afraid of his own indiscretions being publicized, and I'm not bound for a chain gang, I have a job to finish.

I spent the morning wrapping up the unit from yesterday, which seems like weeks ago now. Around noon, I head down to the gas station and say my daily hello to Rufus, use the restroom, and pick up a coffee and a protein bar. The lunch of champions.

I wonder if Rufus would notice if I just stopped appearing one day to annoy the hell out of him with my mere presence. I get the feeling he wouldn't be the least bit surprised or bothered if he saw me on the news for celebrity extortion.

If anything, I could see him being a witness for Caspian's side. Rufus isn't the warmest of fellows.

I add an extra big smile as I pay today. Rufus remains, as always, not particularly impressed.

I head back to the units and maneuver Brutus in front of the next one on my list. After a leisurely ten minutes of sipping bad coffee and eating my peanut butter–flavored cardboard, I sigh and dive back into the task at hand.

As I undo the padlock, I get a tiny sliver of metal stuck on the end of my finger. Some of these locks look scratched to hell and back, and this one has wounds that bite back, for some reason. I'm glad when I manage to dig the metal splinter out on my own. Somehow, I don't imagine Rufus would leap with joy at seeing me come back on a quest for tweezers.

This unit seems less ancient than the others, and it makes me sad. Some of these you can tell were abandoned ages before they were taken back by Charlie, but this one looks like the remnants of someone's actual life.

It mirrors the contents of my own unit more than I care to acknowledge. My stomach aches when I see a mattress propped up against the back wall.

Please, please don't let my unit end up with this fate, I quietly beg whomever might be listening to such pleading.

There's a flat-screen TV off to one side that I feel terrible about putting into Brutus, but maybe it will be a good find for the guys at the dump tonight. I stack up a few boxes with more than acceptable clothing and books to take by the shelter later, and fill the back of the truck with various containers of small electronics and assorted tchotchkes.

There's a love seat that will have to wait until Charlie's

boys pop by at a later date, so I mark that down on my sheet to let him know before kneeling down to sort through a box of old paperwork.

"Find anything you can use to destroy someone else's life today?" a disgustingly familiar British voice asks.

For a moment, I honestly wonder if I've become so paranoid about Caspian as a general entity that I'm now hallucinating. I turn around slowly and, unfortunately, he's all too real, standing at the entrance of the unit.

"You have *got* to be kidding me," I complain. "What, you don't get enough thrills tormenting me on your own time, so you felt the need to come all the way down here?"

Caspian leans against the entrance, looking far too comfortable. Today he's in black slacks and a burgundy button-up under his long black wool coat. He looks like an FBI agent who's trying too hard *not* to look like an FBI agent.

"So," he says calmly, "this is where the magic happens? It's really the Lord's work you do here."

"Oh, shut up," I snap, wishing I had a handy box of shoes to throw at him. "Was I unclear yesterday? Our time together has come to a merciful end, dude. Unless you've decided you need to be here in person to watch them drag me off in handcuffs. I can see where that would be your prime source of jollies in life."

"You're awfully glib for someone who spends her days sorting through trash to find extortion fodder."

That's it. I turn back to the boxes in front of me and start tearing open lids.

"Exactly what are you doing?" he asks.

"At the moment, I'm looking for things to fling at your pompous head," I say with a growl. Every remaining box contains either papers or pillows or other, less aerodynamic items. "Seriously, what the hell could you possibly want from me at this point?"

"I came here to speak with you, but as you can't contain yourself for even a minute without resorting to illegal activity or violence, I've obviously wasted my time, haven't I?"

A growling noise tears out of me, and I open up a box full of dishes. Dishes will do.

Before I can even grab one of the plates sitting on top, a sound of shattering glass explodes behind Caspian. He leaps out of the way and looks back toward Brutus, and for a very ridiculous instant, I wonder if I blacked out with rage and actually threw something at him.

Another shattering explosion rings out, and I glance up to see a man with a crowbar standing beside the truck, broken glass at his feet. Caspian looks back at me for a second, either seeing if this is somehow my doing, or in general shock, and I stand up.

"Hey!" I call to the man with the crowbar. "I know you! You're the creepy guy who was wandering around the other day."

I try to resist smacking myself in the forehead for actually saying those words out loud.

He's dressed almost identically to what I saw him in when he appeared at the door of the other unit I was working on. The same tattered puffy coat and jeans.

The crowbar, however—that's a new accessory.

His response is to swing hard and shatter the back window of the truck. I yelp a little in response. Caspian backs away, joining me inside the unit.

"You think you can just steal someone's shit?" the crowbar-wielding, angry man shouts. "Who the fuck do you think you are?" He turns around and swings again, this time taking off the driver's side mirror on Brutus.

"Is this…is this your unit?" I ask foolishly. "Did you try to cut open the lock?"

His response is an eloquent one. He brings the crowbar down on Brutus's windshield, and I yelp again, this time in terror.

"Gimme your phones," the man yells. I'm deep enough in the unit that his voice echoes like the surround sound in a horror movie.

"I'm sorry?" Caspian asks, looking utterly stupefied.

"Gimme your fucking phones!" the guy shouts, taking another crack at the windshield.

Out of sheer reflex, my hand goes into my pocket, and I start walking forward with my phone outstretched. I only make it a few feet before Caspian yanks it away from me, bundles it with his own, and calmly hands both of them out the opening of the unit.

Crowbar Man stomps over and snatches our phones from Caspian. Without saying anything, he drops them to his feet and starts beating them to death with the crowbar. Over and over and over he hits them. It's like the more he destroys them, the more it fuels his anger, and his face turns into an absolutely terrifying mask.

I'm not the only one noticing this. Without taking his eyes off the intruder for even a split second, Caspian reaches behind himself, grabs me by the arm, and starts pushing me back farther into the unit. Even when my shoulder bumps into the concrete wall, he doesn't release his vise grip on my forearm.

By now, all that's left of our phones are some case shards and dust in lieu of glass. With a guttural scream, the man suddenly kicks the fragments in our direction. I flinch hard and try to squish myself against the wall even tighter, but Caspian doesn't move a muscle.

For a blood-chilling moment, the intruder just stares at us, panting with his teeth bared and clenched. Caspian's grip gets even tighter, and I whimper.

The man wheels around, swings the crowbar again, and shatters one of Brutus's taillights.

My speechless shock has long since worn off, replaced by a legitimate fear that I'm about to be murdered with a movie star in E-Z Storage unit 278.

Instead—and I'm not sure if this is much better—the man whips back to face us, reaches up, and pulls the unit door shut, slamming it into the ground with so much force, it bounces up a good two feet before crashing down again. It makes an impossibly loud blasting sound that reverberates off the concrete walls and makes my teeth shake.

It's darker than black inside now, and my terror only grows as I hear Crowbar Man secure the padlock he'd previously attempted to chip away at, sealing Caspian and me inside.

The tiniest sliver of light peeks under the door, and I see the man's shadow walking back and forth. A second later, I hear the sound of another vehicle, and I feel a sense of dread, thinking of some poor stranger coming by to visit their own unit and being greeted by a monster with a crowbar.

I start to run toward the entrance, prepared to scream a warning, but Caspian doesn't release my arm. The blackness is beyond disorienting, and we both grab on to each other to keep from falling.

"We have to do something," I say, not at all sure what that might be other than shouting until my lungs bleed. Since he still hasn't let go, I drag him up near the door with me. "What if he hurts whoever that is!?"

"I don't think that's a random visitor," Caspian says quietly. I look up and see the faintest outline of his face in the minimum light we've been allotted. He seems to be listening carefully. The sound of things being slammed into the back of a truck echoes into the unit, and I try to picture what's happening on the other side of that door. "I think he came for his belongings," he adds.

I hold my breath and try to picture what's happening outside. Yeah, it definitely sounds like he's moving things from the back of Brutus to another truck.

For a few minutes, that's all we can make out. Then I hear the unmistakable sound of shattering glass again, peppered with the slamming of the crowbar against metal.

"Hey!" I shout, pounding on the door with my free hand. "You leave Brutus alone, asshole!"

Caspian yanks my arm so hard I stumble into him again.

"Are you mad?" he hisses at me.

"They're beating up Charlie's truck!" I yell.

"Better the truck than us!"

"He can't get back in here, because the creepy fucker left the keys with me!" I continue banging on the door, and Caspian tries to shush me again. I angrily yank my arm from his hand and blindly push him away. After a few more sickening cracks, I hear vehicle doors shut and the squealing of tires. "Yeah, you'd better run!" I scream at the door.

"My god," Caspian says from a few feet away. "You are truly unhinged."

"Oh, shut up!" I shriek at him. "Just shut up! Not everything needs your pompous commentary!"

"Yes, screaming obscenities at the violent man who brought friends seems like a positively brilliant idea!"

"I told you, they can't get back in here!" I say, taking the keys out of my pocket and jangling them in front of his face. "I have the goddamn keys!"

"Right," he shouts back. "Because that seemed like a man who would be stopped by a missing set of keys!"

I stare at the keys in the outline of my hand, illuminated by the minuscule streak of light. "Oh my god."

"What now?"

"We…we are locked in here."

He scoffs. "Worked that out, have you?"

I walk up to the door and put my hands on it, feeling every ounce of my body starting to panic with claustrophobia.

"Oh Christ," Caspian says as the same realization hits him, suddenly sounding detached. "We're locked in here."

I hear him walk up beside me and stand by the door as well. I strain to hear any sounds at all, but there's nothing.

"I don't suppose you have some burly driver outside who is proficient in picking locks?" I ask.

"I took a car from the theater and was dropped off," he says, still sounding terribly far away, even though he's less than two feet to my right. "I was going to call another one when I was ready."

Whatever pocket of adrenaline that's been fueling me through the bulk of this ordeal wears off, and my heart is pounding in a different way now. "Our phones. We can't even call for help." I push away from the door and feel the entire unit closing in around me in the darkness. I try to take a breath, but it stalls with only a fraction of the air I needed. "Oh god, what if we suffocate in here?" I gasp, either from shock or lack of oxygen, I'm not sure which. I lurch back to the door and fall into it with one hand outstretched. Dropping to my knees, the panic takes me, and I can't breathe.

"You're hyperventilating," he says, and just as I pull in

enough air to make a biting comment, I feel his hand on my shoulder. "Lean forward."

I collapse down onto my elbows, curling up in a little ball, and wonder if I can suck enough air through the crack. "We won't suffocate," he tells me. "There's plenty of air in here."

"Oh, yeah?" I gasp. "Do you know that for sure? Do you somehow know the exact rate of oxygen usage for two people in a unit this size?"

"I mean, I'd look it up, but some lunatic broke my phone."

My head jerks up, and I realize his hand is still on my shoulder. "Was that a *joke*? Is this what it takes for you to make jokes that aren't at the expense of other people? Near-death experiences?"

Caspian chuckles. "Evidently." He sighs and moves away to sit against the cement wall behind me. "So...in the absence of my burly, lock-picking driver, I don't suppose you have anyone on standby outside, or set to check on you anytime soon?"

"Nope," I say, letting my head drop back down to my arms.

"Is someone expecting you for anything? What time do you normally head back to your brother's?"

I shrug before remembering he can't see me. "It depends. Sometimes it's early. Sometimes I go hang out with my friend and don't get in until after Tom and Trina are asleep."

"And they have no problem with you spending your days at an empty storage unit lot? Seems a bit sketchy at best to have you out here all by yourself."

My head snaps up. "Excuse you, I can take care of myself. I don't need permission from anyone to have a job."

"Easy now," he says, and I swear I can hear him rolling his eyes. "That wasn't a woman-related jab. I have no doubt you can handle yourself. But I think the fact that we were just quite literally attacked makes my point for me."

"I'll give you that one." Thinking about potential rescuers, I add, "My friend CiCi will probably come looking if she hasn't heard from me by the time she gets off work."

I realize a piece of broken phone is cutting into my knee, so I sit up and put my back against the door. Then a horrible thought pops into my head, and I choke on a second burst of hysterics.

"What?"

"It's just…" I try and fail to regain a little composure. "She's going to think you had me arrested. That's what we spent all last night talking about. How I would just suddenly disappear when you finally dropped the hammer, and she'd be the only one who knew what happened."

"You really do have a dramatic sense of imagination."

"Says the actor," I retort bitterly. "The actor who kept threatening to have me arrested, by the way, so it's not like our theory was really that far-fetched."

In the faint glow of light, I watch as he stretches his extraordinarily long legs out and crosses them at the ankle. "That's fair."

There's a very restless silence for a few moments. Figuring I have nothing to lose while locked in a storage unit, hoping we don't run out of air, I say, "We got interrupted by the dude with the crowbar and all, so you never got around to telling me exactly why you're here. It's slightly out of the way of the theater."

"A bit." He starts gently straightening his watch. "I meant what I said. I really did come with the intention of speaking with you." I can see a hint of a smile on his face now. "But before the crowbar man appeared, technically we were interrupted by you preparing to throw things at me."

"I'd like to think we were interrupted by you not knowing how to say hello to someone without it coming out as an insult," I offer. "Makes it hard to feel particularly conversational."

"Also a fair point."

"Honestly, are you that rude to everyone?"

"God, I hope not."

His admission startles a laugh out of me. "So you *do* hear how big of an ass you are when you talk to me? That's nice to know. I'd hate for that kind of venom to go unnoticed."

"If we're being honest, you're not exactly kind when we chat, either. Are you always that vicious?"

"Only to physically imposing celebrities who blackmail me."

"I'm not physically imposing," he says, and I almost laugh again, but he sounds so genuinely surprised, I reel myself in.

"Have you *met* you?" I ask. "You're really, really tall, and you have this icy stare that makes regular humans cry. And oh my god, when you do that thing where you stand up really fast and start shouting? That shit is terrifying."

He starts fidgeting with his watch again. "I was trying to be intimidating, not terrifying."

"Intimidating is you on a regular Tuesday. You could dial it back by a mile and still get the point across."

"I'm sorry about that," he says.

I eye him suspiciously, even though I know he can't see my expression. "I can't tell if you're being serious or not."

"Of course I am." I find myself actually believing him. "I guess I didn't stop to think about how all that must have looked from your perspective. I never meant to scare you. Well, not that badly, anyway."

"Thank you," I say fervently. "For future reference, if you're doing something you would do on-screen while playing a villain, it's probably a hair too far in real life. Particularly if you're a good foot taller than the person you're trying to intimidate."

"Duly noted." A moment goes by, him still toying with his watch, and he adds, "You've had some solid moments of terrifying yourself."

I sigh. "I wasn't going to actually throw anything at you. I don't think. If it helps, I've got horrible aim, anyway."

"That's not what I'm referring to."

I try to think back to any time I might have let my talk of potential murder or open manhole cover comments slip into our conversations. "What, then?"

"You have no idea what it felt like to get that voice mail you left."

I shrink down against the wall. "Oh. That."

"It was the first thing I saw when I woke up," he elaborates quietly. "I hadn't even gotten out of bed. And there you were, laughing your way through the details of the most traumatic point of my life. I actually Googled myself for the first time that day. To see if you'd already sold the story. All I could think about was my mum seeing it before I had a chance to tell her."

His voice sounds so uncharacteristically fragile, and the imagery is so horrific, I can't help the tears that start to fall. "I am so, so sorry." I try to clear my throat, but there are more tears than I can cough away. "I truly never meant to do that to you. I know that doesn't magically make it not exist, but I swear, I would give anything to undo it. I really am so sorry for everything." I pull my coat sleeves down over my hands. "I know you don't have any reason to trust my word on it, but I promise you, I was never going to do anything with those papers. It probably doesn't ease your mind any at this point, but it's the truth."

"Thank you," he says, reaching out to put his hand on my shoulder again. "I believe that."

I don't know what else to do, so I pat his hand with my coat sleeve–covered palm. "Thanks."

"For the record… I was never actually going to have you arrested," he says, giving my shoulder a squeeze before pulling away. "Well, not after I met you, anyway."

"Seriously?"

"Quite serious, yes. The whole ordeal in your brother's apartment was so…unsettling. I believed you then, honestly."

I gape at him for half a second, then reflexively slap him on the arm. "Dude."

He laughs. "I'm sorry about that. But not really, I suppose, because there was always the chance that you could have tried to sell the story later on, and while I believed what you said, I wasn't going to take any chances."

"So I've been having daily panic attacks and picturing myself in orange this whole time, and you were never going to actually do it?"

"No," he says, and I swear he sounds almost sheepish. "That's actually what I came here to talk with you about. But, as our interactions tend to do, things got off on the wrong foot."

"I'm waiting for you to accept responsibility for the bulk of those wrong feet."

Another laugh. "All right, I accept. In my defense, I didn't realize how— What was the phrase you used? How 'physically imposing' I was being along with my jabs. That sort of takes things to a level of cruel I wasn't intending."

Now I have to laugh, both from the absurdity of the situation and from relief. "You know," I say, "when you're not threatening me or growing to the size of an angry tree right before my eyes, you're not quite the monster I had you pegged to be."

"I do believe that's the nicest thing you've ever said to me," he says, and I hear a smile in his voice. "And when you're not calling me a prick or preparing to throw dishes at my head, you're quite pleasant company."

I blush and, in the moment, am glad he can't see my face. "Well, now you're just sucking up." He laughs again, and I let loose a giggle of my own. "So, I'm curious. Is this what you're normally like? With people who didn't accidentally uproot your life, I mean."

He moves a bit, and I take it as a shrug. "I think so? What about you?"

"I'm pretty sure it is, but I guess it's hard to say, isn't it?"

"I suppose it is."

We're silent for a moment, and I become painfully aware of how very cold it is. The lack of sunlight and the cement floor have turned this experience into what I imagine sitting on a block of ice feels like. I shudder so hard, the door vibrates behind me.

"What was that?" Caspian asks.

"My body rebelling against only a thin layer of denim between it and the frozen floor. It's like being locked in a freezer. Why couldn't Crowbar Guy have locked us in here in, say, July?"

"I imagine that would be rather like being locked in an oven."

"Yes, but waaaaaaarmth." I shiver again, making the door wiggle loudly.

"Why don't you come sit beside me?" he offers.

I blink slowly, certain I didn't hear him correctly. "Uh. Are you serious?"

"Yes? Why wouldn't I be?"

"Because we hate each other?"

He moves slightly again, which I take to mean another shrug. "Not at the moment, I don't hate you. And didn't we just discuss our mutual hatred being dialed back?"

"I guess we did," I say, only now realizing it.

"In the spirit of our honest discussion in captivity, I would even be prepared to say I'm discovering I may not actually hate you at all."

"Aww, just what every girl wants to hear," I tell him.

He chuckles. "How about this, then—I've got a long wool coat that's probably better to sit on than nothing, and I'm guessing it's safe to say it's warmer for two people to be huddled together than spread apart when ensconced in frigid concrete."

I consider all this for a moment. "You're freezing your ass off, too, aren't you?"

"So very much."

I laugh so hard it echoes through the unit. "Okay, fine."

I crawl over to where he's sitting and have the damnedest time figuring out where all of him actually is. He reaches out and guides my shoulder until I'm curled up inside his coat with him, with one of his arms wrapped around me.

"Okay, full points for the sitting-on-the-coat advice." I notice he's shivering a little as well. I tuck my knees to my chest and lean in as much as I can. "Not to go fully morbid here, but aside from my lack of air concerns, should we be more worried that if no one finds us, we are definitely going to freeze to death in here?"

"I'm hoping your friend comes looking for you before that happens, but I'd say that might be a concern, yes."

I shudder again, but this time not from the cold. "I am

having the worst mental image of someone finding us days from now, all Popsicle-y like Jack Nicholson in *The Shining*."

"That's rarely a good look for anyone."

I turn my head and give him an amused and incredulous look before remembering he still can't freaking see me. "Ugh. I never realized exactly how much of my communication is through nonverbal facial expressions. This is really throwing me off my game."

"Sticking your tongue out at me, are you?"

I snort. "Well, I am *now*."

"See, it hasn't slowed you down as much as you th—" He stops talking suddenly, and I hear the sound of a car pulling up outside.

I jump away from the wall as though it's burned me, trying to move as far back from the door as I can, but my feet get tangled up in Caspian's coat. "What if it's Crowbar Guy again?"

"You said he can't get back in here, right?" Caspian says, reaching out to steady me before I tumble backward. "Should we call out for help? Whoever it is probably has a phone."

"I guess if it's the creepy guy, at the very worst, he would just ignore us or beat up Brutus again."

"Who is Brutus?"

"The truck," I say, staring at the crack of light to see if I can make anything out. "I name inanimate objects. It's a thing."

A shadow appears at the base of the unit, and Caspian and I both scramble to stand. The sound of the padlock being fidgeted with causes my heart to stop.

"What if he went to get something to cut the lock?" I whisper, feeling panic rush through me again.

The door starts to roll open. Caspian pulls me behind him, and I hope he's about to use some of that physically imposing stuff on whomever is on the other side. I clench his hand so hard it has to be painful.

The door opens all the way, and the afternoon light makes me squint. Caspian hangs on to me just as tight while using his other hand to shield his eyes.

I make out a familiar, bearded outline and cry out, "Charlie!" Caspian looks down at me for confirmation, because I'm assuming that to a person outside the know, Charlie isn't any less scary-looking than the guy with the crowbar. "It's okay," I assure him. "He owns the units." I have to stop myself from lunging at Charlie and tackling him with a grateful hug. "What are you doing here?"

"Security firm called and said they saw the tail end of some punk smashing my truck and played back the tape." In the near-distance, I hear sirens. "Either of you hurt? They couldn't see inside the unit, just that you never came out before he locked it up."

"We're fine," I say, and deflate with relief. I realize freedom is ours, so I race out of the unit, still clutching Caspian's hand, and take a moment to bask in the few glorious rays of sunlight that are gleaming through the November clouds. The sound of broken glass crunches under my boots. "Oh no, Brutus!"

I look at my poor vehicular friend, and it's absolutely mangled. Every window is broken, and while I can tell the creepy man tried to beat the hell out of the body of the truck, other than a little chipped paint, there aren't any real scars. "I'm so sorry, Charlie! He just appeared, and it all happened so fast. I feel horrible about Brutus."

"Brutus?"

"The truck," Caspian offers.

Charlie nods, as if that's a perfectly reasonable answer. "Trust me," he says as the flashing lights of police cars appear at the entrance of E-Z Storage. "It's a lot gentler than what's going to happen to the guy who did it."

Caspian looks down at me to see whether or not he should be alarmed, and I give him a slightly wide-eyed look.

I guess that answers my question as to whether Charlie is the cement-shoes kind of guy.

22

Tom, Trina, CiCi, and I are all crammed onto Gertrude, each with a mug of coffee, staring slack-jawed at the television.

On the screen, the morning news program is going into great detail about the startling heroics of one Caspian Tiddleswich, who, according to the newscaster, survived a horrific attack with his girlfriend last night, complete with video from the scene taken through the chain-link fence surrounding E-Z Storage.

It took less than forty-five minutes from the moment the police arrived for news crews and paparazzi to appear. Bless Charlie for banning them from the grounds.

I don't think he had a clue who Caspian was or cared, but he could see how stressed we were, and, well, Charlie looks after his people.

Tom and CiCi appeared within ten minutes of each other

soon after the TV crews set up. Caspian's handlers arrived around the same time, and we were separated for the rest of the night.

With our phones rendered a step past unsalvageable by the lunatic with the crowbar, the news crews certainly saved us a lot of calls to be made. If I ever see the creepy bastard who locked us in that unit again, I may actually thank him for the broken phone. He's saved me from the 742,000 calls and messages poor Tom has had to field from our mother, demanding any and all information.

"Welp," CiCi says, still staring in awe at the TV, "this is sure happening."

"Are you sure you don't want me to stay home with you today?" Tom asks, not looking away from the screen. I can't blame him—it's like watching a televised car accident. "Seriously, I feel weird leaving you here alone."

"I'm not alone," I say, sounding slightly disembodied. "CiCi already called in. And I have no intention of leaving Gertrude for the foreseeable future, so there's no sense in all of us staying crammed on here."

"You're on the *news*," Trina says, looking as stunned as I feel. "In real life, you're on the news with your movie-star boyfriend."

"You're sure you don't want me to stay?" Tom asks again, slowly sipping his coffee.

"I've got this, little brother," CiCi says, reaching behind me to ruffle Tom's hair. "I'll keep her safe and locked down, I promise."

"*The news*," Trina repeats.

It takes a good fifteen more minutes to convince Tom I won't fall to pieces should he leave, but finally, he and Trina head off to work with Trina periodically whispering, *"The news..."* as he ushers her out the door.

"Remember when you were just a regular person and your life wasn't like watching a surreal documentary?" CiCi asks once they're gone.

"I really don't," I say, watching her flip to the other morning shows to see who else is running the story.

They all are.

"I think your days of the quiet editor life are over, cupcake," she says, getting up to refill her coffee.

"Safe to assume," I agree.

When she returns and drops back down onto Gertrude with me, she asks, "So...he really apologized? And you believe him that he's not going to the police? Because I really want to revel in being right about that."

"He did," I say, taking a drink from my *Write On!* mug. "And technically, you said he wouldn't go because he wouldn't risk implicating himself, when it seems like he actually just decided not to be that level of a dick."

"Po-tay-to, po-tah-to. Either way, you're not going to prison."

"I'll gladly drink to that," I say, reaching over to clink my mug with hers.

"This is all so weird," she says as paparazzi-taken pictures of Caspian and me flash across the screen. "And I'm so freaking glad you're okay. That had to be scary as fuck."

"That's my official stance on it."

"I wonder if they'll catch the guy."

My eyes go a little wide. "He'd better hope the police do before Charlie does. He doesn't strike me as the 'forgive and forget' type."

"Do you ever wonder if maybe Charlie is a—"

"Mob boss?"

"Yes!"

"Every single time I talk to him. Whoever the crowbar guy was, he'd better sleep with one eye open."

"Or he'll be sleeping with the fishes?"

We both chuckle, but stop after a second. There may be too much truth in that to laugh.

"Want me to take you to get a new phone?" CiCi asks, changing the subject from theoretical murder.

I sigh. "No, I have to call my company and see if the insurance I have on the phone covers acts of crowbar-wielding first."

"I think I might have an old one in a drawer somewhere," she offers. "I can dig it out so you don't have to be cut off from civilization."

I smile. "Thank you, but honestly, I'm not minding missing out on the onslaught Tom is getting from Mom. I checked my inbox this morning, and hand to god, I had eighty-seven emails from her. And let's be honest, you know there are probably going to be new publishers calling now, trying to work the Caspian connection even harder."

"About that," she says, turning on Gertrude to face me. "Now that he's, well, slightly less evil at the very least, can you please start considering the two job offers you've got? Getting your foot in the door because of him isn't the worst thing that could happen."

I wrinkle my nose. "I guess it's not. But come on—you'd be pissed, too, if people offered you a job that was based on anything other than your own badass reputation and skills. I would care a lot less about the interviews coming around because people think I'm with Caspian if they even hinted at having read my actual résumé and knowing what I'm capable of."

"Ugh, I hate it when you're right." She huffs. "But you *could* always wow them with your capabilities once you start, you know. They'd think they were just hiring a puff person, but in reality, you'll blow them all away."

I think on her point, but am interrupted by the doorbell. I look at CiCi with dread. "What do you think the odds are my mother spent the night driving all the way down here from home?"

CiCi winces. "That does seem very Mama Montgomery." She sets her mug on the end table and hops up to get the door. "If it's her, hide. I'll tell her you…moved. Or that you're shacking up with your movie-star lover."

"Madam, I will strike you down where you stand if you say the word *lover* to my mom."

CiCi laughs hard and opens the door. Her laugh cuts off instantly, and for a hot second, I worry that Crowbar Guy somehow figured out where I live.

"Is Clara here?" a familiar voice sounds out.

"Caspian?" I say, my voice far more high-pitched than normal as I leap off the couch.

"Oh my god," CiCi half gasps, moving out of the way to let him in. She closes the door behind him and stares, mouth open. Another victim of the celebrity sheen.

"I, uh…" he says, glancing back at CiCi's frozen expression. "I thought I'd bring this by." He holds up a brand-new phone, still in the box. It's the latest version of my relic that died an unnatural death yesterday.

"That is so thoughtful," CiCi says, coming to stand beside me. "Isn't that thoughtful, Clara?"

"Very thoughtful," I say automatically. "Oh, erm, CiCi, this is Caspian. Caspian, this is my friend CiCi."

"Pleasure to meet you," he says, extending his hand.

"Damn right it is," she purrs as she shakes it.

"CiCi," I say pleadingly. Caspian looks down at the floor and chuckles awkwardly. CiCi is still shaking his hand. "Lady, let the man go."

She releases her grip, but keeps staring at him with a hilarious expression on her face. I'm probably a little too delighted by how fidgety she's making him.

"You know what?" she says, turning to me. "I forgot I have to pop into the office for a bit."

"No, you don't," I say, frowning.

"You don't know my life," she insists with a wink. "I'll stop by again later. Text me with the awesome new phone you just got." She turns back to Caspian and adds, "You be nice. I mean it. If you thought the guy yesterday was bad, you ain't seen nothing yet, fella."

I close my eyes and shake my head. "CiCi."

"I'm just letting him know I take my best-pal duties very seriously." She shrugs. "You kids have fun." She passes behind him and grabs her coat off the gray chair before heading out the front door. As it closes behind her, she turns back and mouths *OH MY GOD* before she disappears.

"She seems terribly shy," Caspian says with a laugh.

"Oh, yes." I nod. "Really working on getting her to come out of her shell."

"Here you are," he says, holding the phone out. "I wasn't sure of your carrier, so I bought one that's unlocked. Well, my assistant did, anyway. I was on hotel arrest all night."

"You really didn't have to do that," I say, shuffling my feet. I'm suddenly very aware that I'm still in my jammies—a Captain America T-shirt and pants with little cartoon penguins on them. "That had to be really expensive to buy one outright."

"Take it," he insists. "I figure I owe you a kindness or two."

"I'm torn here, because on the one hand, that is an absurd amount of money," I tell him. "But on the other hand, it's rude to refuse gifts, and I can almost hear my mom gasping with horror."

"See? It's meant to be."

I take the phone from him, and dear Lord, I can't believe how nervous I am. "For the record, you don't owe me anything. I think we established last night that we've both made some huge, mutual cock-ups."

"Still," he says, "it's something I could do, so I did."

We stand in silence for a few moments that feel more like eons before I say, "You can sit? Sorry, I don't know why that came out as a question."

"Thank you," he says, and peels off his coat, laying it across the back of the gray chair as he sits down.

I stand stiffly for another few seconds before flopping back on the couch, still holding the phone box.

"This may be weird to say, but I'm kind of waiting for you to turn all Evil Cas again. Like, now that you're not locked in a cement tomb after a traumatic event and you've had time to think about it, our truce is over or something."

He exhales and looks oddly relieved. "I honestly wondered the same thing about you."

"Is that why you came over? To see if I would start throwing plates?"

He snorts and replies, "No, but I'm glad nothing has been hurled yet, verbally or otherwise. Although I will admit the phone was my excuse and buffer, just in case."

Now it's my turn to laugh. "As far as excuses go, this was a good one. I couldn't have afforded this phone even if I wasn't living it up all unemployed on Gertrude here."

"Gertrude?"

"The couch."

He nods. "The naming-inanimate-objects thing. I see what you mean."

I giggle. "So, why are you here? Aside from making sure I didn't turn back into a bitter pumpkin."

"Truthfully?" When I look at him expectantly, Caspian huffs out a breath and says, "I was feeling a little more freaked out by yesterday than I was prepared for, and my handlers were trying to get me to do all sorts of press about what happened. They mean well, but not everything needs to be spun into promotion for the film."

"Ew, yeah," I say with a frown. "That is kind of gross."

"This was the only place they would let me go without demanding a reporter follow me, when I told them I needed to come see how you were doing."

I wave my hand. "Glad to be of service as an excuse."

"I mean, I obviously did want to make sure you're all right as well," he adds, looking contrite. "I didn't mean to imply otherwise."

"I knew what you meant," I say with a smile. "If I'd had the ability, I would have at least texted to see how you were feeling. I'm freaked out, too. But then, part of my freaking has to do with seeing myself all over every morning show, but I suppose you're probably used to that?"

"There's a vast difference between showing up on the television for my job, and when it's focused on something like last night that's part of my actual life."

"Oh, wow, yeah. I bet that's…"

"Unsettling."

"I'm sorry," I say. "It has to be so surreal, seeing everything you do plastered on the news." It occurs to me to ask, "So, wait. Does that mean you're here hiding out?"

A sheepish expression spreads over his face. "If you'd rather I left, please don't feel obligated to let me stay."

I'm surprised when I answer honestly with, "Not at all. It's actually nice to have someone here who gets how bizarre this all is." I point at the TV, which is still running quietly in the background. Our faces are plastered on the screen again, and I wince. "Seriously, *how* do you get used to that?"

He sighs. "If I ever manage to get used to it, I'll let you know."

"Fair enough."

We both watch the TV in silence for a bit as the peppy host goes into the details of our ordeal. I've been watching these stories all morning, and it hasn't stopped being the weirdest thing I've ever seen.

"I, um, actually have a confession," Caspian says suddenly. When I look at him, I'm kind of shocked to see how very strained he looks. In fact, I immediately feel nervous by proxy.

"Okay. I'm listening."

"There's no way for me to say this without sounding like a prat, because, well, having done it makes me a prat." He stress-runs his hands through his hair.

"Doing what? I'm on a knife's edge here."

Caspian breathes deeply and then pushes it out in a loud gust. "I've been acting."

I stare at him for a good thirty seconds. "You're an actor. That's kind of your job."

"No, I mean, I've been acting with you. This whole time. Well, up until yesterday, anyway."

I'm even more confused. "I mean, haven't we both? Wasn't that the deal? Acting like we're a couple?"

He leans back in the chair, gripping the arms in frustration. But the way it reads, the frustration is with himself, not with me. "I'm trying to tell you I've been playing a role, a character, since the moment I knocked on your door that first night. You asked me yesterday if I'm as big an ass to everyone as I am to you, and I should have come clean about it then, but I'm so damn embarrassed by all my behavior, I didn't."

"You're telling me you've been playing a character since we met," I say slowly. "As in, I haven't actually met…you?"

"Essentially," he says, the word dripping with shame. "Although, if you want to mark the exact second you did meet me, I'd say it was about five minutes into our frozen captive situation yesterday."

I can't seem to focus my eyes. "This may be the creepiest thing I've ever heard."

He squeezes the arms of the throne again. "It really is. And I'm so sorry. But I've never had to actually be intimidating in real life in a way that would have been convincing, and when I made up my mind to track you down, it occurred to me to treat this as just another part to play, and it all sort of just…happened."

"Dude."

He shakes his head as if he can throw off his mortification. "It went so much further than I ever intended. I might've taken it all to the grave, but you were being so honest yesterday, and I wanted to return the favor. And when you said the things about how I'd gone well past intimidating and delved fully into terrifying… I can't actually think of a time I've felt more guilty about something and disgusted with myself. I wanted to scare you into decency, not *scare* you, if that makes sense."

"Only just," I say, my voice sounding detached.

"And…" My eyes go wide, wondering how there could possibly be an *and*. "There were more than a few occasions when I rather panicked in the moment, if I couldn't manage to ad-lib anything." He looks so beyond humiliated right now that I can't sit still. "And so—god, this is mortifying—there were several times when I…recycled lines from characters I've played. I started to get really scared I would end up quoting something you'd seen and you'd realize what I was doing."

I am so stunned by the scenario he's describing, I have to purse my lips shut tight to keep from bursting out laughing. Not because it's particularly funny—although it kind of is—but the whole thing is just so absurdly ridiculous, it's the only acknowledgment that seems appropriate.

Based on his squirming discomfort, I don't think he'd agree.

"I, uh…" I stammer. "I don't even know how to respond to this."

He leans forward and closes his eyes. "I just wanted to apologize again for scaring you. And I felt like you deserved to know what was really going on. Plus, I didn't like the way I felt knowing what you thought of me. The idea that you had no reason to think all of that was anything other than my actual personality made me sick. I really am terribly sorry, Clara."

I shrug stiffly and huff a little. "I mean, I guess it's a good thing that acting like a sociopath is out of the norm for you enough that you had to create a fictional sociopath? I think, anyway?"

"Let's hope Saint Peter comes to the same conclusion."

Now I do chuckle. "If I'm being honest, I'm glad to hear it's not, like, the hallmark of your personality, the things I've seen thus far. So, I suppose I should say it's nice to finally meet you, Caspian."

He smiles a little. "Likewise."

"Is that it?" I ask. "Is that all of the confession? You don't have bodies hidden in your hotel room in preparation for a film role, do you? Because I think Saint Peter might have some specific thoughts on that."

"That I can honestly say no to. But I do, uh…" He nervously rubs his hands down his pant legs. "I actually have a favor to ask."

I raise an eyebrow. "Wow, you're on a freaking roll today, my dude. So the confession and phone are also excuses and bribes?"

"No," he says so earnestly that I feel bad he didn't catch the joke I was going for. And his expression is serious enough that I actually start to feel concerned about what he might say next. "Not at all. That really is just a gift to replace the one that was broken. And maybe subconsciously a bit of a balm for my guilty conscience, if I'm being truly transparent."

"I was just messing with you," I say, unwilling to keep him on that hook. "What's the favor?"

"You can absolutely refuse," he insists. "I meant what I said yesterday. I have no intention of lording calling the police over you anymore."

"Just tell me what the favor is so I can decide if I need to refuse."

He's fidgeting so much, it's starting to make me squirm, too. "Again, you can say no, so please don't feel pressured—"

"Spit it out, sir."

He takes a deep breath and finally stills. "Would you be willing to keep up our arrangement and accompany me here and there until I'm due back to London?"

I blink very slowly at him. "I thought we were dropping the whole extortion thing?"

"Oh god, not like that," he says and resumes fidgeting. "Not at all. This wouldn't be in exchange for anything. It would just be…helping me out. I was being honest when I said I'm under a lot of pressure from my team to appear in a relationship, and, well, you've gotten them off my case."

"Huh." I genuinely don't know what else to say.

"This wouldn't be you at my disposal, or me being the prick who demands you jump when I call. Truly. It would be what we discussed before, but without the animosity or bullshit games. I could even give you a schedule ahead of time, whenever possible." He sighs and shakes his head. "I know it's a lot to ask."

I ponder the task at hand. "What would that even look like? I mean, no offense, but your fake boyfriend track record isn't the best."

"I know, trust me." He looks so ashamed, I can't not believe him. "And as I said, you owe me nothing, here. You can tell me to fuck off, and I would completely understand."

"I'll keep that option under consideration," I say, frowning again. "So, are we talking all the same stuff as before? But what? Without ditching me in VIP rooms and chucking me out on the curb to catch the last train of the night?"

He looks mortified. "I see now why you wanted to throw things at me. My god, I'm an ass."

"I want to argue with you, but…"

"I really am so sorry about how I behaved," he says genuinely. "It's unforgivable. I have no right to even ask this."

"I mean, thank you for that," I offer. "But I haven't said no or anything. I'm just trying to picture it." I try to put the Caspian of the last fifteen hours or so in our previous scenarios together, and the juxtaposition is jarring. "No shenanigans? No tricks?"

"Absolutely not."

"And if something like a job interview comes up, I wouldn't be tarred and feathered or threatened with police action?"

"Not in the slightest."

"I get the feeling there's something in particular you have in mind, here."

"Well, the premiere and the play, for starters."

I eye him suspiciously. "And?"

His expression turns sheepish. "And…there's a dinner tonight that you've been requested for."

"And the shoe drops," I say with a little laugh. "What does that mean?"

"There's a part I'm considering, and the director and producer want to meet tonight to discuss things. They're bringing their significant others and asked to meet you." He rests his elbows on his knees and clasps his hands. "They just contacted my team this morning, so I promise I wasn't going to spring this on you under our prior arrangement."

"That's nice to know." I shrug because I don't know what else to do. "So this is just because people think I'm your girlfriend, and it's easier than trying to explain otherwise?"

Caspian thinks about that for a moment, almost like he's trying to find a way to put a more positive spin on my summation. Eventually, he says, "Basically, yes."

I turn the phone box over in my hands and internally debate the proposal. This time yesterday, I would have sold both my kidneys to get out of being Caspian Tiddleswich's fake girlfriend. And yet here I am, debating whether or not to stay in the role on purpose.

"I think I can handle that," I say slowly.

He looks just as surprised as I feel hearing the words leave my mouth. "Seriously?"

I point a finger at him. "As long as you promise to treat me like an actual person. I'm talking dignity and respect, here, mister. And that will go both ways. I promise to do the same. And no throwing things. Probably."

"I promise." He looks both stunned and relieved. "You really are doing me a tremendous favor, Clara. Thank you."

Hearing the way he says my name—"Cl-AHR-a"—reminds me of the first few seconds of our initial meeting, when I found it endearing.

That feeling has returned a bit.

"Well," I say, dropping the phone on the couch beside me. "I figure I owe you a kindness or two."

23

As soon as we pull up to Fromage, I begin to feel like I've made a horrible mistake.

I've never seen so many photographers in one place. There has to be at least forty of them, all crammed together on the sidewalk looking into the window of the restaurant, and when one of them spots our car pulling up, most of their heads turn in unison like a flock of flamingos with giant cameras hanging from their spindly necks.

"Oh Jesus," I whisper, staring out at the throng.

"God," Caspian mutters. "I knew it would be bad, but this…"

I turn to him, my horror uncontained. "Why is it like this? I thought the ten or fifteen you usually have was awful."

He shakes his head and looks past me. They're starting to aim their cameras at us, and I've never been more grateful for tinted glass in my life. "Part of this is just because this restaurant is always littered with people hoping to get their pictures taken. And I'm assuming part of it is probaby because someone we're meeting with called a handful of the paparazzi themselves to let them know we'd be here. As for the rest... I'm guessing they're here because, well, you and I caused quite the stir with our adventure yesterday."

"Lucky us."

"Indeed."

The driver is outside the car now and heading around to Caspian's side to let us out, and I have to fight the urge to leap across his lap and lock the door. Or possibly fuse it shut forever with a blowtorch.

Caspian takes my hand in preparation, and I grip him tight. "I swear, if you let go of me, I will die in that stampede and come back and haunt you until the end of your days, Tiddleswich."

"I was going to tell *you* not to let go of *me*," he says with a wink.

Then the door is open, and it's somehow so much worse than I had anticipated. I don't know what the car is made out of, but it very effectively muffled the now-deafening volume that is echoing through the back seat as we move to climb out. The driver is trying to block people as best he can, but he's only one man in a sea of clicking desperation.

What makes this all the more horrifying is, through the chorus of "Caspian!" and "Mr. Tiddleswich!", for the first time I hear multiple people yelling, "Clara! Miss Montgomery!" as well.

Nope. He definitely doesn't have to worry about me letting go.

I don't think we ever discussed whether it was okay for me

to hang on to him like a tiny monkey, but that's pretty damn close to what's happening.

It can't be more than twenty feet to the door, but it feels like a mile-long walk of nightmares—and once we are inside, it somehow doesn't feel any less smothering.

The hostess is a woman in her very early twenties with her hair sleeked back into a perfect low chignon. She's wearing a white blouse that is so low-cut, I can see her actual navel, which has me questioning again how people wear shirts like that without their boobs making public appearances. She's the second hostess I've seen in a similar top, and I'm starting to wonder if there's some sort of citywide regulation that requires these women to stand at the ready with their sternums on display. I make a mental note to hit the internet for answers later.

"Welcome, Mr. Tiddleswich, Miss Montgomery," she says in a low purr. I am not a huge fan of this new trend of people I don't know calling me by my name with no introductions. "The rest of your party is already seated. If you'll follow me, please."

"Hmph," I mutter as we trail behind her. Caspian looks down at me curiously. "Every reservation I've ever made, they won't seat until the entire party is present." He grins, and I roll my eyes at him in mock exasperation. *"Celebrities."*

We're escorted to a large round table by the front window. Five people already seated and, by the looks of it, a drink or two in.

"May I take your coats?" the hostess asks. Caspian pulls his off smoothly and hands it over. Before I can finish unbuttoning mine, he takes the collar and waits for me to slide out.

"So gentlemanly," I say quietly. He gives me another wink, and I swear, this chivalrous new habit of his is a little unsettling and a lot more appealing than I care to admit.

We turn and face the other diners. "Hello, everyone," Caspian says in his perfectly Shakespearean voice. "My apologies for the lateness. I'd like to introduce my date, Clara Montgomery. Clara—" He starts gesturing at our dining companions. "This is Geoffrey VanHousten, and his wife, Deanna."

A gray-bearded man in his fifties wearing a polo shirt and suit jacket smiles and gives me a wave. His slightly younger wife, looking masterfully elegant in a navy cocktail dress, smiles at me as well.

Caspian continues. "This is Walter Donahue and his fiancée, Arabella Quinn. And last, but never least, David Bishop."

I wave awkwardly at the table. "Hello," I say. "It's a pleasure to meet you all."

Caspian pulls out a chair for me, and I sit, enjoying this gentlemanly side of him. As soon as he joins the table, the comments start flying.

"So, Clara," Deanna asks kindly. She has a friendly face, framed by light brown hair sprinkled with a few grays, and a soothing voice. "What do you do? How'd you manage to lock down our Caspian?"

"Um." I look at my date. "I'm not sure I've locked anything down." His mouth twitches, and I add an annoyingly coquettish giggle for good measure. "I work in publishing. I'm an editor, but between houses currently."

"Oh, yeah?" Walter, who kind of resembles a cliché Wall Street businessman from the eighties with his loosely worn tie and slicked-back blond hair, pipes up. "An editor? Arabella here has been wanting to write a book, haven't you?"

Arabella lights up. "I have! I think it'll be a big seller."

"What kind of book?" I ask her. I take a slow, measured breath that I've rehearsed a thousand times. Enough to calm my irritation, but not so obvious that anyone can tell what I'm doing.

Why have I rehearsed this? Because anytime I meet someone new and they find out I work—well, *worked*—in publishing, I am immediately bombarded with claims that they have an idea for the next *Harry Potter*. Other times, people give me a lengthy and often unfathomably detailed account of their lives, which they think would make just the *greatest book ever*, but they don't have time to write it, so could I do it for them?

It's exhausting.

"Well, I don't know what someone in *publishing* would call it." She says "publishing" in a tone I'm taking either as reverie, or mockery. It's a tough call. "But there's these teenage vampires, and their city was destroyed by the government. Then the main character gets cancer and has to lead the revolution while going through chemo."

I bite my lip, and my hand jumps out to grab Caspian's knee in a death grip. "That sounds really fascinating!" I say with more fake enthusiasm than I've ever mustered in my life. "I bet it will be a lot of fun to write!"

"Don't I just sell the idea and someone helps me write it? What are those people called?"

Her fiancé offers, "Ghostwriters?"

"Yeah!" Arabella smiles. "You'd buy an idea like that, right?" She turns to Geoffrey. "And you'd scoop the movie rights up, I'm sure." She laughs as though this is the most obvious course of action, and I squeeze Caspian's knee harder. He has a casual smile on, but I can see the muscle in his jaw straining to hold back laughter.

I would wager what little money I possess that Arabella was the one who tipped off the paparazzi. Her short sequincovered violet cocktail dress seems purposely designed for sidewalk-posing.

Geoffrey smiles a far more genuine smile than I'm managing and turns to me. "What sort of books do you edit, Clara?"

It's hard to hold back the flood of personal grousing about the life of an unemployed editor, but I'm on a mission for Caspian's sake. I release his knee, and he drapes his arm over the back of my chair, listening intently.

"Well, I focus on children's literature. I did a lot of young adult, but I've always had a huge soft spot for middle grade."

"Have you worked on any books that I might have heard of?" Deanna asks kindly. "We have a daughter who's eleven."

I decide right there I like Deanna and Geoffrey. "Well, let's see. Oh! Last year one of my authors released a book about the daughter of a pirate who takes over a rival ship after her father tells her girls aren't meant to be captains."

"Captain Featherwig?" Geoffrey says.

"Oh my gosh, yes!" I'm thrilled that they recognize it, and my stomach flops excitedly.

They both laugh. "It's one of her favorites," Deanna says fondly. "For three months straight after that book came out, she dressed like a pirate. It took us weeks to figure out she'd torn open a feather pillow and hidden it under her bed, and that's where her 'wig' had come from."

I'm beaming. "That is so wonderful. It really is a great book."

"I'd been looking into the rights," Geoffrey says. "Are you still involved with the project?"

And there comes the sinking depression. I keep my smile magnanimous. "Unfortunately, our house didn't survive the merger with Alkatraz over the summer. But I still have so much love for that book and the author. I hope it works out."

"Oh, that awful e-retailer?" Walter makes a disgusted noise. "They're the downfall of society, mark my words."

"Does anyone even read books anymore?" Arabella ponders. "Isn't everything digital now?"

"They're still books," I insist, using everything I've got to keep my smile intact. "Even on an e-reader, it's still a book."

"I read print books," Caspian chimes in—his first full sentence since we sat down. "I appreciate the convenience of a digital book when I'm traveling, of course, but nothing will ever replace bound pages."

I look at him gratefully, which is a jarring change of pace from my previous pledge to curse his entire existence.

The waiter comes by to take our drink orders. I'd been so busy talking I didn't think to look at the menu, so I just reflexively order my usual G&T.

The conversation steers to various enterprises. I study my menu with extra concentration in hopes of having a moment to catch my breath. From what I overhear, it sounds like Geoffrey is a fairly bigwig Hollywood director attached to Caspian's possible next film project. I wonder if it's the Top Secret watermarked script. Deanna—whom I've decided I really want to be friends with—is a stay-at-home mom to three and active on the boards of at least four thousand charities.

Walter is a producer on whatever film this is, I think. Arabella is… Aside from a wannabe writer, I'm not really sure. She seems to have a lot of opinions on things, though. David Bishop is unnervingly silent, and I can't figure out what he's here for.

Caspian is a completely different person in front of people he knows well. He's got a great sense of humor, and it doesn't take much to get him to laugh until his teeth show and the sound echoes through the restaurant. It's very endearing.

I'm liking this side of him more and more by the minute.

However, much to my dismay, our table by the window has given the photographers prime access to our little party. I'm angled just enough that the flashes aren't directly in my eyes, but it's still obnoxious, like sitting near a strobe light. I'm probably judging, but I feel as if Arabella chose her seat at the table with care to be in full view.

When the waiter comes back with our drinks and prepares to take our orders, I flash back to CiCi repeatedly suggesting the lobster, but think better of it, remembering my newfound truce with Caspian. I go for a very autumnal-sounding salmon dish with sweet potato hash instead.

When the waiter hits Caspian, I don't know what I expected, but the slow-roasted pork with apples seems surprising to me. I suppose I need a minute to adjust to this new version of him who feasts on traditional fare as opposed to the one I pictured feeding on the hopes and dreams of small children.

I hear my shiny new phone buzzing nonstop in my purse hanging on the back of my chair, and I whisper an apology to the group as I pull it out.

I try to hold back my sigh, but my shoulders slump a bit of their own accord. Dozens upon dozens of texts and calls. I ignore all but CiCi's and see multiple pictures attached. Caspian and I in the car. Caspian and I exiting the car, making me terribly thankful I didn't wear a dress, because holy shit, that photographer had to be low to the ground.

A picture of us sitting here at the table taken through the window.

This is the creepiest thing I've ever seen.

I text back. Where are these coming from?

She answers immediately. They're all over Twitter and the Page Six site.

I suck in a breath and tuck my phone back in my purse.

"Everything all right?" Caspian asks softly.

"Absolutely," I say, and turn my attention back to the table. Caspian rejoins the conversation, and I'm sure I should as well, but I'm distracted by the horde of people outside the window. They aren't just focused on our table, and I know there must be other celebrities here. I don't have a clue who they are, but the flashing lights outside are nonstop.

Out of the corner of my eye, I notice people at other tables subtly trying to take pictures of us with their phones. They're not even paying attention to their own companions; they're just rubbernecking all the tables in hopes of spotting someone outlandish.

I take a deep drink and feel grateful they make 'em strong here. I'm not used to the feeling of people staring at me, but that's exactly what's happening. People who have no idea who I am are snapping photos of me sitting next to Caspian and posting them to god knows what on the internet.

Someone pounds on the window just to the right of where Deanna is sitting, and we all jump. It's a photographer trying to get everyone to turn and face him—which we all absolutely do, in shock, and he starts shooting pictures to the point where I see little stars from the residual flash again.

Our waiter comes running over. "I'm so sorry," he pleads. "Management is having that man removed from the property. Is there anything I can do for you all?"

Geoffrey looks at David with great annoyance. "You wanted the table by the window," he says, exasperated. David just shrugs in response and throws back the rest of the bourbon in his glass. He's not a chatty man.

Deanna puts a hand over her heart, but Arabella turns

slightly in her seat so her legs are crossed and visible to the window. I decide right then I *don't* like Arabella.

"Will you excuse me for a moment?" I say to the table, and stand up before anyone can respond. I scurry away in search of the ladies' room and find an attendant who leads me into my own luxurious personal bathroom. It's nicer than any NYC bathroom I've ever been in. All that's missing is a claw-footed bathtub, and I'd never leave this place.

I lean over the sink and take a few breaths. I've been able to fake my way through this evening pretty well so far, but I'm getting overwhelmed fast.

People always say publishing is a lot like the entertainment field, but with a bit less drama. Sure, we have our own high school–level crap and obnoxious people, but unless you've written the hot new thing about teenage lovers gone awry and it's been made into a major motion picture, no one really gives a shit about publishing folk. Especially not the editors. I've been very content to sit at a desk in silence and watch words become books.

It's a wonderful life.

Now my mom is going to see all those pictures and she's going to call me over and over and over. As is everyone else I know.

I reach for my phone to text CiCi and beg for a pep talk, then realize I left my purse hanging on the back of my chair. I try to take another deep breath, and it comes in shuddering. My eyes are starting to burn.

How is this my life? This isn't me. I'm not fancy restaurants and storage unit robberies and paparazzi. I'm pizza and manuscripts under a blanket.

There's a knock on the door. "Just a moment," I call in a shaky voice.

"Clara?" It's Caspian.

"Yes, just a moment!" I trill. I'm starting to hyperventilate.

The bathroom door starts opening, and I scramble away from the sink, trying to keep my composure.

"Is everything all right?" he asks, closing the door behind him.

"What the hell are you doing?" I demand. "You can't just come into an occupied bathroom. What if I was, uh, bathrooming?"

He makes a face at me. "You seemed uncomfortable when you stepped away. I wanted to see if you needed anything." He holds out my purse. "Also, I brought this."

I mean to take it gently, but rather rudely yank it out of his hand instead. "Of course I'm uncomfortable! There are pictures of me popping up all over Twitter and people are banging on windows to get your attention and I'm on a pretend date with a freak who followed me into the bathroom!"

My legs go wobbly, and I fling my hands out to steady myself on the wall.

Caspian the Great very calmly sits down on the floor with his back to the door. "I am a bit of a freak, aren't I?"

I'm sucking in very unsatisfyingly shallow breaths. "Less so than I thought yesterday, if that helps. And I can't believe you're sitting on a New York bathroom floor. That's how the zombie apocalypse is going to start, you know."

He gives a little laugh and stretches his long legs out across the tiled floor, crossing them at the ankle, calling back my memory of him in the storage unit. "Care to join me?"

I eye him suspiciously. My legs are still feeling rubbery, but I'm not about to crawl over to him. I carefully sink down to my knees and lean forward a bit to catch my breath.

"I was going to be a bastard and give you a MetroCard the other day at lunch," he says.

"What?" I say in confusion, trying to casually brush the tears out of my eyes and hoping he doesn't notice. "I have a MetroCard."

"I assumed you did. I was going to give you one for the sole purpose of rubbing it in that I'd be making you dance back and forth into the city at my whim on the train. I have cars at my disposal that you could have easily used, but I wanted to make a point. I was trying to be cruel."

I frown. This would be a lot easier to take in if I weren't gasping for air on the floor of a bathroom, for crying out loud. "I don't really know what to say to that."

"The others find you very charming."

I'm feeling a bit of whiplash at the sudden change of subject. "Yeah, I don't know what to say to that, either."

Caspian smiles at me. "I apologize. This is a lot to ask of someone, and you're doing a wonderful job. I'll have my driver take you back to your brother's tonight."

I pull in a full breath and nearly yelp with joy at the feeling of expanded lungs. "There's no need, honestly. The train's fine. Just as long as the not-dropping-me-off-in-the-middle-of-nowhere agreement stands."

"It stands. And consider the offer of a lift to be part of my apology."

"You've already apologized," I remind him, exhaling slowly. "Which I appreciated, by the way."

"I know, but I keep remembering all the horrible little things I had planned. And while you may not need to hear them, I feel the need to continue to apologize for them." I want to cut him off and insist it's all not necessary, but he

looks so sincere and bizarrely out of place sitting on a bathroom freaking floor, I don't stop him.

"You're really on a confession kick lately." I reach over and
poke at his shoe. "If it makes you feel any less awful, I rou-
tinely imagined you falling into open sewer grates."

He laughs hard. "The *Looney Tunes* demise. I admire that."

I snort a little. "Yeah, okay, it was a tad Bugs Bunny."

"Do you feel up to finishing dinner? If you'd rather call it
a night, I understand."

I take another deep breath and shrug. "I'm good. It was just
a little overwhelming for a minute."

"I have to admit, I've spent the last week hoping you'd fail
spectacularly at this, so I'd have cause to gloat. But you really
have been doing amazingly well."

"You're kind of a jerk sometimes, aren't you?"

He nods. "I can't argue. I'm disappointed that it's accurate."

"I was joking," I say, poking his foot again. "Come on. We
were both assholes to each other. It was our thing."

"I guess I don't like having a guilty conscience."

I intend to be supportive, but an unfortunate thought bar-
rels into focus. "Uh. Do you realize that if anyone saw you
come in after me, they probably 100 percent think we're in
here having sex."

Caspian cycles through several expressions. A furrowed
brow. Wide eyes. His mouth popping open.

Finally, he deflates and drops his head in defeat. "Christ.
That'll make for an interesting headline tomorrow."

I have to giggle. "I look forward to my mother's apoplectic reaction to that headline. But hey, we've been in here long
enough, I think you'll be portrayed as appropriately virile.
Your handlers will probably dig that." I sigh. "That said, there
is such a thing as too virile, so we should probably get back."

Chuckling, he stands up and brushes off his pants. He takes a few steps forward and holds his hand out to help me up.

I accept the proffered hand, and he easily pulls me to my feet. "You're sure you're all right to continue?"

"Yep. I've got this. One solid freak-out'll do me."

He gestures to the door. "Shall we?"

I gape at him. "Dude. You just sat on a bathroom floor. If you even try to walk out of here without washing your hands, the deal's off."

With a deep and genuine laugh, he joins me at the sink.

24

Charlie called early this morning with the news that Brutus is repaired and back on the lot. I was surprised by how enthused I was at the prospect of returning to my work at E-Z Storage, but with only four units left to go, the promise of getting the albatross off my back seems quite thrilling.

Plus the endless anxiety remains excellent fuel for hauling shit around. Not quite as good as my rage from the last week, but preferable, overall.

As I'd predicted, I woke up this morning to infuriated text messages from my mother, appalled that I spent last night having bathroom sex with my movie-star boyfriend.

You need to get off the TMZ website, Mom.

I don't hear you denying it, Clara. I didn't raise you to behave this way. And I'm not on that website. I have a Google Alert set up for your name.

MOM. No. No, no, no. Undo it. And I didn't have sex with Caspian in a restaurant bathroom. God.

I ignored all her other responses, as they're serving only to raise my blood pressure.

Before I headed over to E-Z Storage, I'd checked my email and discovered I have three other houses wanting to set up interviews with me. I responded to each of them, full of professional hope, but now, a couple of hours later, I can't shake the feeling that they're all Tiddle-based.

"Seriously," CiCi says, pulling me out of my moody thoughts, "it's not the worst thing in the world for them to want to hire you."

CiCi, ever the best pal—and possibly on orders from Tom, who is likely on orders from my mother to not let me stay at the units alone for very long—has sacrificed her Saturday morning and vowed to help me finish at least one unit before I have to go fluff myself up for the fancy Manhattanites. Tonight, Caspian and I are set to have dinner together again.

"Because of who I'm dating," I scoff. "Correction—who they *think* I'm dating. Who I'm not *actually* dating, but who I originally started gallivanting all over town with because Trina has the same stellar impulse control that I do."

CiCi pauses to think. "I'm still shocked she did that. It's always the quiet ones."

"And we have exactly zero room to judge her, don't we?"

Bashfully, she mutters something about different motivations.

We work in silence for a few minutes until she says, "This unit is gross. Why would someone keep a bunch of canned food in a storage place?"

I look around. "I don't know. End-of-the-world planning?"

"This is a lot of spoiled planning." She holds up a rusty can. "This says it expired seven years ago. Ever wonder what happens to canned potatoes that expired seven years ago?"

"Not even a little."

She tosses the can back into the box and tries to lift it, but the cardboard hasn't handled time well and shreds under the weight of the cans. They clatter all over the cement floor, and CiCi dances out of the way to avoid losing a toe.

"Oh, shit! There were jars in there, too!"

Then she claps her hands over her face and screams.

"What the hell is that smell!?" I shout.

"Run, oh my god, run!" she says through her fingers.

We flee the unit together, but the stench appears to have fused to us in some way. "Jesus, did you get some of it on you?" I gasp.

"I don't know," she wails. "But I swear to god, it looked like eyeballs, dude. Disgusting gray eyeballs. I love you, but I didn't sign up to haul off fucking eyeballs."

"Bad day at the office, then?" a familiar male and British voice says from the other side of Brutus.

"Ahhhhhhh!" CiCi and I scream together, wheeling around.

"What. The hell. Are you doing here?" I demand, clutching at my chest. "You can't just sneak up on people after one of them was robbed the last time she was here."

"I was going to see if you'd like to grab drinks before dinner, but your sister said you were here working," Caspian explains, looking slightly apologetic.

"Sister-in-law," I say, still clutching my chest. "Well, future sister-in-law."

"Noted. So," he says, looking around. "Eyeballs, eh?"

I shake my head, and CiCi catches my gaze. She's got that half-stunned, half-sexpot smile on her face, just like she did yesterday.

"CiCi, breathe," I command, poking her in the ribs. "Caspian, you remember CiCi."

"Of course. Pleasure to see you again," he says, but she's still frozen, stunned and smirking. He looks at me, and I shrug. "Oh, Clara," he adds, pulling something out of the inside pocket of his coat. "I wanted to give this back to you."

He hands a small piece of paper to me. I unfold it, then look up at him and sigh. "I told you I don't want it."

"What is it?" CiCi asks, finally unfreezing and coming over to look.

"It's the check from that picture," I tell her, handing it back to Caspian. "And I'm really not taking it, but thank you, Caspian."

"Whoa, wait! What are you doing?" CiCi gasps. "Clara!"

"I don't want it," I insist stubbornly. I pull in a deep breath and start throwing loose cans into Brutus.

"That's ridiculous!" CiCi squeals. "Come on—that's seventy-five hundred bucks! You've been slaving for weeks cleaning out these stupid units for five thousand!"

"I agree," Caspian says, sounding mildly frustrated. "I know it wasn't you who sold it, and otherwise the money will just go back to that horrid place. It's got your name on it. You might as well benefit from the whole mess."

"I'm not taking it," I insist firmly. "If you refuse to burn it or whatever, I will go with you and cash it, and you can donate the money somewhere. If somebody benefits from that picture, it's not going to be me. And holy damn, those seriously do look like eyeballs."

"Spider!" CiCi shrieks.

"What?"

"THERE IS A SPIDER ON YOUR ARM!"

I'm not proud of how I flail around. I'm really not. Nor

am I particularly proud of the girlish cries that fall out of me as I thrash out of the unit, ripping my sweater off over my head in a panic.

"Where did it go!? Is it still on me!?" My entire body shudders, and I can't stop clawing at myself.

I'm knocked totally motionless by two long-fingered hands on my shoulders. "Stand still," Caspian says in his übercalm manner. I whimper. He releases my shoulders and scans me, even walking around behind me and checking my hair. "You're spider-free." He steps past both CiCi and me and heads into the unit, making a slight face when the stench hits him. "And those appear to be ancient pickled eggs, although I can see the eyeball confusion."

"Well, okay, then," CiCi says. "That settles that."

"And as we have plans to get to, Clara," he says, pulling his suit jacket off, "we'd best get started cleaning this up."

"Oh god, no, don't touch anything!" I say desperately. "You're all…clean and stuff."

He walks out to where we're still standing and sets his jacket on the front seat of Brutus. "And I intend to stay that way." He rolls up his sleeves and heads back inside. "Do mind the broken glass."

CiCi stares at me. I stare at CiCi. We both turn our heads slowly and stare at Caspian.

"Erm," I say delicately. "Well, uh. Here we go, I guess."

All hopes of finishing that unit came crashing down when the pickled eyeball smell became infused in all our clothing. We abandoned ship, with CiCi heading home to savor the rest of her Saturday, while Caspian gave me a lift to Tom's so I could attempt to shower the stench off and change before heading back into the city.

With the promise that I'd be no longer than ten minutes, tops, I left Caspian hanging out in his fancy black town car, tending to various business needs on his phone, and scrambled up the stairs to Tom's bathroom, desperate to rid myself of the putrid eyeball cloud.

As I wait for the water in the shower to warm up, it occurs to me that I don't really have time to properly wash my hair, dry it, and manage to put on a quick shellac of makeup, plus get dressed.

Looks like it's a quick body scrub and dry shampoo/perfume kind of day.

I manage to get in and out of the shower in about ninety seconds, but it isn't until I'm standing in front of the mirror, wrapped in a towel and emptying a bottle of dry shampoo onto my head, that I realize, in my hurry to de-stench, I forgot to grab clothes to change into. I assume I'll have to burn what I was wearing at the unit.

I've only got about six minutes left, so I abandon the mirror and rush back into the living room.

And I scream.

Loudly.

My brain literally can't process what it's seeing.

Tom and Trina are standing awkwardly by the door to the kitchen holding several large bags of take-out food, but worse—oh, so *very* much worse—is Caspian, standing in the middle of the living room.

Next to my mother.

My actual mother is standing right. The fuck. Beside him.

"Mom!" I shriek. "What are you doing here?"

"Honey!" she trills, as though this is perfectly normal. She walks over and gives me a quick hug. "I'm heading up to see your great-aunt Wanda for a few days, and I thought I would pop in for a late lunch with my babies!"

I gape at her. "Great-Aunt Wanda lives in Connecticut, Mom. This is ever so slightly out of the way."

"Well, since I was making the drive regardless, a few hours out of the way wasn't a big deal," she explains, while simultaneously picking up a lock of my hair and making a face.

"Uh, sis," Tom says quietly, and I look over at him, too stunned to function.

"What?"

He points at me, still holding a sizable bag of food. "You're... kind of naked."

I look down, and yep—clad in nothing but a towel and hair full of whatever powder dry shampoo is made of, I am, in fact, quite nude.

My brain is working about a minute behind where it needs to be. I look up and realize Caspian is 100 percent still standing there.

"Oh Christ."

"Language, honey," my mother hisses.

"Hey," Tom announces loudly, "Mom, Caspian, how about a tour of the apartment?"

Trina quickly takes the take-out bags from him and scuttles into the kitchen, and Tom walks over and starts to lead Mom away from me.

"I don't need a tour," she says, indignant. "I have been here before, Thomas."

"Yeah, but Caspian hasn't," Tom says through a clenched-teeth smile. "And you'd hate to miss him seeing this Valhalla of ours for the first time, right?"

I mouth *Bless you* at him as he drags Mom toward the bedroom, followed closely by Caspian, who has yet to actually look up from the floor. Or speak.

As much as the urge to stand here and stare blinking forever is hitting me, the second they pass through the door frame, I fling myself at the closet, clutching my towel for dear life, and grab an armful of clothing, hoping to all the gods I've gotten an actual outfit—and, more important, underwear—before I bolt back into the bathroom.

I can feel my heartbeat palpitating as I throw on jeans and a drapey black shirt, then do my best to tame my overly pow-dered hair while also trying to slap on a few coats of mascara.

I run back out to the living room, where Trina is silently setting trays of food out on the coffee table. It's a pretty im-pressive deli spread, by the looks of things.

Caspian is sitting on the Gertrude, next to my mother, looking… I'm not even sure. Floundering? Mortified? Des-perate to be literally anywhere else in the known universe?

Maybe I'm confusing his mood for mine.

"Uh," I say, clearing my throat. "Can I borrow you for a moment, Caspian?"

He stands up in that ridiculously fluid movement he does, and my mother seems both startled and charmed by it. I start to head to the kitchen, but Tom quickly hops over, grabbing me by the shoulders, and turns me around.

"Why don't you use our room," he suggests. "If you want some privacy."

The only room with a door we can actually shut, other than the bathroom. My brother is a god.

"I don't deserve you," I whisper as I dart away, grabbing Caspian by the sleeve and dragging him behind me.

As soon as we are in Tom and Trina's room with the door

shut, and reflexively locked, I turn to Caspian and unleash my panic.

"I'm sorry, I'm sorry, I'm sorry, I'm sorry," I chant.

"So," he says, staring blankly at me, "that's your mum."

"I'm sorry, I'm sorry, I'm sorry, I'm sorry..."

"She seems..."

"Unhinged," I offer. "How did this even happen!?"

He slowly shakes his head. "I'm not sure, entirely. I was on the phone, and suddenly there was a knock on the car window and her face was just...there."

"Oh my god."

"Next thing I know, she's got the door open, and I'm climbing out, and your brother was standing there on the sidewalk looking like he'd sort of died inside, and then she pulled me into the building."

"I'm sorry, I'm sorry, I'm sorry, I'm sorry."

There's a knock on the door, followed by someone attempting to turn the doorknob.

"Ack!" I yelp. And this is why it's my natural instinct to lock doors whenever my mom is around.

"We are about to eat," she calls through the door. "It's rude to keep everyone waiting, Clara."

"Yes, because it's definitely not rude to show up unannounced," I mutter in the general direction of the living room. I hang my head in defeat. "Be right there, Mom." I look up at Caspian and grab him by the arms. "Save yourself. Flee. Tell her you have to get back to the theater or something. Or, better yet, let's just climb out the window and run."

Caspian finally cracks a smile. "I think I can survive a meal with your mother after all I've forced you to do."

"Okay, but see, you only think that because you've never actually had to sit through anything with my mother."

There's a louder knock at the door, and my body jumps like it's going to dive for the window without an actual order from me to do so.

"It'll be fine," he says, putting a hand on my shoulder, leading me back to the door. "Most likely."

I reluctantly unlock it, and we rejoin the others.

"I apologize for having to eat in the living room," Mom announces as she sits on Gertrude again. "But it appears having an actual dining room table to sit at is out of fashion these days."

Tom sits on the floor in front of the coffee table with Trina by his side. "Where exactly would we put a dining room table, Mom?"

"You don't have to live in a place this small," she says haughtily.

"We haven't hit Rockefeller status yet," he reminds her with a sigh. "Which is the only way we'd be able to afford a place here with a dining room."

"You could buy a place in Buffalo, and the mortgage would be a third of the price of your monthly rent, you know."

"Yes, but then he'd have to live in Buffalo," I say with a smile. "And, Tom, please, you and Trina take the couch. I'll sit on the floor and Caspian can have the chair."

"No, I want to sit with your new beau," Mom counters. She pats the cushion beside her. "Both of you, sit."

Every time I think I've seen all seven circles of Hell, a new circle appears and Satan says, "Hold my beer."

I glance at Caspian, and we both seem to remember at this moment that my mom thinks he and I are dating, and therefore we have to appear couple-y. He gives me an almost imperceptible shrug and puts his hand on my back, leading me to Gertrude.

Mom tries to urge Caspian to sit beside her, but I quickly leap onto the middle cushion. He and I may have had our differences, but I don't want to see anyone suffer that much.

Everyone starts piling greens and pasta salad and smoked salmon onto plates, and I try to casually ask, "So, Mom. What's with the surprise visit?"

"I told you, I'm visiting my aunt."

"Yes, but why didn't you tell us you were on your way?"

Mom laughs. "I can't get you to answer an email or return a call these days! I figured it wouldn't matter if I tried to let you know."

"You get ahold of Tom just fine," I counter. "And judging by his expression, he didn't have a clue you were coming, either."

"I can't visit my children without a month's notice?" Mom says, adequately feigning hurt.

"Who said a month?" Tom asks, a forkful of salad frozen a few inches from his face.

"I mean, it's always nice to have as much advance notice as possible before a flagellation," I say, taking a bite of pasta. "How's Dad? Why didn't he make the trip?"

"Oh, he's fine. He sends his love. He and Uncle Jack are going ice fishing for the week, which made this the perfect time for me to head down this way." Before I can respond, she coos, "Trina!" and Trina literally jumps, dropping a cherry tomato onto the floor. "How goes the wedding planning?"

"Erm," Trina says, trying to find where the tomato rolled under the coffee table. "It's good. A little stressful, but mostly smooth so far. Clara and I just had our first dress fittings, and that went really well."

My mother nods and sends Caspian a meaningful glance. "Have you ever been married, Caspian?"

"Mom!" Tom and I snap in unison.

Caspian, who up until now has been poking rather piti-fully at his plate, looks up, stunned. "I have not, Mrs. Mont-gomery."

"Are you wanting to get married?"

I'm trying not to lose it, but Caspian just looks amused. "I don't have any immediate plans, but it's only the afternoon, so who knows what the day may hold?"

I try to hold in a laugh and almost inhale an artichoke heart.

Mom shakes her head and tuts. "You actors do tend to just run off and get married at the drop of a hat, though, don't you?"

"Indeed. Sudden marriage, substance abuse, and joining cults are really what we're known for. I personally request those things be written into my contracts for good measure."

Poor Tom was taking a drink at that moment, and now his lap is covered with spat water. I press my lips together as hard as I can to try to hold the laughter in. Trina is outrageously focused on the tray of salmon.

Caspian, however, is all smiles and maintaining steady eye contact with my mother.

"So I suppose we'll be seeing you at the wedding?" Mom continues, undeterred. "It would be nice to see Clara use her plus-one."

I look at Caspian. "Can you actually die from extended periods of mortification? Asking for a friend."

"I'm going to get a bottle of wine," Trina mutters, setting her plate down and standing up.

"It's a little early for that, don't you think?" Mom asks in a judgmental tone.

"Well, if ever an occasion called for day-drinking," I say.

"Cheers to that," Caspian says under his breath while stabbing a piece of asparagus with his fork.

"How's the job hunt going?" Mom asks me.

I drop my head to my chest. "You are truly the reigning queen of non sequiturs, Mom. And the job search is swell. I should be ready to fling myself off a cliff at any moment."

She takes a bite of salad and continues, "I spoke with Jack the other day, and he says the district's middle school English teacher will be going on maternity leave over the summer, and they'll need to find a replacement."

"Mom, stop. I'm not a teacher. I'm not certified to be a teacher. I don't want to be a teacher."

She carries on as if those things mean nothing. "He told me you can get your certification in a matter of months, and he wants to discuss it over Thanksgiving."

"Mom, no!" I say, and loudly drop my plate onto the coffee table. "We aren't doing this again! I'm not moving back home, I'm not going to work for Uncle Jack, end of discussion."

"Well, things obviously aren't working out for you here," she counters, waving her arm as though the living room represents all of my NYC failures. "You can't find a job, you've got nowhere to live, the crime here is out of control—"

"No, it's not!"

"You were attacked two days ago!"

"Okay, one time!"

"Excellent save," Tom murmurs.

I turn and face her head-on. "What's going on, Mom? You're being especially hostile today, even for you."

"And exactly what is that supposed to mean?"

My jaw drops. "It means exactly what I said! You show up with no warning, you're lobbing passive-aggressive gre-

nades like it's your job, you're being astonishingly rude to
Caspian—"

"Oh, you mean your fancy boyfriend that you never felt the
need to inform me you had? The boyfriend I learned about
by watching *the news*? That Caspian?"

Looking at Tom, Caspian asks, "Does she know I'm still
sitting right here?"

Tom sighs. "She knows."

"Is that what this is about?" I snap. "You're pissed I didn't
tell you I was seeing someone?"

"Language!"

Trina comes back in carrying a tray of wineglasses, all containing white wine. She successfully sets it down while managing to avoid making direct eye contact with anyone in the
room. I reach over and grab a glass and drink as though my
mother's life depends on me getting tipsy enough to let her
barbs roll off me.

Because it just might.

"This is all your doing, I know it," my mother snaps, pointing at Caspian.

"I'm sorry?" he stammers, absolutely floored.

"You swoop in and pull her into your hedonistic Hollywood lifestyle, and now she can't get her life together!"

"Oh, I disagree," he retorts with his steely glare and a smirk.
"Having one's life together is really just a matter of structure,
is it not? I've scheduled her cult initiation ceremony for five,
we've got dinner reservations at seven, and while I'm remiss
to have overlooked it thus far, thank you for reminding me
about the celebrity rule of at least one spur-of-the-moment
wedding, so I think I'll call in a few favors to see if a justice
of the peace can squeeze us in at nine. After that, I thought
we might start our honeymoon early by walking around Port

Authority wearing coats made entirely of hundred-dollar bills to try and do our part to boost the crime rate statistics."

I swear to Odin, I think I just heard a record needle scratch this room to a screaming halt. While Caspian sits like an icy-eyed statue, still smiling, everyone else is frozen, jaws on the floor. I'm not even sure anyone is still breathing. I know I'm not. I sit, holding my now-empty wineglass, and just stare.

I've never seen my mother speechless. It's somehow both equally amazing and unnerving.

Her face seems to be spiraling through every possible reaction. Will she explode and start shouting? Break out the crocodile tears? Spackle the walls of the apartment with guilt?

Suddenly she squints and looks away from Caspian, her eyes searching the room. This is a new one.

"What's that smell?" she asks.

"Oh, that's me," Caspian says casually. "Eyeballs. I'd explain, but if I do, the cult leaders will be very cross, and I won't be allowed to pass level five thousand and have tea with our alien overlords when they return for us all."

He reaches out, takes my empty hand, and kisses the back of it before turning his attention back to his plate and nonchalantly popping a slice of cucumber in his mouth.

25

After the longest lunch ever in the history of all time—which was surprisingly calm after Caspian's monologue—we got Mom packed up and off to Great-Aunt Wanda's. Tom and Trina collapsed with a pitcher of much-needed early evening martinis, and now that I've changed into a dress that wasn't soaked with mother-induced flop sweat, Caspian and I are on our way back to Manhattan, aiming for his hotel. Mom was right; the pickled eyeball smell is really clinging to him.

"I can't believe you touched that stuff. And in your fancy suit." I laugh beside him. "I mean, I had gloves, and I still wasn't about to touch an eyeball."

"I'm 90 percent certain they were eggs. Although one did appear to be looking at me."

"Well, they proved successful as a diversionary tactic against my mother, so cheers to the eggs."

"A charming woman, your mother."

"She certainly has a presence," I admit. "CiCi came home with me for Easter once and wore a shirt with a gemstone vagina on the front, and my mom had one of those boot things put on the tire of CiCi's rental car."

Caspian laughs. "Well, I'm glad I didn't wear *my* bejeweled vagina shirt, then. That would have been terribly embarrassing."

I giggle and catch a glimpse of the time on the car's dashboard. "Ugh, I'm so sorry about all of that. I can't believe she just showed up and hijacked you. How badly did it mess up your schedule for the day?"

Caspian waves his hand. "This wasn't a set-in-stone meeting. I was advised to be seen with you in public, just the two of us, and I thought dinner would be easiest."

"What does that mean? 'Advised' to be seen with me?"

"My handlers," he answers, as if this is perfectly normal. "Especially leading up to a release date, they tend to become very bossy about my personal appearances and image. They seem to think you are beneficial to that image."

Thinking back to my hideous McEnroe and Polar House interviews, I make a snort noise. "I know that feeling."

He looks surprised. "Do you?"

"Well, getting the image boost, not the handlers. That's weird."

"It is."

I slump in my seat a little and come clean about my frustrating job prospects.

"Did you take either job?"

"No. I mean, I need a job—like, a lot—but they didn't seem to care what I was even capable of. I want someone to hire me because I'm damn good at what I do." Staring wistfully out the window for a second, I reach over and poke him in the shoulder. "And I am, you know. *Damn* good."

"I believe you," he offers sincerely. "Geoffrey was quite taken with you. I think he'll try extra hard to option that pirate book you spoke of now."

"Really?" A surge of pride washes through me. "That's great. The author deserves that. And if you're working with him, I'll assume he's a good enough director not to screw it up."

Caspian slaps his hand dramatically to his chest. "Was that... was that a compliment? The tides have truly turned."

I roll my eyes. "Don't go getting too big a head," I warn. "You still smell like eyeballs."

We reach the hotel and make our way through the everpresent gaggle of photographers, then take the elevator up to the penthouse.

As I hang my coat up, Caspian says, "Make yourself at home while I un-eyeball."

I'm grateful for that plan, as it was getting a wee bit hard to breathe in the town car. He heads into his bedroom, and I hesitantly stand by the elevator door for a few minutes before I work up the courage to meander about the apartment-like hotel room.

Glancing at the table full of scripts, which is now tainted by memories of awkward "can we hold hands?" agreements, I bypass the area entirely and head for the couch. There's a stack of books sitting on the end table, and after I flop down on the squashy cushions, I peek at the covers.

Okay, so my first thought is that he's got mildly pretentious taste in upscale literature. But my second thought is that he's reading books, and I can't fault a guy for that.

Well, maybe I can. Chaucer?

I hear the sounds of a running shower and take his invitation to make myself at home a little too seriously. The lunch/ flogging with Mom has me beyond drained. Stretching as long as I can, I fan myself out over his couch.

"Oh, sweet, upholstered magic of the gods, this is a great couch," I purr into the empty room. This is a *magnificent* couch. This isn't even in the same universe as Gertrude. This is what all couches aspire to be in life.

I grab one of the obscenely soft pillows and smoosh my face against it. This could be upholstered with baby unicorn fur and stuffed with the feathers of fallen angels, and I wouldn't feel even the slightest bit bad about drooling on it.

The exhaustion of my day is coupling with the bliss of this couch in an unfortunate way. If I don't move soon, I'm going to pass out into the sleep of the dead. But at the same time, I haven't been this comfortable in months.

"Oh, sweet, glorious couch. I shall call you Jasmine. When I sleep on Gertrude, I'll be thinking only of you."

"Shall I leave you two alone?"

I pull the pillow over my face. "Naturally you'd be standing in the room. Because of course you would. Damn it."

"I can come back later if you need a few more minutes."

I tilt my head back and see him standing a few feet away. Using all my strength, I fling the pillow at his head. He catches it easily. "Shut up. You'll never understand the forbidden love of a girl and the couch of her dreams."

"Should I be alarmed by your attachment to these objects you name?"

Trying to sit up from a couch caress while wearing a short dress isn't as easy as I'd hoped. "We should probably *all* be alarmed. But you don't know the horror of sleeping on a couch for weeks because you're a loser and homeless and have to live at your little brother's.'"

He drops the pillow down beside me and comes to sit on the other side of the couch. His hair is still very damp, and he's changed into what I suspect is an identical suit, but in a slightly darker blue color than before. Either way, he no longer smells like pickled eyeballs, so there's improvement.

Actually, he smells like some kind of expensive men's shower gel that is the olfactory equivalent of this couch.

"I do, though, actually," he says, pulling me from the cocoon of shower gel and unicorn fur.

"You do what?"

"Know what it's like to be a loser and homeless and sleeping on a couch."

I throw the pillow at him again. "Playing a poor person in a movie does not a poor experience make, sir."

He tosses the pillow back. "I wasn't born a working actor, you know. It hasn't all been fancy hotels and cars and big paychecks."

His face is shadowed slightly by the expensive lamp on the end table behind him. It hollows his cheekbones, making him look more like the assassin in the Nebula Force movie posters plastered all over the city. But just beyond the sinister cheekbones are his lovely blue eyes, gleaming with sincerity.

"Didn't I read something about one of your parents being an actor in England? They were famous, too, right?"

"And did you grow up wanting your parents to hand you all of your opportunities? Judging by your reaction to those publishers dropping my name and your outrage at your mother trying to finagle you a teaching spot, you're the type who wants to make it on her own merits. We have that in common."

I consider this. "Ohhh, I get it now. You tried to make it

as an actor on your own, didn't you? When you were nineteen." My mind flashes back to the picture of young Caspian in the Cranson files, and my stomach flips uncomfortably.

"The day I signed that contract, I'd used my last dollar for train fare to an audition." His eyes take on a foggy appearance as he remembers. "I was desperate. I could either call my parents and beg for help, or I could be a foolish, stubborn ass and make my own way, no matter how destructive that way would prove."

"That's really sad," I offer quietly. "I saw the stuff from that…place, but I guess I never thought about what it would have been like to actually have to go through with doing it. It must have been so scary."

"God, I was terrified," he breathes. "Make no mistake—absolutely petrified. But I never got further than a booking. The day of my *appointment*, I got the call casting me in my first show. It wasn't much, but it was enough to eat for a few weeks. Things came more steadily after that."

"Oh my god, so you never had to…do stuff?" I wince a little. "Sorry, is that inappropriate?"

"You're fine. And no, I took the coward's way out and never showed my face in Cranson's ever again. Eventually they stopped ringing, and I put it all behind me. I still think back to that appointment, though. Often. I'd been too afraid to even look at what I was being hired for. I thought I'd just deal with it once it came about. I think the sheer possibilities of who it could have been and what I would have done are a suitable punishment for my youthful bull-headishness."

"Because it probably couldn't have been as bad in real life as what you can imagine?"

He nods. "I tell myself that, but I sometimes feel as though even the darkest parts of my mind couldn't possibly compete with the horrors of reality."

I pull the pillow up to my chest and squeeze it tightly. "And I'm the horrible bitch who left you a drunk message pushing it all back up in your face." Burying my face in the pillow, I groan. "I am so sorry. Nothing like this ever occurred to me. I am a horrible person, Caspian. I'm sorry."

The pillow is whisked away from my face and right out of my hands. "You're supposed to call me Cas," he says with a wink. "And remember, I already told you that I believe you. That you never meant to sell what you found."

"I really wouldn't have. I swear, Casp—I mean, Cas. I wouldn't have."

"I know." He pulls at the seam of the pillow with his impossibly long fingers. "And, while we're in such a contemplative place, I'm willing to admit that perhaps some of my initial anger toward you was possibly rooted in a bit of latent self-loathing. I'd always assumed that anyone who signed up for that life had to be in the same place I was—desperate, broke, hungry, scared. And I'm sure some are, but I met quite a few of the other escorts in a training program of sorts, and none of them seemed motivated by those things. They genuinely enjoyed the job. They were good at what they did, and they took a great deal of pride in it."

He looks down at the pillow and swallows hard. "It made me ashamed. Not because of what I was signing up for, but because I'd signed up for all the wrong reasons. I was looking down on the job as an absolute last resort before I handed over what little dignity I had left by that point, when really, I'd made up an entire judgmental scenario in my head to punish myself when I could have easily swallowed my pride and asked my parents for help. The others... They seemed content—*happy,* even. They wanted to be there. Or if they didn't, they did a spectacular job of hiding it. But I was just trying to hurt myself because I felt like I'd failed.

"This may sound ridiculous," he says, glancing up at me through his eyelashes, "but the thing I was most afraid of when I got your voice mail was my mum's reaction. She wouldn't have really cared about the actual profession, honestly, if that's what I'd wanted to do. But she would have been horrified that I was so fucking stubborn and dishonest with her and Dad. That's what I didn't want her to know. The bad choices I'd made based entirely on foolish pride. The idea of her being disappointed in me was just…too much."

It feels like one of the couch cushions is stuck in my throat, and I can't find any words to do the situation justice. The picture of kid Caspian, all gangly limbs and cheeks still sheltered by residual baby fat, is flashing violently in my mind, and it makes my heart hurt to think of how scared he must have been. But I'm also unspeakably sad about how he's still punishing himself for youthful obstinacy. I don't know anyone who doesn't look back at their teenage motivations and cringe.

He continues, "That said, again, I've made damn sure I'm properly haunted by imagining all the outlandish scenarios that could have played out if I'd kept that appointment. Maternal disappointment or not, those possibilities make my blood run cold."

Caspian finally raises his head, and for a moment, he looks almost startled. Like he forgot I'm here, or realizes what he's been saying. "I'm sorry," he says. "I didn't mean to pour all of that on you. I haven't ever actually said any of that out loud before. Bit self-indulgent, isn't it?"

I know he's trying to defuse the tension, because he smiles a not-at-all convincing smile and resumes running his fingers over the pillow. I want to say something, *anything*, that would alleviate even some of the stress he's put on himself, to apologize a thousand times over for the stress *I* put on him with that blasted phone call. But no matter what words I consider, they all seem woefully inadequate.

Accepting the absence of a "right thing" to say here, I calmly slide across the couch and wrap my arms around Caspian's neck.

"I'm so sorry you've been carrying this alone," I say quietly. "But I think holding a bitter grudge against yourself for over two decades is probably penance enough."

It takes a few seconds, but eventually, he puts a hand on my back and rests his chin on my shoulder. "Thank you."

We stay like that for a moment, and I find myself utterly confused by a myriad of sensations. My stomach is doing a little twist, my heart is beating faster than it should, and my skin feels tingly where his hands are resting.

I don't have the extra brain space to sort any of it out at the moment, so instead I pull back to look him in the eye. "And thank you for telling me all of that. I'm glad you got it out. Do you feel a little better about things now?"

Caspian stares at me, his eyes moving across my face, and I start to wonder if I managed to say something horribly insensitive when I was going for comforting. That fear, combined with his unreadable expression, and the fact that I'm all but sitting on his lap with his hand on my back and my hands still resting on his shoulders is starting to feel rather overwhelming.

"What?" I ask finally.

"I just…" he says, his eyes still focused intently on me. "I'm trying to figure out if you'd actually punch me."

"Wait—what?" I say, utterly confused. "Why? Why would

you think I'd—" Then my mind bounces back to my first visit to this hotel room, and our discussion of boundaries.

I'd been very specific about what would earn him a sock to the jaw.

My stomach goes from a twist to a complete free fall, my heart takes on the rhythm of a hummingbird's wings, and the tingle on my skin spreads far beyond where his hands still lie.

"Um," I say, certain I've misinterpreted what he's saying. "I'm not feeling particularly punchy at the moment?"

His hand slowly moves from my back and slides up to my jaw, and I am so stunned, I don't know whether to gasp or giggle.

And then, quite suddenly, I am kissing Caspian Tiddleswich.

I'm kissing Caspian Tiddleswich on a couch called Jasmine while a unicorn fur pillow rests in his lap.

It's more amazing and more odd than I can wrap my head around in the moment.

He kisses the way his voice sounds.

He kisses the way he says Cl-AHR-a.

Apparently, the universe *does* occasionally give with both hands.

I pull in a deep lungful of the scent of his luxurious body wash and allow my fingers to tangle themselves in his hair, still damp from the shower. He shifts slightly in his seat, and his free hand comes to rest on my waist, pulling me closer still. My breath catches in my throat, and my mind goes all cloudy.

I could happily do this all night.

But, very regrettably, I draw myself away. Only because I know if I don't do it right this very second, I don't think I'll ever be able to force myself to detach.

I can feel the same stunned feeling that's flopping around

in the place where my stomach used to live playing out in real time on my face, and I'm gasping for air a little, but while he's just as out of breath, his face is both amused and thoughtful.

"All right," he says. His voice has a new, scratchy edge to it. "If you've rethought your position on punching, all I ask is that you try to avoid my nose." One side of his mouth quirks up. "I have to do the *Today* show on Monday."

I damn near snort. Instead, I reach over and steal the pillow back. "Stop taking my pillow. It's made of baby unicorn fur, and it's my friend."

"If I wake up tomorrow and that pillow is missing, I know where to find you."

"Okay, Mr. Creepypants." We're back to our easy banter, but on the inside, I'm hysterically giggling and fighting the urge to hide in his bathroom and call CiCi to share this most unexpected and surprisingly welcome development. "Now leave me alone. I'm going to nap with my new friends."

He slaps his palms on his knees and stands up in a swift and fluid motion. It's the first time I've seen him do it when it hasn't been unnerving.

It is, in fact, kind of hot? Like in a way that makes me wonder how he might move in…other situations.

I try to casually lift the pillow up to my face until just my eyes are showing, because I definitely just set my own cheeks on fire.

"Alas, madam, I'm under strict orders for a public outing with my lady friend." He holds his hand out to me. "A deal's a deal."

I clutch the pillow tighter and whine, mostly to give my blush a chance to flee my face, but also because the idea of leaving this couch makes me feel pouty. "But, but, but."

He reaches down and takes me by the wrists, gently pulling me up from Jasmine and my unicorn pillow.

"I'll make it worth your while," he promises in a throaty voice, sending a delightful chill running down my spine. Leading me toward the door, he adds, "A late dinner, your choice of location, and I promise, absolutely no tables by any windows."

I cock an eyebrow at him. "Ooh, I'm sold. But—and I swear, I mean this in a really normal way—but sometime, could I just sleep on that couch for, like, half an hour, tops? I'll even pay you. Like, rent-a-couch!"

He helps me with my coat before pulling on a new one of his own that wasn't involved in the eyeball fiasco. "I'm sure we can work something out."

The elevator door opens and we step inside. Just as the doors close behind us, I call back, in front of Caspian, Jacob the elevator attendant, and Odin himself, "I'll be back for you, Jasmine! Our love is real!"

26

"I'm sorry—YOU WHAT!?" CiCi shrieks at a decibel that could shatter glass.

"Shh," I hiss. "I think I hear dogs in the next borough howling."

I spent my morning juggling two different interviews with two different publishing houses. I'd planned to get a few hours in at the units this afternoon, what with being so very close to being done, but CiCi insisted I meet her for lunch, and honestly, I could stand to eat in a place where people don't try to shove cameras up my skirt as I exit a car.

Plus, after the crowbar and pickled eyeball incidents, I'm starting to think the units are saving the worst surprises for the end. And, if I'm being honest, I was delighted to blow off my trash-sorting to deliver the news about my night with Caspian in person, so I could savor the look on her face.

Which, aside from her earsplitting volume, hasn't disappointed.

Coming with exactly zero shock to me, she doesn't seem to care much about my job interviews compared to the details of my Cas kiss. After my third straight rundown of every single tiny detail of our interlude, I finally put an embargo on any smooch talk until I get a chance to dive into my professional prospects. I came to the diner where we're having lunch straight from my second meeting, and I'm dying to get her opinion on my chances.

At the first—Carmichael Press—the VP launched into her love of all things Caspian immediately after we were introduced, and asked if I could snag her an autograph. And despite the seismic shift in my relationship with Cas, it's getting harder and harder to sit through these encounters without screaming, "I AM FULLY QUALIFIED FOR THIS JOB PLEASE CARE."

He's a mighty fine kisser and all, but I still want to get a job based on *my* merits, not *his* cheekbones.

His sexy, sexy cheekbones.

Ahem.

The second—Fogler Publishing, a midsize house with a solid reputation—had impressed me by making it through the entire interview without mentioning my faux beloved once. I had to give the guy who interviewed me credit; if he was holding in his Tiddle-squee, he did a good job. But he was just a preinterview for the president, who may yet drop the Cas bomb.

Which would be a damn shame. I'd actually really liked Trey, my interviewer, and I've heard great things about Joan McInerney, the semilegendary boss of all. Bigger pubs have been trying to lure her away for years, but she has yet to be wooed.

"That's great news, right? The guy not even mentioning Caspian?" CiCi asks as our food arrives, and I can see how hard she is physically restraining herself to stay on topic.

"I hope so," I say, picking up half my BLT. "I'm almost done at E-Z Storage, and I think I'm getting to the point where I can't turn down the other offers just because they don't give the foggiest fuck about my actual skill as an editor."

Through an enormous mouthful of baby greens, CiCi mumbles, "That's the spirit."

"Is there a reason you're attacking that salad like it owes you money?" I ask. "Do you have to get back to the office?"

CiCi snorts, and I worry she may choke on a crouton. "No. Good one. But I do have a surprise for you after this. We have an appointment."

I pause with my sandwich an inch from my mouth. "What kind of appointment?"

She swallows quickly and grins. "The good kind. Now snarf faster, lady."

I manage half my sandwich and five whole fries before she's up, paying the check, and dragging me out behind her.

A moderate cab ride later, the time of which is passed with a fourth and fifth retelling of the kiss, we arrive at our destination.

"We're...at your apartment," I observe.

"Nothing gets by you," CiCi says as she tucks her debit card back in her wallet. She grabs my hand and pulls me in through the doors after her.

In the elevator, I watch as she hits the fifth floor instead of her usual third floor.

"What are you up to?" I frown, suspicious and dying of curiosity.

She's practically bouncing in place, making the elevator shake a little. It's not one of my more rational fears, but I don't care much for elevators, and making them shake on purpose amplifies that paranoia. I reach out and try to hold her in place.

When the doors open, she heads out down the hall, and I don't have much choice but to follow her.

There's a woman standing by a doorway, and CiCi beams. "Hi, Mrs. Esposito," she calls out.

"Hello, Cindy," the woman says.

I pause midstep. "Who's Cindy?" I ask.

CiCi turns and sighs. "I am. Shh."

She grabs my hand and continues pulling me along with her, but I am in shock.

Cindy? What?

Mrs. Esposito opens up an apartment door and says, "Just send me a text when you're done, and lock the door when you leave."

"Yes, ma'am!" my friend trills. Without giving me a chance to do anything but wave a hello to the woman with the keys, I'm being yanked inside.

"How have we known each other for years and years, and I'm just now finding out your name is Cindy?" I ask.

"Because no one but my grandma and people who read my credit report even know that it is," she says. "Now, let that go and look around."

"Let it go?" I laugh. "No way! What other secrets are you hiding, Miss Cindy Raleigh Winchester? *If* that's even your real name."

"Oh, it's all too real," she mutters, and starts hopping in place with frustration. "But seriously, what do you think?"

"About what?"

"The *apartment*," she sighs. "You're kind of killing this for me."

I suddenly feel like an idiot. "Oh my gosh, are you getting a new place? That's so cool! Good for you!"

"No, *we* are getting a new place," she says, positively beaming.

"Beg your pardon?"

CiCi goes into the kitchen that opens up into the living area and starts poking around at the appliances. "I knew this was opening up, and I asked the managers to let me have first crack at it," she says, turning back to me and grinning. "It's almost the same as my place, but it's a two-bedroom, and the bathroom is, like, twice as big."

"I'm sorry—you're going to have to fill in some information here. We're getting an apartment?"

"Damn right, we are," she sings. She's so giddy, I don't know what questions to ask first. "It's move-in ready, so we can take it over immediately. They'll roll my lease over onto this place so I don't have to worry about breaking my contract, and add you."

"Okay, slow down here, Secretariat," I say, looking around, stunned. "I can't sign anything right now. I live on a couch. No one is going to rent anything to me. I'm an unemployed financial undesirable."

"I could get this place on my own, madam," she says with a wink. "I'm a hell of a tenant, and my income more than qualifies me for the lease on my own. I was planning to snag this apartment no matter what, but if you're planning on suffering through another roommate—which, let's be honest, you know you will—why not me? I was hoping it was going to open up last month so you could have stayed here instead of on Gertrude at Tom's, but the people living here needed a few extra weeks while they bought their new place."

"I...I can't..." I stutter. "I can't sign a lease with you, lady. What if I can't pay rent? I can't let you pay for me. I love you, but I would sooner die than let you pay my way."

She walks over and puts her hands on my shoulders. "I know that, you dork. And I would never offer, because I know you'd sooner die, like the stubborn ass that I know and love. But you have three pending job offers, and I doubt they'll be the last. And I know you have savings, so you can live on that while you wait to get settled at the amazing new job you're going to be accepting any day now. In the meantime—and I'm genuinely anticipating that meantime to be, like, a week— you'll stay with me instead of Tom. Except here, you can have your bed back, and your own room."

"This is nuts!" I say, trying really hard not to fall in love with the super-tall windows flooding the living room with light. "What if all of those jobs pull their offers when Caspian leaves?"

"Then you stay with me instead of Tom while you keep looking," she says with a shrug. "Come on—we'll have so much fun! It'll be like a big-ass slumber party all the time, except no sleeping bags and I won't put your bra in the freezer every night. Probably."

"Okay, this feels like counting all the possible eggs before they've hatched."

"Fine," she says, grinning. "Time to break out the big guns."

"Big guns?"

She reaches out and takes my hand. "You could get your mattress out of that storage unit. Like, immediately."

I gasp. My mattress.

"That's a very manipulative move."

She keeps grinning. "I have zero regrets. And look, even if you don't want to live here, I still plan on dragging your ass out of your brother's apartment to stay with me until you find a place of your own. I'll just turn the second room into an office or a sewing room or a sex dungeon or something. The bottom line is, I'm taking this place one way or another, but I would much rather take it with you as my roommate. Come on, cupcake. This is the first time you and I have ever had a chance to live together since we moved to the city."

I look around the apartment, sort of stuck where I stand. She makes a hell of a solid case, I have to give her that. And she's right. If she'd had the second bedroom as an office when I moved out of my last place, I would have gladly thrown my mattress on her floor and lived here. And, as the list of awful roommates I've had over the years scrolls through my mind, I honestly can't think of anyone who could hold a candle to the amazing Cindy...

"Oh my god," I say, puzzle pieces latching in my mind.

"What?"

"Cindy Raleigh Winchester. *Cindy Raleigh.* Like Cinderelly from the movie?"

"I hate you."

I purse my lips to keep from laughing. "Your parents named you after the thing a cartoon mouse called Cinderella. On purpose." Another piece clicks into place, and I completely lose my chill. "Fuck me, you even have the blond hair and blue eyes!"

"I will set fire to everything you love if you so much as breathe a word of this to anyone."

I manage to stop openly guffawing, but I can't quite hold in my cackle. "I love you so much, CiCi."

"So? What do you think? Wanna be roomies?"

I bite my lip. "What if I end up not finding a job for months, lady? That could happen. And I don't want to go from being your best friend to being that horrible burden you used to like back in the day."

"Look," she says in a rare moment of pure seriousness, "I don't think that's going to happen at all. But if it does, how about you let me be your friend and help you? I'm pretty sure that's the crux of the whole best-friend thing. We have each other's backs, always. I talk you into loosening up from time to time, you serve as my much-appreciated moral compass when needed."

I raise an eyebrow.

"Okay, fine. It's always needed. All the more reason to lock this shit down."

I slowly walk through the open space and drink it in. The bedrooms are fairly good-sized, especially by New York City standards, and the bathroom is even bigger than the one at Tom's. Plus the giant windows reveal a semi-awesome view of the nearby park instead of the bricks of a building five feet away, like at my last apartment.

"Okay," I say at last. "But I'm not going to let you just carry me. I have my savings, and I refuse to be your freeloading pal. You know that would wear down my sanity."

"Understood. But you also have to accept that if you need help, I am going to give it, whether you like it or not."

I twist my hands nervously. "So… I could really move my mattress in right away?"

She squeals and comes running over to hug me, jumping up and down. "The second we get the keys, baby!"

"And you're sure you want to do this?"

She's still dancing in place, holding on to my wrists now. "So, so very much! This is going to be great!"

Now it's my turn to be serious. "There really isn't anyone else I would want to be my roommate. I kind of love you a little."

"Love you back, nerd," she says. "But hey." Her mouth sets in a stony line. "At the first 'Mop the floors, Cinderelly' joke, you're out on your ass." She can't fight the smirk that follows.

"We should write that into the lease, just to be safe."

27

I haven't been to a Broadway show in ages, and I have definitely never been to one where I'm basking in a front-and-center seat, and where I'm treated by the theater staff as someone who is anything other than one of hundreds crammed into a small space in the hope of seeing something magical for the price of a car payment.

Or, in the case of the seat I'm sitting in, a month or two of rent money and the mortal souls of three virgins.

I've always followed the rules of dressing nice when going to the theater, but I certainly never had to go as far as I've gone tonight. I'm in a proper cocktail dress and heels, all pilfered from CiCi's closet after she sprang our impending cohabitation on me. She was so chipper after officially putting forth the paperwork to Mrs. Esposito that she gladly spent the afternoon playing Barbie with me.

So here I sit, dressed and coiffed to the nines.

I've never managed higher than the fives, maybe a six at my very best, on my own.

CiCi may have gone a little overboard with the primping. Although, while the shoes are killing me one toe at a time, I'm not hating this smoky eye. I never could pull one off myself without looking like a toddler who found their mother's makeup stash. She tried to talk me into red lipstick, too, but even with her expert hand, there was no getting out of the mischievous toddler look with that.

Some people look amazing in red lipstick. These people have magical powers, and I remain forever awed and envious of their sorcery.

I'm especially thankful for CiCi and her makeover skills when I catch more than a few people using their phones to sneak pictures of me sitting here. I send a silent shout-out to the ones who use the sneak attack, as opposed to the three separate people who apparently felt no need for cloaks and daggers and just pointed their cameras right at me, gawking openly.

I'm reserving a special place in hell for the person who used their flash.

What value these pictures would have to anyone for any reason, I will never understand. In a few short days, I'll be forgotten forever. Maybe called into some random piece on Caspian about that nameless nobody he used to "date."

My treasured anonymity is soon to return, and I am counting down those days.

However, while I *am* relishing the thought of returning to my normal life, I'm a lot less thrilled about the weird, heavy feeling in my chest when I think about never seeing Caspian again. The kiss notwithstanding—although it's my new favorite memory—I've gotten rather attached to hanging out with regular Cas. He's surprisingly funny and charismatic and sincere.

On the one hand, I'm kind of bummed that most of my time with him was choked under a cloud of mutual hatred when it didn't need to be. On the other, if I hadn't made some very questionable life choices that spawned that hatred, I never would have met him in the first place.

The overhead lights flash, and everyone takes their seats. The few remaining gawkers lose interest in watching me sit here, pretending to be very fascinated in the random things I see posted on Facebook. I'm less than amused when I see multiple posts from my mother with links to various gossip sites and my pictures with Caspian as the thumbnails.

I click on her page and see that all her content is equally split between Caspian and me, recipe videos, and articles about all the things millennials are ruining in the world.

Why, Mom? Why?

Thankfully, the show is starting, so I tuck my phone into the little bejeweled clutch that joins the CiCi Winchester collection I'm sporting for the night. I haven't seen *A Midsummer Night's Dream* since I was dating a theater tech major in college who was doing the lighting for the performance, and I went to show support. I remember really liking the play, but that relationship lasted an even shorter amount of time than the fake one with my current drama enthusiast will.

As the first actors take the stage, it occurs to me that I have no idea what Caspian's role is. All I know about this adaptation is that it uses the original dialogue, but it's set in modern times. Which, even from the get-go, is fascinating. The dichotomy of watching Shakespeare's words spoken in coffee shops and accented with cell phones is both amusing and odd. It fits the tone of the work surprisingly well.

Soon, Caspian makes his entrance, and a random smatter-
ing of applause from the back of the theater breaks out, almost
as if they couldn't control themselves.

Caspian is Oberon, King of the Fairies.

Okay, so that's sort of expert casting.

I don't know who the actor playing Puck is, but their chem-
istry is freaking hilarious. Caspian's comedic timing while
playing someone so annoyed is a thing of genuine marvel.
He hits every mark, and the audience erupts in all the right
places. Even when the laughter drags on longer than the beats
they've worked into the show, his ability to vamp for time is
kind of an art in itself.

I'd seen Caspian as Poirot and in various film roles, but
watching him live on stage is something else altogether. He
definitely takes the notion of a commanding presence to some
next-level master class.

As the show goes on, I honestly don't think I'll ever be
able to read the play again without picturing him as the Fairy
King, either in the spiffy suit from this version, or the imagined fairy garb from the original—which, now that it's in my
head, is a surprisingly appealing visual.

I'm honestly not sure what I was expecting from the play,
but it surpasses anything I could have imagined. It's a goddamn delight, and I'm kicking myself for not begging for an
extra ticket for CiCi, but I have a sneaking suspicion I would
have had to fight another theatergoer to the death to get it.

I kind of feel bad for the prospective audience members who
will never get to see the play in its limited run with Caspian
in this role. No disrespect to whomever takes on the Oberon
role next, but he's setting a really high bar here. Even if we
were still locked in our barb-flinging hate duel, I would have

had to give it up to him—silently, of course—for positively owning the stage up there.

After the show ends—far too soon, if I'm being honest—I head back to the stage door, as Caspian instructed me earlier today. I'm not at all thrilled about my shoes as I stand in a line of about twenty other significant others and family members, waiting to be allowed backstage for a quick tour while we wait for our thespian counterparts to shuck off their costumes and makeup.

The weirdest part of this line is watching the mob of people who don't have Golden Tickets—and by that, I mean small VIP passes that let us past the wooden barrier set up near the sidewalk to keep fans away for the time being. They stare at us all with a mixture of envy and disdain and curiosity as to what we all managed to do to get those hallowed pieces of cardboard.

Somehow, I don't think my particular scenario would cross any of their minds.

It's fun for me to listen to the conversations of the other people in line with me. Some are the parents of bit players, delighted for their baby making their big break in a real Broadway show, gleaming with pride at getting to see the backstage experience.

Honestly, I'm geeking out a little on the inside myself. I've heard tales from friends who have gotten pulled out of the throngs of waiting fans for tours now and then, and it's always been some kind of life-changing experience for them.

I suddenly feel incredibly guilty for being privy to the perks of this night for no other reason than I fell ass-backward into the situation—though I have certainly paid several steep prices for the pleasure.

When the back door finally opens up, and we're allowed

into the caverns, I am beyond grateful. This outfit may be suitable for the "girlfriend" of the starring actor, but it's not particularly conducive to comfort or warmth in the November air.

The actual tour kind of lives up to the expectation set by those friends. I wasn't sure what to expect other than what I saw backstage during my brief time as a theater girlfriend back in the day, but this is absolutely nothing like a college theater.

My favorite part is listening to the awed and inexpressibly proud trilling of the parents of those bit players, who frequently pause to take pictures. On more than one occasion, I offer to take group shots of them in various locations. When we get onto the actual stage, I stand there for a good five minutes, being handed phone after phone to take photos of people bursting with unabashed cheer.

I don't get to finish the tour, however. Before we're whisked from the set, a stagehand who was waiting patiently for me to finish my photographer duties runs over and introduces himself.

"Miss Montgomery?" he says, and everyone turns to rubberneck the interaction. "I'm Carlos, and I'm to take you to meet Mr. Tiddleswich in his dressing room."

If there was rubbernecking a second ago, there are people with literal whiplash now. Almost as a reflex, several folks lift their phones to take pictures of me, on the off chance I might be someone of import.

"Oh my gosh," I hear a woman whisper as Carlos leads me away. "She took our picture! Who is she? How come she gets to go meet him?"

"Thank you, Carlos," I say, trying to keep from giggling at the not-so-hushed whispers behind me, and also fighting the urge to stop and reassure those people I am of exactly zero importance, so don't waste any of the room on their cameras on me. "It's nice to meet you, by the way."

"You, too, ma'am," he says, both appearing focused on me and listening to something on the little black earpiece he's got in.

If I could make it just one day without getting ma'amed, I would be a happy gal.

There are people coming and going in every direction as we make our way through the corridors, but it's definitely a much more pleasant experience coming through this way than it was from the stage door. Not nearly as "you will 100 percent get lost in here and your body will be found weeks later" as my previous adventure.

Back at the shiny green door with "Caspian Tiddleswich" posted on the front, once again, a long and loud knock is issued. I notice now that both my escorts avoided eye contact during and after the knocking, which lends more credence to my theory that they're giving the stars chances to hide something as much as it is for the sake of privacy for a potentially undressed actor.

A few seconds later, the door opens, and Caspian smiles kindly at us both. He leans down to kiss me on the cheek, and I find myself blushing, which is rather out of character for me.

"Thank you, Carlos," he says. I turn to say my own thank-you and realize Carlos is, in fact, not wearing any sort of name tag, and I wonder if Caspian has memorized all the stagehands' names, or if Carlos is someone he deals with specifically on a regular basis.

My escort scurries away, once again listening intently to his little black earpiece, and Caspian escorts me inside the dressing room.

"Thank you for coming," he says, closing the door. As I

turn to face him, I wonder if he may not have been quite ready for my arrival, because while he's wearing pants, he's also still wearing a robe.

"I'm sorry," I say, jutting my thumb at the door behind me. "Am I early? I can wait in the hall while you finish?"

In the time it took me to say those words, Caspian's already pulled the robe off and is yanking a T-shirt over his head.

"What for?"

I barely hear him. It's only a split-second view, but I'm thrown back to the night I spent sitting on the couch with CiCi and swooning over a shirtless Caspian as Poirot before this all began.

And now...seeing him shirtless in real life?

It's running laps around the on-screen version by a whole lot.

"Holy *shit*," I whisper-gasp.

His shirt is all the way on now, and he's looking at me with sudden concern. "What's wrong? Are you all right?"

My vision feels a little hazy, like I've had a few too many cocktails, and it's only now I realize I said that *holy shit* out loud.

I quickly try to blink the image of shirtless Caspian from my eyes and stammer, "Oh, yeah, I, uh..." I glance around the room, desperately looking for something that was *holy shit*–worthy. "I was just so blown away by the...play! And that backstage tour! Wow, that was sure an incredible experience!" I perk up and cling to the inspiration, as it is totally believable and far less mortifying than the truth.

He smiles at me, and his concern melts away. "I'm very glad you enjoyed it. I'm terribly sorry to have kept you waiting. Again, thank you for coming tonight."

Momentary shirtlessness aside, I realize this is by far the

most casual I've seen him dressed since we met, and it's kind of fascinating.

Clad in black slacks with a dark gray T-shirt and no shoes, I don't think I've ever seen him look so…normal. Every other time I've laid eyes on the man, he looked like he was on his way to a particularly well-dressed office or photo shoot of some sort.

Right now he looks, dare I say, *human*.

"Thank you for asking nicely," I say with a grin. "I may have a little PTSD about this room, I'm not going to lie."

He chuckles a little and reaches for a plum-colored button-up laid over the chair by the mirror, seeming a bit rushed. "Your last visit was on the more volatile side, wasn't it?"

"How do you manage to make everything sound so sophisticated?" I ponder aloud. "I would have said it was a clusterfuck, and you go for *on the more volatile side*."

"*Clusterfuck* does roll off the tongue with a bit more clarity," he says with a genuine laugh as he shrugs into the plum shirt.

I laugh with him. "Okay, hearing you say 'clusterfuck' is easily the best part of my night."

Well, maybe the second-best part, but I'm sure as shit not going to admit that out loud.

Caspian looks amused as he finishes buttoning. "Was the show so disappointing that the highlight is my delving into the profane?"

"Oh my gosh, no," I say, with the utmost sincerity. "You were incredible. Like, I honestly can't put into words how amazing you were up there."

Now he shifts into embarrassed as he seeks out his shoes. "I wasn't fishing for compliments," he says, sitting on the red couch and starting to lace up.

"No need to fish," I insist. "That was a hell of a performance. Truly. I fully plan to spend the remainder of our time together gushing in explicit detail."

His face fills with what I find to be comic mortification. "Oh god, please don't. I don't think I could stand it."

"Of all the things for you to be shy about," I say, grinning again. "Compliments are what does it?"

He smirks and stands up, looking for his coat. "Apparently."

"That's kind of charming," I say. "You really were fantastic, though. But I promise I'll try to contain my accolades."

He pulls on his long wool coat and grabs a forest green scarf off the table with the flowers. "I tend to spend the time after a performance mentally replaying all the bits I cocked up."

"I definitely didn't see any of those."

He comes to stand beside me at the door and, with a little half smile, says, "Well, then, maybe I did my job all right."

"So, uh," I say, looking around, "do we have somewhere to be I don't know about? You seem to be in quite the rush."

"I just don't like to make everyone wait longer than they have to. It's terribly cold out."

He holds out his arm, and I scurry out the door beside him, feeling awkward. "Everyone who? Does your driver, like, stand outside the car waiting for you or something?"

He chuckles again. "No. I mean the people who line up after the show. It feels rude to keep them waiting while I lounge about the dressing room."

"Oh man," I say, feeling like a huge jerk. "I know I kind of yelled at you about that, but I didn't mean you had to scramble out or anything. And I saw that crowd tonight. It's definitely more than fifteen people lined up after a rehearsal."

He turns to me and smiles as we walk through the labyrinth. "As much as I admired that aspect of your lashing the other day, I always make a point to go out. I try to when I can, anyway. They stand out there for such a long time, it would be unkind not to."

I'm so stunned I stop dead in my tracks. "Are you serious?"

He stops a few feet ahead of me and turns, uneasy. "Yes? Why?"

"That is the least famous-person thing I've ever heard anyone ever say."

"Ha!" Caspian's baritone reverberates through the concrete tunnels. "That is high praise, indeed."

He reaches out and guides me forward again, his hand on my shoulder.

Pre-truce, I imagine he would have kept a pace that left me running after him in these blasted shoes. Tonight, though, we move swiftly, but in a very short-person-wearing-heels-friendly way.

I am very much digging this version of Caspian.

When we come upon the exit, he takes my hand without even looking, as though we've comfortably done that exact maneuver a hundred times. "Fair warning," he says. "This will be quite loud."

A security guard on this side opens the door for him, and sweet baby Jesus, he was not wrong. There is screaming from down the alley, on the other side of the wooden barrier, that I imagine echoes for miles. Those screams feel as though they will hang above the city forever.

Leaning down to half shout in my ear in an effort to be heard, he says, "If you want to wait with Podrick here—" he gestures to the absurdly large security guy on the outside of the door "—or even pop back inside where it's warm, I'll try to be quick."

I look up at Podrick, a behemoth specimen of a human

being if I've ever seen one, and say, "Take your time. I'm in no hurry."

If I thought watching Caspian on stage was something to awe at, watching him try to sign autographs and take pictures with everyone shoving head shots and magazines in his face is truly something to behold. Some of the people can't seem to contain themselves and reach out to touch him, whether he consents to it or not, which would make me more uncomfortable than just about anything else in the world.

He poses for selfies with groups of squealing girls and hugs those who ask and signs so many things that I have to assume his hand has lost all feeling from overuse.

Several security personnel who were guarding the barriers do their best to control the overzealous fans who try to get too handsy, or who try to push others out of the way, but Caspian remains calm and smiling through all of it.

There's a moment when a small girl is pulled to the front of the barrier, clutching a picture of Caspian as the Nebula Force assassin, and for a moment, I think the poor child is going to be crushed by a group of twentysomethings who don't seem to care about trampling any of the people they're pushing past to try to get their hands on the actor of their dreams.

For the first time, Caspian seems frustrated and bends down, inviting the little girl, who can't be more than seven, to slide under the wooden barrier with her mother. At first, the security guys look annoyed, and start watching for anyone else who might try the maneuver uninvited, but they soon shift their attention to making sure the barrier stays in place.

I'm not going to lie: when he takes extra time to stay there on one knee, having an in-depth conversation with the little girl, I feel myself swoon pretty hard.

She's quiet at first, clutching her photo of him and looking up through long blond bangs, but eventually, she's all smiles and excitement, looking up at her mother as Caspian takes her picture to sign. Her mom is holding up her phone, recording the entire interaction, and I am honestly delighted for the little gal. She will watch this back over and over again and show it to all of her friends. She will be the envy of the first grade.

Or most grades, to be honest.

Finally, he appears to ask her a question, and she nods excitedly. He gives her a hug.

He was asking her if he could hug her.

Yep. There's another swoon. Damn it.

There is now a tie for the sexiest thing I've seen tonight.

He finally stands up and shakes the mother's hand before handing the now-signed picture back to the glowing tot.

Speaking to the closest security guard, he points, and I can see him trying to instruct them on the safest way through the crowd, to make sure the girl and her mother aren't trampled by the now-supersonic masses.

Apparently I'm not the only one who felt punched in the ovaries by Caspian and the towheaded lass.

He says a goodbye to those who can hear him, and waves to everyone as one of the guards escorts him back to where I'm standing with Podrick the Silent.

When he reaches me, he takes my hand again as if by genuine habit, and leans down to say, "I apologize that took so long."

As we're escorted down the alley in the opposite direction, it occurs to me that it's been at least an hour of standing there watching the festivities. It honestly seemed like only a few minutes.

"That was the most adorable thing I've ever seen," I say

as the screaming behind us begins to fade. "That little girl is going to grow up determined to marry you."

At the end of the alley waits his black car, and the driver steps out to open the back door for us.

"Someone needs to tell that poor girl she can do loads better," he says, allowing me to climb in first.

"I'll allow no such thing," I declare as he joins me. Within mere seconds, his driver returns to his seat, and we're already moving. "That was really kind, what you did for everyone. Especially that kiddo." I make an executive decision to leave my ovaries out of my commentary.

He shrugs, leaning forward in the seat and taking off his scarf. "I wouldn't get to have any roles at all if it weren't for people who stand in line for my silly signature. I figure it's the least I can do."

"The least you could do would be to run out that door and pretend there isn't a mob of people vying for your attention like damn near every other celebrity does, so no, it's definitely not the least."

"Well, that would make me a bit of a prat, wouldn't it?"

I laugh. "Well, that hasn't stopped any of them from doing it, but I prefer your take on it."

I can't contain myself any longer, so I launch into a detailed commentary on the show, and while I don't want to come across as one of the screaming fans, I also kind of can't help it. To lessen the complimentary blow and save him some quality blushes, I pepper my praise with questions about the show itself, including the other cast members I was wowed by.

Those things, he can't help but gush about. He really does seem to be in love with the whole process, not just his own part in it all. He lists everyone he discusses by name, from the director to the people running the curtains, who he says are some of the most spot-on with timing he's ever worked with.

I'm fairly floored by his attention to detail for everyone he's working with. I've never been particularly good with names, and I know I'd be one of those asshole actors who ends up calling everyone "Buddy!" when I saw them, out of necessity. Based on the sheer volume of people he must come into contact with during each show and film set, I can't even fathom the number of names rattling around in his head.

Every time I point out a specific part of the show where he stood out as notably impressive, he shifts the conversation to the people working around him—the other actors, the stagehands, anyone involved—and explains how they were the reason that scene or moment worked. At first, I assume he's just being unnaturally humble, but as the car ride continues, I realize he actually believes what he is saying to be the facts of the matter.

I'm so engrossed in the discussion and his left-field replies that it takes me far longer than it should to realize we aren't anywhere near his hotel.

Nor, according to the view whizzing past the windows, are we even in Manhattan any longer.

"Whoa," I say, whipping around in my seat to get my bearings. "Where are we going?" I turn back to him. "Did I just fall for some clever ruse? Are you taking me to some deserted part of New York to have me murdered or something?"

"An awful lot of your theories seem to end in someone being offed. Have you ever noticed that?"

I raise an eyebrow. "And yet that's not a no to the murder prospect."

He laughs, and I can even see the driver shaking a little in silent amusement. "I'm taking you home. No murders tonight. But now that I know a good conversation is all it takes to throw you off the scent…"

"Why on earth are you taking me all the way to Astoria?" I gape. "That couldn't possibly be more out of your way. And you've just spent the night owning the stage and posing for adoring fans and precocious tots. Aren't you exhausted?"

"You've ventured into the city many times on my behalf. And sat through a tediously long show tonight. I figure seeing you safely home is a fair trade."

"Well, now I know it's a murder plot," I say.

He smiles, slightly visible in the passing streetlights. "If I went right back to the hotel, I'd end up spending the rest of the night alone and working. And, truthfully, when you're not pledged to hate everything about me, I find you to be excellent company. So this is really a selfish trip on my end."

"I…I mean…" I am so genuinely at a loss for words, my self-deprecating nature kicks in, and I start filtering through a list of the sarcastic quips I could make to ease the building tension.

In the end, more to my surprise than anything else, I discover I don't particularly want to ease the tension, so I reach over and bump his wrist with mine. "You don't suck as company yourself, sir."

It's only when I look out the window to find absolutely anything else to stare at that I realize we're parked in front of Tom's apartment building.

And I have exactly zero clue how long we've been here.

Before my brain can pull all the pieces together, Caspian Tiddleswich is kissing me on the cheek.

"Thank you for coming tonight," he says, not entirely pulling away. "And for everything, Clara."

I kiss him. I kiss him real good.

It's all too much. The actual humble behavior, the dedication to making sure everyone around him knows they are valued, the care given to that little girl.

The smell of his shower gel. The memory of him shirtless. Dear god, the shirtlessness.

I'm only human.

It's not a classy move, but I can't help myself. Without breaking away, I pull myself up onto my knees and lean into the kiss, hard. He wraps his arms around me and eagerly returns the favor, so I appreciate the assurance that I'm not out of line.

I can feel myself losing any semblance of control here, and as my fingers lock in his hair once more, I start to curse the universe that I'm still staying on my little brother's couch and not, say, at an apartment of my very own with my glorious mattress.

When he twists in the seat and pulls me tightly against his chest, I decide that maybe it wouldn't be the worst thing to suggest driving back to his hotel room under the pretense of cashing in on my date with Jasmine.

I pull away, breathless and a little dizzy, and just as I'm about to drop the world's most laughable pick-up line, I look to my left and blink at the front seat.

"Uh," I say, staring at the emptiness, "wasn't there a driver there a second ago?"

Cas grins and points over my shoulder. "Derrick is particularly skilled at giving privacy."

I turn around, and sure enough, standing by the very front of the town car is our driver.

"I didn't even hear him get out," I say, awed.

"As I said, the man is skilled. Though you did seem a bit preoccupied."

I turn back to Caspian and smirk. "Yeah, I kind of was." The longer I sit here, the more I realize I can't pull off casually suggesting another hour-long car ride for the purpose of possible sex under the guise of being reunited with the couch of my dreams.

Plus I'm feeling some privileged guilt, here. "Jesus, it's mid-November. He has to be freezing." I can't contain the sigh that slips out. "I suppose I should go?"

Without looking away from Cas, I reach for the handle to suavely extricate myself, but then the door opens beside me, and the blast of frosty night air is so jarring, I half fall out of the car. I only miss eating pavement thanks to the quick movements of Caspian, who grabs my waist, and Derrick, who catches my arm.

I look up at Derrick and say, "My god, you really are good."

"Thank you, ma'am," he replies while smoothly helping to extricate me from the car.

"I'm sorry I made you stand out here in the cold," I add, once I'm back on my own two feet.

"It's no problem, ma'am," he says with a smile. "It doesn't bother me at all. I'm pretty hot-blooded."

"Check it and see?" I ask with a goofy smile.

He tilts his head and stares at me. "Ma'am?"

Caspian is laughing so hard, the car is shaking. My shoulders deflate a little, and I sigh. "I'm never going to be able to explain that in a way that doesn't make me look like a huge dork, so just ignore me. And thank you, Derrick."

Before moving out of the way so he can close the door again, I look into the back seat and say, "Thanks, uh...for the ride. *Cas.*"

He smiles, and his eyes darken in an inviting way that

makes my stomach flip. I damn near dive back onto his lap. "Absolutely anytime."

I almost trip over the curb backing away from the car. I wait for Derrick to shut the door, then make my way across the sidewalk and up the steps of Tom's building, pausing once to look back at the car, half-convinced I just hallucinated everything from the theater until now, and that I really dreamed the whole thing while sitting on the train.

But no. There sits the black car, still idling at the curb.

It was a hell of a ride.

28

With just two and a half units until I'm free of E-Z Storage forever—other than jail-breaking my own belongings, hopefully sooner rather than later—I spent the day sorting through boxes of old receipts from what seems like decades of tax returns for someone who owned a Laundromat somewhere in Queens.

It's been tedious, but it's allowed me to replay the events of last night several hundred times. I'm stuck in a loop where I congratulate myself on my restraint for not leaping back into that car, and mentally kicking my own ass for not leaping right the fuck back into that car.

I will say, envisioning what might have happened if we'd headed back to his hotel certainly makes the time pass faster.

Around five, CiCi appears to offer me some company while I wrap the unit up. She wisely doesn't ask if I've found any incriminating information among these financial records.

I'd say lessons have been learned all around.

She listens intently as I run down the details of my night at the theater, and she's uncharacteristically quiet the entire time.

"So…" she says eventually, staring off at nothing from the tailgate of Brutus. "He kissed you again?"

"My cheek," I clarify, putting the lid back on a box and lugging it to the truck. "He kissed my cheek. And not in the way we've been doing the fake-girlfriend kissing on the cheek in public. It was…different. Sweeter. But then I kissed him. Like…a lot. And he definitely kissed me back."

"If you two get married, I want to be your extra plus-one to every event. Can you ask him if he knows Chris Hemsworth?"

"Isn't he married with kids and stuff?"

CiCi looks genuinely disappointed. "Fine. Whatever unmarried superhero hotties he may know, then."

The topic reminds me of the little girl, and I relay that story in great detail.

"I swear, CiCi, when he asked her if he could hug her, I almost died watching it."

CiCi blinks at me. "That is unfairly hot, if I'm being honest."

"Right?" I agree, loading up another box. "I'm convinced I ruptured an ovary."

"I think I did just hearing about it."

"Okay, but I'm not hallucinating that this is totally weird, right?" I huddle on the floor in front of one of three remaining boxes and dive in. "Like, this has taken a really bizarre turn."

CiCi shrugs, hopping off Brutus and joining me to sort through a box of her own. "I don't know. It's not completely absurd. Thin line between love and hate and fake British boyfriends and all that." She pauses with a stack of papers in her hand. "Maybe he's about to be a less fake British boyfriend."

"Now, *that's* completely absurd," I say with a snort.

My phone buzzes, and it's a message from Caspian.

Free for a late dinner after my show tonight?

I purse my lips together to keep from smiling, and I can't for the life of me understand why I'm having to purse my lips together to keep from smiling...

I think I could swing that, I send back.

Meet me at the hotel around 9. I'll do my best to be on time. You can head up to the room and spend as much quality alone time with Jasmine as you'd like, and I'll meet you there? I do promise to knock before entering, lest I catch the two of you in a moment of passionate bliss.

I laugh out loud. CiCi eyes me suspiciously.

It's a deal. I did promise Jasmine I'd be back for her, after all.

I tuck my phone in my pocket and try to carry on working, but CiCi will have none of it.

"That line is looking pretty damn thin, judging by that look on your face."

"Shut up," I say, fighting to wipe away the ridiculous smile.

CiCi looks at the time on her phone. "Do you realize he must have been about to walk onto the stage, and he stopped to send you that message?"

I ponder what she's said and feel my face burning. "Shut up harder."

"Okay, but if he knows the guy who plays Loki, I call dibs.

Oh! Or Chris Evans. Please ask him to set me up with Chris Evans, who is clearly the superior Chris."

I focus way more than is necessary on the papers I'm sorting, and we work in silence. Silence is a relative term, though, because I can practically hear all sorts of filthy scenarios running through CiCi's mind, like she's announcing them through a bullhorn.

I distract myself from her mildly smug grins by internally debating exactly how creepy of me it would be to take him up on his offer of a nap on Jasmine. My guess is that answer would be very, but when I remember the unicorn pillow, I'm tempted to risk it.

Unicorn pillows and couches from Narnia aside, is CiCi right? Is it possible the love/hate line, at least on my end, has gotten thinner?

I've been working really hard to avoid allowing thoughts like that to fully form, but based on my delighted reactions to his messages...and how when I read the words *passionate bliss* regarding the couch, I immediately started picturing passionate bliss with Cas...and since the image of him pulling on that shirt is serving now as my mental screen saver...and the fact that I was about two seconds from a carnal throw-down in the car last night...

I think I might have to face some facts, here.

I know Caspian and I agreed that our mutual hatred had come to an end, but at some point, I seem to have shifted over into...actually liking him.

It hits me that since I'm meeting Cas at the hotel, it's entirely possible that if I play my cards right, maybe there's a chance to pick up where we left off last night, but in the cozier confines of his room. And while I do long for a nap on Jasmine, I think this may be an even more preferable idea.

The scenario forms in my mind, and it suddenly feels like my chest is too big to fit inside my body.

It's not an unwelcome feeling at all.

My head snaps up.

Holy shit.

I...I *really like* Caspian.

"You okay, cupcake?"

I whip around to look at CiCi. "What? Why?"

She looks appropriately confused. "You sort of jumped just now. And your cheeks are all red."

I can feel my eyes bulging. "Uh, bad cold chill. It's freezing back here."

"Yeah, we need a portable space heater or something," she says, evidently appeased.

I let out a silent whoosh of relief when she turns back to her task and pledge to deal with this development of mine later—partly because it's a lot to unpack, and I feel a little blindsided by it all, and partly thanks to my inability to experience a single emotion without it tap-dancing right across my face for the easy reading of others.

CiCi stands up and deposits her box in Brutus, pausing after to check her phone. "Ooh," she says gleefully, leaning against the truck. "I know I should have learned my lesson and all, but I love when news alerts involve skeezy politicians being outed for quality sleaze."

"Anyone good?" I ask, attempting to sound cool, as I'm having zero luck pushing the Cas-centric mental pictures away. I finish up the next-to-last box and walk over to join her.

"That senator from Jersey," she specifies as she reads. "The one who keeps insisting rape wouldn't happen if women would wear less makeup."

"Ew," I say, heaving the box in the bed, grateful for the

distraction. "Good. I hope they got him on something really gross."

CiCi keeps scrolling as I head for the last box, thinking that all too soon, I will be snuggled up on the world's comfiest couch, trying very hard to not actually be caught snoring and drooling into unicorn fur when Caspian finally arrives, but making no promises.

And despite my best efforts, I can't shake the other things I'm picturing doing on that couch.

I flush at my overly presumptuous thinking and dive into the final box before CiCi's superhuman filth radar picks up on my deviant thoughts.

"Oh my fucking fuck," she gasps, her hand going to her mouth.

"What?" I ask, dropping to the ground and popping the last lid off. Maybe her radar really is that strong. I blush harder and try to deflect, prepared to go into great detail about a very targeted blast of frigid air that would explain my rosy cheeks. "Grosser than normal?"

"Clara," she says, and her voice is so panicked I look up and see her running over to me, phone outstretched. She clicks a video and kneels down beside me.

A newscaster appears beside a floating picture of the senator from Jersey, and the bubble beneath the woman speaking reads, "Senator Crum Caught in Prostitution Scandal."

A strangled noise rips through me, and my hands jump to my chest. "No."

"Evidence was brought to public attention today in a story first broken by the gossip website TMZ that shows detailed receipts of Senator Crum frequenting an escort service in the midnineties."

The screen cuts to scanned copies of the Cranson receipts,

and my heart stops beating for several seconds. I drag in a strangled breath as the woman continues. "The senator, who has campaigned for the last fifteen years on a strict morality platform, was found to have utilized the services of both male and female escorts, and according to the records submitted by an anonymous source, involved very specific requests. Peter Cargill is here with a more detailed analysis of what was found."

"Oh my fucking FUCK," CiCi repeats as Peter appears with printouts in his hands.

"Thank you, Betsy," he says, diving right in. "Now, at first glance, these receipts don't show much other than Senator Crum being a very loyal customer of Cranson Escorts, but when paired with what I can only describe as a sort of sexual menu, you'll see his tastes were quite consistent."

A picture of the menu pops up on the screen. One of the same menus CiCi and I giggled our way through reading what feels like a lifetime ago.

"Let's just say," Peter says with a laugh, "he didn't often pay for just cuddling."

I'm unspeakably grateful I'm already on the ground, as I've lost feeling in every part of my body, and I can't even maintain a sitting position anymore. I drop forward onto the box and start rocking back and forth.

"No, no, no, no..."

"Okay, look," CiCi says, muting her phone as Peter goes into greater detail dissecting the menu. "They're only talking about *this* guy. If they knew about Caspian, they would have said so. They wouldn't have just mentioned the senator. They would have called it some kind of giant scandal and listed everyone they knew about."

I whip up, holding on to the box for support. "Did you sell it?"

"What? No!"

"Be honest with me, CiCi," I snap. "Did you sell that stuff? You were on a quest·looking for a family-values asshat to fry, and now here one is!"

She leans back on her heels and looks horrified. "How can you even ask me that? Of course I didn't sell it! For starters, I never would have done anything like that without telling you or getting your okay, and for another, I wouldn't even think about fucking around with something like that after what we did to Caspian. I'm not an idiot, Clara. Come on!"

"Are you sure? Are you absolutely sure?"

She waves her arms around angrily. "Am I really fucking sure I didn't forget I sold sex-worker records that could get you thrown in jail by Caspian? Yes, Clara! I'm really fucking sure!"

"Oh god," I whimper. "I'm sorry. You're right. I'm so sorry. I'm panicking. I know you wouldn't have done it. Seriously, I'm sorry."

"I'm panicking with you," she says, calming her justified rage. "How? How could this possibly have gotten out? We took it all to the dump ourselves!"

"CiCi," I gasp. "He's going to see this. Caspian is going to see this, and he's going to completely freak out."

"Fuck, fuck, fuck," she hisses, looking back at her phone as if it will hold the answer. "But he's on stage right now, right? Are you meeting him tonight?"

I try to pull in air, but nothing is happening. I nod shakily. "I'm supposed to meet him at his hotel right after his show for dinner."

"Maybe you'll see him before he has a chance to read anything about this?" CiCi offers desperately. "If he comes straight from the theater, that's totally possible! You could explain to him before he even knows it's happening!"

"Do you really think so?" I ask, panting for absolutely any air at all.

"Yes?" She doesn't sound entirely convinced. "But I know I don't give a fuck what's in this last box, and that you need to get over there *now*, so there's no chance he'll have a chance to kick back and turn on the TV before he sees you."

Before I can agree, she pockets her phone and grabs me up from the floor with one hand, the remaining box with the other, and drags us both out of the unit.

29

All dreams of snuggling on Jasmine dashed, I've spent the last two hours sitting here, clutching the unicorn pillow to my chest, legs bouncing nervously, watching the clock on the wall tick closer and closer to nine while frantically trying to put together some sort of explanatory monologue to tackle Caspian with when he arrives.

Two hours of desperate pondering, and you'd think I'd have something better than bursting into tears and wildly waving my arms by means of clarification, but every time I picture his face upon hearing the news, I can't come up with anything beyond the Muppet flail.

When I hear the elevator bell ding at 8:45 sharp, I fall into a full-fledged panic, thinking that if I just had those extra fifteen minutes, the perfect answer would have come to me.

The door opens, and in he walks. I fly up off the couch, still clutching the pillow.

"I have to talk to you about something important," I blurt out as the door closes behind him.

He's frozen in place, staring at me. "What are you doing here?" he asks flatly.

"You told me to meet you here," I say, confused. "But seriously, I have to tell you something."

Caspian stands there for an endless moment, just looking at me. No emotion. No response. My stomach drops to my feet.

He knows.

Peeling off his scarf, he walks over to the nearest chair and drops it and his coat, still expressionless and silent.

"Cas?"

He looks back at me, and the deadness in his eyes tells me I'm definitely too late.

"What did you think would happen by coming here?" he asks. "That somehow retroactively confessing would undo it?"

"I'm not here to confess *anything*, because I didn't do it," I say, my voice pleading. "I didn't out that senator. And I came here because I was hoping you hadn't seen it yet, so I could warn you."

"*Warn* me? Warn me that you'd—what? Finally found the highest bidder?"

"No!" I throw the pillow on the couch and try to make my way closer, but the tension wafting off of him stills me. "To warn you that, somehow, the information got out. I can't imagine how awful it felt to see that out of nowhere. I was hoping that if I could tell you before you saw it, maybe it wouldn't freak you out as much."

"Is this honestly the angle you're going with?" His voice is rising, and his eyes are no longer dull, but filling with rage. "That you're merely playing the Good Samaritan, here to spare my feelings?"

"Please, please listen to me," I beg, growing frustrated. "I didn't sell that information. I never even saw anything about the senator in the stuff we went through! And even if I had found it, I wouldn't have done anything with it, Cas. Come on. I would never do that to anyone, but more importantly, I wouldn't do that to you. I know how terrifying any of this getting out would be for you."

"Oh, come off it," he scoffs. "You expect me to believe that, somehow, by some magical coincidence, the exact kind of information you found on me, almost certainly from the same files you dug me out of, just ended up being publicly distributed, and you had nothing to do with that?"

I use everything I have in me to try to appear as calm as possible, but I'm a raw nerve inside. "Honestly? Yes. Because that's what happened. I don't know how that information ended up with TMZ and CNN and everyone else who probably has it, but it wasn't *me*. I am begging you to believe me, Cas, please. Please, just listen to me."

"No, enough!" he shouts, and I jump a little. "Whatever this is, whatever sick game or twisted plot you have going, I'm done being the fool who falls for it!"

"Please, oh my god," I say, feeling tears pool in my eyes, spurred by anger now as much as the stress of it all. "There's no plot, you're not a fool, and I didn't *do* this."

"Are you even capable of not lying when you speak?" he chides, wholly unconvinced by anything I've said. "I spend my life surrounded by people pretending to be anyone but themselves, and I've never come across anyone with your skills. I'd be impressed if it weren't so disgusting what you're doing. At least the rest of us know when we're playing a part."

"Look," I snap, "if you've reverted to that Evil Cas villain character of yours, you're taking it way too far."

"Did you call that senator, too?" he asks, his voice dripping with disdain. "Did you even give him the chance to try and keep you from ruining his life, or did you just go right for the easy sell?"

"Oh my god, I didn't—"

"Was I your practice run?" Caspian pulls his hands through his hair. He's pissed, for sure, but he seems to be rapidly shifting from anger to fear to hurt. It's like he can't land on an emotion as he starts pacing in front of the kitchen area. "Was this all your extortion starter class? When you saw it wasn't as easy as you thought, you just went right for the kill with the next one?"

"Cas, I know you don't know me very well, but I swear to you I would never—"

"Know you very well?" He laughs a forced, quick, bitter laugh. "Don't act like I have any goddamn clue who you are."

The first tears start to fall, and I clench my jaw. I know he's in pain, but he's also being a monster, and I want to tear into him claws first. But as much as I want to draw that metaphorical blood, I know he's wounded, and if I have any chance of getting him to listen, shouting back is probably not the wisest approach.

I square my shoulders and try to keep my voice from shaking. "I have never been anyone but myself with you. Even when we were at each other's throats, I was honest with you the entire time. You know that's true. Please, *please* hear what I'm saying. I know how scared you must have been to see that on the news, but I'm trying to tell you I didn't have anything to do with this, and you don't have to worry about your stuff coming out. I gave you all the papers we found on you, and we took the rest of the Cranson files to the dump."

For a moment, his mask of anger falters ever so slightly,

and I catch a glimpse of reason, but just as fast, he regroups. "Where's your phone?"

"What?"

"Your phone!"

I reach into my pocket and hold it out. "Of course you can have it back."

He stomps over, all concerns of accidentally being physically imposing gone the way of the dinosaurs, and grabs the phone out of my hand.

This doesn't feel like his attempt at being intimidating gone wrong. In fact, the more I watch him, the more I'm convinced this isn't a character he's playing in the hopes of scaring me straight. This feels more like witnessing an injured animal that's been backed into a corner. As angry and overwhelmed by his reactions as I am, I still have an undeniable urge to try to find a way to soothe that injured part.

"I don't want the bloody thing back," he snarls, trying to unlock my phone. Quietly, I give him the passcode. "I want to see what you've recorded."

"Wait—what? What does that even mean?"

"How fucking idiotic was I to fall for any of your play," he says, scrolling through things on my phone. "When we'd talk, how much of that were you videoing? What pictures do you have? Do you think you'll get more money now that I was a complete fool and confessed every detail about my time at Cranson?"

"What? That's demented! I didn't record anything!"

"Stop lying to me!" he barks. He's losing his icy exterior and slipping into actual panic now. I want to reach out and calm him, find whatever words will fix the terror he's feeling, but he's so emotionally all over the place, I don't know where to start.

"Where is it?" Caspian demands. "Did you already upload it somewhere else as a safeguard?" He curses and flings the phone back at me, and I just manage to catch it, out of sheer reflex. "Of course you did. You wouldn't want to lose your biggest payoff yet, would you?"

"Please stop," I say, tears falling freely now. "I know you're upset, but you're scaring me."

"Oh, really? What's that like? To have someone you foolishly started to trust suddenly fuck you over and be terrified of what they might do next? I can't possibly fathom how that would feel."

"I'm telling you I didn't fuck you over, and you don't have to be afraid of what will happen next, because nothing will!"

"Why did you do this?" His entire posture shifts suddenly. His voice breaks, and tears pool in his eyes, and I feel like a huge crack rips through my chest. The pain is so sudden, I wrap my arms around myself. "Why? How could you do something like this, after all of it? I thought we... I thought—"

He stops himself and shakes his head. It's like he thinks if he can just shake hard enough, whatever words he had forming will fly out of his mind.

When he looks up at me again, the suspicion and hate aren't there anymore, but what's left feels so much worse. It's all betrayal and pain. "Just tell me when," he pleads. "When is it coming? Please, Clara. Give me enough warning to speak with my parents first. Can you at least be decent enough to give me that?"

When his tears begin to fall, everything in my chest shatters at once, and I can't control my sobs. "Nothing is coming," I say, begging with every syllable. "I swear to you, nothing is coming. Please, Cas, please—"

"Stop calling me that," he shouts, the fire returning as he

angrily brushes the tears from his face. "And fine, if you can't be human enough to give me even the slightest bit of warning, then to hell with you."

I don't know what to say or how to get him to hear me. I look around the hotel room in desperation, but find nothing to help me convince him of the truth. "I'm sorry," I say between gasping sobs. "I'm sorry this is happening. I'm sorry you're so afraid. I don't know how to make you understand I had nothing to do with this, but I wanted you to know you don't have anything to worry about. You're safe." I stop for a moment, as the tears are coming too fast for me to speak through them. I pull in a shuddering breath through an impending wail and try to carry on. "You never have to see me again, I promise. But please believe me that you're safe. I promise."

"Your words mean nothing to me," he says, locking his expression down again. His eyes are still rimmed red with lingering tears. "But no, you don't get to just walk away while I wait for you to destroy my life."

I try to wipe my own tears away, but they're coming too fast to manage. "I don't understand what that means."

"You conned me into this nightmare, and you're going to finish it," he says, his voice an audible threat. "Thanks to you, I have a team who thinks you're part of my life. And you're going to follow through with our deal, or so help me, I will ruin you in every way I can possibly find to do so."

I desperately bounce in place and pull my hands through my hair. "How? Nothing about you is even out there to be sold to anyone. If there's no story about you, why would you try to make one?"

"Enough with the utter bullshit that there won't be a story," he growls. "When it comes out, I will tell everyone my *girlfriend* turned out to be nothing but a fame-whoring liar who tricked me into opening up about a painful past so she could make a fast buck from Page Six."

I wring my hands, shaking my head. "But it's not true. None of that is true, Caspian. I *know* you know it's not true."

"Like you give a good goddamn about what's true."

Another pitiful sob escapes me, and I want nothing more than to somehow calm him and pull my own self together, but there is no control to be found in this room.

"But I do," I say quietly. "I do care about what's true. You and me? We were—"

"We were nothing. *Nothing*," he says with more conviction than any of his other declarations. I don't know which of us he's trying to convince more. "Don't ever think otherwise."

I nod, the tears still flowing. I don't know what else to say. What to do. How to fix any of what's happened.

"Fine," I say, a numbness spreading through my entire body. "What do you want me to do?"

"What do I want you to do?" he repeats with a spiteful laugh. "I want you to suffer the way you thrive on making others hurt."

"Okay," I say, my voice a cracking squeak. "If that's what you want, just tell me what I have to do."

"You're going to follow through with the rest of our deal," he commands. "You'll be at my final show and the event after. And then at the premiere, you will stand there as I end this pathetic sham of a relationship."

I bite my lip to keep the sobs in. "Fine." I shake my head and try to control my body, which is now practically convulsing all over. "What else do you want?"

"For you to get out," he says coldly. The icy veneer has returned, and I'm once again looking at the character I met that first night in Tom's living room. "Leave. Now. I don't want to look at you a second longer than I absolutely have to."

I quietly pick my coat up off the arm of Jasmine the couch and make my way to his door, pressing the elevator's down button.

While I wait for it to arrive, without looking back at him, I say, "I am so sorry, Caspian. I'm sorry for how afraid you are, and for bringing this back into your life."

As the elevator pings, he snarls, "Fuck you and your apologies."

The door opens, and the elevator operator goes from smiling to concerned upon seeing my face. As I step inside, I murmur, "Goodbye, Caspian."

The doors shut, and the operator and I head down in silence.

30

I call CiCi the next morning, once I'm able to speak without blubbering incoherently, and let her know the plan failed spectacularly. She offers to spend the day with me cleaning out the last two units, but more than anything right now, I just want to be alone.

Alone with my pain and my fear and the guilt of what I've done.

I may not have had anything to do with selling out that senator, but all the pain Caspian is feeling is a direct result of every mistake I've made from the moment I opened the Cranson unit. Whether I want to admit it out loud or not, that hideous phone call I made to him makes me culpable.

Midmorning, I receive an email from Joan McInerney herself, requesting an interview at Fogler for tomorrow. I should be thrilled, but I'm only a small step above dead inside. I send a reply, sounding as professional as I can, agreeing to meet with her tomorrow morning and thanking her for her consideration.

I wonder how long it will be before every publisher I've applied to sees my public evisceration at the hands of Caspian at the premiere. All my job offers thus far have rested entirely on my relationship with him, and publishing is almost exclusively rooted in a person's reputation. After mine shifts from fully competent editor to moneygrubbing, untrustworthy starfucker, there won't be a publishing house in the country that will touch me.

How long before everyone I know finds out what a horrible person he thinks I am?

How long before I stop wondering if maybe he's right?

Around noon, I receive a text from my mother.

We're going to set a place for Caspian at Thanksgiving. Your father is looking forward to meeting him!

My stomach lurches, and I nearly vomit into an old box of stuffed animals in the unit.

I can't handle confessing right now. I know it's coming, and I'll eventually have to do it, but right now, I can barely handle existing.

He's leaving for London in a few days, Mom, so I don't think he'll be back for Thanksgiving. I don't think Brits even celebrate it.

She quickly replies.

Nevertheless, I'll have a place set for him just in case. Please tell him we hope he can make it! Love you, honey!

I can't explain the why or the how, but he really seems to have won her over during that caustic lunch. It figures that when I finally introduce her to a boyfriend she approves of, it's all a lie.

She's not the only one who was fooled. I'd started to think it wasn't a lie as well.

I'll make sure to tell him, Mom. Love you, too.

I feel sick. I wish I wasn't such a coward and could come clean to her. My mom is the queen of judgment in most instances, but the best thing about her parenting approach is that she is the queen of mama bears. All her predilections toward sniping about my life choices would fall away if I were to fess up, and she'd be supportive and listen to me cry and likely threaten to find someone on Craigslist to maim Caspian for hurting her baby.

And even though I'm to blame for the ember that blazed into the inferno, she wouldn't hear anything of the sort.

I really need that kind of mom hug right now. But I'm not ready to share my shame with anyone yet.

Maybe the less palatable things Mom said at her impromptu lunch visit weren't that far off. I *am* screwing everything up here, and there's no visible sign that my luck is preparing to change for the better.

Thanksgiving is in two weeks. Maybe it wouldn't be the worst thing in the world to sit down with Uncle Jack and talk. It's possible I haven't given the idea of a career change into teaching a fair shake. After all, the reason I love words and books as much as I do is solely because of the amazing teachers I had when I was a kid.

I've had it in my head for years that the worst possible fate would be to slink back home to my old suburban black hole in Buffalo and accept that the big bad city was too much for me to conquer. But that was all long before I was poised to become known as a corrupter of the rich and famous.

I would miss my life here, for sure. But CiCi was very clear that she was planning to get the new apartment on her own anyway, so it's not like I'd be leaving her in a financial lurch if I left. I doubt her parents had this in mind when they set up her trust fund, but I'm grateful for their foresight, regardless.

I'd miss her, and Tom and Trina. But the idea of not having to see their looks of pity and disappointment is openly appealing.

This all feels like taking the quitter's way out, running home to Mom and Dad and hiding out in my hometown for the next few decades until the guilt and humiliation die down, but even without those things, the fact is that all too soon, my finances will demand action.

Well, my student loans will demand finances, anyway, and I've successfully damned my chances to regroup my current career about as much as anyone can. I'm tempted to break out my phone right this second to start looking up exactly what would be involved in going back for my teaching certification, so I don't sound like a complete dunce when I speak with Uncle Jack, but I don't want to break the momentum I've got going.

My pain is oddly effective as a source of motivation in the units, and today looks like it might be my last day at E-Z Storage.

Another thing I should be thrilled about.

Instead, I just feel sad. Sad that the few strange but consistent things I've had going in my life are coming to sudden ends.

As much as I've struggled and whined—and at times, momentarily feared for my life here—I am going to miss the routine I've created. I'll miss the chance to peek into the lives of others through these forgotten memories. I'll miss Charlie and his mafioso presence. I'll miss dear Brutus, who was bloodied in battle, but not beaten.

I wish I were more like Brutus. Solid and demonstrably unbreakable.

I pile up the boxes of ancient stuffed animals in the bed of my faded orange friend and carry on in the unit.

After an ignored lunchtime, Charlie appears. I'm both happy to see him and afraid he'll see the shame dripping all over me.

"How're things?" he asks, eyeing the nearly empty unit.

"I think I'll have them all finished today," I say. I mean to sound proud, but my voice is weak and despondent.

"You've done real good, kid," he says with a smile, looking more like a kindly mustachioed uncle and less like a man who severs the kneecaps of those who have wronged him.

"Honestly, I think just about anybody else could have done this in half the time or less," I say with a pathetic attempt at a laugh. "But I really appreciate you giving me the job."

"I'd rather have it done right than fast," he says with a wink. "I just stopped by to pick up the checks from the drop box, but I wanted to see if you needed anything."

I smile, one I don't have to force for the first time since the news of the senator broke. "I'm good, Charlie. But thank you so much for everything." A thought hits me, and I change lanes. "Actually, I forgot to ask. Would it be all right if I rent Brutus for a few hours later this week?"

"Rent Brutus? What for?"

"I need to move some things from my unit into the city, and I just realized I don't have a way to do it," I tell him. "I'm happy to pay for the time, and I'll be really careful with him.

Plus, I've grown awfully attached to this truck, and I guess I'm not quite ready to say goodbye."

He laughs, deep and sincere. "He is a hell of a truck." He pats the side of Brutus, and it makes a satisfying metallic *thud*. "But, hon, you don't have to rent anything. You're family. I'll loan him out to you whenever you need."

"Oh, Charlie," I say, more emotional than anyone should ever be over a truck. "Are you sure?"

"I wouldn't take the money even if you tried to hand it to me," he insists. "I'm glad to do it. You're a good kid. I trust you to take care of him."

I feel myself about to cry. If only Charlie knew how very wrong he was about my goodness.

"Thank you, Charlie. Truly. For everything."

"Just gimme a call and let me know when you need him, and I'll make sure he's gassed up with the keys inside, okay?"

I don't know what makes me do it, other than I am so very grateful for everything he's done, but I walk forward and hug Charlie as tight as I can.

"You're a great guy, Charlie. I'm really glad I got to know you during all of this."

He pats my shoulder. "You've done good."

I pull away and feel the tears starting to well up. Charlie seems to sense that my show of emotion has little to do with him, and bless him for granting me my dignity.

Or maybe I've just made him uncomfortable.

"I'll let you get back to work. You be careful, okay?"

"I'll certainly try. And thanks again."

He nods and walks off toward the office. I watch him disappear behind the depository, and I head back into the unit to finish up.

By early afternoon, long after Charlie has gone, I'm opening the final unit and practically choking on a thousand emotions I can't seem to compartmentalize or process.

My last task is a neatly organized space of people who clearly took care of what they kept in here. I can't help but wonder what happened to keep them from coming back.

There's a comfortable-looking Barcalounger up front that I mark on my list of large items. Boxes of CDs and DVDs. Old photo albums stacked neatly in plastic storage containers, meant to keep them safe and secure and protected from moisture that would ruin the pictures inside.

Toward the back, I see a large garment bag hanging from a hook on the wall, and I carefully unzip it.

Inside is a gorgeous, perfectly preserved wedding gown. It's white and crisp and covered with delicate beadwork and sequins.

This was the gown of someone who put a lot of effort into making their dress, and their day, as special as possible.

And now here it sits, abandoned and alone, surrounded by hundreds of other lost memories, waiting for me to chuck them into the back of a truck, where they will head for the dump, never to be crisp or clean or cared for ever again.

Here they sit, left behind by some horrible mistake that has caused them to be forgotten and alone. Irreplaceable and unable to be rescued. Things once so carefully protected, now abandoned by everyone who believed in their value, destined for a shapeless heap of nothingness in a city dump.

These lost treasures are me.

I carefully pull the wedding dress off the hook and hold it, running my fingers over the carefully laid beadwork. Walking over to the Barcalounger, I sit down, still holding the dress and feeling that if I can just find the right spot in the stitches, I can save it. I can spare it from the fate I will be forcing it into when I place it in the back of Brutus, never to be seen again.

The thousand emotions I can't contain bubble up, grabbing hold of me, and I start to cry. I cry for all the lost memories I've been responsible for erasing from existence. I cry for this perfectly preserved unit and all the items I'm going to push toward destruction.

I cry for Caspian and the pain he's feeling. The fear. The shame.

He believes he's suffering all those things because of me.

If I'd never made that call, he'd be blissfully unaware of all this madness. He'd be focused on finishing up his run in the play and his upcoming movie release.

Maybe I've earned the fate of being publicly mangled for the things I've done.

My tears fall onto this perfectly preserved and gorgeous dress that deserves better than the hand it was dealt, staining it with saltwater regrets.

I sit there for I don't know how long. Hours could have passed. Days.

I cry until I have no more tears to give.

Then I carefully zip the dress back up and put it in the front seat of Brutus to donate. I doubt the shelter will find much use for this magnificent gown, but I can't bear to place it in the back, destined for a garbage heap.

I cram the boxes of DVDs and CDs in there as well.

The boxes of photo albums, I can't bring myself to open. I can't look at the people whose past I'm about to erase. I carefully place them in the back of the truck and feel my stomach wrench as I do so.

I work steadily, saving everything I can to donate in the hopes that these items will find a home and a future with someone else. Someone who needs them and can use them and can try to give them a fate better than the one I would have in store for them.

By the time the sun goes down, I'm pushing the last box of perfectly preserved clothes into the front seat, a seat packed so full I will barely have room to sit and drive. But I refuse to part with any of the things I've placed in here.

I close up the last unit, carefully locking it behind me.

Climbing into Brutus, wedged tightly against boxes stacked to the roof of the cab, I pull away, headed for the shelter.

I will save these memories in hopes of creating new ones for others. I will save anything I can, knowing that nothing and no one can save the parts of me that I've lost over the last few months.

I drive out of E-Z Storage for the last time in my official capacity, feeling like the person I thought I was is lying, unsalvageable, in the bed of this truck, along with the rest of the things I've sentenced to the same fate.

31

The next morning, I head to my interview with Fogler Publishing, a gray cloud of misery hanging over me. Tom and Trina both know something is wrong, but I'm so despondent that they've just tiptoed around me and left me to my wallowing. For that, I am grateful. If they were to press me to find out the source of my mood, I wouldn't have the strength to keep up the facade anymore. I know the whole nightmare would come tumbling out, and I'd stand there, watching any respect my little brother ever had for me fall away right before my eyes.

When I get to Fogler, I'm taken with the office right away. Everything is a hodgepodge of mismatched office furniture and ancient bookshelves crammed to bursting with books. Everything is beautiful, well-worn oak and weirdly thick gray carpet that seems like it would be better suited to someone's living room than an office. It radiates comfort and warmth under my sensible heels as I walk through.

Everything feels genuine and inviting, and the people working away in their cubicles seem calm and focused and driven. It almost feels like walking into my favorite library, filled with people who care as much about the books crammed on those shelves as I do.

I'm led by Trey, my original interviewer, through the maze of cubes and toward the office of the president. After a quick knock, he opens the door and sticks his head in.

"Your ten o'clock is here, Joan," he says casually.

"Yes, thank you," she says without looking up from whatever she's typing on the laptop at her desk.

Trey motions me inside. "Have a seat."

"Thank you so much, Trey. And it's nice to see you again."

"You, too," he says with a friendly smile. He's all business, but not in a sycophantic or contents-under-pressure way. I like this about him.

I walk into the office, letting the door close behind me, and take a seat in one of the smooshy chairs located in front of Joan McInerney's desk.

In person, she looks absolutely nothing like her reputation would suggest. She's known in the industry as a lioness, and with good reason. She fights hard for the books she wants to acquire, and has on more than several occasions beaten out the biggest houses who have far more money to offer in auctions.

People want to work with her because they know she'll fight to the death to see a book sent on its most successful journey. She leads one of the only midsize houses that consistently sees books on the bestseller lists, and she somehow manages to do it without the resources of the Top Five houses.

When I hear tales of her escapades, I've always pictured various forms of some polished, cliché businesswoman in power pantsuits.

But the woman in front of me looks like someone's gray-haired Catholic auntie, complete with an elaborate rosary around her neck. She sports nothing resembling a power suit, and instead wears a comfortable-looking floral dress with a blazer over it. This is not a woman who wastes time on some performative outward appearance, and instead spends that time focusing on her authors and her team.

She's a formidable woman who gives off the vibe that she's made entirely of salt and bourbon, even as she sits here and types, completely ignoring the fact that I'm sitting in front of her.

Eventually, Joan finishes whatever she was working on and turns to me. I instinctively sit up straighter in my chair.

"So," she says, her voice exactly that of salty bourbon. "You're Clara Montgomery."

It's not a question. "Yes, hi. It's such a pleasure to meet you. It's an honor, really."

"Well, I can see I'm bribing the right people to keep my reputation intact," she deadpans. "Trey filled me in on your first interview, and he seems to think you're worth considering for our open associate editor spot. Do you agree?"

Wow. She cuts right to the chase. "I do, actually. I think I'd be a great fit here, and I feel like my tastes match up really well with the projects your house puts out. I think I could bring a lot to the table, and I know I could learn an awful lot working here."

"Confidence without pretending to know everything," she says. "I admire that."

"I admire your take-no-shit approach to publishing," I say bluntly. "I've never known anyone to advocate for their authors the way you're known for doing, and I can't think of a better sign of a solid house to be a part of."

She leans back in her chair. "And you think you can maintain that standard?"

I grin. "What's the point of doing the job if you're not willing to fight hard for the people you work for?"

"Trey wasn't wrong," she says, tapping her fingers on the arm of her mahogany-and-leather chair. "You do seem like you'd fit in here."

My first impulse is to be impossibly flattered, but a nagging thought pulls at me, and I can't shake it loose.

"I'm sorry, but I have to ask," I say, without giving my mouth permission to do so. "Did you bring me in here because of Caspian Tiddleswich?"

She frowns. "What the hell is a Caspian Tiddleswich?"

My eyes go wide. "He's this actor I'm…seeing. Several houses have seemed more interested in trying to lock him down as an author than in what I'm capable of bringing to the table as an editor."

Joan leans forward and stares me down. "I don't give a damn who you're dating. I can't imagine why that would be relevant here in the slightest."

My hands feel suddenly icy, and I know I've made a horrible mistake. "I apologize," I say with maybe more intensity than is advisable. "I just want to be considered on my merits alone."

"Trust me when I say I don't ever do anything but that," she says, leaning back again.

"Which I really appreciate," I say uncomfortably.

She raises an eyebrow. "I'm certainly not doing it for your benefit," she says plainly. "I do it because it's how a business should be run. And I run this business my way. You were brought in because you have a solid résumé and had an admirable list of authors at your former house. That's it."

I swallow a little too hard. "That's high praise coming from someone with your standards. I would be honored to be considered for a place here."

She glances over at the clock hanging on her wall. It's made of a mahogany that perfectly matches her chair, surrounded by a selection of framed covers of the many successful books she's been responsible for championing.

"I have a lunch with one of my authors to get to, so I need to get back to this if I'm going to finish in time," she says resolutely. "Thank you for coming in, Miss Montgomery. I'm sure we'll be in touch."

I'm being dismissed, and I want to beg her to start over before I cocked it all up by bringing Caspian into the conversation, but I find the sense to keep my mouth shut.

I stand up and wait for an invitation to shake her hand, but I remember hearing a rumor that she doesn't touch anyone under nearly any circumstance. Instead, I awkwardly smooth down the sides of my blazer and say, "Thank you very much for meeting with me. I genuinely look forward to hearing from you. Have a great rest of your day, Ms. McInerney."

She gives me a solid nod before turning her attention to her laptop and diving back into something that will keep her focus long after I leave this office.

I close the door behind me and make my way back through the admirable floor plan, wondering if my feet will ever have the opportunity to walk across the inviting carpet again.

I smile at Trey, sitting at his desk hard at work, on my way out.

I finally found a house that had no knowledge of Caspian, and I somehow managed to fuck it up by inserting him into the mix, likely destroying any chance I had at being seen as a competent editor, and instead coming off as an insecure basket case with name-dropping delusions of importance.

My gray cloud of despondence returns, and I head off to catch a train to meet CiCi at her apartment.

I take the ride in absentminded silence, staring off into the distance, unable to form full thoughts beyond flashes of Joan's frowning expression or forgotten wedding dresses or Caspian's tear-streaked face.

When I get to CiCi's place, she's waiting in the lobby for me, all smiles. When she sees me, those smiles become slightly forced.

"How'd it go?" she asks carefully.

"I stupidly brought up Caspian, because I was sure they couldn't have asked me there just because they liked what I had to offer," I confess. "But it turns out she doesn't even know who he is, and she seemed immediately displeased with me mentioning anything of the sort, and I'm pretty sure I sank any shot I had."

"Oh, honey," she says, taking my hand. "I'm so sorry."

"Even when I'm determined not to let my Caspian mistakes mess up any more of my life, I manage to strangle any opportunities of my own in his name."

"Maybe it wasn't as bad as you think?"

"That's my problem," I say with a sigh. "I keep hoping that things won't be as bad as I think, and I'm never prepared when they turn out to be worse."

"That seems like a really disappointing way to look at the world, cupcake."

"My choices recently beg to differ."

She smiles again, sincerely, and pulls on my hand. "Come on. Today is going to get better right now."

She leads me to the elevator, and we head to the fifth floor. Stepping out, there stands Mrs. Esposito, keys and a stack of paperwork in hand, waiting for us in front of apartment 524.

We say our hellos and head inside to do a final walkthrough. CiCi is on her game and points out all the little things scuffed up in the apartment that she wants to make sure we're not held responsible for in the lease, and I trail behind, useless and staring at my soon-to-be new home, terrified I'm making a horrible decision that could harm one of the few great things I have left—my friendship with CiCi, who, as time goes by, I worry I don't deserve.

After a thorough inspection, we sidle up to the kitchen counters and the lease is laid out in triplicate. I wish I could push this off until after I talk with Uncle Jack at Thanksgiving, but selfishly, I'm desperate to have a room with a door and a place to sleep that isn't in full view of Tom and Trina while I'm sorting through the dregs of the last few days I have to deal with Caspian.

With every set of initials and every signature I scribble out, my stomach clenches more and more, the fear of a looming mistake in the form of a two-year, legally binding commitment staring me in the face.

Before I'm ready to accept the things I could lose by doing this, Mrs. Esposito hands us both a set of keys, smiles at CiCi, and says, "Congratulations! We're happy you've decided to stick around." She turns to me with the same friendly look and says, "Welcome to the building, Miss Montgomery. I hope you'll feel at home here. Please let me know if there's anything you need."

I reach out and shake her hand, putting a smile on. "Thank you so very much, Mrs. Esposito. I think I'll be very happy here."

"I'll leave you ladies to your new place," she says, gathering up her copy of the lease. "CiCi, you know how to get in touch if you have any issues. We'll do your final walkthrough downstairs when you're all moved out this weekend. Keep me posted on things. And congratulations again."

CiCi bounces in place and clutches her new set of keys with unbridled joy. "I will, thank you, Mrs. Esposito. Thank you so very much." She reaches over and hugs her landlady, and I envy that kind of happiness.

Mrs. Esposito leaves us and pulls the apartment door shut behind her. As soon as she's clear of the room, CiCi squeals and grabs me in the tightest possible bear hug and starts jumping up and down.

"We did it!" she says, still jumping. "We're roommates! You're no longer homeless! Things are looking up, lady. I know it's hard to see right now, but I promise, this is the start of better things to come."

I hug her back with sincerity. "Thank you so much for being my friend, CiCi."

She pulls away to look at me, but keeps her arms wrapped around my waist. "Hey. I always will be. No matter what happens, Clara, no matter what he does, or what awful things he sends your way, I'm yours. And there's not a damn thing you can do to get rid of me. You're stuck with me, so there."

I feel more tears working their way up. "You promise?"

"Always," she says, and pulls me into another hug. No jumping, no squealing. Just love and support. "You're my people, and nothing is ever going to change that."

"Love yer face, lady," I say, a single, grateful tear falling.

"Love yers right back, cupcake."

32

The flicker of security and hope I feel lasts only until I have to make my appearance at the theater to watch Caspian's final performance. Once again, I'm dolled up with CiCi's help and wearing more of her fancy clothes.

She went with a meticulously applied cat eye tonight. I worried liquid liner would be a much more dangerous smudging risk if the night ends with tears, as it seems to take exactly nothing to set me off these days. But CiCi assured me this is waterproof liner, and I was so grateful for her foresight, I hugged her until she nearly broke.

I'm sitting in nearly the same seat I was the other night, but the experience is in a whole separate universe than the last time. When the few people who spot me try to sneakily take photos, I hide behind my program. This is not a night I want photographic evidence of. Not in any capacity.

The lights go down, and the show begins. When Caspian finally appears, it's like a punch in the face. It's the first time I've seen him since the verbal shoot-out in his hotel room, and it's physically painful to watch him move across the stage.

Everything he does is just as brilliant as it was the other night, but I sense a slight edge to his performance that wasn't there before, and I feel responsible for that. The good news, if there is any, is that the role works well with that edge.

But it shouldn't be there. I know it shouldn't. And I couldn't stop it from forming.

Every perfectly delivered line, every nailed beat of comedic timing—it's all as magnificent as it was before, but I sit here, watching it all and remembering what it led to only nights ago. Knowing what it will drag me into tonight is almost more than I can stand.

The news over the past few days has been a nonstop loop of every newscaster and their dog analyzing every letter of the Cranson papers. Delightedly discussing every aspect of Senator Crum's life as it crumbles in real time.

For the first twenty-four hours, his wife stood beside him as he tried to denounce the "unfounded" allegations, but as the evidence proved too concrete to ignore, he issued a new statement, confessing his "sins" and announcing he was going into a treatment facility to deal with his past indiscretions.

A few hours later, his wife, whom he was married to during those indiscretions, issued her own statement to the press that she was separating from her husband.

His political party has also called for his resignation. They seemed less bothered by the fact that he frequented sex workers than they were that about half of those sex workers were male. Which makes me all the more disgusted by that party as a whole.

It also makes me feel genuinely sorry for Senator Crum.

I've always considered him to be a garbage fire of a human being, since he's made a career out of demeaning women for political gain, but I can't help pitying a man who felt he had to hide his true sexual orientation to have a shot at a career.

Then again, he spent the last fifteen years buoying up that political machine, ensuring it would be just as crushing to anyone else battling the same struggles. And he did it while simultaneously blaming women for being sexually assaulted and submitting bill after bill to restrict nearly anything a uterus has a need for.

So, I guess while I feel genuine pain for his internal turmoil, I would also take the opportunity to punch him in the throat should the chance arise.

I think back to the moments CiCi and I laughed at the thought of watching some vile politician go down at our hands by finding details about them in the Cranson unit. It's all a hell of a lot less hilarious watching it happen now, in real time, even if we didn't have anything to do with it.

As the performance continues, everyone in the theater laughs heartily when Caspian nails his marks, and he never misses a beat. I'm grateful for the darkened setting, so no one can see me sitting here, quiet and struggling, as opposed to playing the part of the charmed girlfriend.

Still, even with the horror surrounding all things Caspian, I watch him move across that stage in awe. Our massive fallout hasn't changed my opinion of his skills in the slightest, even if it has stolen my ability to watch him without feeling devastated.

The show ends, and the theater erupts with seemingly never-ending cheers and whistles. When the actors come out for their curtain call, the man who plays Puck takes a special moment to single out Caspian specifically.

"This man," the elfin actor declares, "has made this one of the best experiences I—or any of us, for that matter—have had on stage. And it's a damn shame he's leaving us to go back to being a big-deal movie star." Caspian laughs genuinely with the others, while also managing to look endearingly embarrassed. The other actor continues, "We all want to say a huge 'thank you' to you, Caspian. You've not only made ticket prices twice what we could have charged otherwise—" there's more laughter from everyone in the building "—but you've also made us all better at our jobs, and for that, we thank you, friend."

Two stagehands come out with an absolutely mammoth floral arrangement and hand it to Caspian as the entire theater rumbles with joyful screams and applause. The standing ovation goes on and on, and gives Caspian more than enough time to accept a hug from everyone he shared the stage with.

Eventually, he raises a hand and gives a heartfelt smile and wave to the audience, and the curtain begins to close, the applause never waning.

Finally, the theater begins to empty, and I head off to follow the rest of my instructions for the night.

Slowly, I make my way through the mass of people around to the stage door, where a considerably larger number of friends and family of the cast are lined up. At the end of the alley where Caspian's car met us the other night, there are cabs lined up to whisk us off to the cast party.

I want nothing more than to run back to Tom's and hide with my shame away from Caspian's hate-filled eyes. Instead, I'm crammed into the back seat of a cab with two others—I can't tell which actor they're associated with. Thankfully, they couldn't care less about who I am or why I'm there. If anything, they seem mildly annoyed that I'm invading their space.

I appreciate the opportunity for personal silence.

We arrive at the venue, and my car-mates jump out without a second thought for me, which I'm grateful for. There are photographers lined up on either side of the roped-off entrance. I try to tuck myself in behind my fellow riders and go unnoticed as we head inside.

Inside, there's music playing and food and an open bar. My plan was to stick to a corner and not touch anything, as I'm not at all who these accoutrements were set out for, but the longer I stand here, watching people file up to the bar, the more I realize I may have to consider having a glass of wine or two if I'm going to make it through this evening in one piece.

Somehow I don't think my sulking around looking lifeless is what Caspian intended when he demanded I make a good showing in his name tonight. So I make small talk with several folks in line for drinks, and I do my best to play the role of glowing and proud girlfriend when they begin gushing about Oberon's performance.

When the actors start to arrive, Caspian is naturally nowhere to be found. I imagine him back in the alley, signing and posing for fan after fan. Picturing the small, blond-haired girl from the other night, I start to feel queasy, and carefully hand the last half of my second glass of wine to a passing waiter clearing tables.

I smile and chitchat with people who are in the highest of spirits. For anyone I recognize from the stage, I make sure to compliment their performances and gush appropriately.

After what feels like hours, Caspian enters the party. I only notice at first because everyone breaks into applause and cheers for their treasured King of the Fairies.

I honestly don't know what I'm supposed to do here. Do I run to him, pretending to be the smitten girlfriend? Nothing about that feels right, so I hang back to the side and watch as he makes his way through the crush of people all vying for his attention. He's obviously the man of the hour in a room full of people being honored.

The show will continue on without him, with the same cast, if I recall correctly, but with others stepping into his newly vacant role. His fellow cast members seem sincerely delighted by his presence, and equally heartbroken to say goodbye.

Eventually, he spots me against the wall. It's only a flicker of recognition, and I doubt anyone else noticed, but I did. I saw the way his face went from genuine lightheartedness to a flash of darkness before he turned back to the people whose existence doesn't disgust him.

Eventually, he breaks away, excusing himself politely, and makes his way over to me. Most of the other partygoers are several cocktails in and don't notice our immediate mutual discomfort in our little darkened corner.

"You were really great again tonight," I say by way of greeting, hoping to lessen the tension even slightly.

He looks down at me, the set of his eyes stony, and for the first time since I've known him, he looks tired. But only, it seems, because he's in my presence.

"I don't want you here," he says finally. Quietly.

"What?"

"I want you to go," he says, looking past me at the wall. Off to the side. At the floor. Anywhere that isn't my face. "These people are important to me, and I want to enjoy my last night with them, not thinking about you."

While I'm grateful for the excuse to leave, it doesn't make his words hurt any less. "I understand. I can see myself out."

He raises his hand and attracts the attention of one of the

waitstaff. The young woman quickly comes trotting over. "Can I get something for you, sir?" she asks.

"Yes," he says, all authentic kindness for the stranger. "Clara, here, isn't feeling well. I was wondering if you'd be able to have one of the cars take her home, please."

"I'm sorry to hear that," she says to me, and turns back to him. "Yes, sir, I'll take care of that."

"Thank you," he says, quickly glancing at her name tag. "Melanie, I appreciate that." Turning back to me, he adds, "I hope you feel better, Clara. We have a big day tomorrow. I'll see you to your car."

To the waitress, it probably seems like chivalry.

I take it as a threat.

"That's okay," I say, thankful for my new part as the ill companion. It allows me to embrace the deadness I actually feel instead of trying to force an adoring smile. "I wouldn't want to take you away from your party. I'm in good hands with Melanie, here." I give her a grateful look as she holds her arm up, preparing to guide me out. I turn back before I follow her and say, quietly, "Good night, Caspian."

At least this time, my tears have the good sense to wait until I'm back in a cab before they make their appearance.

33

I back Brutus up to unit 118, unfathomably relieved to be the one removing the items, thus ending my great fear of watching my belongings become abandoned relics to be removed by whomever Charlie has to hire next year to sort through repossessed units.

This particular trip, CiCi and I are loading up my beloved mattress and several boxes to take to our new place. I'll be staying there tonight, once again reunited with the sheer joy of sleeping on a proper bed and not Gertrude. With all the other hell the day has in store for me, this highlight almost makes up for the rest of it.

Almost.

And, I suppose, it's not really a proper bed if it's just my mattress on the floor, but it's better than Gertrude, and it's a considerably more dignified option than shuffling back to Astoria tonight with my tail between my legs and having to explain my feeble emotional state to Tom and Trina, once Caspian takes his final revenge after the premiere.

"How," CiCi groans as the two of us try to haul the mattress into the bed of Brutus, "how can one mattress be this heavy?"

"Shh," I say, equally out of breath. "She can hear you."

Finally, it thumps, still safely shrink-wrapped, into the back of Brutus, and we stand gasping for a few seconds.

"We have got to get you back out into the world so you can stop making friends with inanimate objects," CiCi observes.

"It's okay, Brutus," I say, patting my giant orange friend. "She doesn't understand our bond."

I'm weirdly touched to have Brutus be the carrier for the few items I'm christening our new place with. This old truck and I have been through a lot over the last few weeks.

I'm renting a van with Tom over the weekend to unload the rest while we help CiCi move her stuff in as well, but for now, I'm thrilled to have access to the handful of things I'm taking with me.

Unfortunately, one of the boxes we dig out is for the purpose of pulling out my fanciest dress, so I can wear it to the premiere tonight. It's a black ankle-length slip dress I bought to wear to a semiformal party my old publisher threw a few years ago. Admittedly, it's not actually fancy, but it passes, I think.

I imagine I'll never be able to wear it again after it's been drenched with public humiliation.

We carefully select a few more boxes and load them into Brutus. After this, we'll swing by Tom's to grab my things from their living room floor and the infamous coat closet. Tom and Trina made a big show this morning of appearing to be heartbroken to see me leave, but I can't imagine they'll be too devastated to have their home to themselves again. The ever-present big sister occupying the couch after a long day at work had to have become a tired notion almost instantly.

I plan on rewarding their hospitality with many, many dinners, bottles of wine, and an elaborate wedding present.

I still maintain a new couch is the way to go.

As we pack up my meager belongings at Tom's, I glance over at Caspian's Iron Throne and think maybe I'll replace that, too, just for good measure. I can't imagine ever reaching a time when I can look at that chair without feeling every ounce of shame and guilt and horror that's accumulated since he appeared, larger than life and too British for words, in this living room.

There's a knock at the door, and for a brief, terrifying moment, I fear Caspian will be on the other side.

CiCi sees the look on my face. "No way," she says as she heads to the door. "I saw him on the news this morning doing an interview for his new movie. He said he'd be doing press basically nonstop from now until it's in theaters."

I exhale and resume rolling things up to stuff back into my suitcases. "Bully for him."

CiCi opens the door, and I'm almost more shocked to see Charlie standing there than I would have been to see Caspian.

"Hi," I say, standing up. "Come on in."

"Nice to see you ladies," he says, carrying himself and his mustache inside.

I don't know why, but seeing Charlie in his neon orange vest standing in my brother's living room is oddly disconcerting. It's like suddenly seeing a bear sitting at the table next to you in a restaurant.

"Did I forget something?" I ask him. "Or was I not supposed to take Brutus today?"

He looks at me like he can't figure out if I'm being serious.

"I left the keys in there for you, kid. I knew you was taking the truck."

"Oh, right," I say, feeling, if possible, even less competent than normal. "Then what's up?"

He reaches into his pocket and pulls out an envelope. "I owe you money, remember? Figured it was time to get that squared away."

I squeak with joy. "Oh my gosh, I guess I forgot about that part!"

He grins. "I figured you might have been distracted. You seemed a little off the other day."

CiCi turns to me. "You did?"

I give her an impatient, knowing look. "It's been a long week."

Now CiCi looks sheepish. "Oh, right."

I take the envelope from Charlie. "Thank you for this," I say, clutching my hard-earned wages. "Truly, I appreciate absolutely everything you've done for me, Charlie."

"Nothing to it," he says with a shrug. "Good help is hard to find, and you were good help."

"Somehow I can't imagine you ever having a shortage of people wanting to work hard for you," I say, smiling.

"You know," he says, stuffing his hands into the pockets of his Technicolor vest. "The work I do, I see a lot of people's lives. A lot of times, there's really private stuff in those units. It's hard to find people you can trust with things like that."

I look over at CiCi, who looks appropriately intimidated. "I hope I lived up to that expectation," I reply to Charlie.

"*You* did," he says, rocking back and forth onto his heels. "But I found out one of my guys at the dump was goin' through the stuff you brought. You hear about that senator who just got fired or whatever?"

It takes everything I have not to gulp audibly. I manage a nod.

"The guy who was workin' for me is the one who sold that stuff to the news." CiCi and I look at each other in horror. "Now, I'm not sad to see that senator get what's comin' to him, but I'll be damned if it's someone working for me who does it with stuff they found in my units. That's not how I do business. Plus, I never had much use for those gossip sites. Do you?"

I shake my head and try to find any moisture in my mouth to speak. "No, I really don't."

"I'm just glad you showed yourself trustworthy," Charlie continues. "I know you had to have come across those things, too, and you did the right thing."

I can't do anything but keep my mouth shut and keep nodding.

"How did you even find out who did it?" CiCi asks bravely.

"Damn fool was running his mouth down there, braggin' on the money he got for it," Charlie says in disgust, shaking his head. "Hope that money is a big comfort to him now, because he don't work there anymore. I took care of him."

I stand up straighter. Is this one of those things where Charlie is subtly confessing to having someone killed? Which reminds me…

"Hey," I ask, desperate to change the subject. "Did you ever find out who robbed the unit that day?"

Charlie laughs. "Course I found out. He robbed his own unit. I had his name and address, the damn fool." With a big grin, he adds, "Took care a' him, too."

CiCi has officially reached the bug-eyed stage.

I have so many questions, but I'm wise enough to keep them to myself. "I bet you did," I offer, finally.

Charlie grins again. "Like I said, I'm glad I had you on those units. Someone I knew who'd do the right thing."

"I...I sure tried."

"I know," he says, and I have to wonder exactly *how much* Charlie knows. I think back to the security cameras that caught Caspian and I being locked in that unit as Crowbar—now possibly lifeless—Guy beat the hell out of Brutus.

"Anyway, I just wanted to drop that check by. You can leave Brutus back at the lot when you're finished." He turns to CiCi and nods. "Nice to see you again." Facing me once more, he smiles, making his mighty mustache turn all the way up at the ends, and says, "You take it easy, kid. Don't be a stranger."

"You got it, Charlie. And thanks again."

He tips his head to us both, and turns to let himself out.

I don't know how long CiCi and I stand there staring at the spot where Charlie stood, processing everything he just said.

Finally, eons later, CiCi turns to me, eyes still in a fishlike state, and whispers, "Ho...ly...shit..."

"I'm pretty sure we're lucky to be alive," CiCi says an hour or so later, once we're safely inside our new apartment, finally dropping the mattress on the floor.

"I get the feeling Charlie wouldn't just go right to murder," I muse, digging out a pair of scissors from one of my boxes to cut the shrink-wrap off my mattress. "He seems like the kind of guy who would enjoy the interrogation process a little too much."

CiCi debates this silently. "Do you think Trina knows whether he's really in the mob?"

I raise an eyebrow at her. "I doubt it. And even if she does, we will *never, ever ask her.* Would you really want Charlie to know we'd even thought about asking?"

She looks good and terrified. "Nope. Solid point."

"Well," I say as I hack away at the plastic, freeing my mattress, "at least we know how the stuff about the senator got out. Mystery solved."

CiCi gasps. "You can tell Caspian what really happened! He can't seriously stay mad at you now."

I scoff, balling up the sticky wrapping. "Right. Because he has every reason to trust anything I tell him."

"Oh, come on," she says, pulling my sheets out of a box. "You have to at least try. He's planning to give you a public smackdown tonight that you don't deserve. That's not fair."

"It's not *that* unfair," I counter, taking one end of the fitted sheet from her and bending down to tuck it in under the corners of the mattress. "Trust me, I have enough bad karma built up from the things I did. This is getting off easy, as far as I'm concerned. I'm not thrilled about it, but come on. I could have ended up like Crowbar Guy or the dude at the dump."

CiCi pauses midtuck. "Charlie wouldn't have really…offed you, right? Or us?"

I keep applying the sheet. "I think we should be counting our lucky stars, is what I think."

We work silently for a few moments, fully adorning my bed. It's missing the bed frame and box springs for now, but it's mine, and it's covered with sheets and a comforter I own. It's mine, and I've never been so happy to see a mass of fabric in all my years.

She and I both take a pillow and start stuffing them into my pillowcases. Soon, we drop them down at the head of the mattress, placed up against the wall under the tall window in my room, and I stare at our good work.

"Welcome home, Clara," CiCi says, smiling.

I walk over and give her a tight hug. "Thank you so much for being wonderful."

Never one to let a touching moment go by untarnished, she kicks my foot out from under me, and we go toppling over onto my freshly made bed.

"Nerd," she says, as we giggle and poke at each other. She rolls up onto her elbow and says again, "Okay, but I am going to need you to come around on the whole telling-Caspian-what-really-happened thing. I can't stand the thought of you taking a public lashing over this."

"CiCi…"

"No, listen! You have already been good and punished for what we did, which, let's be honest, was bullshit in the first place. I was guiltier than you were, and you're the one who keeps getting her ass kicked. And you suffered plenty in those early days with him. You're done. You don't have anything else to atone for."

"Debatable."

CiCi reaches out and slaps me on the arm. "You're too god-damn hard on yourself," she insists. "You've paid your penance. What he's going to do to you tonight, you don't deserve. I don't care how much you think otherwise—I'm telling you, it's not fair, and I won't stand for it."

I reach out and smack her back for good measure. "I don't think you refusing to stand for it is going to matter much. Caspian has it in his head what happened, and I can't blame him. The optics are really bad. If I could think of some way to make it stop—even just to finally reassure him there's no escort record guillotine hanging over his head—believe me, I'd do it."

CiCi looks sad. "You really liked him, didn't you?"

I slide up and lay my head on my pillow. "I did. And it was

completely misguided of me, but I kind of thought we had some weird actual friendship forming there for a minute."

"Yeah," she says, joining me on the other pillow. "I think that might have squeaked past friendship into something else, cupcake."

I make a face at her. "Dude. Even you wouldn't have been able to keep your shit together, between the no-shirt thing and seeing him hug that little girl. That was, like, super-concentrated swoon fodder."

"Damn right, I wouldn't have been able," she agrees. "Seriously. That was hot. I saw pictures of it online."

I shake my head. "After everything we've been through, how you can still stand to even look at tabloid stuff, I will never know."

"Because I was getting to see updates of your nightmares slash adventures," she explains. "Trust me, my desire for juicy gossip died a swift death early on. But that was *my* punishment— having to see you in all those awful places and not being able to help. That sucked."

"Aww," I say, a little choked up. "I love you, you majestic misfit."

She looks at me, a rare serious face on. "If you love me, please try to talk to Caspian tonight. I don't want to watch him flay you on a red carpet."

"I do love you," I say, and reach over to hold her hand, "but I think this is past salvaging. I just want to survive the night and put all of this Tiddle-drama behind me for good. Think about it this way—yes, I am going to be publicly flogged, but at least that'll be the end of it. This will be a bizarre chapter of our lives we'll someday look back on and wonder if we had some kind of joint hallucination for three weeks."

CiCi sighs and flops back on the pillow. "It's been a hell of a month, that's for sure."

"But this part is finished," I say, trying to sound positive, even knowing there's an ax hovering above my neck for the rest of the day. "And now we get to focus on making this place ours and being roommates and me finding a new job. A life without Caspian stinking up every corner of it seems pretty damn exciting to me."

Staring at the ceiling, she makes a noncommittal noise.

I sigh. "You're not going to let this go, are you?"

She shakes her head. "I'm really not."

"I'm about two seconds from making a 'Wash the windows, Cinderelly!' joke."

She grabs the pillow from behind her head and swiftly smacks me with it. "Jerk."

I laugh and dodge another blow. "So we can agree that wasting time trying to convince Caspian Tiddleswich of anything is pointless, yes?"

"Says you," she laughs. "Anyway, you need to be resting. You've got a red carpet to walk tonight, and a Prince Never-Charming to spend the evening with."

I groan. "*Red carpet.* The two most terrifying words I can think of right now."

"Yeah? If you ask me, Uncle Charlie is a hell of a lot scarier."

Mental images of the two recent men who have wronged Charlie flash through my mind, and I shudder.

"Touché."

34

"Aside from the constant humiliation," I say as CiCi once again coifs me up, "I'm definitely not going to miss having to get dressed up like this. It's a Thursday night. I should be going out for drinks with you in jeans, not having makeup put on my cleavage." I frown at her as she pulls a brush across my sternum again. "Is there a reason you keep putting stuff on my boobs? Shouldn't you buy me dinner first?"

She snorts. "It's contour. The lights you're going to walk under are going to make you look like a dead woman without stuff like this." She steps back to check her work. "Your tits have really never looked more fabulous."

"I kind of feel like my breasts were just insulted."

"We definitely made the right choice going with this dress," she says, apparently pleased with her décolletage efforts and setting the brush back on her desk. "No offense, but yours did kind of have that librarian-off-to-a-high-class-funeral look."

"How in the hell does one make a funeral high-class?"

Grinning, she says, "I'm in PR. I can make anything high-class. Your tits are examples A and B." I try to smack her, but she moves out of the way too quickly. "And besides, you're going to a Hollywood premiere. If you don't wear something with a label, you're doing it wrong."

I pout. "My dress had a label."

"GAP doesn't count."

I eye the dress in her mirror. "I bet this thing cost more than my first car."

"Well, that dress *is* vintage Gucci," CiCi says, pointing her finger at me. "It's a classic."

"What it must be like to be rich," I wonder, still evaluating the dress from all angles. "I feel like a twisted version of Cind—" I catch myself and slap my hand over my mouth.

She rolls her eyes. "Just say it."

"I swear that was accidental," I say, trying to keep a straight face. "Anyway, in this version, instead of turning into a pumpkin at midnight, someone drops one on my head from really, really high up, and I die."

"Somehow I don't think Disney would have gone for that ending."

"And my fairy godmother swears a lot."

"Okay, Disney *should* have gone with that version."

I stand up and try to sell myself on my appearance. I can't really think of anything I could wear that would make me feel comfortable, but at least when I'm dressed like myself, it's easier to deflect. The spaghetti straps on the long black dress are so thin, I worry they may snap if I so much as sneeze. It's also super low-cut compared to my normal look, with slits that go up to my thighs on each side. I had to borrow a special strapless bra from CiCi to keep everything in place, and as I have a full cup size on her, my boobs are a bit squished, but pretty impressive-looking.

All in all, I suppose I *do* look pretty great. My hair is straightened and lying perfectly, and we once again went with a cat eye, this time thicker. Plus, CiCi's not wrong—the ladies are looking pretty boss. Shame to waste them on a night like tonight.

"We used the waterproof stuff again?" I ask, pointing to my eyes.

"Yep. Never thought to do otherwise."

"Ahh, self-preservational makeup. What a time to be alive."

CiCi checks her phone. "Okay, your car will be outside in five, so let's get you going."

"I can't believe you sent for a car. This is all so wasteful. God, I hate him."

"No, you don't," she says, as though that's an actual fact. Before I can vehemently argue, she holds up a long teal coat for me to slide into. "And it's not like I was going to let you ride the subway. You would be late, for starters, but you can't show up to his hotel like that. Plus, I dare you to walk to and from the train in those shoes."

I look down at the strappy four-inch heels as I hoist the coat up onto my shoulders. "Oi. Good point. I already can't feel my toes."

"That's how you know the shoes are working."

I grab a little sparkling clutch off her desk and shove in my phone and whatever peach-colored lip goo she has on my mouth, plus a small collection of things like my debit card, MetroCard, and some cash with it.

"Okay, but consider this," I say, turning to her suddenly. "How bad would it be if I just didn't go, or faked my death or something? What's the worst that could happen?"

She gives me a suspicious look. "Do you really want to know the answer to that? It's like asking what Charlie did to the guy who beat up his truck. There are things that are best left unknown for the sake of our sanity. And safety."

I whine. "Damn it."

"Look, text me often, and I can come get you as soon as it's over if you want. I'll keep my phone with me all night. You say the word, and I'm there." She pauses for a second. "Well, I'll be a few blocks away where you would have to meet me, because they don't let regular people anywhere near stuff like this unless they're on the list, and I'm in no mood to get tackled by an overzealous bodyguard tonight."

"I think I'll be fine," I say, giving her a quick hug. "I'm probably just going to come back here and embrace my pathetic state alone for the night. Wallow in misery with a pizza or something. I'll let you know I made it back alive, and we can have lunch tomorrow?"

"Are you *sure* you won't even try to talk to him?" she says one last time. "Even if he doesn't believe you, at least you'll know you gave it your best shot."

"Oh, hey," I say, pointing at an empty spot on her floor. "That poor dead horse is being beaten again."

CiCi smirks and grabs me by the shoulders, pushing me out of her apartment. "Smart-ass."

"Rest in peace, little horse."

"You be careful, know I'm a sobbing call away, and good luck, cupcake."

"Thanks, hon. Love you."

"Love you back."

I catch a glimpse of the clock in her living room as she closes the door. If I don't haul, I'm going to miss the car, and

CiCi's right—these are not the shoes in which to be a stubborn hero and prance across town.

It's a lot easier to keep my mood in one piece when I've got my best friend to banter with, but it's another story altogether when I'm in the back of the car, alone, headed to the hotel of the man who hates me more than I realized people could hate.

When we finally pull up to the hotel, I'm treated to the doorman opening the car door for me. So far, I've only been privy to that sort of attention when Caspian is with me. And sure, they do that for every single person who rolls up to their sidewalk, but it's still nice to be treated like a human, and not just because I'm standing with someone like Caspian.

I walk into the lobby, my shoes clacking loudly against the marble floor, and make my way toward the elevator. When the door slides open, I'm almost too relieved when I see the operator from my first trip here. "It's nice to see you again, Jacob," I say. "How are things?"

"I'm well, Miss Montgomery," he says. "Mr. Tiddleswich's room?"

I try not to visibly deflate. "Yes, please. Thank you."

I wish the ride were longer. I wish I could cling to Jacob and ask him to turn the elevator around. I wish I could kick the emergency stop button and hide in here until I'm sure Caspian has long since headed back to England.

As I step into the penthouse, prepared to meet my unmaker, I instead find a flurry of people in the living area, talking on phones and to each other. Sometimes both at the same time.

A woman sitting on my beloved Jasmine spots me first, and her face lights up. "You must be Clara," she says. Another Brit. She quickly crosses the room, and two of the other people, both on their phones, glance over, still engrossed in their conversations. "It's such a pleasure to meet you finally!" the woman exclaims, holding out her hand. "I'm Margot, Cas's agent."

I shake her hand and reply, "Likewise! I've heard such wonderful things about you!"

Truthfully, I don't remember hearing anything about her, other than the references to the amorphous "team" Caspian has made periodically. I don't know what I expected his agent to look like—possibly a crusty old white dude with slicked-back hair and a 1992 cell phone strapped to his hand—but Margot is none of those things. She's in her fifties, I'd guess, and she looks alert, trendy, and genuinely friendly. By the way she's dressed, I gather she'll be attending the night's events as well.

"Those two over there are Nathaniel and Devon," Margot explains, gesturing to the folks still on their phones. "Caspian's manager and publicist, respectively."

Nathaniel vaguely resembles the older white guy I pictured, but he's not crusty or talking on an original Nokia. He seems terribly posh and dignified, even as he paces the room intently in his tuxedo.

Devon looks more like someone's quirky best friend pulled from the screen of a rom-com. Her dress is a strapless tea-length gown in a fabulous bright print that I'm honestly dying of jealousy to see her pull off so magnificently. I make a mental note to invest in more vibrant colors the next time I'm able to shop. Life suddenly feels too short to hide behind a neutral palette.

Nathaniel gives a dignified hint of a smile and a quick flick of his hand in greeting before carrying on, and Devon lets loose a very cheerful wave, followed by a deeply apologetic look as she points to her phone, still pressed to her ear.

"We're all so glad you could make it," Margot says, motioning me inside the room. "Can I get you a drink?"

I shake my head. "No, but thank you for the offer."

She walks over to the table and refills a mostly empty champagne glass from a bottle of bubbly amid several other empty bottles. "I'm sorry none of us have had the chance to say a proper hello before now," she continues, taking a sip, "but you know how Cas likes to keep things separated. I think he was set to sack us all when we first heard about you."

"Oh, gosh, I would hope not," I say, trying to laugh. I look awkwardly around the room, wondering if Caspian is crammed into a corner somewhere watching all of this.

"Well, thanks for being such a good sport about it all," she says genuinely. "The way I hear Geoffrey tell it, I think Cas has you to thank directly for landing the Aperture role. We'd been pushing for that for months, but after one dinner with you, they offered him the part."

I scan through my brain, trying to think if I ever heard Caspian mention Aperture, and I almost squeal when I realize Margot's talking about a graphic novel series from the eighties about a mad scientist who does all manner of vile things until an experiment goes horribly wrong and gives him powers. When he uses them for evil, his body starts to rapidly deteriorate, and when he uses them for good, he gets stronger and stronger and his powers grow. It's a really dark series, but man, is it good. It's the only time my mom banned a book from the house—which, of course, made me all the more obsessed with it.

Some teens hide porn under their mattresses. I hid Aperture.

That inner squeal comes crashing back to reality when I remember there's no way I'll be able to watch Caspian in anything ever again, and now that stain has bled over into my beloved Aperture.

"Geoffrey is being far too kind," I insist with a smile I hope doesn't look as forced as it actually is. "I had a wonderful time meeting him and his wife. And everyone else, of course!"

Margot scoffs into her glass. "You're among friends. Arabella is a twit, and you're a gem for pretending otherwise."

"I knew I liked you," I say with an honest laugh.

The damn shame is that I *do* actually like her. And I'm really not looking forward to being verbally shredded in her presence later tonight.

The door to the bedroom opens, and a very feisty-looking woman carrying two giant cases comes walking out. She's got an undercut with the tips of her black faux hawk dyed the same neon orange as Charlie's vest. It's not a look many could pull off, but damn, is she nailing it.

Caspian strolls in behind her, buttoning up the jacket of his tuxedo, looking incomprehensibly hot, as always.

This night would be a lot easier if I could go back to the days before I realized his hotness was an undeniable fact.

"Thank you, Tai," he says to my new hair idol as she sets down her mammoth cases and grabs a luminous blue coat made of some sort of fur.

"Knock 'em dead tonight, Cas," she tells him, grabbing the cases back up and heading for the elevator. I'm guessing stylist or hair and makeup?

Margot snaps her fingers to her two counterparts, still deep in conversations on their phones, and looks back at me. "We'll let you two have a little peace and quiet before you head to the theater. But do try to control yourselves, as Tai can't come back to get that hair of his under control again." She throws a wink at Caspian, and I can't help the blush that swirls across every inch of my overly visible skin.

She and the others join Tai at the elevator and start pulling on coats. All the more an impressive feat for the ones on the phone.

"Sorry about this," Devon says, covering the bottom of her phone. She's also English. I get the feeling this crew follows Caspian from London when he travels. "I look forward to meeting you properly later tonight!"

Nathaniel makes a nearly identical gesture to the one he greeted me with just as the door opens and the four of them pile in, with Jacob still at the helm.

When the door pings shut, I am very aware that Caspian and I are alone again. The last time we stood in this room, there was a great deal of shouting, and none of it was in my favor.

"They, uh," I say, looking for anything to cut through the silence, "they all seem really nice."

"They are," Caspian says, adjusting a cuff link. He walks over to the couch and sits, reaching past the empty bottles of champagne to riffle through a stack of papers.

"Um, oh, hey," I offer, "congratulations on the Aperture role. That's really cool. That was my favorite series in high school."

Without looking up, Caspian shakes his head. "Wonderful. Another bit of sensitive information for you to sell. I should have warned Margot not to answer any of your questions."

I fight down the flash of anger. "I didn't ask. She talked about it like she thought I knew, was all." I shuffle my feet. "I was trying to be polite to you, which I'm aware is a lost cause, but I'm a sucker for hopeless cases, I guess."

"Do try to restrain yourself from emailing your favorite gossip site as you stand there," he says, still sorting through papers. "That would be extraordinarily crass, even by your standards."

Yep. I was right. I could stand here and make my case about

the truth of the senator and the Cranson papers until I bled the room of all available air, and it wouldn't do a damn bit of good.

It's only now, as I look around the room, trying to bite down any vicious retorts that may be building, that I realize everything looks…off. Over by the giant picture window sits a small stack of boxes and suitcases.

Caspian will be heading home in the morning, and it appears as though he's already all packed up.

This really is it. He'll be leaving, taking his delusions with him, and there won't be anything I can do to stop either of those things.

I shouldn't care. I should be thrilled to have him out of my life forever, and not give a single fuck about the misguided impression of me he'll be taking with him.

But I *do* care. Whether it's because I can't stand the idea of anyone thinking so poorly of me, or because I thought we'd gotten to a place of friendship…or because of the other things I still feel for him, despite my desperate quest to avoid thinking about those feelings since that night.

None of that matters now.

And the worst of it has yet to come.

I swallow down the feeling of dread climbing in my chest. "I'm sorry. I was just trying to make conversation. I don't know what else to say."

"Feel free to say nothing," he says, not missing a beat.

It's going to be a long-ass night.

35

By all measurement, the most painful part of the night thus far was the endless limo ride from the hotel to the premiere.

Everything after that wasn't as bad as I'd feared it would be.

There was the wildly uncomfortable exit from the car onto the red carpet, where doting boyfriend Caspian made somewhat of an appearance. It occurs to me somewhat later that he wasn't going above and beyond, because he no longer has to. His plan is for us to have a very public breakup later tonight, so slathering on fake romance doesn't really suit the part anymore.

After we're welcomed by screaming and the light of a thousand suns in the form of camera flashes, I'm whisked off to the side with Margot and Nathaniel while Devon earns her big bucks.

It's so very odd watching the circus of getting someone to pose for pictures of this nature. Hundreds of people are screaming his name, trying to get his attention. He has to angle himself in all sorts of ways to try to make sure the screamers' needs are being met. Devon runs up periodically and whispers things to him or adjusts his tie to make sure he is looking his most movie star–ish, no matter what.

The entire spectacle feels endless to watch, and I can't imagine what it's like to actually experience.

Caspian stops to sign autographs and pose for selfies with fans lined up behind wooden barriers and the arms of police and private security called in to block for the event. I watch as other actors from the franchise arrive and start doing the same dance.

Other famous folk who I'm fairly certain have nothing to do with the movie but are here for their own promotion take the same walk, with slightly less zealous results.

It's all so surreal. This is their lives. Caspian and all of them. This is their job.

Their job is weird as hell.

I'm led down the edge of the carpet as Caspian makes his way up to other members of the cast, and it's here that a slew of managers and publicists and other team members all pile in together to set up group shots for the photographers in front of the mammoth movie posters and cutouts and other promotional materials littering the front of the theater.

Looking over, I realize I'm not the only companion banished to the outskirts of the carpet, and for the most part, most of us look far happier to be outcasts. There are a few who seem to be chomping at the bit to find a way into the edge of shots, and there's even one girl who runs over as though she has something terribly important to tell one of the male stars of the movie. She's quickly escorted back to the frays with the rest of us by one of that actor's handlers.

It's all such an odd experience, and yet it seems so perfectly choreographed. I don't see how anything with this amount of chaos and the sheer volume of people involved could ever work in a well-oiled manner, but everyone seems very certain of the parts they're playing in making sure that exact thing happens.

It's honestly fascinating to watch as a bystander.

As the cast lines up in front of the television crews, those of us who are waiting for our respective actors to return are offered the chance to retreat inside, out of the glare of the burning portable studio lights, to grab a drink and take our seats if so desired.

It is so very desired. These shoes were a horrible mistake. I'll add it to my list.

From there, things are the picture of calm from where I'm sitting. I tinker on my phone and say hello to a few people who are either trying to spark conversation with someone, or who recognize me from my tabloid antics with Caspian. I'm as friendly as I can be, but mostly, I want to melt into the theater seat and be left to my own devices. Though I suppose I don't have to go out of my way to make an impeccable showing as his girlfriend, given the way this night is destined to end.

It's at least an hour before the actors start filing into the theater. They're all brought in by their teams, the actors chatting and laughing away with each other, obviously glad to be reunited for the premiere tonight. I see more than a few famous folk I admire, and I want to shrivel up and die when I imagine them witnessing my evisceration in a few short hours.

Finally, *finally*, the lights go down, and each actor is taken to their respective seats. Whether it's dark enough that he doesn't feel the need to put on a show, or because he doesn't care how out of love we appear now, Caspian is silent when he takes his seat between Margot and me.

The movie itself is actually quite good, although the parts where Caspian is in full-villain mode are less enjoyable now that I've seen him make those same terrifying expressions in real life.

When your date has too much in common with an intergalactic assassin, you know you've gone wrong somewhere in your life.

The movie ends with much cheering and applause that lasts forever. Nearly all of the actors look embarrassed to some degree as the lights come back on, and they take solace either in cracking jokes with their significant others or with members of their managerial squads. Caspian is talking with Nathaniel and one of the other lead actors, pointing out various places he wishes he'd stuck his landings better, or played off the brilliant acting of whomever else in a more organic way.

If he were anyone else, I would want to roll my eyes and gag at all the fake self-deprecation. But this is all par for the course with what I learned of Caspian during our genuine moments together. He seems honestly uncomfortable having had to watch himself on screen, and looks to have taken mental notes, much like an athlete watching back a game to learn from their mistakes.

From the theater, we're led back outside, past the flashing cameras and to our car, and I'm suddenly trapped in a tiny space filled with intimidating animosity. As we make our way to the premiere party venue, Caspian says absolutely nothing as loudly as a person possibly can.

He occasionally checks his phone, responding to various texts and other alerts, completely ignoring my presence. I finally pull out my own phone and see a few missed texts from CiCi, asking how things are going.

If I make it out alive, I will consider myself very, very lucky, I reply.

Traffic is particularly horrid, but I guess that's to be expected when hundreds of people are leaving a theater and heading to the exact same location across town. Expected, but not particularly forgiven, because it's making this car ride last longer than anyone should ever have to suffer through such uncomfortable silence.

Actually, uncomfortable would be a welcome step up from whatever adjective applies to this mess.

Once again, after the initial walk up, most of us are separated from our partners and brought inside, where a raging party is already in full swing, even without the guests of honor. I'm tempted to find the nearest dark corner and hide there until my beheading, but after the third tray of food passes my way and I remember I haven't had anything to eat since lunch, and it's now pushing midnight, I am reminded of CiCi's advice from my first Caspian outing.

I decide I've earned a lobster puff. Or twelve.

When the actors do start appearing, I realize part of what held them all up is that most of them appear to have changed into more party-appropriate clothing, compared to their previous tuxedos and gowns.

This is the first time tonight I haven't been able to control the annoyance on my face.

If I'd known I could have changed, I would have gone to great lengths to accomplish it. Facing what's about to be unleashed on me while wearing these godforsaken shoes and with my contoured jumblies hanging out isn't doing anything for my mood at all.

"Fuck it," I mutter to myself, and grab another puff.

Caspian finally appears, now clad in a more casual suit, sans tie.

Oh, sure. He gets to be dressed more like himself to drop the hammer, while I look like I'm about to strut off to the prom. I have no doubt he was well aware I could have brought a costume change and elected to leave that information out.

Or, judging by the look on his face when he spots me, he knew it would be pointless to let me take the time to change. I can actually see him shift out of whatever he was feeling a second ago and into the dead-eyed, icy glare of the Evil Cas character.

His expression is clear: I'm not going to be standing here much longer.

Oh god.

It's one thing to know something like this is coming, days and even weeks in advance, and try to make my peace with it.

It's another thing altogether when that thing is barreling down on you with a bitter stare as gaggles of actors and managers and agents and waiters and god knows who else stand a few feet away.

I can't tell if I'm hallucinating or just trying to do whatever I can to delay the inevitable, but I swear he's walking in slow motion as he makes his way over to me.

A thousand things jump into my head. Am I supposed to cry? Look gutted? Beg him to keep me to make him look better in front of his associates? Fight back and act like an aggressive bitch, so he looks like the victim? If I stand here and take whatever is about to come my way with a stiff upper lip, will he just keep going until I finally crack?

I wish I had asked for clarification as to what's expected of me, but somehow, I doubt he would have been particularly forthcoming with instructions.

Millennia later, it seems, when he finally reaches where I'm standing, I mentally kick myself for not going to the dark corner. I doubt he would have actually gone to the trouble of dragging me back into the center ring for our bout.

I try to look as composed as possible, but my hands are shaking. Squaring my shoulders and pulling in a breath that is 90 percent shudder, I look up at him and brace for impact.

"Well, then," Caspian says, his eyes resembling the blankness of a shark's as it circles its prey in the water.

Now that the moment is here, I may not have a say in whether I cry or not. I can feel the burning sensation in my throat already.

His dead stare is broken for the briefest instant, and I see a sliver of real emotion on his face. I'm close to a full-fledged panic attack and am barely holding it together as it is, so there's nothing left in me to try to decipher the look.

"Clara," he says, his voice low. It doesn't have the same virulent animosity or cold tone as everything else he's said to me over the last few days, and I don't know what to make of it. If he's trying to inject humanity into his performance so it's believable to everyone around us, he's doing a good job, because even I'm thrown off balance by it.

Suddenly, whatever the emotion was disappears, and he does the last thing I would have expected: he reaches into his pocket and pulls out his phone.

Is he…is he going to record this or something? Have we devolved so far that he wants evidence of the massacre?

He looks back up at me, even more irritated than before, if possible, and then back down at his phone.

I don't know what he's looking at, but somehow, this is

worse than him preparing to verbally maul me in public. I'm tempted to scream, "JUST DO IT ALREADY!" but I can't pull in enough air to get my voice above a squeak, even if I wanted to.

His phone lights up in his hand, and he looks away, pursing his lips, frustration clearly building. He looks at me again, shaking his head before he puts his phone to his ear and...

Walks away?

Uh.

Now what the hell am I supposed to do?

Is he coming back?

Do I make a run for it?

Vomit on my feet-strangling shoes?

Burst into tears now and hope they dry up before he returns?

I'm frozen in place, watching him speak with great annoyance into his phone as he finds a dark corner of his own to take the call. I don't know who is on the other end of the line, but I don't feel particularly grateful to them for winding him up even more.

Suddenly, Devon is in front of me, still rocking her amazing multicolored dress. "Clara!" she says, reaching out to hug me.

Okay, so she's one of those people.

I hug her back, hoping my shaking hands aren't detectable.

"Are you having a good time?" she asks, grabbing a glass of champagne from a passing tray.

"I am," I lie. "Thank you for asking! How about you?"

It's nice to see the debilitating terror hasn't dulled my manners.

"I'm ready to get back to the hotel and out of these bloody shoes," she says, taking a powerful swig of her drink. I get the feeling it's to dull the aching in her feet more than anything.

"We have that in common," I say with a genuine smile of solidarity. "By the way," I add, realizing I won't have the chance to make casual conversation again in a matter of minutes, "I've been meaning to say all night that you are wearing the hell out of that dress. You look fabulous."

She giggles. "I can see why Cas likes you so much. You really are as charming as I've heard!"

Oh, hey, an emotional punch to the chest. Neat.

"I don't know who I need to pay for all that good press," I say, "but if I figure it out, the check is in the mail."

"You are such a delight," she says, reaching out to take my hand. Yup, she's definitely a toucher. "I'm so glad I finally got a chance to meet you before we head back to London. Have you made any plans to come visit? Maybe for the holidays? I'd love to set up some tours for you if Cas is working while you're in town!"

Now my stomach really hurts, and I regret every single lobster puff. "Well, uh, we haven't really finalized any plans yet," I fib, knowing damn well what my final plans are to be. "But when we do, I'll make sure he lets you know?"

"Absolutely, please do!"

Over her shoulder, I see Caspian making his way back, staring at his phone while somehow managing to navigate the crowds. Either that, or he's Caspian Tiddleswich, and people just hop out of his way.

I cringe inwardly and look at Devon, sipping on her champagne, and think I can't imagine a more painful audience for what's about to happen. It's one thing to be yelled at in front of a bunch of actors who have barely looked at me twice, but it's quite another to be torn down in front of a woman I am genuinely beginning to like.

But, in the end, I suppose that's the point.

I want to excuse myself and run off, meeting him before he can get to where the two of us are standing, but with his damnably long legs, I know I wouldn't make it if I tried, especially since I'm wearing shoes that have effectively hobbled me.

I can't help it—I look down at the floor, shifting uncomfortably.

"Hey, Cas," Devon trills, "hell of a party! Can I get you anything?"

"Thank you, Devon, no," he says, before adding, "Actually, if I could have a moment with Clara?"

I look up. Maybe he doesn't want someone he cares about having a front-row seat for my smiting.

"Of course!" Devon says, trilling again. "I'm off to find the bar." She holds up her empty champagne glass. "I can do better than this." She winks at me and reaches over to give me another hug. "I do hope I see you in London, Clara. Enjoy the party!"

She skips off, leaving Caspian to his task.

"I didn't say anything to her about visiting," I blurt out. "She brought it up, and I said we hadn't made any plans, that's all. I know you won't believe that, but I didn't—"

He leans down and kisses me on the cheek, pausing to whisper, "Clara, I'm so sorry."

I'm so stunned, I leap back a good two feet. "Excuse me?"

He steps forward and leans in, so I can hear him over the commotion of the party. "I know it wasn't you who sold out the senator. I truly am so very sorry. I swear to you I'm not going to embarrass you here. You have my word."

I stare at him, quickly shaking my head, certain I've had some sort of aneurysm and misheard everything he's just said.

Before I can open my mouth to respond, the actor who played the leader of the space resistance pops over and introduces his date, one of the women who had been trying to hop into the peripheral of the red-carpet photos.

Caspian reaches down and takes my hand, looking down at me with heartless conviction before turning his attention back to his friend.

I look down at our hands, then up at him, and back down again.

With my free hand, I yank a glass of champagne off a tray and start drinking.

36

Due to a constant stream of well-wishers, Caspian and I don't get a moment alone for me to ask what in the merry fuck just happened.

He holds tight to my hand and introduces me to everyone who stops by to say hello, and he does so with an open fondness. He seems honestly relaxed and happy the entire time.

It hits me that maybe asking what changed would be looking a gift horse in the mouth and then punching it in the teeth. Whatever stroke or sudden-onset drunkenness caused his change of heart, I don't particularly trust it, but I also really don't want to scare it off.

I keep waiting for the party to die down at least a little, but if anything, it gets more and more raucous as the night goes on.

I thought publishing folk could hold their own at an open bar, but man, these people can really throw back the booze.

Finally, sometime around three in the morning, when it

becomes clear this isn't going to let up, Caspian leans down and asks, "Would you like to leave?"

I frown, not sure if I'm being set up for some elaborate rug pulling, but I nod anyway. He raises his hand and flags down Devon, who immediately comes running over on slightly wobbly feet. Guess she found the bar.

"I'm going to take Clara home," he tells her. "Could you have the car pulled around?"

"Absolutely!" She reaches up and hugs him, saying, "You did amazing tonight, Cas." She turns to me and grabs me in a slightly sloppy hug. "I'm so glad I met you," she says, pulling away, all toothy smiles. "I hope I get a chance to show you around at Christmas! London is brilliant during the holidays!"

I do my best to look hopeful and pleased. "I've heard that! I hope it happens. It was a pleasure to meet you, Devon."

She releases us both and prances off to track down the limo, and Caspian laughs to himself. "Let's go fetch your coat," he says, taking my hand again.

He says some quick goodbyes as we make our way through the ballroom, but most people seem either too drunk or too tired to do much beyond wave and promise to call him later.

There is little line for the coats, as damn near everyone is still inside, partying the night away, and it takes the check guy a while to dig out both our coats. I don't know what to do or say, so I avoid looking at Caspian and focus on the counter in front of us as if it's the most interesting cherry wood to ever exist.

Devon comes back through and smiles, nodding to let him know the limo is at the ready. When our coats are passed over the fascinating slab of wood, Caspian, full to the very brim of surprises, helps me pull mine on before shrugging into his.

Out on the sidewalk, sure enough, there's a driver waiting

to open the limo door as soon as he sees Caspian emerge. A few photographers are still lingering, but the long night has gotten to them as well, and their reflexes are a little slower than normal. I think they've hung around in hopes of seeing one of the more famous attendees stumble out completely smashed, so our sober walk is of little interest.

We get inside the limo, and Caspian calls up Tom's address. I'm both impressed and confused that he has it memorized, but considering his entire job is based around his ability to remember lines, I guess it's not that out of the ordinary for him.

It takes me a full city block before I remember I'm not headed back to Astoria. I find my voice for the first time in hours and correct the course, giving the driver my new address.

Caspian looks over at me, confused.

"I...I moved," I say, fidgeting with my clutch. "Well, I'm moving, anyway. It's my first night there."

"That's wonderful," he says, sounding as though he really believes that to be true. "I'm glad you and Gertrude were able to part ways. Amicably, I hope."

I look up at him, so far beyond lost that there aren't words to describe the place I'm currently in. I don't know what's happening or who this Caspian-shaped person is beside me, so I resume poking at the zipper on my little purse, doing my best to ignore the thousands of questions swirling in my head.

Caspian's phone buzzes, and he pulls it out of his suit pocket and replies to something. We make the rest of the trip in silence, which is perfectly fine with me. The mood in the limo is considerably different from the silence from our earlier drives, and I'm grateful for it.

The late night/early morning traffic is all but nonexistent, and we make it to my new apartment building in a sanity-saving amount of time. The driver hops out as soon as the car stops, and I have a moment where I hate not being able to fly out of this vehicle like I'm on fire.

"It's, uh…" I say, waiting for the door to open. "It's been real, Caspian. Good luck with…stuff."

Now I do flee the limo like I'm ablaze.

Before I can dig out my keys to get into the building, I realize I'm not alone.

"Could we talk?" Caspian asks, sounding uncertain.

I whirl around to face him, my eyes bulging with disbelief.

"You can't be serious. What's the point of it if there's not a party full of people here to watch?"

"I think there are a few things that deserve clearing up," he explains, nervously pushing his hands into his coat pockets.

I shake my head, more out of the impending madness than to disagree. "But we're done! You're finally rid of me! Ding, dong, the failed extortionist is gone!"

He walks forward until he's only a few feet away and says calmly, "I want to apologize. And I understand if you aren't willing to hear it, but if you'll allow me, I'd really like the chance to talk to you, Clara."

"I…" The driver, sensing our need for privacy, quietly gets back into the limo. For whatever reason, this infuriates me. I don't want Caspian to have a calm, private moment to get his way. Again. I don't want to be reasonable. I don't want any of this.

I raise my arms and let them drop to my sides with frustration. "You know what? No! I'm tired of this! Look, I know you were pissed and scared, but guess what, Caspian, King of the Narcissists? So was I! You keep saying I took the worst part of your life and shoved it right into your face, which we both know I can't take back, but we also know it was unintentional.

Yet here *I* am, right in the middle of the worst goddamn period of *my* life, and you've done nothing but make it worse, over and over and over again, and completely on purpose! So you can spare me the explanation of how afraid or stressed out you've been these last few weeks, because none of that excuses the things you've done. None of it!"

I pause for a breath, trying incredibly hard not to cry. "I don't care what happened tonight that caused you to see the light, or whatever," I say wearily. "Because I *tried* to tell you what happened. I told you everything, and you wouldn't listen. I had to stand there, terrified and sobbing like a fool and begging you to stop. But you just kept yelling and saying horrible, cruel things, and you put me through hell!"

His expression is pained and his eyes are wet, and every single emotion—all the things I've felt and even the ones I've tried to ignore—comes rushing up, and I feel like I may be sick.

"Clara, please—"

"Stop!" I shout, my voice shattering as the tears begin to fall. I hastily brush them off my cheeks, feeling betrayed by my own body. "I don't want to hear any of it. It doesn't matter. Never in my entire life have I ever treated someone the way you treated me, no matter how angry or confused or scared I was. I *never* hurt you on purpose, but you hurt me repeatedly, knowing exactly what you were doing. Your explanations and apologies mean less than nothing to me. *Nothing!* Even if I did listen and believe you, all I can think is you'd immediately find something else to take completely wrong and come back swinging, and I won't do that to myself again.

"I already gave you a second chance. I started to trust you, and god save me, I liked you. And as ridiculous as it is, I thought you...or we...or... I don't know. That we...had something there. I *cared* about you." I choke on the last words and look down at the sidewalk, shifting my weight from foot to foot, hoping he can't see my tears hitting the concrete.

"It isn't ridiculous, Clara," he says, his voice thick and strained. "I felt—"

I hold up a hand to stop him. I pick my head up, square my shoulders, and pull in a shaky breath. I can't bear to look at his face again. There is nothing up there that will make this situation any better, so I pick a button on his tux to stare at.

"I don't want to know what you felt. I don't want to hear your apology," I say quietly, clenching my teeth together so hard it hurts. "I did what you asked. I followed through with my end. And now we're done. You're leaving tomorrow, and I'm going to do everything I can to repress every fucking second of this mess."

I won't look up, I won't look up, I won't look up…

But with zero permission from me, my eyes glance up, and I see his face locked in an expression of helplessness, with tears pooled and falling. I slam my traitor eyes shut. "Goodbye, Caspian," I say, my voice cracked and wobbly. "Good luck with everything."

I can feel a body-fracturing sob building up, so I turn and half run to the door, digging my keys out of the little clutch as I go.

I don't look back as I twist the lock.

I don't look back while I repeatedly push the elevator buttons, willing it to appear faster.

I don't look back at all.

37

After our long separation, my dream of being reunited with my cherished mattress fell mighty short in reality.

Instead of sprawling out and reveling in the gloriousness and support, I spent the night lying there, wide awake, alternating between bursts of incoherent rage and inconsolable sobbing.

Neither made me feel particularly proud.

I watched the sun rise and never managed to fall asleep, which is especially unfortunate, given the rest of my day is to be spent helping CiCi pack her apartment and start hauling things up here.

Finally, just after eight, I decide to give up on the quest for even a single Z and get up.

I open a box of clothes that's been locked in my storage unit for weeks and feel a real shot of happiness when I pull out my Wonder Woman graphic tee and a pair of well-worn and distressed jeans. There's nothing particularly special about either item, but they're *here*. In a place that's mine.

After getting dressed and ignoring that sort of hollow, musty storage unit scent that seems to have infiltrated my boxes of clothes, I head to the still-empty living room and grab my coat. In the absence of sleep, the best course of action seems to be schlepping down to the bodega across the street and buying the absolute largest coffees they sell for both CiCi and me.

I shoot her a text. Are you awake? I'm going for coffee.

A second after I hit Send, the apartment door swings open, and I yelp.

"Of course I'm up," CiCi says, strolling in carrying a tray with two giant coffees and a bag that I am hoping contains some kind of chocolate-based baked goods.

"You scared the hell out of me, lady."

CiCi plops the tray down on the counter, turns to me, and puts her hands on her hips, glaring.

"Uh. What's wrong? You're giving me your scold face."

"You didn't even let him explain? Are you freaking serious?"

I gape. "How, *how* could you possibly know about that?"

She flails her arms out wide and shouts, "Who the fuck do you think told him everything in the first place!"

"CiCi! What!?"

"Cupcake, I called in every favor I had and then some to get the invoice from TMZ showing it was the junkyard guy who sold it and not you. And you didn't even let him tell you!"

I close my eyes and shake my head. I think my synapses have ruptured. "Okay. Slow down. One, what do you mean, you got the invoice? And two, how do you even know I didn't let him explain?"

"Because he told me!"

"He wh—"

"Look, I spent the whole day playing email and phone Tetris until I managed to get ahold of someone who sent me a copy of the receipt of payment to the guy." She takes out her phone, scrolls quickly, and holds it up for me to see a picture of a piece of paper.

It's a copy of the contract for the Cranson story from TMZ, complete with the name of the person who sold it.

Chris Brunman.

"How in the *fuck*?" I gasp.

"I didn't get it until late last night, so I dug Caspian's number out of our old texts from the night I sent it to you, and texted him the picture. I didn't hear back right away, so I called him over and over until I got the bastard to pick up."

"Oh my god, *you're* who he was talking to?"

"Yes! I called that motherfucker a good ten times in a row before he answered, but he finally did, and I explained everything. He was really upset and kept apologizing and said he was going to tell you everything and promised he wasn't going to do the breaking-up-with-you thing."

My legs feel gelatinous, so I lean against the counter. "I can't believe this."

"And when I didn't hear from you, I figured you guys had been talking or doing it or something, so I didn't bother you."

"CiCi!"

"I was on my way back from grabbing the coffee and I got *this*," she says, poking at her phone again. She holds it up once more.

Thank you for all your help, CiCi. I'm sorry I made it necessary. Clara is very lucky to have a friend like you.

Not a problem! Although, next time, maybe pick up your phone sooner, ;) I hope it helped. Are you still with Clara? I was about to go see her, but if you guys are still hanging out, I can make myself scarce.

I'm on my way to the airport. Unfortunately, my actions were far too little, far too late, and I didn't get the chance to relay any of the information you sent. I don't blame her in the slightest for not wanting to hear anything I had to say. I made a terrible mess of things. But I truly appreciate everything you did. I'm very glad to have met you. Cheers.

I look from CiCi to the phone and back again.

"Why didn't you tell me!?"

She looks half past exasperated. "Because *he* was supposed to tell you! And then I would get to hear the sordid makeup details from you over packing today!" She shifts into soothing best-friend mode. "What the hell happened last night?"

I poke at the cardboard coffee tray with my finger. "We spent the whole night on edge, and I waited for him to do the thing, and then he got your call and it all shifted, but we were at the stupid party, so it's not like we could talk, you know?"

"Okay, so what about after the party?"

"I don't know!" I wail, feeling a little desperate. "We rode in, like, absolute silence all the way here, and then he asked to talk and explain and I just sort of…lost it. I shouted, I screamed, I cried, and I walked away, and that was the end of it."

"Clara, come on."

My cheeks are burning. "No! Come on, nothing! Okay, fine, so he finally realized what actually happened, but that doesn't change any of the things he did! He still tortured me for days, and he freaked the hell out of me in that hotel room! I've never seen someone so angry! This man has been responsible for the complete and total fuckification of my life since I met him! Am I just supposed to forget everything he said to me because he finally listened to you?"

"No, not at all! He had some major ass-kissing to do after all of that."

"Goddamn right, he did."

"So why didn't you give him the chance to do it!?"

I huff. "Look, I get that you want to look after me, but this is not that big a deal. So we don't end up pen pals. It's not the end of the world."

She furrows her brow at me. "I can't tell if you're being deliberately dense, or if you're just really that good at lying to yourself."

I blanch. "What the hell does that mean?"

"He has feelings for you, you dork!"

"No, he doesn't!"

"Lying it is." She shakes her head at me. "Okay, so, setting aside the kissing and the bonding and the fact that you were having googly eyes when you got his texts before the senator thing happened—tell me how he reacted when you shut him down last night."

I stare at her, mouth open a little, but I can't seem to make any words come out.

"Lay it on me, Clara. How did he react?"

"He was…fine."

"Cupcake."

I shake my head again. "He cried, okay?"

"FEELINGS."

"Hey, if someone was calling me on all my bullshit, I would cry, too! I wouldn't read anything into it."

CiCi sighs dramatically. "Look, he's probably not on his plane yet. Why don't you call him and see if he can take a later flight, so you guys can actually freaking talk."

"No way!" I cry. "Absolutely not. I'm not going to be the girl who goes racing through the airport to chase down some guy who was horrible to her. I've made an ass of myself in his presence too many times to count as it is. If someone was going to make a grand gesture and risk humiliation and rejection, it sure as shit deserves to be him." I drag the toe of my sneaker across the wood floor. "Besides, even if we had talked, and I'd swallowed the one shred of dignity I have left and forgave him, he'd still be leaving today. I'd still be here, and we wouldn't have ever seen each other again, anyway. This way, I keep that dignity sliver, and maybe the next time he gets the urge to go all Shouty McPrimadonna at someone, he'll walk it off instead."

"Clara."

"What?"

"I'm not an idiot. You think you did some great job hiding the fact that you've been head over heels for the guy, but I have eyes, and you're a shitty actress. You liked him. You *still* like him. It's okay to admit you have feelings for the guy."

I shake my head and feel tears welling up. With a shrug and a pathetic attempt at a smile, I say, "It doesn't matter either way. It's done."

CiCi reaches out and takes my hand, giving it a squeeze. "It doesn't necessarily have to be."

I sniff, take a deep breath, and give her hand a return squeeze before letting go and picking up one of the coffees she brought. "So, what's in that bag? Please tell me it's chocolate croissants."

"Clara, come on."

"Hey, man, if you still want me to help you pack up today, I'm going to need the fuel."

She opens her mouth, I assume determined to argue further, but my phone rings on the counter.

"Oh my god, is it—"

I roll my eyes and grab it to answer. "Even without looking, I can assure you it's not." I hit Answer. "Hello?"

"Is this Clara?" an unfamiliar voice asks.

"This is she," I say, stifling a yawn and reaching again for the coffee.

"Am I interrupting something?" the voice asks, a take-no-shit cadence coming through clear as day.

Oh my god. It's salt and bourbon.

"Uh, not at all, Ms. McInerney," I say, setting the coffee back down and flailing my arm wildly at CiCi. "I'm glad to be hearing from you."

"You should be," she says with what I assume, for her, is a modest chuckle. "I'm officially offering you the associate editor position on our kidlit imprint."

A thousand inappropriate things play on the tip of my tongue. Squeeing. Bursting into tears. Shrieking, "Are you fucking serious OH MY GAWD."

Instead, I calmly but enthusiastically say, "That's wonderful! Thank you!"

Nailed it.

She goes into details about the position, hours expected (long ones), a work-from-home day each week, pay, a quick overview of benefits, etc., etc. She also promises that while I will have a comfortable level of freedom over my list, she insists on working as a tight-knit group, and she thinks I'll be a quality team player.

All the while, CiCi stands in front of me, desperately trying to hear anything.

"From what I hear," Joan adds, "you've got quite a few offers on your plate, and from houses that are likely offering you more money than I am. You gotta do what's best for you, so no hard feelings if you turn me down. But I will say, I was impressed with the list you'd curated at your old house, and I think you'd fit in well here. And I can promise I will do my best to help ensure you're able to keep growing with the kind of titles you have an obvious talent for nurturing. I would look forward to the chance to build that list together. Anyway, you take the time you need to make your decision, and I hope you find a good home, even if it's not with us."

I clutch my hand to my heart so hard it starts to hurt. "Ms. McInerney, I don't need the time. Yes, a couple of the other offers might have more money attached to them, but I know I would never have the opportunity at those houses to learn the things I could learn working with you. I'm incredibly flattered you see the value in my work, and I'd be honored to join Fogler Publishing. I accept your offer."

"Good," she says, and I can hear her typing in the background. She can't be contained, this woman. "Those other houses are shit, anyway." I laugh hard. "Glad to have you on board, Clara Montgomery. I'll have Trey send over all the details, and you can look over the contract. If you have any questions, let one of us know."

"I'll do that, Ms. McInerney. Thank you."

"It's Joan," she clarifies. "Welcome to the team."

"Thank you, Joan," I say.

The line goes dead, and I stand there for a second, just staring at my phone.

"You got the job?"

"I got the job!" I squeal. "Based on my actual skills and merit and everything!"

We mutually devolve into excited shrieks and jumping up and down and hugging.

"I'm so happy for you!"

"Oh my god, now I don't have to admit to my mom that she was right about me being a big failure and go get my teaching certification and move home to Buffalo and have my uncle Jack as a boss and purposely drink myself into an early death!"

CiCi stops jumping. "Was...was that an option?"

"Not a good one," I admit, picking up my coffee again. "All right, lady. Let's get your shit packed up and let the roommate adventure begin!"

38

Two weeks later...

"**O**kay, I know why we're here," Tom says, taking the exit that leads to our parents' house. "But why would you do this to yourself, CiCi?"

"On purpose, even," I add.

She shrugs beside me in the back of Tom's rental car. "My folks are going to Italy for a romantic vacation Thanksgiving this year. Plus I'd never miss a chance to see Mama Montgomery in her natural habitat."

"Oh god," I say. "I didn't see you before you put your coat on. What shirt are you wearing?"

She grins, and I half expect canary feathers to fall out of her mouth. "It's a surprise."

We all start laughing. "The holiday is definitely looking up," Trina says.

Pulling onto my parents' street, all my customary child-like panic comes flooding back. "I hate that no matter how old I get, every time we come back here, I get this feeling of dread, like she's going to retroactively ground me for breaking curfew in high school."

"I don't know," CiCi says thoughtfully. "Maybe it won't suck as much this year."

I turn to her and glare. "You have a penis on your shirt, don't you? A giant rhinestone penis."

"If she has this car towed, you're paying the fee," Tom mutters as he slides into a spot on the crowded street. It looks like we must be some of the last to arrive.

"If it gets towed over a rhinestone penis, I'd be willing to chip in for that," Trina says.

We're all giggling like children as we gather the stuff we've brought—a host of store-bought pies and breads put into our own dishes to make it look like any of us has an iota of the skill required to make such things.

"You know she's going to be pissed we're all staying at a hotel, right?" I grumble as we make our way up the sidewalk. "We should have warned her."

"Like she wouldn't have called every hotel within a two-hour radius and canceled the reservations," Tom argues.

"And it's a great hotel!" CiCi adds as we hit the porch.

"I really wish you'd let us pay for the rooms, CiCi," I whine. "It's too expensive. I start my new job in a few weeks, so it's not like I need the charity anymore."

She reaches over and pats my head. "Trust fund, cupcake. Plus, I had points, so it was practically nothing."

Without speaking, we all take a deep breath in unison, and Tom rings the bell.

"We could just go in," CiCi says with a laugh.

Tom and I look at her like she's lost it.

Then the door opens, and there's Mom. "Hi, everyone! You're late!"

I drop my head. "Nice to see you, Mom."

She ushers us all inside, and my dad comes in to relieve us of our Thanksgiving offerings. "Hey, Dad!" I say, giving him a big hug. I haven't seen Dad in a few months, and his hair is noticeably thinner, but still the same dark brown that genetics passed on to me and Tom. We both got the hazel part of our greenzel eyes from Dad, too.

"Hi, Bug," he says, managing the hug despite the parcels. "Son!" More hugs to Tom, Trina, and CiCi.

"May I take your coats?" Mom asks, in full hostess mode.

Those of us who rode with CiCi all turn to stare at her as she unbuttons.

With a perfect smirk, she peels off her coat and reveals a low-cut black tank top with big glittering letters that say, MY IDEAL WEIGHT IS CHRIS EVANS ON TOP OF ME.

Tom, Trina, and I can't help it. We snicker as my mom purses her lips and scowls.

"So nice to see you again, Mama Montgomery," CiCi says and hands over her coat, all smiles.

Mom turns on her heel and goes to tuck the coats away. I put my arm around CiCi's shoulders and whisper, "I fucking love you so much right now."

She wraps her arm around my waist and leads me toward the living room. "Remember that feeling in three...two...one..."

I turn to her, confused. Tom and Trina are walking in front of us and stop dead in their tracks with a loud gasp, and I slam into them.

"Uh, your brake lights are out, guys."

Tom reaches around and grabs me by the arm, yanking me into the living room.

Standing by the coffee table, surrounded by my uncle Jack and aunt Susan and a dozen or so cousins, is what is obviously a hallucination.

"Hello, Clara," says Caspian Tiddleswich.

Cl-AHR-a

I blink. I blink harder.

My mouth opens and closes like a fish, the ability to form words completely lost.

I also appear to have forgotten how to breathe.

CiCi slams a hand between my shoulder blades, and I suck in air.

"What…what are you doing here?" I manage to squeak.

"I invited him, remember?" Mom says, pushing past us into the kitchen.

"I—I do, but I didn't… I mean, I never…"

"You never told him?" she says with a smile. "I know, dear. Who taught you to behave so rudely, I'll never know."

I look at CiCi desperately. "I don't understand what's happening right now. Am I dying? I feel like I'm dying."

CiCi smiles beatifically at the room, takes my hand, and says, "Excuse us. Clara and I need a minute to freshen up after the car ride."

I'm glad she keeps hold of me and pulls me along down the hall, because I have no control over my legs anymore. She shoves me into the half bath and shuts the door behind us, wisely locking it.

"What's happening?" I gasp, dropping my head down to my knees and trying to breathe.

"Remember how you said you love me?"

I whip up so fast I almost fall over. "What did you do?"

CiCi looks very pleased with herself. "Do you also remember how you said that if there was going to be a grand gesture, it should be him doing the gesturing?"

"What did you *DO*?"

"I sent him a text and asked for his email address and maybe implied it was for you and then I gave it to your mom."

"CiCi!"

"Well, I didn't want to give her his phone number. I didn't want to kill the poor guy."

"I'm going to kill *you*!"

"Totally worth it," she says with a grin. "All right, so, the facts are, he was pestered to death by your mother to come here, a few thousand miles out of his way, and he showed up. He showed up, because seeing you and talking to you is *that* important to him. Because feelings."

"You're cracked!"

"Yes, I am," she says, looking way too pleased with herself. "And I also told him Mama Montgomery changed the schedule, and it started two hours ago, which means he's been here this whole time alone with your parents, and he hasn't run away screaming."

"Okay, so *he's* cracked."

"If he wasn't before, he is now." She nods. "But put all that together, and this is the picture of a man who really, really wants to try to make things up to you. Now, if you hear what he has to say and you still want to tell him to fuck off, then I support you 100 percent, and we will spend the rest of our days having a good laugh over the well-earned payback he's currently suffering through.

"But if you can manage not to kill him, and realize that possibly a big motivator for you refusing to hear him out at all was because you didn't want to admit to having the gooey feelings for him and getting your heart broken when he left town—well, I'd say the fact that he's willing to put up with your mother and come all of this way just to see you is a pretty solid indicator he's not going to fly off into the sunset unless you want him to."

"Oh my god," I hiss, "I feel like you should be twirling a spindly little mustache or something."

"Definitely. But you've been miserable since he left, cupcake. Like, peel-off-the-floor sad. And I know you think you're doing a bang-up job of hiding that, but like I said before, you're a shitty actress. You dig him, he digs you, and if you're too stubborn to do something to mutually express the digging, or at the very least get some closure from the situation, then it's my job as your best friend to do what needs doing." She reaches out and opens the bathroom door. "Oh, and he's staying at our hotel, which is why I picked it. So, good luck, and remember you loved me three minutes ago!"

"CiCi!" I shriek after her, but she's already gone.

I wonder if I stayed locked in here for the rest of the day, would anyone notice?

Who am I kidding? I figure I have maybe sixty seconds until my mom takes a nail file to the doorknob.

All right. Okay. This is all fine. I've got all of dinner to get through before I have to decide what I'm going to do. I put my hands on the sink for support and take in as many deep breaths as I can while mentally counting down.

There's a knock on the door. Son of a bitch, Mom.

"Clara, we have company."

I look up at myself in the mirror and make an annoyed, incredulous face. I call out, "Yes, Mom, I am aware. I am part of that company."

"Well, if you're aware, it makes it all the more disrespectful for you to stay hidden in there, doesn't it?"

I need to get really drunk, really fast.

I sigh and head back out. Mom is still standing by the bathroom door, arms crossed. "I'm here, I'm going, god," I mutter and walk past her.

Back in the living room, I still have trouble comprehending what I'm seeing. Caspian stands out like he's actively on fire. He looks so shiny and out of place.

Huh. Maybe he does have the full Anthony Hopkins sheen after all.

He's staring directly at me, I assume waiting for some acknowledgment of his presence that isn't hyperventilating.

I raise my eyebrows and give him a small smile while stiffly swinging my arms at my sides.

"Excuse me, please," he says to the gaggle of my family surrounding him, and carefully extricates himself to walk over to me. "Hello."

"Uh. Hi."

Smooth.

I feel horribly on display. Everyone is gawking at the pair of us, and I want to crawl out of my skin.

He leans in slightly and whispers, "I know this is unfair, and I'm sorry. If you want me to go, I'll tell everyone something came up and leave immediately. I just… I needed to see you."

I nervously slide my foot over the carpet. "You really must have, to come here willingly. I only showed up because Mom would have sent a strike team to get me if I hadn't." I look up at him, and he's got a half smile going. "Have you really been here for two hours already?"

Caspian nods. "I really have. Credit where credit's due to CiCi for that one."

"Crafty little minx, she is."

"Indeed." He looks nervous, and in a way that has nothing to do with being surrounded by the bulk of my immediate and extended family. "Do you want me to leave? No hard feelings whatsoever if you do."

I press my lips together and try to look very interested in the ancient painting of peonies in a vase hanging on the wall beside us. "I guess it's okay if you stay."

"You're sure?"

I look up again and feel a bit annoyed at the flip in my stomach. "I'm sure. But you realize, the tables have kind of turned here."

He seems confused. "How so?"

"Now you have to pretend to be the boyfriend. And this isn't for some gross gossip magazine. This is for my family. You'd better sell that shit."

He tries to hide it, but he chuckles. "I'll do my best."

"Oh, it's going to take more than that. My mom is like a dog that can smell fear, but put her in a room with the rest of her family, and you've got a wolf-pack situation on your hands."

"I see," he says, still smiling. "Same parameters?"

"Ahh, the hand-holding and whatnot," I say with mock seriousness. I try to weigh the potential damage I'll do to myself if I spend the night back in this place with him versus having my mom shout across the table demanding to know why we aren't holding hands over the cranberry sauce, and decide I can take the personal hit if it's coming. "Yeah, sure. Same parameters."

He tries to keep his tone light, but his eyes look a little pained when he softly asks, "Would you punch me?"

My stomach flips again, and I am so not ready to have this

conversation while standing by watercolor peonies in front of my entire family. "I don't know yet, but Mama Montgomery definitely would."

I take him by the hand and lead him into the fray, and he quietly says, "Duly noted."

39

"What do you mean, you're staying at a hotel!?" Mom shrieks, making the entire room of twenty-five people jump. "All of you?"

"CiCi had points!" I point at her with mock accusation.

Mom glares a glare that makes Caspian's iciest gaze look pathetic.

Caspian manages to extricate himself from the horde demanding to know whether they'll see him again at Tom and Trina's wedding and comes over with his coat already on. "I'm afraid that's my fault, Mrs. Montgomery," he says, helping me into my own coat. "I don't get to see much of Clara right now while I'm promoting my new film, so I booked the rooms to give us some more time together."

"Well, what about you two?" Mom says, turning to Tom and Trina with maternal guilt locked and loaded.

Tom has gone full deer-in-headlights and mutters, "Uh…"

Rolling my eyes, I say, "Maybe it's because they're engaged and living together, and you still make them sleep in separate rooms, Mom."

She looks positively scandalized. "Well, they aren't married *yet*!"

"Again, my apologies," Caspian intercedes, shaking his head. "That's on me, too. Did I forget to mention they've joined the cult as well?"

Mom has fully devolved into a scowl. Tom, Trina, CiCi, and I all submit to giggles that can't be contained. Even Dad is chortling off to the side.

"You think that's so funny?" Mom snaps.

"Oh, it's quite serious," Caspian says, without even a hint of a smile in his voice. I am absolutely dying from internal laughter and doing a poor job of hiding it. "The hotel just made more sense, what with our communal head-shaving ceremony happening at dawn."

She turns her outrage on me. "I don't know what you see in this man."

Shrugging and trying to keep a straight face, I reply, "He doesn't make the rules. The alien overlords do. Sorry, Mom."

Dad comes over and gives us all hugs. Poor guy is looking slightly worse for the wear after the events of the day. Or maybe it was the three scotches. Either/or.

Before Mom can fully reach an apoplectic state, we all shout goodbyes to everyone and start pushing our way out the door. We hit the sidewalk at a run before the guffawing begins.

Caspian's car is already waiting at the curb. Tom, still laughing, comes over and shakes Caspian's hand as the driver climbs out. "It was great to see you again, man. How much would I have to pay to get you to come to all of these things? Anyone who can make my mom fume that hard is always welcome."

"I appreciate that," Caspian says fondly. "Although I confess I might have too much fun with it."

"No such thing," Tom says, clapping him on the shoulder.

"I really do hope we'll see you at the wedding," Trina says, and shakes his hand as well. "Clara looks fantastic in her dress. It's not to be missed."

I give her a pointed look, but realize it's probably falling short in the dark of night.

CiCi, ever the diplomat, walks up to Caspian, pokes him in the chest, and says, "Make it count, fella." Before he can respond, and before I can open my mouth to say literally anything, CiCi pushes me toward his car and calls out, "I'll bring your stuff up to the room, and I'll be asleep within minutes, so no need to hurry back on my account, byeeeeeee!"

"I don't have a key to our room!" I bark. "Wait—I don't even know what room we're *in*! CiCi!"

As I watch my people head to the rental car, I scowl in their direction. Caspian's driver stands calmly to the side, waiting for our cue to open the door.

Finally, Caspian offers, "I swear I didn't know she was going to do that."

I sigh and shake my head. "I believe you. CiCi is definitely not known for her subtlety."

"If you're uncomfortable, I can easily call myself another car and you can take this one."

I exhale loudly. "That's ridiculous. I can handle riding in a car with you, Caspian. It's not like I hate you that much."

"So you do hate me to some degree?"

"What, like just right now, or...?"

"To start, I suppose."

I look awkwardly around. "Could we maybe not have this conversation on the sidewalk in front of my parents' house? There's no way my mom isn't spying through a window with some kind of sophisticated long-range listening device. And it's about three degrees out, which makes it hard to focus. Plus, if the driver freezes to death, that complicates our travel arrangements."

I've got him by siege of manners. "Oh, yes, Logan, my apologies," he says, preparing to reach for the door himself, but stepping aside when Logan beats him to it.

I don't know where these drivers get trained, but they anticipate needs like nobody's business. I climb into the back seat first, immediately soothed by the blissful, sauna-like temperature. It's like settling into a hug.

Caspian follows, and soon the door is closed and we're pulling away from my parents' house.

I've never felt more twitchy in my life. And let's face it, the bar is set pretty high on that one.

I turn in my seat to face him. "So. Care to elaborate on... well, any of this?"

His eyes seem to involuntarily dart to the driver. "If it's all right with you, I'd rather discuss things at the hotel."

I suddenly feel silly for even asking for clarification right now. If I've learned anything about Caspian over the last month, it's that he values his personal privacy above just about anything else. And the idea of me potentially verbal whaling on him in the presence of Logan is probably making Caspian break out in hives.

A residually bitter part of me wants to punish him further and say, "Actually, it's not all right with me. We're having this out now, witness be damned," just to see him squirm. But a bigger part of me is disgusted to even have that level of desire for revenge burning through me.

He's sort of half looking at me, with his eyes going back and forth between my face and his feet. The part of me that wants to delight in his discomfort is squashed down by the part of me that wants to make him feel at ease.

This constant shifting between polar opposite emotions is making me dizzy.

"I learned a lot about you tonight," I say, by way of desperately hoping to break the silence. "Like this is your first visit to Buffalo, you hate corn but love corn bread, and you have a genuine skill for politely navigating seven thousand simultaneous questions being hurled at you by people you don't know."

He chuckles. "Years of red carpets and press junkets finally come to good use. Although, I will say, a line of reporters is ever so slightly less intimidating than your family."

I've got to give him that one. "Touché."

"I heard you discussing a new job at the table," he says. "I believe congratulations are in order."

I feel oddly embarrassed for reasons I can't explain. "Uh, thank you."

"I apologize for not saying anything when you brought it up, but under the guise of being a couple, I figured that would be something I'd already know, and I didn't want to give anything away."

I can feel myself starting to blush a little and try to shrug it off. "In all fairness, you played the part of supportive significant other very well in the moment."

Now it's his turn to look twitchy. He starts smoothing out his pants at the knee, even though they're perfectly straight already. "Well, I'm proud of you," he says, straightening up and looking strangely formal. "Sorry, that wasn't meant in a condescending way. I just know how very hard you worked to get the position, and I'm happy that it all worked out."

He's absolutely radiating discomfort, and instinct takes over me. I reach out and give his hand a squeeze. "I knew what you meant. And thank you."

Before he can react to my unexpected touch, I yank my hand back and start fidgeting with one of my rings.

The rest of the ride is the same kind of cordial conversation. I ask how his film is doing, and he explains how exhausting the promo tour is. He asks how the move to the new apartment went, and I go into exhaustingly specific detail about the experience, hoping to draw it out long enough to finish the car ride.

Eventually, we make it to the hotel, and I exhale with relief. I'm amazed by how much tension can be crammed into one tiny car.

It's all uncomfortable silence as we make our way into the hotel. There's a pretty huge difference here from the giant, elegant, penthouse-having behemoth I'm used to visiting him at while in NYC. Although, the Curtiss Hotel is pretty spectacular in its own right. It's lit up beautifully on the outside, glowing a gorgeous blue against the night sky.

He must've checked in before heading to my parents' place, because he has no bags to lug and heads right to the elevator as soon as we walk in.

God, the atmosphere between us is so painfully stiff and ceremonial. Every move is like a choreographed dance of what people are supposed to do. The elevator ride to the top floor has the same interminable, suffocating vibe we had in the car, and I am half past done with being trapped in enclosed spaces with this kind of air around us. As soon as the doors open, I practically leap out.

Nothing is being said whatsoever, which makes this all so much worse. He leads the way down the hall, and I follow a step behind, noticing he's attempting to be polite and walk with me, rather than leave me trailing after him like a little duck. Truthfully, I'd prefer to be quacking along in my own space at the moment.

We reach his room, and I almost collapse with relief.

I'm ready to get this over with.

Caspian deftly swipes his keycard, and in we go.

It's a gorgeous room. He's got a large suite, because of course he does, and it's all modern furniture with a comfortable feel to it. Squishy-looking couches and chairs, a neutral but inviting color scheme, and a hell of a view. As I walk inside, I casually notice a suitcase and garment bags neatly tucked away in the closet.

I'm not really sure where to go or what to do, so I just stand like a perplexed statue over by the coffee table. Words do not exist to describe the discomfort I'm feeling.

"May I take your coat?" he asks as he hangs up his own. I stare at him for a beat before quickly tearing mine off and handing it to him. "Please, have a seat."

At least he seems to be in an equal state of unease.

I scurry over to the couch and ungracefully plop myself down on the cushions as fast as I can.

"Can I offer you a drink?" he says, placing his keycard and wallet down on the table by the closet.

Determined to break the tension, even by a little, I ask, "Do you think this will go easier for you if you get me drunk first?"

"I think I'm less likely to get kicked in the shins if you're drunk."

I shrug. "At the very least, my aim would be less accurate,

so maybe you're onto something." I shuffle my feet over the carpet. "Uh, I guess I'll take some wine, if you've got it?"

He walks over to the mini-fridge by the giant TV and opens it. "We do have wine. Red? White? Sparkling?"

"I'll take something fizzy," I reply.

"Can do," he says, grabbing a bottle for me and a tiny scotch for himself. "Glass or bottle?"

"Erm, bottle," I say. "I kind of love the shrunken wine bottles. As short as I am, the tiny bottle makes me feel like I'm not from Munchkinland. Plus, it gives me that kind of whimsical feeling from college, where we all thought we were the tits drinking Boone's Farm straight from the tap."

He laughs a very genuine laugh. "I can't say I'm familiar with Boone's Farm, but I definitely relate to the bottle memory. I drank many a mate under the table during my one year at university in that manner."

He hands me the mini-wine, and I crack it open. "Just a year?"

"I very stupidly dropped out," he says, pouring his scotch into a glass tumbler, "before moving to the States to make it on my own. Which, as we both know, didn't quite work in my favor for some time."

"Oh, right," I say rather pathetically. I resume shuffling my feet across the plush carpet and take a long drink. He's not wrong; this occasion absolutely mandates a need for alcohol.

"So, on a scale of Gertrude to Jasmine, how's the couch rate?"

I smile and look down. "I'd say solidly in the middle. But then, what couch could ever hold a candle to Jasmine?"

"What couch, indeed," Caspian says with a soft chuckle.

He takes his scotch and walks across the room to the chair adjacent to where I'm sitting. There's more than enough room on the couch to sit beside me, but I get the sense that he is purposely trying to give me as much space as possible. Whether this is for my comfort or out of fear for his own physical safety is unclear.

We sip in silence for a few moments, deliberately avoiding eye contact. To an outside observer, we look like a pair who really enjoys studying the minutiae of carpet fibers. The entire scene is night and day from the memories I have of him in his charcoal-gray throne in Tom's living room. There's no bravado, no essence of a master plan, no role being played.

I'm seeing Caspian again. The real-life Caspian.

I don't know why I'm finding it so unsettling. Maybe it's because I've been missing that Caspian.

I shut my eyes hard until I'm able to cram that thought into the securely roped-off part of my brain that feels any sort of fondness for him.

Sip. Shuffle. Repeat.

After an age and a half, he sighs and says, "I suppose I'd best get on with it, then."

I sit up a little straighter and internally brace myself for emotional impact.

"What's on your mind, Cas...pian?" I groan inwardly. I'm not handling this well.

He throws back the rest of his scotch and sets the now-empty glass on the coffee table. He takes a deep breath, and I don't think I'm hallucinating how shaky it sounds. "I messed up," he begins. "I messed it all up. A horrible, unforgivable, preventable series of cock-ups. I don't blame you in the slightest for not wanting to hear a word from me that last night. If anything, I'm surprised you didn't actually slap me, which I would have had coming and then some."

"I mean, I'd be lying if I said I didn't fight the urge a couple of times," I offer, trying to defuse the horrific tension and failing miserably.

"I don't know how much CiCi told you about our conversation," he says, "but she made me realize that thanks to you pulling my information out of the Cranson unit, it wasn't there to be found with that senator's. The biggest irony of all is that you ended up saving me by doing it. And if I'd never gotten that voice mail from you, and never met you... When the news broke about him, I would have been so sure I'd be outed next that I likely would have confessed publicly to try and get ahead of the narrative."

He heaves a great sigh. "You spared me in every possible way, and I did nothing but punish you for it."

I shift uncomfortably on the couch. "Okay, you're not wrong about the punishment, but I can't really take credit for any of what happened. It wasn't some great, calculated humanitarian thing I did. It was a failed attempt at altruism that just happened to work out."

"I suppose. Still, I'm grateful for it." Caspian leans forward, placing his elbows on his knees and clasping his hands. "I almost stayed, you know. I had my phone in my hand to cancel my flight, and I was going to stay and try to do whatever it took to beg for your forgiveness." He shakes his head at the memory. "But I knew how unfair that would be to you. And moreover, I realized I didn't deserve that forgiveness, even if I did manage to convince you otherwise. So, instead of calling the airline, I sent that message to CiCi, and accepted that was the end of it. That my punishment would be living with the memories of every horrible thing I'd done, every single expression of pain I'd watched play across your face as a direct result of my behavior. I spent the entire flight home playing those moments in my head over and over, and I honestly hoped they'd haunt me forever."

I open my mouth to say I have no clue what, but he keeps going. "And that's exactly what happened. The whole ordeal kept playing on a loop in my mind from the instant I left that sidewalk. Through every interview for the film tour, every meeting, every second. Several reporters even brought you up and asked how things were going, and each time, it was like a punch to the stomach, and I almost savored that pain because it felt like nothing less than I deserved.

"I stuck with my standard line of keeping my private life separate, so I didn't have to publicly share my shame, like a coward. But every time your name was brought up, it hurt. It *physically* hurt. I got scolded repeatedly by my team for being so solemn in those interviews. I'm normally fairly at ease, and can manage professional banter, or at least embarrassing moments mixed with the impression that I'm not always a complete buffoon. But no matter how much effort I gave it, I couldn't be that person. Or maybe I wouldn't be that person. I don't really know.

"The last thing I would think of before I fell asleep was one of the hundreds of moments I'd caused you pain. And the first thing in my mind when I woke up was your face in those scenarios.

"And I tried to ignore this next bit, Clara. I swear I did. I felt it creeping up over and over long before that night with the senator and the night of the premiere. I pushed it away and pretended that it didn't exist. But no matter how hard I hid from it, I finally admitted to myself that long before I began using the memory of you to punish myself, you were still the last thing I was thinking of before I fell asleep, and the first thing I saw in my mind when I woke."

My entire body has gone rigid, and I realize I've stopped breathing. I try to gasp in a breath, but only manage what amounts to a weak, inhaled breeze.

"I wasn't supposed to do it," he says desperately. "It wasn't supposed to happen. It's the absolute opposite of what I intended when all this started. But despite my best efforts, I completely fell for you, Clara."

Okay. Now I gasp. Not enough to get actual air into my lungs, but enough that it's *loud*.

"Everything I did was wrong. From start to finish," he carries on. "From swooping into your life playing a damned character to try and intimidate you into silence, to believing any of the nonsense things I did were justified, when it was clear from the moment we first met that you were being genuine.

"And worst of all, that night in the hotel." Caspian's voice breaks. "I will *never* forgive myself for my actions. For the vicious things I said. None of what I'm about to say excuses what I've done, but I feel like if this is my final chance to speak with you, I want to lay it all out as best I can."

His eyes have filled to the brim with tears, and as I fight to maintain my own composure—a battle which I can feel myself losing—I randomly wonder if he can even see clearly at this point.

"I was so ashamed, Clara. Of my history with Cranson, of you knowing about it, of my behavior toward you. And then to feel like I'd finally, after years of childishly hiding so much of myself, and letting that side out to you, only to think I'd been conned. I think I knew, even as I threw that disgusting tantrum, that you hadn't done any of it, but I was so sure I hadn't deserved the good you'd brought into my world, that it had to have been a trick. I was ashamed I'd been so foolish, and ashamed of the way I felt for you when I had no right to feel anything of the sort.

"And I was afraid. Afraid that maybe it *was* all a game that I'd lost. Afraid that it wasn't, and I'd already taken things light-years away from a place where you could consider forgiving me. I took all of that—all of the angst and contempt I had for myself—and refused to hear you that night. I was clouded by all of my own bullshit, and I unleashed every bit of that panic and fear and self-loathing directly onto you. And even as I heard myself doing it, I was screaming at myself inside my head to stop."

The tears are falling freely now, but he pays them no mind that I can see, and soldiers on. I've seen Caspian open up before, but I've never seen him this vulnerable.

I'm not sure I've ever seen *anyone* this vulnerable.

My instinct to comfort him is so strong, I grip the couch cushions to keep from involuntarily leaping up and running to him.

"After I made you leave, I sat there, replaying it over and over, and maybe it was pride, or maybe I was just scared of admitting what I'd done, and what I knew I'd lost, but I wouldn't acknowledge any of it. I doubled down, lying to myself as hard as I possibly could, and ran with it."

I no longer possess the physical ability to breathe or speak or form solid thoughts.

"I didn't want to be wrong, and I didn't want to be right. I just clung to the course of action I'd picked, and I was hell-bent on following through and ignoring anything in myself that was trying to show reason. When I was walking toward you at the premiere, I thought I was going to be sick. And when I got to you, I felt so broken, and I wanted to make it all stop and find something to say to take us back to a place where we could just talk things through, but I already knew it'd gone too far for that. Even now, I can't tell if I would have actually gone through with it, but I'm such a stubborn ass, I worry I might have.

"And when I got the call from CiCi, my first reaction was pure joy at learning I'd been an utter fool. That all the things I'd felt for you and the trust I'd put in you had been right. And the next second, I was overtaken by the thought that it didn't matter. That no matter what I said or did, it would never erase what I'd done. I spent the rest of the night carrying on calmly at the party, but the entire time I was inside my head, in a full spiral, trying to think of something, *anything*, I could say that would undo the colossal fuckup I'd caused."

I'm staring. It's all I can do. My chest hurts. The back of my throat is burning. My fingers are in actual pain from digging into the couch cushions so hard.

But I'm afraid to let go. Because if I let go, I don't know if I can control what my body does next.

"But of course there was nothing. I stalled as long as I could, thinking that if I just had a few more moments, it would come to me, but there was nothing to come. The damage was irreparable, and I knew that. I *still* know that."

Caspian runs his hands through his hair. "When I got that message from your mother about Thanksgiving, I honestly didn't know what to do or how to respond. At first I planned to just ignore it and leave you be. But she messaged again and again, angry with me for both my lack of messaging etiquette, and for being the cause of whatever had you sounding so very sad since I'd left. I think she thought you were just missing the man she thought was your significant other, and was pissed I wasn't jumping at her offer to come see you sooner. I didn't know how to explain anything to her, so I didn't.

"But the more I thought about it, the more I realized that meant you hadn't told her I was gone for good. And I hate to admit that it gave me a glimmer of hope. I couldn't shake it, and I definitely couldn't shake your mother. My god, can she lay on the emotional warfare." A look of grudging admiration crosses his face. "I finally broke down and sent a text to CiCi asking for her perspective, and she laid into me even harder. All of which I had coming."

My jaw falls straight to the floor, and a hollow place in my mind starts plotting out the various ways I'm going to murder CiCi and my mother.

Caspian looks up at me, real desperation in his eyes. "I expect nothing from you. You owe me nothing. But I owe you everything, and I couldn't bear the thought of you continuing to suffer after everything I'd done. And I knew I probably wouldn't have the chance again, so here I am. Selfishly trying to clear a sliver of my conscience. Knowing that you'll always carry those things with you, and no matter how many times I apologize, I can't wipe them away, but I'm promising to try anyway. Hoping that maybe a small part of you finds relief in knowing that I will never stop hating myself for what I did to you. And if you can think of literally anything I can do to ease any of the pain I've caused you, I will do it a thousand times over.

"I'm sorry, Clara. I'm so very, impossibly sorry. You never deserved a moment of the time you were forced to spend with me. Saying I'm sorry feels like the most useless and lackluster thing I could present to you, but, regrettably, it's all I have to offer."

Caspian finally sits back in his chair, quickly wiping away the tears on his face, and clears his throat. "I apologize for the endless monologue. Thank you for listening."

There are no words. Words as a concept no longer exist in this piece of space and time. I don't know what I expected to come out of Caspian in this room, but it sure as shit wasn't a single syllable of that. I keep trying to replay it in my head, but every sentence is sounding off over another, and it's all ringing out as gibberish.

I feel tingly all over and compressed and combustible. One errant spark, and I'll ignite, taking out a full city block.

Tick.

I fly up off the couch without meaning to and start pacing beside the coffee table.

Tick.

Seemingly out of instinct, Caspian rises from his chair as well.

Tick.

Watching his movement is the spark. I can sincerely feel myself become totally unhinged.

BOOM.

"What the *hell* was that?"

He looks startled. "I beg your pardon?"

"You standing up just now?" I shriek, flailing my arms wildly. "That's not how you stand up! You always do that superfast, otherworldly fluid thing that looks like CGI, so what the fresh hell did you just do?"

"I…" He looks down at himself, as if the answer might lie there. "I was trying not to do the thing you said was physically imposing. I never realized I did it until you told me, and I've been trying to be more aware of it."

"Excuse me?"

He's still looking from me to himself and back again with blatant confusion. "Trust me when I say that while I know all the evidence I've given you is to the contrary, I don't particularly want to be a monster. I saw so many things about myself through your eyes, and I don't want to keep making those mistakes."

Caspian lifts his arms slightly, drops them, and lifts them again, like if he can just gesture properly, this'll all somehow make sense to him. He looks like a bird that's just realized it has wings. If I weren't spiraling into a rage blackout, it would be endearing, which just makes me all the angrier that he's even allowed to be endearing.

"However," he continues cautiously, "of all the things I've said and done today, I can safely say I never considered standing up to be the thing that infuriated you."

I throw up my hands in complete frustration. "Shows what you know, doesn't it?"

"I suppose it does." He looks alarmed, and rightfully so.

I'm off in my own realm of emotional overload, and I barely hear him. "Okay, let's compare the standing thing to some of the other gems you've dropped, shall we?" I start pacing again. "How about the fact that you felt compelled to tell me any of this in the first place? Or that you knew straight away what a huge mistake you'd made freaking out at the hotel and you just. Kept. Doing it. Or how about the fact that you found out what really happened, and you still kept me at that party for hours while you tried to think of a way out of the mess you'd created?"

Caspian drops his head and pushes his hands into his pants pockets. I swear I see a tear fall onto the carpet. "*Or*," I'm yelling now, "let's talk about you thinking you have any right whatsoever to casually slide the fact that you had feelings for me into that fucking trilogy's worth of information? Exactly what is wrong with you that you felt entitled enough to drop that on me?"

"Have," he says, lifting his head again. I was right. There are tears.

"What?"

"Not *had* feelings. I *have* feelings." As the words leave his mouth, he immediately starts fervently shaking his head. "Which I now realize is the absolute wrong thing to say at this moment. Christ."

"Are you kidding me right now!?" I've become so shrill, there's a real risk of the windows shattering. "Why would you tell me that? What in the hell can I possibly say in response to that, Caspian!?"

He looks up, sincere and desperate. "Nothing, Clara. You don't have to say anything. That was immeasurably selfish of me. All of this is." For the first time since I met him, Caspian seems to shrink right before my eyes. "I am so truly sorry. Whatever you need to do, please do it. Keep screaming at me. Throw something. If you want to try that kick, I won't move. If you decide to tell me to go fuck myself and walk out of here, I promise I won't follow you. I won't bother you ever again. You'll never have to hear another word from me. I swear to you."

I don't know what to do. How to respond. I can feel tears working their way up, and I start silently chanting to myself that they're tears of rage, nothing else. They have to be rage. I need them to be rage.

But no matter how many times I repeat the wishful lie, it doesn't become the truth.

I walk toward him, and I honestly think he believes I've come in for the kick, because he keeps his eyes on the floor and his hands in his pockets.

My next move is all one dance-like motion. I make my

way up right in front of him, put one hand on his chest, the other on the back of his neck, and I kiss him.

It's a coin toss as to which of us is more stunned by the action, but here it is. I finally find my lungs and pull in a long, deep breath, savoring the shouldn't-be-but-absolutely-is familiar scent of his shower gel, and I kiss him again.

By now, at least a smidge of the shock has worn off, and after he stumbles back a step, his hands are out of his pockets and coming up to rest on my waist.

The time for speeches and debating and analyzing has ended.

I tangle both my hands in his hair as he moves his to my face, kissing me with all the urgency of a drowning man who's finally managed to break the surface of the water. But no matter how tightly I pull him against me, it doesn't feel close enough. For a moment, I worry I'm taking things too far, that I've become so captivated by it all that I'm crossing every available line, but he matches me beat for beat, touch for touch, movement for movement, and I commit to letting us both be carried away, wholeheartedly.

This may be madness, but it's my madness, and I welcome it.

40

I wake up to the sound of my phone buzzing against wood. There's so much about the room around me that doesn't make sense, it takes me a few seconds to piece together what's happened.

I'm not on Gertrude. I don't live at Tom's anymore. I'm not on Tessa, my freshly monikered mattress. I'm not at my and CiCi's apartment.

I'm in a hotel room.

I am not wearing…anything. And there's a deliciously shower gel–scented arm attached to a man who was recently named one of the Sexiest Men Alive by *People* magazine draped over my back.

With the sun scorching my retinas, I fumble for the phone on the nightstand and try to will vision back into my eyes.

I have eleven missed calls from CiCi and seventeen unread text messages. The most recent reads: I am giving you exactly five minutes to respond to this before I kick down Caspian's door while simultaneously filing a missing persons report, because neither of you are replying and I'm solidly freaked out.

I blink slowly at the screen and fire off a quick reply. Stand down. I'm alive and well, and I'm upstairs. Will report back all developments when I fully regain consciousness later.

Wait. Are you…are you with Caspian right now?

Yes.

Were you with Caspian all NIGHT????????

Yes.

I swear to every god I just heard a screeching sound from somewhere in this hotel.

I send: Shut up. You'll wake the entire city.

DON'T CARE omg you have to tell me everything everything EVERY LITTLE THING

Done. Now shh and go back to sleep, nerd.

GO GET EM CUPCAKE

"Everything all right?" a sleepy English voice asks beside me.

"Just CiCi being her overprotective self," I say with a yawn. "By the way, I apologize in advance if you ended up with the same number of missed calls and texts as I did."

Without moving his arm, I feel him reach over and grab his

own phone. Still on my stomach, I turn my head on my pillow to face him. He curls up on his side and starts scrolling.

"I have to say, I'm impressed by how quickly she jumped from concern for us both to threatening my life. Bonus points for creativity, though. How exactly would one dismember someone whilst they are already submerged in acid, I wonder?"

"Oh my god." I groan and laugh into the pillow. "That's a classy message right there."

"Did you happen to talk her down from actual murder, or should I be climbing out the window carrying my trousers?"

I giggle way too hard at the imagery. "You're good. I know she's excited, because by the end, she'd stopped using punctuation and her caps lock key seemed to be stuck."

"That's an interesting litmus." He drops his phone on the bed behind him. "I admire her dedication to being a good friend."

"She is that," I agree. "Although she's going to be downright insufferable after this. I may have to hide in here forever if I'm going to escape her gloating."

He kisses my shoulder. "I can live with that."

I'm feeling a little swoony. "Not to look a naked gift horse in the mouth or anything," I say sleepily, "but somehow I think your team would take issue with you abandoning real life to live in a hotel room." A thought occurs to me. "Actually, how is it you're even here right now? Aren't you in the middle of a press tour?"

Caspian yawns. "Technically, I'm at the end of one, and for the first time in a decade, I asked to have my schedule cleared until Monday."

I prop myself up on my elbows. "Monday? Were you that confident I was going to accept your apology, or…?"

He looks shocked. "God, no. I genuinely assumed you'd

throw something at my head or punch me in the face, and honestly, I figured I'd need a few days after to come to terms with it all. Process the situation." He pulls me slightly closer. "And to give myself time for the swelling to go down before I had to be on camera again, of course."

"Of course."

He gazes at me, radiating sincerity. "I was very serious about everything I said last night," he says. "I never expected anything from you. I never anticipated you'd speak to me again, let alone—" he grins a little "—this particular development."

"Vegas bookies would have given some tremendous odds on this one." I ponder those odds. "If you'd asked me yesterday morning where my bet would have fallen, I would have lost a lot of money last night, is all I'm saying."

I roll onto my back and wriggle into a little nook next to him. I am very, very comfortable.

"Clara," he says, and the corner of my mouth pulls up at the way he says it. "Can I ask you something?"

"Sure."

"What are your thoughts on seeing me again after our time in this room comes to a close?"

I frown. "Wow. Way to bring the mood to a crashing halt there, sir."

"I apologize," he says, leaning his head back onto his pillow. "I was just hoping to get an idea of where you're at, I suppose. I wanted to manage my expectations accordingly. Knowing you're thinking of this as a onetime event is—"

"Okay, I didn't say that?" I say, a little too sharply. "Also, you get oddly formal when you start to close up about things. Do you realize that?"

He smiles. "I do, don't I?"

"And I didn't say I wanted anything to be a onetime whatever, but, Caspian, come on. What else is there? Realistically, you can't keep dumping your schedule to show up at my family functions."

He tilts his head until he's looking at me again. "That's not necessarily what I meant."

"What, then?"

"That, should you be so inclined, we could make a point to see each other again."

"Overly formal."

"Sorry," he laughs. "I'm asking if you'd be willing to... spend time with me. In an official capacity of some sort."

"How would that even be possible? We don't even live in the same country. We'd never see each other."

"Long distance isn't that terrible, and I'm in New York all the time. And you could come visit. I'd like that very much, actually. And I know Devon already has at least a month's worth of sightseeing lined up for you."

"Okay, I know I'm technically employed again," I say, "but I'm not rich, dude. I can't afford to jet across the Atlantic at whim."

"Clara, I have approximately seven billion frequent-flier miles that I never get to use because I'm always being flown for work. I'd be delighted to put them to such a worthy endeavor." He smiles again. "Assuming that's a thing you'd be interested in doing." His smile rapidly devolves into a frown. "I realize as I'm saying all this that springing an intentions conversation on you while trapped in bed naked is maybe not the fairest way I could have approached this."

I shrug. "I don't know. I think it's a good way to be sure you're getting an honest answer from someone, at the very least. No armor, nowhere to hide."

He looks pleased. "I like the positive spin."

I stare up at the ceiling and ponder. While it's debatably been a hoot and a half to spend the last few weeks in total denial about my feelings for Caspian, both for and against, the idea of…what, dating him? That seems surreal, and after everything, my barometer for the odd is wildly skewed compared to most.

"What's going through your mind right now?" he asks. "You look very deep in thought."

I turn on my side to face him, and he mirrors the action. "Are you…? Do you feel guilty, or something?"

"I hope I always feel guilty for what happened," he says quickly. "But what do you mean, exactly?"

I sigh. "I'm trying to think of a way to say this that doesn't sound self-deprecating, or like I'm fishing for a compliment, but while I get what made you roll with the fake-girlfriend angle before, I'm falling back to my original thoughts on the subject. You're a super good-looking, famous actor with a voice that's essentially audible sex. You don't strike me as the type who would need to go to such great lengths to date. Or get laid. Or whatever it is you're suggesting. I just wonder if your guilt is motivating you into thinking you need to do this to make amends or something."

"I have so many issues with so many of the things you just said."

"I'm serious, Caspian."

His brow furrows hard. "For starters, I would never even imply I was suggesting we spend time together just so I can get *laid*. I'm a tad offended. Secondly, you seem to think I'm looking to just date *someone*. I'm not. I want to date *you*."

"Why?" The word falls out of my mouth before it's properly formed in my brain. "Oh my god, that's the most irritating thing I've ever said. But still, I guess it just doesn't make sense to me."

"The fact that you even asked it shows you can't see what I see, Clara."

"I swear I wasn't fishing for an ego boost. Ugh, I'm not explaining myself well," I say with a groan. I take a deep breath. "I guess I'm trying to tell you that if you think you have to fly over three thousand miles again and again or shuttle me the same way out of guilt, there's no need. I just did the whole relationship-for-fake-slash-wrong-reasons thing, and I wouldn't want to get into a situation like that again because you feel like you owe me periodic atonements or something."

He props himself up on an elbow and looks down at me. "Do you realize how absurd this is? You're trying to let me off a hook I don't want to be let off, and I'm trying to delicately beg you to not walk away from the idea of us being an actual *us*."

I stare at him for a really, really long time, breathing slowly. "I think we might need to work on our communication skills."

"I think I have a long way to go before I've earned your trust in the things I say."

I chuckle a little. "So, you're serious? You want to…what? Do the whole dating, boyfriend-girlfriend thing, but for real this time?"

"If you'll have me, yes," he says fervently. "That's exactly what I'm saying." He brings his hand to my neck and starts running his thumb across my cheek. "Look, it's a lot to consider regardless, especially after all I've put you through. And if you're not up for it, or it's more of a question than you're willing to answer right now, I'll understand, and no harm, no foul. I came here to see you again, and to try to relieve some of the terrible strain I put on you. That you were willing to hear me out at all, let alone for things to have ended the way they have, is a miracle in the same category as loaves and fishes. I've gotten more from this trip, and you, than I ever dreamed, let alone deserved. And if all this has given you some closure, I'm glad for that, and I'm happy to have been given a chance to be a part of you finding it."

I quickly boost myself up onto my elbow and poke him in the chest. "Look here, mister." My tone is solid, and the sudden transition is jarring to us both. "I want to be really clear, here. If I were going to do…this? It means doing it in real life. No locking down completely if we have an argument, no turning into Evil Character Cas if you're upset with me, and never, under any circumstance, are you allowed to hold any of those threats over me again. *Ever.* For all the rest of time."

"That's all more than fair."

"Overly formal," I repeat. "But I'm serious. Because a single whiff of that stuff again means you weren't driven by shame and fear. It means that's who you really are. And I don't want to believe that's the case. I *don't* believe that's the case. I wouldn't be here right now if I did. I'm choosing to believe the things you said last night, but I like myself way too much to ever allow anyone to treat me as less than an equal human ever again. So, at the first hint that you are going to any of those places, I'm out."

I've expelled my ultimatum reserve and flop back on the pillow, holding eye contact. "Wow, yeah, this is all a little more awkward with the naked thing—it's true." I take a deep breath and let it out slowly. "I know that all probably sounds overly harsh at the moment, but I want to be very clear where I'm at. If I'm going into something with you, I want those cards face up on the table from minute one."

"I appreciate that," he says, looking a little pained, but sincere. "I won't insult you by unleashing a flowery speech of how I swear to you those things will never happen, and that I really am not the person I gave you every indication I was. But if you're generous enough to offer it, I very much look forward to the opportunity to prove to you through my actions that I was just as horrified by that version of myself."

"I think I'd like to see that," I say, taking his hand and planting a quick kiss on his wrist. "All things considered, it wouldn't suck to see you again. I suppose," I add with a wink.

His face stays still, but his eyes flash with delight. "Really?"

"Really, Cas." Grinning, I say, "Charlie did say if I found anything in the units I liked, I should keep it. This feels like a worthy finder's fee."

I can see how hard he's working to control the smile on his face, but he seems to be losing the battle. He bends down and kisses me on the forehead, then pulls me closer until my head is resting on his shoulder and he's got me snuggled up against him.

Then he reaches down, grabs his phone, and starts intently poking away at it with his one free hand.

"Wow, the romance sure dies quick in these parts," I say dryly. "Four seconds into it all, and you're already surfing Facebook while we're in bed together."

He gently pokes me in the ribs, and I squeal, unable—and not particularly willing—to wriggle too far away. "I'm not on Facebook," he says. "I am just—" he stalls for time as he clicks various things with his thumb "—committing to one of those grand romantic gestures, as CiCi calls them." He pauses for a moment. "Well, what I hope is a grand romantic gesture, anyway."

"Okay, now you have to share," I say, excitedly bouncing my feet under the blankets.

"One second," he says, punching away. "And there we go."

He turns his phone to me, and I read the screen. "It's a... flight confirmation in February?"

"It is."

I frown with confusion and keep reading. "For... Oh my gosh. That's the morning before Tom and Trina's wedding. You're not serious."

"Very serious. And, to show you exactly how serious, you'll notice I made sure it's nonrefundable, yes?"

I laugh. "For someone who is likely richer than God, I'm not sure how impactful that actually is."

"You're rather stepping on my gesture," he says, poking my ribs again.

I squeak and say, "Okay, okay! But that's almost three months away. Are you sure you want to commit to something that far out?"

"Absolutely. I've heard your dress is not to be missed."

I snap back up on my elbow. "Wait. How did you know when the wedding is?"

"Mama Montgomery. And then CiCi. And then Mama Montgomery again. And then literally every single member of your extended family at the dinner table yesterday."

I snort and flop back onto his shoulder. "So subtle, these people of mine."

"I'm rather excited to go," he says as he reaches over to place his phone on the nightstand and then turns back to me, wrapping both arms tightly around my back. "I quite like your brother and Trina. I look forward to getting to know them better."

My brain feels a delectable rush of swoon. "That's really sweet. I know they'd like that, too. Your ability to stop my mother in her passive-aggressive tracks has made you their hero."

He tilts his head down into my hair, deeply inhales, and lets it out slowly. "I hate to press my luck here, but does this mean you've somehow found it in your heart to forgive me?"

I grin into his chest. "I'm thinking about it."

A breath whooshes out of him in a contented way. "Any thoughts on what might tip the scales in my favor?"

I look up at him and smile. "Tell you what. Find a way to introduce me to David Tennant, and we'll call it square."

"Consider it done."

I start to laugh, but as I replay his words in my head, I notice a glaring absence of a joking tone. "Wait. I'm sorry—what?"

He shrugs and runs his fingers gently down my shoulder. "Dave's a mate. We play squash. Next time he's in town, I'll set up dinner with him and his wife. She's very charming. I think you'd get on well."

"Caspian." I gape. "I was kidding. I wouldn't actually make my forgiveness conditional on you introducing me to a celebrity."

"I was just so pleased the condition was something I could so easily check off," he says into my hair. "Not like you requesting I get a tattoo on my face or similar."

"Well, damn." I sigh dramatically. "There goes my *actual* caveat." He chuckles for a good long while as he continues to absentmindedly stroke my shoulder. "I can't believe you *play squash* with David Tennant. And that you call him *Dave*."

"It's his name."

I consider that. "Okay, it's definitely not a condition, especially now that we've agreed on the face tattoo, but if it ever comes up, could you please tell him that I think he's awesome and I'm a huge fan?"

"I know you are," he says with a grin in his voice. "I remember the T-shirt."

I push back from him slightly, giving him a confused look. "What t—" A horrific flashback to our first meeting in which I was wearing flying-cat pajama pants and a *Doctor Who* shirt comes screaming into mental focus. "Uh. That…that was a gift from CiCi. I was just wearing it to be nice."

"You must be a very, very good friend," he says, now grinning ear to ear. "Since it looked like you'd worn it several hundred times."

"Oh god!" I groan, grabbing a pillow from behind his arm and slapping it over my face. I mutter through the down, "Please, oh please, don't tell David freaking Tennant I have a shirt with his face on it."

The pillow suddenly disappears. "I tell you what," he says with a teasing, conspiratorial edge. "I'll keep this secret of yours if you promise to accept a ticket from me to fly out to visit for a weekend in a few weeks." He plops the pillow down beside my head. "What say you, Miss Montgomery?"

I issue a tremendous fake gasp. "Why, Mr. Tiddleswich, are you blackmailing me?"

"Ahh, yes," he says, and laughs. "We've now come full circle."

"Scoundrel." I click my tongue.

"And don't you ever forget it." He moves just enough, until his face is hovering over mine.

"Are you really going to kiss me right now?" I say with a giggle. "That would be *soooo* cliché."

"I'll gladly risk it."

And he does exactly that.

★ ★ ★ ★ ★

ACKNOWLEDGMENTS

To Lauren Smulski, my cherished Ketchup. I'm grateful to have you as an editor, and honored to call you a friend. You make my words better. You make me better. You also protect me from violent pool floaties. Full-service, indeed.

Brent Taylor and Uwe Stender, my dynamic duo! Thank you for all you do, and the support you give. You're truly the greatest agents in all the land, and I'm lucky to have the opportunity to work with you both. Our symbiotic Ride or Die relationship is one for the ages, and may Odin save anyone who forgets it.

Dana Kaye, publicist extraordinaire. You're glorious and magical, and it's been an honor to work with you and the entire Kaye Publicity team!

Sarah Hollowell, you're wonderful and magnificent and the most supportive and loyal friend a gal could ever dream of having. The world is a better place because you're in it. You are eternally loved.

So, so many thanks to Abby Jimenez, an amazing author,

incredible friend, and baker extraordinaire! You never let me wallow in self-doubt over this book, which was a frequent struggle for me, and you made me believe that maybe I don't completely suck after all. I don't deserve you, lady.

Liz Lincoln, who graciously spent an afternoon brainstorming Caspian's last name after I was stuck banging my head on the wall.

Angela Durall, sister-in-law of champions, for always being in my corner, for taking such great care of my family in my absence, and for reminding me in a moment of panic that Mr. Darcy exists and never gets old.

To Mom: thank you for always waving the best pom-poms in my direction. I did promise the second book I published would be either puppies or prostitutes, and I'm nothing if not a woman of my word. Flipping a coin to determine if the next one will be kitties or cults. At least we're edging closer to where you can tell your friends what my books are about! Love you, lady.

Lola and Miles, my darlings, my babies, my whole heart. Lola: the Rory to my Lorelai. Miles: the Loki to my Frigga. I am proud to be your Mama Bun.

To my dearest Drew, we survived a lot over the course of my writing this book. We all lived, even though it seemed certain at times that we couldn't possibly. Thank you for soldiering on, for keeping the kiddos breathing and fed while I worked, and for never judging me when I inexplicably had *Fantastic Beasts* on a loop for five straight days while I binge-wrote the first draft of this book. (We got out of there, baby!)

And finally, to a very specific British actor, the star of my post–heart attack, heavily medicated fever dream that inspired this novel—thanks for the unintentional plot bunny, and for not suing me should you ever discover the existence of this book. Please. Thanks. Cheers.